The
Judas
Conspiracy

Also by Leslie Winfield Williams

A Thing, They Say
When Women Build the Kingdom
Seduction of the Lesser Gods
Night Wrestling
Which Way Is Home?

The
Judas
Conspiracy

Leslie Winfield Williams

Jo
Sara

JoSara MeDia

ISBN: 978-0-9843049-8-1

Published by:
JoSara Media
Tomball, Texas

Front Cover Detail, The Entombment of Christ (1939), Chapel of St. Joseph of Arimathea, Washington National Cathedral, by Jan Henrik DeRosen, used with permission.
Cover design, Mimi McNamara; photograph, Craig Stapert.

1st printing, December 2010

To my grandchildren

"We are healed of a suffering only by experiencing it to the full."

Marcel Proust, *Remembrance of Things Past*

"When through the deep waters I call thee to go,
the rivers of woe shall not thee overflow;
for I will be with thee, thy troubles to bless,
and sanctify to thee thy deepest distress."

K. In John Rippon's *Selection*, 1787

Prologue

In Paris, July 2004, Rodolphe Kasser announced the finding of fragments from an ancient Coptic manuscript, the *Gospel of Judas*. In 2006,
The National Geographic Society translated the document and presented
a televised special on this newly discovered glimpse into antiquity.

Dating from the third or fourth century, the Coptic manuscript was
translated from a Greek Gnostic gospel written between 130 and 180
A.D. The gospel contains theology from a specific religious sect called
the Sethian Gnostics.

In the first few years after its introduction to the public, the *Gospel
of Judas* took the theological world by storm. The manuscript threatened
to overturn the Biblical view that Judas Iscariot betrayed Jesus to the authorities. In contrast to the four New Testament gospels, the *Gospel of
Judas* claims that Judas acted in obedience to Jesus' command to turn
him over. Reflecting the Gnostic view that the human form is a spiritual
prison, Judas was merely releasing Jesus, allowing Him to finish his mission on earth and go to heaven.

⤶

The Judas Conspiracy is the story of how an unknown Greek copy of
the *Gospel of Judas* was discovered and translated by an English monk
during the time of Henry VIII. Brother Caedmon was a member of a powerful secret organization called the Sethian Brotherhood. Already over a
thousand years old in 1539, the Sethian Brotherhood was dedicated to the
destruction of the Church—and devoted to protecting the only known
complete copy of their holy text, the *Gospel of Judas*.

The second son of the Earl of Standby, Brother Caedmon barely escaped with his life and the parchment of his family's lineage when Henry VIII closed down the abbeys and monasteries in 1539. Henry VIII gave the *Gospel of Judas* along with the Stoneleigh Abbey's entire library to Lord Guildford, a member of the king's Privy Council.

Lost for four and a half centuries, the ancient Greek manuscript and a Latin translation surfaced halfway around the world in New England in 2008. Its discovery unleashed an international rampage of death and destruction.

Chapter One
THURSDAY
November 20, 2008

1
Isabella

Finally, after thirteen grueling hours of interrogation, I cuffed the Campus Killer in the interview room of the New Haven Police Department. Baiting me was clearly the suspect's evening entertainment. In response, I'd played good cop, bad cop, bored cop, smart alek, dumb blonde—I'd have played the village idiot to make him confess.

I was exhausted.

In my short tenure in the old boys' club at the police station, I thought I'd seen all the faces of evil—evil in business suits, evil in the gutter, evil with fists of iron, evil in the imagination of Internet porn masters, evil flowering in every neighborhood, in every race, in every class of human being.

Not so. This particular specimen was an in-your-face elitist. Clueless as to why he wasn't naturally entitled to murder twelve women on a whim. He had flaunted a silver Thunderbird around town while I tracked him. As I snapped the cuffs in place I noticed his immaculate manicure. He wore a fawn-colored designer cardigan and hand-sewn leather shoes from Italy.

"You'll enjoy your new orange outfit," I said.

Towering above me, he looked down with eyes blue and cold as glaciers. He said, "I'll be out on bond tomorrow." Then he smiled, revealing perfect, pearly, ten thousand dollar teeth, and whispered, "You're number thirteen."

"Not in this lifetime, you sick scumbag." Heart beating hard, I wanted to kick him where it hurt. Instead, I kicked the metal door shut after him. Then I took a couple of deep breaths, gathered my purse and my composure, and stepped out into a corridor where my colleagues gave me an ovation. "Way to go, Isabella!"

"Excellent work," said Richard Crenshaw, my boss. Crenshaw was the only man I knew who could make a pair of casual jeans look like a Marine uniform.

Everyone patted me on the shoulders with congratulations. I could barely stand up I was so tired. Suddenly, Ted, one of the uniforms, sang, loudly and off-key, a line from one of the Beach Boys' golden oldies, "Well, he had fun, fun, fun—till Isabella took his T-Bird away now."

In one split second, the tension and horror from the last days—weeks— months dissolved into bubbles of laughter, then gulps of guffaws. Everyone in the corridor cracked up, even Richard Crenshaw. We had caught Connecticut's worst serial killer in history. Belly laughs, great convulsions of relief, finally wound down with chortles and snickers.

I couldn't remember the last time I'd laughed like that. Eight years at least.

The next day was a different story. The New Haven PD was lined up in formal attire behind the District Attorney in the courtroom. Except for me. I sat on the back row wearing a black suit and spike heels, the perfect look for a funeral. Or a national press conference, which I had managed to survive earlier without eating my own foot. Looking around the courtroom, I caught glimpses of the families of Harold Spicer III's twelve victims, scattered throughout the courtroom, their faces worn down with grief, but their eyes alive with the hope for justice.

I stuck around at the arraignment long enough to hear Judge Cronin say the three magic words that would guarantee a good night's sleep tonight: "Remanded, without bail."

The courtroom erupted into pandemonium. The victims' families cheered; the defendant's mother wept; a platoon of defense lawyers clamored for attention; and police officers hustled Harold Spicer III, shackled and cuffed, out the side door into the maws of the national press. But not before he had a chance to turn his head and leer again at me. He mouthed, "Just wait."

I had hoped to sneak out the back of the courtroom unnoticed, but I should have known better. I snagged one of my stiletto heels as I opened the courtroom door, almost landing nose first into the microphone of a CNN crime reporter I recognized from earlier in the day.

"Detective O'Leary! Can you comment on the judge's decision for re-mand over a $3 million bond? Any new insights on the Campus Killer?"

A dozen other reporters closed in, straining to catch a sound bite. Still unaccustomed to the bouquets of mikes thrust in my face, I said, "The wonderful thing about America is that justice can still be served, even if the defendant's father and grandfather served on the State Supreme Court."

I smiled for the strobe show of cameras and then got lucky—the horde of photographers and reporters spotted the D.A. and I escaped. I left New Haven's imposing Neo-Classical courthouse for the sanctuary of my Mini Cooper, parked half a block down Elm Street.

The New Haven Green, two blocks of spacious grounds surrounding a few old churches, was a patch of land preserved from earlier centuries— a small, manicured green belt separating town from gown. I ignored the usual crowd of men at the bus stop, who ogled like they'd never seen a pair of legs before. Once inside my Mini Coop, I headed toward the Interstate.

At the light, I glanced down on the seat next to me at the large front-page color photo from the newspaper Crenshaw had given me. Yester-day, a lone photographer from the *New Haven Register* had captured the moment when I'd handcuffed the Campus Killer, a sadistic psychopath who had murdered twelve Yale students and terrorized the city of New Haven for over a year. The story had made the AP.

My picture shared the space above the fold with a photo of a Yale dean named Guildford donating some ancient manuscripts to the Divinity School. The *Gospel of Judas*. At one time, I would have been interested, but not lately and certainly not today.

Moving through the light, I drove east over the harbor bridge as the sun was beginning to set, my car gunning just ahead of the congested traffic that would be leaving New Haven shortly.

Relief from the stress of the past few days felt like a hot shower on a cold day. With the killer locked away, I might actually sleep tonight in-stead of twisting the covers into a knot.

What a year. The Campus Killer had stalked young females alone at night in secluded areas on campus, or jogging along the dark stretches of Grove Cemetery nearby. He strangled his victims, and then branded them on their thighs with a Y.

Not one of the victims had survived to describe the attack. No witnesses. No DNA. No nothing.

After a student found the fourth girl in the stacks of Sterling Memorial Library in yet another clean crime scene, I knew we were dealing with a really, really bad guy. A perp with a deadly combination of ruthlessness and brains. He was either a natural genius at covering his tracks, or he'd studied law and criminal forensics (probably unsuccessfully) right under our noses at Yale University.

I took him on. This nasty piece of humanity was not going to win. I spent months reading FBI psychological profiles, books, and articles. Then I made friends with Ruth Capshaw, the Yale Law School secretary who'd been around longer than Henry Ford's first car. She helped me investigate every male who had failed the program or been expelled. After ten tense months, I'd dropped fifteen pounds to a size four—with no new evidence and no new clues.

Finally, I caught a break. Almost a year after his first crime—just as I was about to give up—I found him. Harold Spicer III, son and grandson of Rhode Island Supreme Court Judges, Harold Spicer I and II. Unemployed for years, he lived at University Towers, a large co-op high-rise at 100 York Street, conveniently located—for his purposes—between the old campus and the Yale Medical School and hospital.

During that first semester, Harold Spicer III had been expelled after exposing himself to three different female law students, on three different occasions, inside the women's restroom of the YGS dining hall.

It took thirteen hours of seemingly guileless questioning to get the confession. I'll never forget the looks of disdain he gave me. He didn't realize that through a fluke of nature my IQ probably outranked his by thirty points—and he was no dummy. He gave himself away over a small heart tattoo on the inner thigh of one of his victims.

Reaching Branford, the next town east on Rt. 1, I approached the Olde Branford Inn, where I planned to relax.

Alone.

Behind the Olde Branford Inn, daylight still lingered on the horizon. A bank of dark, ugly clouds moved in. After turning off the car's motor, I took one more look at the picture on the front page. Who had I become over the last eight years? I saw a tough detective with a small frame but deceptively strong muscles. Dark, shoulder-length hair. Smooth olive skin. In the photo, the brown eyes my Italian mother called "cioccolata" looked almost black with determination. Obsidian black.

I had changed, but the inn had not. After eight years, it still looked like a large New England rock house straight out of Norman Rockwell, with a view of the ocean and a fireplace in every bedroom.

Entering the quiet, quaint bar paneled in dark wood, I asked for the same table I came to every year on the anniversary of the Thursday before Thanksgiving—the table next to the hearth and a window where I could watch the waves rolling in. The hostess, a young teenager in a slinky black dress too big and too sophisticated for her, looked me over. "Are you the lady detective who caught that—"

I nodded. Word got around fast when your face stared out from news bins on every corner.

"Wow. First drink's on the house."

"Thanks." I ordered a Perrier, and then two more, one right after the other. Outside the window, the sun disappeared and the storm rolled in, starting with a light spatter of rain.

Somebody once told me the male personality was like a well-organized tackle box, storing different aspects of life in specific, labeled compartments. The female personality, on the other hand, resembled that one special drawer in the kitchen where twine, paperclips, coins, broken knobs, nuts, bolts, and all the rest of the miscellaneous odds and ends of life were thrown together.

I was getting pretty good at compartmentalizing, especially at work, but not tonight. I couldn't separate the euphoria at collaring the biggest criminal of my career with the sadness that Ronny wasn't here to share it.

I had not spoken Ronny's name aloud for years.

Ronny O'Shaunessy asked me to marry him at this very table, nine years ago today. Tall, buff, with short blonde hair, and smelling like Irish Spring soap—Ronny had fumbled the ring and chased it under the table on his hands and knees. We quit dinner halfway through the filet mignon and took a room upstairs.

After a Christmas wedding—a cream satin gown, red poinsettias—we had a reception back at my parents' house, with more manicotti than the whole neighborhood could eat.

God, I loved Ronny O'Shaunessy. I would never admit it, especially to the guys downtown, but all I ever really wanted out of life was to raise a family.

Out the window of the Olde Branford Inn, darkness from the rising storm gnawed away the rest of the daylight. The Perrier offered no relief from my stomach, tight as a walnut.

Then the wreck. Exactly a year later, I was as big—elephant big, rhinoceros big—with our first child. Ronny and I came back to the Olde Branford Inn for an anniversary drink. He let me out at the door while he parked the car, and all I remember was two headlights coming straight at me before I hit the ground. Some drunk had come out of nowhere.

Two weeks in a coma. When I woke up, Mama was sitting next to my hospital bed, praying the rosary. She looked ten years older around the eyes, like she'd been attacked with tear gas, they were so red. She cried incoherently when I opened my eyes, and immediately I wanted to go back into the soft, dark place from which I had just emerged. Mama dropped the rosary and grabbed my hand.

"The baby," I said.

From the jumble of English, Italian, and tears, I gathered the baby had died on impact; and by the time the ambulance arrived, it looked like I'd bled out. After I got to the hospital, they were filling out paperwork for the morgue when the head of the ER came in to certify time of death. He said, "Just a minute."

Between sobs, Mama called it a miracle. The doctor had revived me and performed an emergency hysterectomy to take the baby.

Mama stopped talking. Even in my drugged state in the hospital bed, I knew there was more bad news. Mama was wringing my hand right off my wrist.

"Tell me."

"Later, mi bambina. Enough sadness for now. You are alive."

"Tell me now."

Mama picked up her rosary from the floor. She began to pray.

One of the nurses came in to fill out the chart. After a flutter of excitement when she found me awake, she left again to call the doctor.

"Mama."

"Please, no. Not yet." Mama had started crying.

"Mama, tell me. Now. I need to know. Where's Ronny?"

Finally, Mama whispered the rest of the story. At the scene of the accident, a rookie EMT had felt for my pulse. Ronny overheard him say, "She's gone. Her and the baby both."

Following the silent ambulance back to New Haven, Ronny had stopped his car on the harbor bridge. With the car still running, he first left a message on my mother's answering machine, telling her he couldn't live with having lost his wife and baby. We were his only family. Then he jumped off the bridge.

Now, eight years later, I took one last sip, paid the bill, and stepped outside the Olde Branford Inn into a cold, driving rain.

The church had refused Ronny a Christian funeral because suicide was a sin.

When would I stop waking up in the middle of the night seeing the car's headlights coming straight at me?

I spent a year at Yale Divinity School, where God slowly sublimated like old dirty snow instead of comforting me with the answers I craved (why had the drunk turned in at that very second? Why didn't the rookie EMS tech keep his mouth shut, leaving Ronny a window of hope? What in the hell was the point of so much suffering?)

The image persisted of God as a tyrannical school master—giving perks to a few pet students, and allowing bullies to make life miserable for the weaker ones. I left the divinity school and, instead, sped through the Ph.D. program in criminal psychology at Yale, followed by training at the Police Academy. I made detective in record time.

Today was the eighth anniversary of Ronny's death. I was almost thirty years old, barren, and had the social life of a nun.

But I was good at catching criminals. At least my job gave my life meaning and paid the bills.

Outside the Olde Branford Inn, near-freezing pellets of rain stung my face. Although each year my suffering eased a little, I still lived with a canker of anger somewhere near the center.

2
Gabriel

In another part of town, Gabriel ran his finger along the shiny blade of the axe he had bought on the way back to New Haven from New York. Small for an axe, this one had an oak handle, sanded smooth, and a fresh steel blade, honed to a razor's edge. The blunt end of the steel wedge flashed with red paint.

Gabriel recalled his first axe, a small scouting hatchet he used on campouts to chop firewood when he was nine years old. He also used it to cut down random trees, fences, and signposts when he took long walks in the woods as a child. His father had taken the axe away when he discovered that Gabriel had chopped a neighbor girl's playhouse into splinters, just for fun.

After that, Gabriel had saved his allowance money and bargained with an older boy for a machete, a sharp, deadly instrument that Gabriel kept hidden under his bed for years.

As he watched dusk and lowering clouds approach outside his window, Gabriel pondered the chain of events that had led him to this threshold of a new start in life. By his late twenties, he was jaded. He'd done it all. He had gotten three girls pregnant and paid for three abortions. He had seen one old woman on the streets murder another old woman over a stick of gum. He had worked in an advertisement firm as an intern and come up with a million dollar idea to sell toilet paper—right before he was fired for telling his boss he'd rather pick nits from a wedgie than work for him.

And he had almost, but not quite, learned to live in the wasteland of his inner life, a Sahara Desert of disappointments, disenchantments, and failure.

Then he was inducted into the Sethian Brotherhood, and his life turned around in a profound and remarkable way.

Gabriel's watch said 4:57. In a little over an hour, he would make the first strike in an international plan that had been several years in the making.

Gabriel sharpened his hatchet, then laid the steely blade next to him on the bed and waited. He closed his eyes, and remembered.

Right after Gabriel was fired from the ad company, he received a phone call from an older man, requesting to meet him in a dim, smoke-filled bar in a neighboring town. Gabriel had gotten there first and downed five or six Scotches while he waited. Although he rarely drank, he was determined to drown his sorrows if it killed him.

When the man arrived, he sat down at the far end of the bar, ordered more drinks, and, when Gabriel joined him, said, "Heard about your job."

"Great." Gabriel felt empty-headed, but he knew he had to say something. He couldn't just sit there. He tried to articulate clearly so he wouldn't slur his words. "I mean, I take a job at this ad company, trying to make everybody happy. So I come up with a million dollar idea to sell toilet paper—the whole idea was a joke. Like the world can't live without triple-ply toilet paper."

The man listened while Gabriel laughed. "Then I'm canned for telling my freaking boss the truth about the way he treats people."

Gabriel drank his Scotch neat, enjoying the smoky taste as he rolled the amber liquid around in his mouth.

"What are you going to do now?" asked the man.

Gabriel's tongue was turning numb. "Don't know." Words and emotions were running around like a pack of devils inside his head—wild, uncontrolled. Gabriel knew he had to start forcing them to make sense, but at the moment, hate was the only emotion he could express. He didn't know whether he'd be able to make himself understood or not, and felt himself on the verge of tears. Yet he felt compelled to start talking, saying anything. "Everything I hate is more powerful than me."

The man nodded. The man was a good listener. The man cared. He had proven that in the past. As Gabriel sat hunched over the bar, the man waited, patient, sipping his own drink with care. He asked, "What is it that you hate?"

Chasing down his thoughts was becoming a major problem. Gabriel leaned forward and with the slender remains of sobriety, forced himself to summon command over the chaos inside him. "What do I hate? Let's start with America. Americans really are as greedy as the Muslims claim they are. Pathetic. Shallow. Hypocritical." He paused. "Did I say greedy?"

The man waited, watching Gabriel.

Gabriel sighed. Gradually, he felt the stampede inside begin to circle into a familiar pattern; he recognized the restless herd of all the grudges and wounds he'd suffered since he could remember. Beasts he could never get rid of. "What do I hate? You really want to know? Okay, I'll tell you. I hate life. I can't do anything right. I hate God. I just about hate everything."

The man lowered his voice, "Do you hate me?"

"Of course not. You're about the only thing I don't hate." He took a slug of his, what—seventh?—Scotch. "You know it's been drummed into my head since I was two years old that I'm supposed to make a difference in this world. If I've heard it once, I've heard it a million times."

"I know."

"So you tell me—how do you make a difference with one crappy, insignificant life? I'm thinking the only way to make a difference is to blow my brains out. That's the only thing I can do to make the world a better place." He finished off his drink and signaled for another. He hadn't meant to get so personal, but there it was.

The man turned his own Scotch around and around on the damp napkin, but didn't say anything.

Gabriel said, "Aren't you supposed to give me advice at this point? Being older and wiser, and all." He was trying to be flippant, but he couldn't disguise his desperation.

Silence.

"Aren't you even going to try and talk me out of it?"

The man watched him, expressionless, as if he were making a decision. Finally, he said, "To make a difference, you band together with other people trying to make the world a better place. Men with high professional profiles, but who meet in secret to take action when action is required."

The bartender filled Gabriel's glass yet again with Scotch from the Highlands. Gabriel wondered if it would be possible to drink himself to death right here on this bar stool. He closed his eyes, inviting the friendly darkness into his mind.

The man said, "Look at Al Qaida. We can learn from their techniques. If you wanted to get the world's attention, what would you do?"

What? Al Qaida? Gabriel opened his eyes and stared at the man. He was too drunk to follow him, but he wasn't too drunk to recognize that the conversation was taking an unusual twist. Why was he talking about terrorism? "The twin towers are already decimated," he said. "They got both of them." Maybe it was the power of suggestion, but Gabriel thought he was seeing two identical men sitting with him at the bar instead of one.

"Yes, but they're not the only monument to what's wrong with the world." The man paused. "Would you agree that the Western World has disintegrated?"

Gabriel laughed. "Yeah. That's a pretty safe statement." Everything had disintegrated as far as Gabriel was concerned.

"What about the government?"

Gabriel rubbed his forehead. "Don't get me started. I don't want—"

"What about the church? Is it safe to say that America is in a spiritual crisis? Pick up any newspaper and read about the latest pillar of the church going to jail for child pornography, for embezzling, you name it. "

"The church." Aha. Gabriel recognized how deftly the man had turned the conversation to the man's obsession, the church. Gabriel wasn't in the mood for a tirade, but out of respect, he played along. "Religion is a dead man walking."

"Correct."

Gabriel placed his chin in his hands. Now all he wanted to do was go home, but he knew he was in for a lecture. The man was hung up on spiritual stuff, and had yammered to Gabriel on several occasions about how Christianity got it wrong. How for two thousand years the church misled and tyrannized the people. He closed his eyes again.

"Pay attention!" shouted the man.

Gabriel jerked himself alert. Something was different today. The man was more intense than Gabriel had ever seen him.

"Yes, sir." He tried to focus. Was Gabriel being tested? Was this the moment of truth the man had hinted at the last time they had talked? Please, not now. Gabriel had already forgotten the question. He nodded because he didn't know what to say.

The man leaned toward Gabriel and almost hissed. "The lies must be stopped."

"Exactly." Gabriel hoped he wouldn't fall off the stool. He was struggling to keep his grip on both the bar stool and the conversation.

"So what needs to happen?"

Gabriel closed his eyes. His head felt dizzy, but he was beginning to pull together strands of their previous conversations. It was almost there, almost coming together. He stalled while he tried to focus. Finally, he said, "The true faith has to make a point."

"And how do we do that?"

Al Qaida. The man was fishing. Something about 9-11 and what it had taken to get America's attention. Gabriel felt suddenly inspired. "A lot of people need to die."

The man nodded and smiled. "And first we must prepare the way."

"Exactly."

"But now we need to get you an ice pack."

What was he talking about? thought Gabriel as he stumbled out of the bar.

Gabriel felt a quiver of anxiety pass through him as he lay on the bed waiting for the action to begin—now his source of fear was whether or not he would be able to fulfill his vows to the Brotherhood.

That night in the bar, the man had paid the bill and whisked Gabriel home. The next day, Gabriel found himself on an airplane to Scotland with a letter of introduction, a list of instructions, and a headache that felt as if someone had smashed his frontal lobe into a bloody mess.

Within twenty-four short, life-changing hours, Gabriel—stone cold sober—had entered into one of his own fantasies. He had penetrated a veil between the reality of his everyday life, and another reality he thought possible only in his own mind, or the mind of Hollywood.

Twenty-four hours after the scene in the bar, and nothing about him was the same. Emotionally, he had ascended from the dark, claustrophobic coffin of despair into an eagle's aerie above the clouds. Spiritually, he was baptized into a faith that tapped his core in a place deeper than he knew existed inside himself.

The Sethian Brotherhood's holy chamber in Scotland was a former dungeon lit with candlelight flickering from sconces strategically placed every two feet or so around the cavernous space. Was Gabriel hallucinating? No. A cold breeze sliced his bare legs and feet, and the dense scent of perfumed incense seeped from old stone walls.

Gabriel had trouble making the leap from the ad agency's pluddy cubicle with a cheesy fake wood desk and glaring fluorescent lights into the magic of this ring of black-hooded men standing around a stone altar with a huge gold—solid gold—symbol of the Sethian Brotherhood gleaming in the shimmering light. How could two so different worlds exist on the same planet?

Instantly, Gabriel knew that the old workaday world of the West's rat race for achievement, its self-serving opportunism and greed was dead to him. True power was spiritual.

After his initiation ceremony, the Grand Patriarch looked Gabriel in the eye and rasped, "I have christened you Gabriel, the Messenger of Life. You have proven yourself fit for the tasks that lie ahead, and you have sworn before the brothers, signing the Book of Life. Now you must listen, for the time is at hand, the dawn of a new age."

Gabriel had knelt on the cold stone floor of the holy chamber while the Grand Patriarch told him the story of the brave wounded monk, Brother Caedmon, who was almost killed by Henry VIII's men. Caedmon had hobbled and stumbled twenty-five miles across the English border of Scotland to entrust his sister's husband with an ancient lineage and to warn the Brotherhood of the disappearance of the only complete copy of their sacred book, the *Gospel of Judas*.

At that moment, nothing else existed for Gabriel outside the dark stone walls with the flickering light. Gabriel had been hand-selected to become part of a sacred tradition two thousand years old. Chills of excitement ran up and down his legs.

Then the Grand Patriarch outlined the plans for this coming week, the week before Thanksgiving. He pointed to the dancing candle flames along the walls. "See how small flames create giant shadows in the light. We are the fire, Gabriel. We are the fire. But the light and shadows that we cast will be very big."

The Grand Patriarch's gaunt and lined face glowed. Gabriel was close enough to smell his breath, spicy from what must have been cabbage and vinegar. Gabriel could hardly breathe himself from excitement—combined with terror and revulsion at the old man's smell and yellow fingernails.

Two days later, Gabriel woke up in his own bed, terrified that the deepest sense of purpose he'd ever experienced was an alcohol-induced reverie, and that the castle in Scotland was a dream. Then he remembered the plan.

Now, as he waited on the bed for the plan to unfold, Gabriel felt his pulse pounding to the rhythm of time itself. *Gabriel was about to make a difference.*

The Sethian Brotherhood had been active for centuries in covert operations against traitors to the truth. The world would never know the Brotherhood's role in the Kennedy assassination, or the support it was giving Al Qaida. Gabriel would never have public accolades, but he would always have the pleasure of knowing that at a crucial juncture in history, he'd been chosen to help change the world.

Now. Gabriel's watch said 6:18. Instructions had been specific. The timing was crucial.

Quietly, he hid the hatchet up the sleeve of his topcoat, placed the slip of paper in his pocket, grabbed his leather briefcase, and let himself out of the room.

3
Victoria

Victoria Guildford stopped in the twilight at the outskirts of New Haven to get a newspaper. Sure enough, there was an article on the front page about the manuscript donation tomorrow. The story featured a picture of her brother-in-law, Dean Andrew Guildford, standing in front of the Yale Divinity School.

The article was eclipsed by a color photo of the detective who had captured New Haven's most notorious serial killer. Victoria studied her photo. The detective, a woman named Isabella O'Leary, looked more like a model than a detective, and wore good clothes.

Victoria hopped back in her Jaguar and headed for St. Ronan Street. Her husband's nephew, Paul St. Clair, was flying in tonight for the manuscript event this weekend. Her husband Malcolm was going to pick up Paul at the airport and take him out to eat. He didn't expect Victoria back from New York until tomorrow.

Good. She would surprise them.

By now, the evening clouds had condensed into a bitterly cold night shower. Victoria pulled into her driveway under the porte-cochere where she could dash inside without getting wet.

As freezing rain pummeled the roof, Victoria pulled her heavy bag from the trunk. She thought she heard the tinkle of sleet against the bay windows on the front of the house.

Fumbling with her keys, Victoria let herself into the dark brick mansion. When she flipped on the Italian chandelier in the foyer, sparkling light revealed her new marble floors and rich cherry wainscoting. She set down her suitcase and turned toward the alarm box. It was disarmed. Maybe her housekeeper Gabby was still here after all.

Or not. The house seemed too quiet. If Gabby had already gone, this was the third time this month she had forgotten to arm the system. Victoria hung up her coat on the rack next to the door. She would have to be firmer with Gabby. No one in New Haven could afford to take chances. Not after the Campus Killer. A jogger had discovered one of the women's bodies only three blocks away. Fear lingered in the streets, even though the killer had been caught.

Just as Victoria started down the marble hallway that led through the house toward the kitchen, she heard the sharp sound of shattering glass. She jumped as a jolt of adrenaline surged through her body—what had broken?

Her nerves were suddenly on edge. But then her no-nonsense reasoning kicked in. It must be the storm, of course. The wind and sleet had probably torn one of the thick branches of the elm tree near the library, sending it crashing into the bay window. Malcolm had already lost one branch—and two windowpanes—in the blizzard of 2005.

Victoria heard someone moaning. In spite of her attempt to remain rational, her pulse began pounding in her head. She walked faster down the hallway toward the library, past a formal living room. Could it be Gabby? But what was Gabby doing in the library? At Malcolm's request, she cleaned there only on Mondays, and today was Thursday.

This time when Victoria heard another groan and a crash from within, a pang of terror shot through her like an icicle. This was not the wind, or a tree branch. She stopped breathing, paralyzed. It sounded like an axe.

Then she softly placed her bag on the floor and took off her Ferragamos.

4
Isabella

Home was a small frame house in the same Hamden working class neighborhood where I grew up. When I first bought the house, my dad helped me paint the outside light sage green with evergreen shutters. We also added a new brass knocker on the door, and did the inside with floral wallpaper and a matching border.

Inside, the furniture was functional. The hallway walls practically sagged with pictures of my parents, four brothers, and my nieces and nephews. Other than that, two prints of the Italian countryside hung over the couch.

I liked my nest. It was clean, uncluttered, and all mine.

The first thing I did when I got home from the Olde Branford Inn was to take off my suit and pull on a deep red, fleece turtleneck. The irony of my life didn't escape me: a world-class figure, totally useless for reproduction.

That first year after Ronny's death, I slept with anything in pants. Don't know what I was trying to prove, but it didn't take long to figure out that each superficial encounter (I didn't want to know their names or anything about them) didn't make me feel better. It just made the canker of anger grow bigger.

Then I went to work on the police force. At first the men called me "the ice queen," but over the last couple of years, they'd accepted me as one of the guys. I focused on catching criminals, sparing myself the unnecessary pain of relationships.

I took off the high heels and wiggled my toes inside my running shoes.

Hungry for the first time in months, I went to the kitchen and munched on leftover spaghetti. Usually, I loved to cook, but tonight I wasn't in the mood. There was the newspaper, which I flipped over, glancing at the article about Yale Divinity School and the Guildford family. The manuscripts were valued at six million dollars. That caught my eye.

The Yale Divinity School. Someone told me that Dean Guildford had turned the place into an international theological center. I hadn't set foot on the property since I sold my books to the incoming, starry-eyed students and left for another part of campus.

The landline rang. This number was unlisted. Only family had access, and I was expecting Mama to call, excited about the article. I picked up the receiver. "Hey—" Alarm spread through me as a smooth, oily voice only too familiar after the last few days said, "Did you enjoy the arraignment?"

I slammed down the receiver. How had Harold Spicer III gotten this phone number?

5
Victoria

Honestly. Get a grip, Victoria Guildford told herself as she tiptoed toward the door of the library. It was silly to be afraid, especially since she didn't know what she was fearing. Still. The blood continued to pound in her brain.

Clutching her cell phone like a weapon, Victoria slowed down and stopped ten feet from the entrance to the library. Its double French doors were closed. She couldn't quite see through the panes of glass from this far away, but she hesitated to creep closer.

Maybe Gabby was exploring where she shouldn't be and had tripped and crashed into something. Dim light (probably from the Lalique lamp on a side table) filtered through the panes of glass from behind the doors.

Victoria heard the moaning again, this time louder and more tortured.

What if something unspeakable were happening to Gabby? Victoria's head began to spin as it had once when she stood up too soon after giving blood. In stocking feet, she crept close enough to peer into the room from an angle. She saw hunter green carpet, the corner of an Oriental rug, and the east wall of books, all intact. Gliding on her toes, she tiptoed up another foot for a wider angle view. Her hand shot to her mouth to cover a gasp. The corner bookcase had been moved away from the wall, and the safe Malcolm had created from a dumb waiter was exposed and empty.

The jewelry her mother had given her. Malcolm's gold coin collection. The $100,000 cash they kept for emergencies. Malcolm's stocks, bonds, legal documents and other valuable papers. Gone.

A scream escaped her throat in spite of herself.

Inside the library, the moans turned to groans, and Victoria heard crashing and grunting along with sounds of breaking wood and lamps shattering. It was definitely an axe, she thought as she pictured Malcolm's desk—from the seventeenth century—splintered into pieces.

Who was in the library? Chills shot down her spine.

In a panic, Victoria turned and began to run back down the hall toward the front door of the house. Dialing 911 with one hand, she tried to brace herself against the wall with the other. Judging from the noise, whoever was in the library seemed determined to trash the place as well as take her and Malcolm's valuables.

Halfway to the front door, she slipped on the slick floor and pitched into a silver samovar resting on an antique sideboard in the hall. She landed full force on the hard marble, hearing the sound of a bone cracking as her body thudded on the floor.

The phone scudded out of her hand.

Horrified, she saw a bone jutting out near her right wrist. She had no time to examine her arm. For a split second, she thought she would black out from the pain. She took three deep breaths. Still trying not to scream, she scooted with her legs toward the front door and the phone, every inch torture for her arm. She could feel her body starting to go into shock.

Almost there. Almost within reach. She strained so hard she nearly passed out again.

For one brief second the racket in the library stopped. In the silent lull, she pushed off against the floorboard in the direction of the phone, desperate. There. She grasped it with her left hand. Fumbling, she tried to turn it around, right side up to get the numbers within dialing range of her awkward left thumb.

Looking behind her, Victoria saw the tip of an axe crash through the glass on the front of the French doors as someone hacked his way through the panes from the library. The grunts and growls he made sounded like a madman.

Victoria grasped the phone, turned it around, and managed to dial a "9" with a thumb shaking from terror. Her other hand, uselessly attached to a catawampus arm, was no help in stabilizing the phone. Nerve endings shrieked up and down her forearm in agony. Gritting her teeth, she forced herself to hit the "1" button. She almost had it.

Again. The phone slipped, but this time her thumb reached up and hit the "1." One more time.

A man in a manic state stepped through the jagged glass and emerged from the library.

Just one more number, just one more. Determined, Victoria stretched her thumb again and pressed another "1." She heard the phone ringing on the other end. "Hurry!" she screamed. "For the love of God, answer!"

When the man heard her screaming, he turned in her direction and charged down the hall, an axe in one hand and her Lalique lamp in the other.

A voice on the end said, "What is your emergency?" Victoria screamed again as the man approached. "No! No!" Her own shrieks almost drowned out the voice on the other end of the phone, telling her to calm down and speak slowly. "Stop!" she yelled, as desperate cries scraped her throat raw. "You don't want to do this!"

The young man ran toward her, raising both the axe and the lamp above his head as he screamed nonsense about a true faith and Pleroma in an insane rage.

"Please stop! No! No!!"

When he reached Victoria lying helplessly on the ground, he swung the lamp, not the axe, at her head, fracturing her skull and killing her instantly.

A disembodied voice from the phone said, "Ma'am, can you give me your location? Ma'am? Ma'am? Are you there?"

6
Gabriel

Gabriel walked down St. Ronan toward downtown carrying the briefcase with the stolen goods and a large green umbrella. He took deep breaths and tried to calm himself down. Nobody was supposed to be at home. *How badly had he messed up the first part of an intricate and carefully choreographed drama?*

The beast of failure began to growl in his belly. No, no. Gabriel would not let this beast eat away his elation. His watch told him he had exactly thirty-two minutes to walk before he arrived at his destination. Rain pelted his umbrella, and his boots were wet. He turned left at Canner Street and walked down Whitney, where he would be less conspicuous.

Gabriel reviewed and analyzed the scene at the house. He'd had no choice. He'd had no time to think. He had to act. Instinctively, he had bashed the woman's skull with the lamp. Only now did he figure out why—because he didn't want to soil the axe blade with human blood. As a tool, the axe had been around as long as the Brotherhood. It was a noble instrument. Gabriel hated the shallow materialism that the woman stood for. She was not one of the chosen, and she deserved to be killed with her fancy lamp—the perfect symbol of what was wrong with the Western world.

As he walked down Whitney, the rain began to let up. Cars passed him as if he were an ordinary human being walking down the street like the other ordinary human beings he passed. Yet on the inside, Gabriel could hardly contain the conflicted rush of emotions he felt surging through his veins.

He would have to contact the Inner Circle with news of the dead woman—a glitch in the plans. A pretty big glitch, he had to admit. Yet he convinced himself he was justified. He knew he'd had no choice. He had to kill her. She had gotten a good look at him.

Gabriel also knew the Grand Patriarch would understand. He'd sized the old man up immediately as so totally committed to the Brotherhood that he was ruthless to the core. He'd even given Gabriel permission to "use his head" if an emergency arose, and Gabriel knew exactly what he meant.

However, dealing with the American Patriarch was different. He had told Gabriel emphatically, "Plans must go without a hitch."

Unfortunately, the chain of command forced Gabriel to communicate only with the American Patriarch. To ensure secrecy, Gabriel was never to contact the Grand Patriarch directly.

As Gabriel walked, he replayed the moment when the woman had first spotted him, when he knew in his groin what he must do. In his imagination, he swung at her skull again and again.

For years he had known the thrill that a hatchet could bring, but he was shocked at the deep titillation he felt when the lamp made contact with her head and she fell to the floor, lifeless.

As he approached downtown New Haven, he felt his confidence grow. Yes, he had no doubt he could fulfill the rest of his assignment.

The surprise was how much he would enjoy it.

7
Paul

Dr. Paul St. Clair saw his uncle, Malcolm Guildford, waiting for him inside the New Haven Regional Airport. Malcolm's pilot had flown him in from Dallas, and Paul had been too excited to sleep or read.

"Victoria is still in New York. We're going to the country club for dinner," said Malcolm when Paul walked through the door. Malcolm wore a hand-tailored pinstriped suit. His nephew wore crisp khakis and a sport coat. The two men were clearly related, with square-jaws and gray-blue eyes, but Paul was six feet, while Malcolm stood an inch shorter and had gray hair. Though a generation apart, Paul and Malcolm were both handsome, striking men who exuded an unconscious air of the kind of breeding that dominated the boardrooms of well-established firms.

"Is the new chef any good?" Paul carried his bag to his uncle's Town Car. His right leg was stiff as he walked across the tarmac.

"Not as good as your Aunt Victoria, but certainly better than the last chef."

At the New Haven Country Club, LeRoy Gautonniere greeted them with his customary dip at the waist. "Hello, Mr. Guildford and Dr. St. Clair. The special tonight is grilled salmon." LeRoy was a young waiter in his late twenties who'd been with the club since he was sixteen. LeRoy was the Guildfords' favorite waiter. He led them straight to Malcolm's reserved table.

"Tell me, LeRoy," said Paul as he seated himself, keeping his right leg straight in front of him. "How are your plans for opening your own restaurant?"

LeRoy hung his head. "Not too good. My mother got sick and I had to spend the money on her hospital bill." LeRoy's light blond was parted down the middle.

"I'm sorry to hear that," said Malcolm. "Maybe good fortune will come your way soon."

"I hope so, sir."

After Malcolm and Paul had both ordered the salmon and a bottle of 2005 Rombauer Chardonnay, Carneros, Paul looked out over the lighted landscape of the golf club his family had joined when the club was founded in 1898. The sleet had stopped, but drops continued to dribble from the tree limbs.

"Big night for Uncle Andrew tomorrow," said Paul. "He'll be remembered for decades as the Dean who donated those manuscripts. They're his legacy."

Malcolm agreed. "Big night for you, too."

"True." Paul could hardly sit still. The *Gospel of Judas* was all he'd thought about the last six months. The discovery had turned Paul's world upside down. He'd be at the center of a scholarly firestorm for months after this conference. He was ready.

LeRoy returned with the wine, and he and Malcolm played out the ritual of tasting, approving, and pouring.

Malcolm nodded. "The new showcase and security system were installed today."

"Is the governor coming for the ceremony?"

"Are you kidding? He wouldn't miss the national publicity." Malcolm scooped a handful of smoked almonds. "First a cocktail party in the YDS Common Room. I hope they have those shrimp and olive things."

Paul laughed. The food lover had, at last, married a woman perfect for him. Victoria had her own cooking show, "Victoria's Secrets to

Cooking Game."

Malcolm continued. "Then the hoopla. The governor, the president of Yale, and the Beinecke Library expert will say a few words. The manuscripts will be revealed in all their glory." Malcolm paused, tossing a couple of almonds in his mouth.

Paul watched his uncle's face. Since Malcolm had married Victoria two years ago, he looked relaxed, happy. He no longer had the calloused second skin that had hardened through thirty years of solitude after his first wife Mary had died.

Paul was bursting to talk about the manuscripts. "After tomorrow, religious circles will go crazy. With the 2004 fragments, the hot topic was Judas as obedient instead of betrayer. This time, the battle will be over suffering. I can't wait."

"Frankly, I think most people wonder about suffering—how God can allow pain."

Paul nodded, excited. "True, but there's much more to it. The *Gospel of Judas* has opened a different can of worms. Not purely theological." He leaned toward his uncle. "Friday's keynote will be an atomic bomb. Dr. Bonnie Barnes from Oxford." Paul reached for the almonds.

"A bomb?" Malcolm's eyes lit up. For seven generations, the Guildford family men had rotated among three careers: scholars, Episcopal priests, and lawyers. Malcolm was the token lawyer in his generation, but his hobby was ancient manuscripts. Andrew and his nephew Paul had both gotten Ph.D.'s in ancient literature. "So what's her topic?"

Paul accepted another glass of wine. "Based on our *Gospel of Judas*, Professor Barnes claims she's traced a secret Gnostic group—the Sethians—from the third century until the present."

"Can't be. The Sethians died out in the third century."

"That's why her topic is a bomb. She claims they're alive and well, and have been up to nefarious activities for centuries."

Malcolm's eyes widened with interest. "Really!" He threw back the rest of the almonds. "A secret group. How intriguing. What do you know about this sect? Are they like the—" Malcolm scratched his head. "Oh, you know. That medieval group of knights."

"The Templars?"

"Yes, the group with the secret jewels in Jerusalem, and the Holy Grail and all that business."

Paul shrugged. "Dr. Barnes will tell us everything tomorrow night." He paused. "She thinks she's uncovered enough evidence to prove they exist. Frankly, I have my doubts. I mean, what's the purpose in the twenty-first century? Why the cloak and dagger stuff?"

LeRoy materialized at their table, carrying plates of salmon, asparagus, and the club's famous cheese garlic potatoes. Malcolm nodded at LeRoy, then said to Paul, "One of our interns is a Gnostic. Interesting fellow. Clyde Sneed. A Brit. A little older than most interns, late twenties, but shows real promise." Malcolm paused. "I wonder if he's a Sethian Gnostic."

Paul took a bite of the salmon, delicately cooked and seasoned. He said, "I'd like to talk with him. See if he has any secret Sethian tendencies." He paused. "Gnostics are everywhere, all over the Internet—regular Gnostics, that is."

Malcolm said, "Give me a good Episcopal liturgy any day."

Paul knew how stuffy and traditional his uncle was. "Oh, come on. You'd be surprised how attractive it is to believe God is purely spiritual. Bad things happen on earth, but there are no messy questions of 'why?'"

Malcolm said, "I'm not suffering at the moment, thank you very much. And I plan to stick with Sunday morning at Trinity on the Green."

At the end of the meal, Malcolm thanked LeRoy as they got up to leave. "If you ever get your restaurant, we'll be your first customers," added Paul.

Going out the main door, Paul and Malcolm ran into Winthrop Smythe, Malcolm's law partner and Paul's godfather. He had Clyde Sneed, the young intern, in tow.

"Speak of the devil," said Malcolm as he shook hands with the young man and introduced him to Paul. Paul looked him over. He and Clyde Sneed were about the same height, except Clyde had a heavy five o'clock shadow and reddish hair contrasting with Paul's lighter hair. Clyde wore the standard conservative suit, but he had loosened his tie.

Winthrop gave Paul a hug while Malcolm ribbed him. "You two are quitting work early. It's only 9:30."

Winthrop replied, "That's the pot calling the kettle black. Clyde spent the day in depositions in Hartford. He showed up for work an hour ago. Since Elizabeth's at some charity dinner, I told him I'd take him out."

Malcolm lowered his voice and asked Winthrop about his son. "How's Jeeter?"

Winthrop shook his head and looked at the ground. "I don't know what I'm going to do with that boy. Elizabeth and I put him on a plane yesterday to a treatment center in Arizona. If they can't fix him, nobody can." Winthrop turned to Paul. "Give me a call if you have a chance."

Paul and Malcolm said goodbye and drove home.

Patches of water on the streets had started to ice over as Malcolm drove carefully home, pulling into his garage at the side of the house. A 1926 Model T roadster gleamed in the berth next to Malcolm's Town Car, followed by an empty space for Victoria's Jaguar and a white Buick Century, Malcolm's extra car that Paul used when he visited.

"Everything is ready for you upstairs," said Malcolm, clicking the remote and locking the garage door behind his car.

"Thanks for dinner," said Paul. "Sleep well."

8
Paul

In the old carriage house over the garage, Paul opened the door to a suite of rooms decorated in rich fabrics, expensive wood, and a fireplace with a fire already going. Paul walked through the sitting room and tossed his suitcase on the huge gilded four-poster bed in his bedroom, his home away from home.

Paul couldn't wait for the Jacuzzi jets in the bathtub. His leg was killing him.

Sixteen years ago, a stallion on his father's ranch in Texas had shied at a rattler on the trail, spooking the horse. Mayday had thrown Paul down a ravine and dislodged a boulder, which crushed Paul's leg. Paul spent the rest of high school in the hospital. He underwent seventeen surgeries, followed by years in physical therapy.

Ranked the number one tennis player in the U.S. at age seventeen, Paul lost his athletic career in one split second. Though his leg still went stiff on him after long plane flights and after sitting too long at his desk, at least he walked—a feat for which he was grateful daily.

Now, sitting on the bed taking off his shirt, Paul heard pounding on the stairs. "Paul!" his uncle called in a distressing voice.

Something was wrong. Terribly wrong.

When the doors opened, Malcolm burst into the room. "Oh, Paul!"

he said. For the first time in his life, Paul saw his uncle weep.

9
Isabella

I called the station and reported the Campus Killer's phone call. Apparently Spicer had been given Internet privileges after the arraignment because of his family connections. Took him two minutes to hack into the phone system and retrieve my unlisted number. The guards moved him into a private cell and put an extra guard on him.

At this point in his career as a prisoner, the only thing Harold Spicer III had going for him was his computer talents, and he had just lost those privileges. He had no friends, in or out of incarceration. I wondered how long he would last in the penitentiary. His "special" status as a relative of two high-powered judges would likely get him killed by the other inmates—convicts stashed in prison for life by his dad and grandfather.

I settled into my recliner, determined to relax. I deserved it. Mindlessly, I flipped to the opening of a made-for-TV movie starring a new male tabloid star and an older actress recycled in her dotage.

My cell phone rang. Caller ID said it was Crenshaw. Probably calling to reassure me Spicer was double guarded.

"Yes, Chief."

"ASAP. 500 St. Ronan."

"What?"

"Get there. Now. Call the top crime scene team."

"I'm on my way," I said, but Crenshaw had already hung up before the words were out of my mouth.

Now what? Had Spicer escaped? Crenshaw never minced words, but this call was unusually cryptic and terse. *Why was Crenshaw personally involved?* I noted the time: 9:56.

Without changing back into my work clothes, I grappled with a jacket, trailing a scarf that I threw around my neck as I rushed out the door and to my car.

In reverse, I shot my Mini Cooper out of the driveway, then shifted into drive and hit the gas. My pulse began to race. The drive down Dixwell seemed to take forever.

The address was one of the mansions on St. Ronan.

Turning the corner, I spotted the CSI van, the Chief's SUV, and two patrol cars out front of 500. Forensics had beaten me to the crime scene. Bob and Maria must have hightailed it from downtown. Someone had already set up a yellow and black perimeter around the entrance.

I ducked under the tape and stepped inside an elegant foyer. *A murder.* A middle-aged woman lay sprawled on the marble, her face and head in a puddle of blood. The tableau was a familiar one, but the setting was not. Few murders took place in homes like this, not in New Haven anyway. The two CSIs knelt by the body, taking pictures, measurements, and fingerprints in the hallway.

"What have we got?" I asked Maria, a young Hispanic forensic tech snapping shots of blood spatter on the floor and the walls.

"Woman, mid-fifties, bludgeoned with that lamp there, or rather what's left of it." Maria pointed to a glass lamp, the base shattered. The shade and the light bulb were still intact. "Looks like the vic's blood and hair on the lamp fragments."

"What's with the axe?" I pointed to a brand new axe lying close by, placed with care next to the lamp base and the vic's shoes and bag. "Hers?"

"Nothing on the axe. The axe is what murdered the library."

I took in the slick floors, the victim's shoes (hmm, Ferragamos) neatly placed next to a small designer suitcase and purse. A chic overcoat hung on the rack. The vic wore a black silk pantsuit. The bone sticking out from the skin of her forearm had torn a hole in the delicate fabric. The vic's other arm clutched a cell phone with a "911" the last number. I'd have to get the tape, if the woman had gotten through. I shook my head. "I don't get the axe."

Bob, a handsome black CSI supervisor with a shaved head was dusting for prints. He said, "Door wiped clean. Axe wiped clean. Prints so far on the shoes, purse, phone, and suitcase belong to the vic." He added, "No forced entry at the front or from the side. Side door's been jacked, though."

I looked around. "Alarm system?"

"Disarmed. Never went off." Stepping over the blood pooled under the victim's head, Maria motioned to me. "Come this way." We walked past a room on the right, high and spacious, with three separate sitting areas and gold threads running through the upholstery fabric. A dining room on the left. "Looks like nothing there, either room." Maria indicated. She pointed to a door up ahead, past the grand room on the right.

"Here." We stepped among glass shards and splinters of wood.

I looked into the ruins of a library. "We haven't processed it yet," said Maria, handing me a pair of shoe booties.

After covering my running shoes, I followed Maria inside. Four walls,ceiling to floor, housed both ancient and contemporary books arranged in some system, probably by topic, judging from the titles. History, theology, literature. None of the books had been damaged, but the furniture—a mahogany desk, reading chairs, tables—had been hacked to pieces, as well as the French doors.

"Anything missing?" I asked.

"Doesn't look like it. We'll know in a minute. Mr. Guildford is in the back with his nephew. They're talking with the Chief."

I was trying to assess the situation. "Is this related to the Campus Killer? Wait." I paused. "Did you say 'Guildford'?"

Maria nodded. "Big wigs. They probably know the Spicers, but I don't see—"

"Of course." The article on the front page. The donation to Yale. I walked back to find a kitchen the size of the whole downstairs of my house. Window seats, a desk, huge pantries, professional refrigerators and dishwashers, as well as an island equipped with everything one could possibly need for culinary adventures.

Then the other shoe fell. Guildford. This was the home of Victoria, the chef on "Victoria's Secrets." I'd caught Victoria's show a couple of times. I loved Victoria's bubbly personality and sense of humor.

I sighed, weary all over again with death. Beautiful home, beautiful life, beautiful woman—another dark beast had slithered into Eden.

To the left, I heard voices, and followed them back to the master bedroom. It was connected to a sitting room with a built-in movie theater and enough technological gadgets to stock Best Buy. Obviously, the intruder wasn't after electronics.

Two men a generation apart sat on the end of the bed. Father and son from their looks, but Maria had said nephew. Still in his dress uniform, Crenshaw had taken a wingback chair to the side. Big wigs, no question. But I'd already figured that out.

"Got your call, Chief."

Crenshaw looked at my casual attire and nodded. "Thanks for getting here so fast." I sensed he was thinking the same thing I was. We all needed a break, but weren't likely to get one tonight. The older man, Mr. Guildford, held his head in both hands with his eyes closed.

The nephew's blue-gray and anguished eyes met mine for a second. Yet another grieving family. I didn't know if I could take it.

Just then, a third man burst into the room, a rounder, fairer version of Mr. Guildford. "Oh, my God! What has happened?" Nobody said a word; they just all looked at each other in disbelief.

"Uncle Andrew," said the young man.

"Some monster has broken into my home and killed Victoria…my Victory," shouted Malcolm, with red-rimmed eyes.

Crenshaw stood up and introduced me. "We've got the best detective on this one. She's the one who caught the Campus Killer."

"We know," said the man whose picture was next to mine in the morning paper, Dean Andrew Guildford. "Thank you."

I blushed, still not used to notoriety. All the men also stood up, good breeding overcoming their grief.

"Dean Guildford, Mr. Guildford, Dr. St. Clair." I shook each hand.

"Call me Andrew, please."

"I'm sorry for your loss," I said sincerely. "I promise you, this case already has my full attention."

Andrew offered me the other wingback chair before sitting down on the bed himself. I heard the arrival of more street cops, sirens screaming as they pulled up. Good, they could help keep the neighbors and gawkers off the property and deal with the press who would no doubt be arriving any minute.

I pulled out the notebook I had hoped to retire for at least a day or two. "Tell me the facts."

10
John

Glenairie Castle lay nestled in the Scottish hills between Glasgow and Callendar to the northwest. John McCullough, Member of Parliament and Grand Patriarch of the Sethian Brotherhood, sat hunched over a computer in his private study at the far end of the only wing he kept open, except for visitors. Cold almost year round even in summertime, the air of the castle felt especially dank tonight. The November wind whistled and sighed outside his leaded glass window, rattling the hinges in an irritating way.

He would hear from the American Patriarch in two more hours, at 5:00 in the morning Scotland time, midnight on the east coast of the United States—and thirty minutes or so before his housekeeper, Mrs. Wallace, got up to light the fires and get breakfast going. He had time for a catnap, but he was too excited.

It had started. The final showdown between the followers of Judas, and the remnant of the faith that had ruled the world for so long. John had trained his whole life for this week.

With time on his hands, he reviewed some of the smaller successes in his life-long mission to undo the damage that Christianity had done. In 1979, Bishop Crike of Durham had died suddenly after giving a BBC broadcast on the subject of John 3:16. McCullough thought, if God so loved the world, then he wouldn't have let his own son die, forcing people to believe that Jesus' suffering—or their own—was how you got eternal life. Getting to heaven was much simpler and easier, but you had to be willing to receive the secret knowledge.

John McCullough had personally overseen the crumbling of a major television evangelist's empire. The vampire had been sucking the blood of millions of people who had paid him their hard-earned money to be healed from crippling pain.

Then there were the two Christian scholars who toured the major universities after the discovery of the *Gospel of Judas* fragments in 2004. They got worldwide publicity debating against brilliant Judas scholars who understood Judas as the only true disciple. The Christian scholars claimed that the *Gospel of Judas* was worthless then and worthless now. Neither of them survived a fire in their hotel room in Chicago.

Just in the last year, John had used his position as MP to great advantage for the Brotherhood. He had won a battle to add extra taxes for church property, making it just a little more difficult to sustain the Christian system of hypocrisy. He had also placed a member of the Brotherhood on the Archbishop of Canterbury's council to encourage the dismantling of redundant churches.

Not to mention a score of mysterious and unsolved deaths over the last fifty years, Christian leaders from pulpits all over the world, beating people into misery by binding them to sin and guilt.

What John couldn't understand was why people continued to allow themselves to remain hostage to a system that denied them true spiritual freedom.

But now. John McCullough was primed to lead an assault that would finally cripple the dying religion. The challenge was to let the world know who was responsible for this new age of spiritual enlightenment and why.... while keeping the Brotherhood itself safe and invisible to the outside world.

Osama Bin Ladin had achieved this delicate balance, and McCullough planned to do the same. With the help of God, Pleroma.

Roaming his favorite Holy Land sites on the Internet, John McCullough felt again the kindred spirit with those denizens of the desert lands. John McCullough possessed an ancient paper that verified what his pulse told him—he had originated in the desert. Only blood could explain the instant and overpowering connection he felt with the sand, the Jordan River, and Qumran.

Ahh, Jerusalem glittered before him on the screen. The Dome of the Rock shone gold in the sun. A mere two months ago, he'd returned from Holy Land heaven to the wet, cold driech of Scotland. Travel to the Middle East was getting more and more difficult, but he didn't care. He wanted to die there instead of in this God-forsaken castle he'd inherited.

However, he had put his inheritance to good use. Four times a year the international Sethian Brotherhood gathered at the castle for meetings and worship. John McCullough ran the international network from this cold, dark room surrounded by some of the world's finest art—sketches, oils, the naked statues of young boys, children.

John McCullough loved the night. A dweller in darkness, he slept during the day in a room with the windows sealed so no light could trickle in. On warm nights he went outside and looked up at the black universe, picking out the brightest star. "Mine," he'd whisper. The darker the night, the brighter the star.

Gabriel, the Messenger of Life. Now there was a pleasant thought. A young man in tune with the universe: strength, passion, brains—and perfectly malleable for the Grand Patriarch's purposes. John had outlined the coming week's plans to him as he knelt in the holy chamber. He told him only once, but Gabriel repeated every detail back to him perfectly.

Gabriel was the son he'd never have. He must have been a beautiful young boy to have turned out so perfectly as a young man.

John McCullough listened to the steady beat of his heart. After his heart attack six months ago, he sped up plans for the Brotherhood. He knew his days were numbered, and he felt the urgency of fulfilling his legacy. John smiled to himself. The culmination of his life's work had already begun. In two hours, he would hear the good news from the American Patriarch.

The Gospel of Judas would at last return to its rightful inheritors.

11
Isabella

In the house on St. Ronan, I took notes and listened. True listening involved bringing all senses—not just hearing—to bear on the person talking. And the context. For instance, when I first walked in the door, I had smelled the coppery odor of spilled blood, but had also noted the scent of recently cooked veal, magnolia potpourri on the hallway's sideboard, as well as the quiet ticking of a large clock in the kitchen.

A vague scent of menthol wafted through the bedroom where we sat. Sitting closest to me, Malcolm smelled slightly like wine, fine wool, and the saltiness of grief. "Victoria had no enemies," he said. "People loved her. Her personality was so sunny, it almost grated on your nerves." Malcolm's eyes were red and swollen in a strong and handsome—but deathly gray—face.

"Any cranks from her show would have ransacked and destroyed the kitchen, not the library, don't you think?" added Andrew, whose clothes added the scent of a fireplace to the mix. His emotions seemed barely contained by his skin.

"She wasn't even supposed to be home until tomorrow." Malcolm blinked hard, unsuccessfully holding back his tears. This poor man. Distinguished, yes. Wealthy, yes. Happy, no. I knew exactly what he was going through.

Usually the spouse was the number one suspect, but Malcolm's grief seemed genuine. More importantly, both he and Paul had an alibi for the time of the murder. Grief could be faked, but you can't fake a solid alibi.

Paul left the room, heading toward a bathroom I'd spotted off the bedroom. His khakis were still starched at the bottom, but creased behind the knees and in the lap area, as if he had been sitting a long time. His leg seemed stiff as he walked. An injury? A congenital defect? He wore an expensive blazer, a Saville Row shirt, tie loosened; and he and his uncle Malcolm both wore cufflinks. He returned with a box of tissues.

Maria appeared in the doorway. "We've finished processing the library and the rest of the downstairs. One hair, some trace, and a partial indentation from a hiking boot," she added.

Paul said to his uncles, "Let's go check the safe."

"What safe?" I asked.

"What safe?" repeated Maria.

"In the library. We don't know if the intruder found it and robbed us or not. Besides, there might be fingerprints on the lever," said Paul.

Both his uncles stared at each other in shock. Paul was the one with the presence of mind to mention the safe. I looked up at him. His facial features were refined, especially the way his patrician nose met full lips. As he moved past me, I caught a whiff of clean skin, and urgency.

"Yes, the safe," said Malcolm. "But the bookcase was in place. You don't suppose—"

Andrew stood up, wringing his hands. "The safe! I was so caught up with Victoria, I forgot the safe. Oh, no. I'm afraid there's going to be some very, very bad news in the library."

Andrew started rambling about an Associate Dean named Bill Pepperling who was—thank God—going to be out of town for the conference. Bill Pepperling had made a snide comment today about people who could afford to buy their way into positions. It had been a horrible day—just terrible—and now this.

Every person reacted differently in shock and grief over the last year. I figured Andrew was the type whose nerves went straight to his mouth.

I followed the brothers back through the kitchen and down the hall. At this point, Crenshaw took leave of the family. "We've got our best people on this," he said, and placed his hand on Malcolm's shoulder for reassurance. He turned to me. "Keep me posted."

Under my breath, I asked him, "Do you think this case is related to the Campus Killer?"

"Doesn't seem to be, but it's too early to tell. Could be just lousy timing."

He got that right. I watched him march down the hall and out the front door, then I followed the family into the library.

Malcolm walked toward the center of the bookshelves on the left side of the room. He pulled out an old, leather-bound volume, and searched behind it to reveal a metal lever, a little larger than a light switch, coated with brown plastic perfect for fingerprints.

"Just a minute," I cautioned as Malcolm reached for the lever.

Bob approached with his fingerprint duster, pulling out several of the books surrounding the switch. Maria shone her small flashlight so he could see what he was doing. After he'd pulled the sticky tape off both sides of the lever, he held it up to the overhead light. "Looks like a partial from the bottom. Nothing from the top."

I nodded to Malcolm. "Okay."

"Stand back," said Malcolm. He reached behind and switched the lever. The corner set of bookshelves swung out, revealing a two-foot by two-foot opening blocked with a sheet of steel and a key code pad next to it.

Bob stepped up and repeated his routine on any surfaces that might produce a fingerprint. Then Malcolm punched in three letters. The steel door slid to the left and disappeared.

Empty. Malcolm closed his eyes and his whole body wilted.

Andrew shouted, "Oh, God, no!" He clutched his chest as if he might have a heart attack. "I knew it, I just knew it."

Bob began dusting inside the safe. He said weakly, "Maybe this time we'll get lucky."

Maria shone the light toward the back of the safe. "Hold on, Bob. There's something here that looks like a business card."

"A business card?" Malcolm and Andrew craned their necks to see.

I stepped in. "I know you gentlemen are eager, but could you give them room to work?"

They moved back with obvious reluctance. I sensed their frustration. Men like these two were used to running the world. It must be tough for them to step aside and let the experts do their jobs.

Bob handed Maria a baggie. She lifted the paper carefully with a gloved hand. "It's not stiff, though. Looks like stationery paper." Once she'd secured the top of the bag, she handed it to me.

Again, the gentlemen craned their necks to see. One typed line on the slip of paper read: "Death: hero on this orb."

A shiver ran through my body. Unlike the Campus Killer who had left every crime scene spotless, this killer had left a deliberate clue.

Why?

Everyone stared at the slip of paper as if it carried anthrax. Considering the dead woman in the hallway and the ransacked safe—the general response seemed to be disgust at what was probably either a taunt, a very bad joke, or a misdirection.

I turned to Malcolm and broke the silence. "Did you have this in your safe? Is it part of the stolen papers?"

"I've never seen it before in my life," said Malcolm.

Andrew shook his head no.

"We'll run it for prints, paper type, and ink," I said. Forensics would help us get started, but then the hard work would begin. We had to figure out 1) what the message meant, 2) why the killer had left it for us to find, and 3) get into the killer's head and discover what the note was trying to hide. My head started to ache thinking about the hours of research I was in for.

Paul stepped up to look. "Trace evidence is good, but what? Why? There's got to be more to it. Death is a hero? Death was not a hero to Victoria. She was happy. She was healthy. Somebody stole her life from her years before she should have died."

Yes. Paul was already on my wavelength while his uncles were still staring at the paper.

"Maybe it's a code," he added.

Andrew looked up. "You're good with puzzles, Paul," he said. "See if you can figure out what the killer was trying to say."

Paul stared at the paper. "I'll have to think about it." He repeated, "Death: Hero on this orb."

"I'll get it to the lab," said Maria.

"Meet you there later," said Bob to me as he packed up his kit to leave.

"Good." As Bob and Maria left, I ushered the family into their dining room, a space that reminded me of the Vanderbilt's dining room I'd seen once on a mansion tour in Newport, Rhode Island.

Once we were seated, I said, "I'm sorry, but I need to ask you some questions. It appears Mrs. Guildford interrupted a burglary, so let's focus on that. What was in the safe?"

"Victoria's jewelry, a coin collection, a few legal papers, $100,000 in cash—"

Andrew broke in, his face flushed with emotion. He was beginning to perspire, and he was no longer able to hold in his distress. "The *Gospel of Judas*," he said. "The original Greek document—what was left of the papyrus, as well as a Latin translation on vellum."

"You were going to donate both manuscripts to Yale tomorrow. Is that right?" I kept my voice even, calm, professional—an anchor for the rough waters around me.

"Yes." Andrew continued, "Those documents were the most valuable thing in there. Cash, no big deal, loose change."

Maybe to this family $100,000 was loose change, but someone in a lower tax bracket could live off that kind of loose change for a long time. I said, "Even so, the money might be a motivation for someone who needed cash in a hurry."

"Maybe," said Malcolm. He began tracing the grain of wood on the table.

"What about the jewelry?" I asked.

"He could hock it, I suppose," said Malcolm.

"We'll put a watch on all the pawnshops in this area and New York. I'll need a list of Mrs. Guildford's items, and pictures, if you have them."

Malcolm nodded. "Our safety deposit box at the bank has the expensive stuff and pictures. We just kept things she liked to wear around town, and documents we might need. Passports, things like that."

"What are the chances of recovering the manuscripts before tomorrow?" Andrew bobbed up from his chair and started pacing, rubbing his hands together as he walked.

I said, a little more cynically than I intended. "Do you believe in miracles? It's happened, but the odds are against it."

"This is a nightmare, a terrible, terrible nightmare." Andrew pulled at his earlobe. "I'll have to hold a press conference and call off the governor. No sense in unveiling an empty case."

"So the whole city knows about this manuscript." I kicked myself. I should have read their article instead of being self-absorbed in my own news.

"Yes," said Malcolm. "The story traced the documents' movements from the Beinecke Library's expert, Dr. Wolfgang Timmerman, to Germany, and back to us. It announced that YDS had ordered a new showcase with special security. The thief probably figured it would be easier to steal from our home than from the new security system."

Andrew groaned. "Tomorrow night was the high point of everything I've worked for. We must find those documents." He seemed more upset over the theft than over his sister-in-law's death.

"How did your family come by the manuscripts in the first place?" I asked.

"I found them," said Paul.

12
Isabella

I watched as Paul leaned forward at the table. If Malcolm and Andrew were Paul's uncles, there had to be another sibling floating around out there—Paul's mother or father. All three men in front of me could have been cloned from the nineteenth-century gentleman whose portrait had been hoisted above the fireplace in the living room.

"Summers in college, I came to New Haven with my mother. Athletics was out because of an accident," said Paul.

So his stiff leg must have resulted from an accident. He still looked athletic and strong—a thoroughbred racer, not a quarter horse.

"This house was built by the Guildford family after the Civil War, with a basement filled with boxes of old stuff nobody wanted to go through. Pappadad—my grandfather—decided he wanted to catalogue the books and ancient papers. It gave me summer projects," continued Paul.

"I see."

"This house fell apart once Mom died," said Malcolm. "When Victoria and I married, we moved Dad to an Alzheimer's unit near the country club. The police had found him wandering around the Yale campus in his pajamas singing at the top of his lungs. He didn't have a clue who or where he was."

I had to work at not smiling, remembering the detectives on that case. They'd called him "Wee Willie Winkie"—a fact I was not going to mention now.

"Victoria and I gutted the house and refinished it two years ago. That's when we built the library," continued Malcolm.

"And the safe," Andrew interjected, "Our father kept his valuables in his socks drawer. We discovered an old dumbwaiter that carried food from the kitchen to Aunt Matilda's bedroom upstairs."

"It was the perfect location, so we walled in the rest of the shaft and put the safe there," said Malcolm.

"Who knew about the safe? Who knew the combination for the key pad?" I asked.

"Only the family," said Paul. "We all knew in case something happened to both Victoria and Malcolm."

"The company that installed the safe knew, too. Failsafe Security," said Andrew.

"What's the code?" I asked

Andrew rolled his eyes in a way that neither other relative could see. "MIG."

"MIG. Like the jet?"

"Yes," said Andrew. "Malcolm's initials. We begged him to use something a little more complicated or less obvious. Anybody could figure it out." He looked displeased, and started pulling at his earlobe again.

"Did you write the code down anywhere?"

"No, that's why I picked something I could remember easily. I didn't want to end up like Dad with no memory at all." Malcolm became defensive as he looked at Andrew, shooting him an angry glare.

It appeared even the best families weren't exempt from sibling rivalry.

Hmm. An inside job? In spite of the looks exchanged by the brothers, I didn't think so. More likely, one of the family members had disclosed the secret to someone who had told someone else.

"Back to the manuscripts," I said.

"Paul found them in the basement. They'd come over on the Mayflower with our ancestors from England," said Andrew.

"Not the Mayflower," corrected Malcolm.

"It doesn't matter. They were crated with a bunch of stuff from the sixteenth century. Paul discovered them when he was cataloguing the library."

"The Latin title caught my eye and I started reading the translation. It sounded interesting, but I was swamped with all the old books, so I filed it away for later."

"Then, a couple of years ago, the Maecenas Foundation bought the Egyptian *Gospel of Judas*. Remember? Rodolphe Kasser announced it in Paris in 2004. Huge international news."

Andrew continued. "Paul brought our copy from the basement. By that time, he had his Ph.D. in New Testament and was teaching at SMU. Perkins Seminary."

So Paul was a university professor. Maybe it was the cufflinks or the tailored blazer, but I would have pegged him as a business executive or a lawyer in a big firm.

Andrew sat down again and gesticulated with his hands. "We'd been sitting on a gold mine in our basement this whole time and didn't know it. We sent both documents to the Beinecke Library just to make sure they were authentic."

"Wasn't there some scandal at the Beinecke a few years back over a Viking manuscript?" I interrupted.

Andrew agreed. "Yes, that's why they hired a new expert from Germany, Wolfgang Timmerman. Even after he'd determined we had the real deal, Timmerman hand-carried the documents to Christian Himmell at Basel, top specialist. Timmerman met with Malcolm and me when he got back from Germany. He was so excited I thought he'd pluck his goatee off."

"That's when we decided to donate them to the Yale Divinity School," said Paul. "The 2004 Judas manuscript is fragmentary. Quite a bit is missing. Also, the provenance is questionable. Our manuscripts piece everything together and fill in the gaps."

Andrew interrupted again. "It's the biggest find since the Dead Sea Scrolls. We wanted to make it available for scholars all over the world." He clutched his chest and slumped down in his chair.

"Were the documents insured?" I asked.

"Of course," answered Malcolm.

"Money isn't the point," said Paul. "Our family has been associated with Yale for three hundred years. Because Andrew was dean, we all agreed it was the right thing to do to donate them."

"It might have been the right thing to do," said Malcolm. "But it's gotten Victoria killed." He started to stand up and leave the table.

It was time to wrap up for tonight. "Can you think of anything else I should know? About the stolen jewelry, the cash, or the manuscripts?" I met the gaze of each man, three sets of gray-blue eyes in varying expressions of grief. All three men shook their heads no.

"Tell you what." I stood up and gathered my purse. "Tomorrow when I hear back from the lab, I'd like to interview anyone who might give some insight. Neighbors. Friends. A housekeeper maybe."

Malcolm nodded. "Gabby."

"Tomorrow evening was going to be the hottest international news in the academic world since Paris. People are coming from all over the world." Andrew's voice was sounding hoarse with distress.

I turned to him. "I'll hold a press conference with your family here tomorrow. If money's not an issue, maybe you can offer a reward for the documents' safe return."

Andrew's face slowly brightened as he looked back at me. "A reward. Yes. Maybe a reward would bring it back." For the first time he looked as if he would survive the night's disaster. "We'll pray somebody returns it for the money. You can always count on human greed."

"Nothing will bring my Victory back," said Malcolm, his voice shaking.

I passed out three copies of my card. "Call me if you think of anything. Otherwise, I'll be back tomorrow morning."

Paul escorted me to the door, as Victoria's body was being zipped up in a body bag. We walked outside through the crowd of police officers and spectators, raising and ducking under the yellow perimeter tape. Members of the press poked microphones at us, and I recognized some of the same reporters from this afternoon. "Detective O'Leary! Can you tell us what happened?"

"The family will give a statement tomorrow morning."

"Is this case connected to the Campus Killer?" More microphones pressed at me until I started to feel hemmed in.

I gave them the standard professional brush-off. "No comment at this time. Please, let us pass."

Paul dodged their cameras and pressing bodies, shielding me.

"Walk with me for a minute, will you?" I asked Paul, motioning for two patrol officers to keep reporters at bay. "I need some basic facts about the *Gospel of Judas.* Your copy. The complete copy." Like what was in it worth killing over.

I remembered the furor surrounding the 2004 fragment's discovery, especially the part that claimed Jesus had instructed Judas to turn him in. Obedience or betrayal? Scholars had debated for months.

After the church refused Ronny a funeral, I'd quit attending mass. But when the Judas craze was at its height, I had run into my priest in the vegetable section of the grocery store and asked him what he thought. "In the first place, this new document is not reliable. Besides, it doesn't change the truth of the gospel."

His arrogance made me angry. I hated the smugness of people who had it all figured out. Gathering steam, I challenged him, "It makes perfect sense that Jesus told Judas to turn Him in."

"It doesn't work that way," said the priest, selecting a peach.

"How do you know it doesn't work that way?" I had insisted.

"Jesus had to be betrayed, turned over to the authorities. Otherwise, there was no struggle at Gethsemane. He had to make the choice to accept the crucifixion."

"Not so. Jesus had already made the choice to die."

"No. Judas acted out of evil motives. That is how Jesus conquered evil."

I had stuffed more tomatoes than I needed into a plastic bag. I knew my priest intended well, but I also knew where good intentions led—to hell, a place I already lived. Since the tragedy, my life was a war zone between wanting to believe in a good God, over and against the evidence of a God who stood by and let innocent people suffer.

Now, I wanted to hear what Paul—with a Ph.D. in New Testament—had to say about the *Gospel of Judas*.

"Like what? It's a complicated document—" Paul began. Frosty air came from his mouth. We hurried down the street away from the crowd.

"Like what could motivate someone to steal the manuscript and murder your aunt. I studied some of the Gnostics in seminary, like the *Gospel of Thomas*," I said. "But none of them encouraged violence. In fact, the opposite."

"You went to seminary?" Although I couldn't see his face clearly in the dark, Paul's tone reflected surprise. And respect.

"One year, at YDS. A lifetime ago. Correct me if I'm wrong, but to the Gnostics earth is matter—a realm of suffering and misery. God and heaven are purely spiritual."

Paul nodded.

"Bottom line—God would never be so tacky and disgusting to become part of a sinful earth."

"Exactly," said Paul. Now that we had left behind the mob scene in front of the Guildford's house, we slowed down a little and stopped under the streetlight at the corner.

I pressed on. "Okay. I need specifics. Give me reasons someone is willing to kill to get the manuscripts." An image of Victoria's bludgeoned body flitted across my mind. "A bunch of ancient words doesn't usually add up to death."

Paul breathed a sigh that sounded deep and troubled. "Correct." He thrust his hands into his pockets. "The *Gospel of Judas* claims Jesus died because He wanted release from his earthly body, not as a sacrifice. Christians believe that Jesus died to redeem our sins."

The release theory only worked if you wanted death—if you considered life unbearable. "So Jesus died to get off the earth and back to heaven, not to save souls." I paused. "So why did Victoria die?"

I watched Paul nod under the streetlamp. "Be patient. I'm getting there. For one thing, if the *Gospel of Judas* is right, the painful, humiliating death on the cross wasn't necessary. Poison would have been more expedient."

Paul had a point. "Okay."

"Here's what I think. The *Gospel of Judas* is dangerous because of what was in it for Judas. Jesus rewards him with the promise, 'You will exceed all of them.' Judas will be the greatest of His disciples."

Paul shifted his weight and leaned forward, intense and eager under the streetlight. Clearly, he loved to teach. If only I'd had him as a seminary professor, maybe I wouldn't be such a cynic. Maybe my faith wouldn't have gone up in smoke.

"In the *Gospel of Judas,* Jesus believes in astrology. A person's destiny is linked to the stars."

Astrology. Astrology was definitely not promoted in the Bible.

"Jesus shows Judas the stars and tells him, 'The star that leads the way is your star.'"

"I see. A promise of the brightest star. A reward. A heavenly reward, no less."

"Yes," said Paul, nodding. "Jesus' promises of greatness probably would have been compelling to someone back then."

"Compelling to someone now."

"Jesus tells Judas that he'll be cursed for generations, but that in the end, he will rule over everyone," Paul continued. "The *Gospel of Judas* is a serious spiritual aphrodisiac."

An idea began to take shape in my mind. "It's got to be a religious fanatic of some kind. Maybe a fanatic Gnostic who wants to be a hero now. A hero like Judas."

"There's more," he said. "Do you want to hear it?"

"I'm listening."

"According to the complete *Gospel of Judas*, Judas Iscariot had twin sons, David and Jesse. David wrote down everything Judas told him. He's the one ultimately responsible for the *Gospel of Judas*. He recorded everything."

Paul had my attention now. I started to get chill bumps. "Tell me if I'm wrong, but doesn't the name 'Thomas' mean 'twin'? Doesn't the Gnostic *Gospel of Thomas* claim to be written by Jesus' twin?"

"Exactly. That's one reason this find was so astounding. Right before our eyes was another set of twins—the progeny of Judas."

"What happened to the other twin?"

"His name was Jesse, and he became a Christian. He's the one portrayed as evil in the *Gospel of Judas*."

I took a minute to absorb what Paul was telling me. This news would rock the Christian world. *Someone had chosen to act on this information.*

Rubbing my hands up and down my arms, I tried to warm myself. *Somebody out there wanted the brightest star for Judas and for himself.* The motive went to the heart of the human condition. We all have our own version of the brightest star, and spend most of our lives working to achieve it. I said, "No wonder your uncle Andrew was so upset."

We started walking back to my car, in silence for a full minute or two.

Paul said, finally, "Aunt Victory was a lovely lady. You know, in the *Gospel of Judas*, death isn't sad. It's liberation from flesh, that's all. A release into the light."

Something clicked. "'Death: hero on this orb.' If that's true, then death is a hero for those trapped in matter on earth. It's a Gnostic belief."

Paul looked at me again with surprise and respect. "Yes. Death, the liberator. It's part of the Sethian creed." He repeated, "'Death: hero on this orb,'" then paused. "Just a minute. Can you hand me a pen and paper?"

I dug in my purse and pulled out my notebook and a pen. In the dim light, I watched him scribbling letters on the page. What was he up to?

"I thought so. Look." Paul moved toward the lights under the porte-cochere. He showed me what he'd written. "'Death: hero on this orb.' These are the same letters that form the phrase 'Sethian Brotherhood'." He added, "It's an anagram."

I stared. "Oh, my God. It is. I would never have figured it out."

Paul smiled in the dim light, light crease lines appearing in his cheeks. He had just saved me hours of research. "The letters—yes. It's a perfect anagram. How did you—?"

He handed me back the notebook. "My accident. All those years in the hospital. I worked puzzles for hours. Learned Latin and Greek. Had to keep my mind busy. At that point, I thought I'd never walk again."

Paul faced me in a cashmere coat that probably cost as much as my salary for a week. He let down his guard, and I saw his eyes go soft for one second.

A flash of something long dead flickered through my abdomen. *Damn it.* For some perverse reason I found Paul attractive, not least because he was an intelligent man (goodness knows, they were hard enough to come by), but because he was schooled in the faith I could no longer accept.

"The Sethian Brotherhood?" I avoided meeting Paul's eyes.

"One of the ancient Gnostic sects. The *Gospel of Judas* is a Sethian document," explained Paul.

"I thought they died out a couple of hundred years after Christ."

"Everybody thought that." Paul hit his forehead with the palm of his hand as if he had just remembered something. "Except Bonnie."

"What? Who's Bonnie?" Paul was clearly excited about something.

"Dr. Bonnie Barnes, the leading Sethian expert. She's coming into town for the conference. She thinks this group is still alive."

"Oh, my God. Is she here yet?"

"She's checking in at the Courtyard early tomorrow. Overseas flight tonight, from England. We'll call her tomorrow."

As much as I wanted to talk with this expert now, I was about to hit a second wall of exhaustion for today, and I was glad we'd have to wait. I walked to my car.

Paul opened the door for me, an extra touch of courtesy. Ronny used to open my car door, but few men since had bothered. "Thank you," I said, beginning to feel major effects of sensory overload. I climbed in my car and closed the door myself.

"You're welcome," he answered, meeting my eyes an instant longer than necessary, before he turned around and walked back inside.

14
Gabriel

Gabriel watched the 11:00 news on his small flat screen television. Toward the end of the newscast, cameras panned the scene of a woman described as "the detective who just yesterday nabbed the Campus Killer," and a man identified as "Paul Guildford, nephew of the deceased." They were walking out of the house where Gabriel had left the body in the foyer.

Nobody knew anything. The police were clueless. Gabriel wondered how long it would take them to figure out the message in the safe.

The broadcast signed off with an excited blonde anchorwoman promising more information tomorrow on the "breaking news of Chef Victoria Guildford's tragic death."

Tonight Victoria's death was a local story. Tomorrow, the Sethian Brotherhood would be international news.

At 11:50, Gabriel called the American Patriarch. Both used throwaway cell phones, and the conversation was short.

"I had to kill her. She saw me." Gabriel began to feel the slow creep of failure, the most familiar part of his psyche, as his spirits began to sink. The approaching darkness was accompanied by the prickly fear of imminent rejection. He added quickly in self-defense, "The Grand Patriarch told me to use my head in an emergency, and this was an emergency." Gabriel held his breath, waiting to see if he would be reprimanded.

"Not a problem," said the American Patriarch. "Collateral damage. Just be prepared for tomorrow."

Gabriel closed his eyes, his bloodstream flooded with relief. "Yes, sir. I'll be ready."

15
Isabella

One last stop before I could put this day to rest. At the CSI lab Maria was in the process of pulling the slip of paper from the safe out of the bag with tweezers and placing it under her microscope.

"It's an anagram," I told her. "Paul figured it out. 'Sethian Brotherhood.' Any forensic evidence that might lead us to the killer? Fingerprints? Paper source?"

"Sorry. Looks like garden variety Times New Roman type on common stationery paper." Maria moved over and I peered into the eyepiece.

I turned the microscope back to Maria. "Look again. We'll have to test the fibers."

Maria gave it a closer inspection, moving the paper to examine all four corners and the edges. "Hey, wait a second. Looks like a watermark." She paused. "Whoa."

I took another look in the microscope.

"Whatcha got?" asked Bob, crossing the room. He stopped to look over my shoulder. I moved aside and he squinted into the eyepiece. "This is interesting."

I peered in again. As I flashed the finding on the screen overhead, the picture of a capital "T" emerged, with a snake coiled around it. "Have you ever seen this symbol?"

Bob shook his head. "Reminds me of a caduceus."

"Yeah," agreed Maria. "But a caduceus has two snakes, wings, and stands for medicine or something."

"This one doesn't look like it stands for anything healthy," said Bob.

I sat down at a nearby computer and googled "Caduceus." After a minute, I agreed. "Look. Every image has a pole, two snakes, and wings. The caduceus is an image for ancient physician, as well as the symbol for Hermes or Mercury."

"So it's not a caduceus. We need to dig deeper and find a T, not a pole, and one snake with no wings."

I thought aloud. "We've got a motto—death as a hero—and the symbol of a snake."

"Death and snakes. Doesn't look promising," said Bob.

Maria continued to study the picture on the large screen. "I'll check iconography first, then analyze for rag content and watermark manufacturers."

"Creepy," said Bob.

"Let me know if you get a hit on any fingerprints. Just leave a full report on my desk for tomorrow," I said. "Bonnie Barnes, the Sethian specialist from Oxford, is supposed to be here. We'll call her first thing."

Chapter Two
FRIDAY

1
John

At 5:00 a.m., John McCullough sat in his private study at Glenairie Castle in Scotland, waiting to hear from the American Patriarch. He had found a new website that brought together his love of the Holy Land and his interest in young boys. Set against a desert background, young Arabs—ripe, perfect—dressed in traditional costume led the observer into a series of brightly colored tents.

Inside, each tent had been decorated like a sultan's harem with hangings, rugs, large jugs, pillows, brass candleholders, and pitchers. Once inside, the Arab lad slowly took off his headdress, then his pantaloons. Underneath, his private parts were swathed in a loincloth, which he slowly unwound.

Another aspect of Christianity that John didn't understand—the current debates and schisms over sexuality. The church had squelched pleasure for so long under the rubric of sin that human beings had lost sight of one of the few earthly gifts that made our temporary material existence worthwhile.

Lost in the desert, John could feel himself reaching a tumescent state, when his email message board beeped.

Midnight already! Quickly he closed the site, having memorized the address.

His message read:

"TO: The Grand Patriarch of the Western World
FROM: American Patriarch

SUBJECT: Day One

"Documents in hand. Collateral damage and complications. Don't be alarmed by news coverage of a murder. The death was accidental and does not—repeat, NOT—affect our plans. Will proceed, with caution."

John answered the email: "Send Gabriel with documents to Glasgow tomorrow, unless too risky."

He waited for five minutes, then read the reply: "As planned. Will sort it out on this end. Red alert, if necessary to abort. D-Day plus six, and counting."

McCullough's heart began to beat erratically from excitement. Quickly, he took a pill from his desk drawer and swallowed it. He had no intentions of dying before the week was out.

Good news. Wonderful news. By tomorrow, he would be holding the *Gospel of Judas* in his own hands—returned to the Brotherhood after five hundred years.

McCullough deleted the emails, and then emptied them from his trash, finally going into his hard drive and wiping them out altogether.

"Will proceed, with caution." John wondered about the collateral damage, and what kind of complications had come up. However, he had faith in his brothers—the American Patriarch could handle whatever the problem was.

He rubbed his hands together for warmth and from excitement. He would eat Mrs. Wallace's breakfast of eggs, fried toast and stewed tomatoes, then sleep for five hours, followed by a jaunt to Glasgow to receive the treasured manuscripts. He would clock the next hours with precision.

The important thing was to synchronize the forthcoming post card messages with the events, so the world would discover the truth as it unfolded.

The legacy of Judas was coming to fulfillment.

2
Isabella

I arrived at work earlier than usual. After I got home last night I didn't have a chance to change into my pajamas before I passed out on the bed. Six hours later, a dream jolted me awake—a squid wrapping its slimy, suctioning tentacles around my arms and legs and neck, instead of a pair of headlights coming at me out of nowhere. I didn't have time to ponder the significance of the change in dream imagery.

Armed with a large cup of Caramel Macchiato coffee, I walked into the CSI lab at 7:00, just as Bob had isolated a fingerprint from the back door. It didn't match the prints from the Guildford family. It didn't match the partial he'd found on the lever in the library either, but it was a start. "I'll get the housekeeper's print this morning," he said.

"Anything new about the axe?" I asked.

He shook his head. "My money's on the killer. Why would Mrs. Guildford bring home an axe, wreck her own library, then wipe her own fingerprints off before she died?"

"What is the psychology of someone who would bring an axe to a crime scene and then kill the victim with a lamp?" I asked.

"And leave both lined up so tidily next to the vic's shoes," said Maria.

"Blood spatter indicates the murder took place in the hallway, not in the library. The vic was already on the ground when she was hit," said Bob.

"She must have broken her arm falling. Probably slipped on the floor running away from him," I said.

"Maybe he was about to smash the lamp in the library when he heard her fall, and he came at her instead. Had the lamp in his right hand and didn't want to switch hands. We determined it was a right-handed attacker," said Maria.

Bob sighed. "I need a break." He turned to me and asked, "Mind if we go out for some pancakes?"

"Be my guest. This is another high profile case. I'm sure we'll all be suffering from sleep deprivation again soon."

"I'm also working on the boot print," yawned Maria. "It's a hiking boot."

"Well, that certainly narrows it down," said Bob.

"Go eat pancakes," I said. "I'll check back by the lab about nine. We'll be heading back over to Malcolm Guildford's pretty fast after that."

3
Isabella

Within an hour, I'd googled the Internet and Wikipedia for information on Sethianism and the *Gospel of Judas*. I found myself pulled into the Mediterranean world of the Israelites, Gnostics, and early Christians—a time of ancient religions, when belief systems met deep human needs. I looked at the pictures of the Holy Land, especially the Sea of Galilee, and felt the tug of homesickness. But homesick for what?

My phone rang. For some odd reason, I felt reluctant to re-enter the twenty-first century, where proof and facts trumped our desire for a relationship with any spiritual transcendent being. Had we lost God, or had God lost us?

"O'Leary."

"This is Paul St. Clair. I hope it's not to early to call."

Immediately, I pictured his face under the light of the porte-cochere, his smile of delight when he figured out the puzzle. "Not at all."

Paul continued. "Dr. Barnes checked in at 6:30 this morning, but she left a request at the front desk. No calls before ten. Said the flight wore her out."

"Is Malcolm awake?"

"Yes. And Andrew's at his YDS office digging through his files trying to find anything Dr. Barnes sent him. Said he remembered a rather colorful rendition of the original Sethian creation story. Seems she wanted to produce a movie based on it. Something like *Lord of the Rings*. Anyway, he'll be over in time for the press conference."

"Good. Bob and Maria and I will be there shortly."

With more public appearances today and the press conference this morning, I had worn another crisp designer suit and stylish shoes to work. Truth to tell, I liked the feel of silk, linen, fine wool against my skin, and I also knew dressing well gave me an edge when I needed it.

Even though I was damaged goods—nobody had to know it.

I stopped by the lab to pick up Bob and Maria, back at work after breakfast. They got me up to speed. The footprint was from a hiking boot sold at every Walmart and Payless store in the country. Size ten. "Great."

"Maria's identified the watermark from the slip of paper in the safe," said Bob. "It's called the 'crucified serpent.' An old alchemical drawing that represents fixing unstable elements. They used to make mercury as a legendary cure by taking out the poisonous or volatile element. Apparently, the picture has biblical roots from the story of Moses. Moses made a statue of the crucified serpent in order to cure snakebites that God sent as a punishment for the Israelites whining in the desert. It's also a charm against plague."

"Biblical roots?"

"Yeah. Old Testament. Numbers 21. I looked it up. It's also included in a stained glass window at Keble College in Oxford."

"What's it been used for lately?"

"Still working on that one."

"Let's go back to the house," I said. "Bring your kits."

When Malcolm answered the door, I thought he looked dignified, but haggard. Skin hung loosely around his eyes. He wore a dark blue wool suit with a light blue pinstripe. The entryway had been cleared of Victoria's body, but not cleaned. "Gabby's supposed to come at 9:30," said Malcolm. "I didn't have the heart to call her and tell her before she gets here."

I followed him into the dining room and sat down. Today in the sunlight, the table looked like a conference table at a prestigious law firm instead of an elegant setting for a meal.

"We need to get Gabby's fingerprints and everyone's DNA. We also need to take a closer look at closets and laundry." I nodded to Maria to get started, then said to Malcolm, "In the meantime, do you mind if I ask you some questions?"

He shook his head no, tracing the grain in the wood of the table as he had last night.

I considered my tack carefully. The focus had to be on the safe and who wanted the contents enough to kill. "Are you sure that you didn't repeat information about your safe and the code to anyone at work?"

He shook his head no, eyes still downcast.

"Is there anyone who works with you at the law office who could overhear you talking on the phone?"

Malcolm's hand stopped tracing patterns in the table. "I have an intern, Clyde Sneed, who has a cubicle right outside my door." He paused. "But he's trustworthy. The firm would never hire someone with a criminal background."

I made a note of Clyde's name. "Can you tell me a little more about him?"

"Yes, well, he's one of the brightest interns we've had. Full of energy. Went to law school. Bounced around a bit, then came to us."

"I see. Who recruited him?"

"Actually, I think Winthrop Smythe found him. Legal background in England. Knew his father or something." Malcolm did not seem to see Clyde Sneed as a threat.

"Did you ever discuss your safe in a public place where a stranger could overhear? At your club?"

Again, no. Malcolm said, "My mother warned us against the public utterance of family business. She always said, 'You never know who is sitting in back of you at the theater.'"

Not exactly like my own background, where everyone within three blocks knew everything about everybody. I pursued, as gently as I could. "What kind of law do you practice?"

Malcolm sighed. "International business law. I travel quite a bit, less in the last two years. But when my first wife died, I spent several years in London, handling the firm's business there. The firm set up a London office, with Winthrop Smythe and myself. He brought his family with him."

"Who is Winthrop Smythe? You mentioned him earlier."

"Law partner."

"Do you socialize with him outside the office?"

Malcolm nodded. "Oh, yes. Our families used to travel together when we were growing up. Now he's a hunting buddy. We travel all over the world looking for exotic game. One reason Victoria started her cooking show. She loved cooking game and it was a unique approach for the cooking channel." Malcolm swallowed hard and I thought for a second that he might lose his collected demeanor.

I paused for a minute and wrote in my notebook, giving him a chance to gather himself together again. "Do you know whether Winthrop knew about the safe?"

Malcolm thought for a moment. "I'm not sure, actually. I don't remember confiding in him any specifics, but he has a similar arrangement at his house. In fact, that's where we got the idea."

Another note in my book.

"But you can count Winthrop out as a suspect. He's like family. His son Jeeter is my godson. No, not Winthrop."

I would make the decisions about who to discount, and I intended to interview Winthrop Smythe, Clyde Sneed, and Jeeter, too, no matter what Malcolm said.

I changed the course of the questions. "Please don't be offended, but…" I hesitated. So many times family and close friends had a bearing on a case. "What is your relationship like with your brother Andrew?"

"What does that have to do with anything?" Malcolm's face was a mix between puzzled and offended.

"Do you trust him? Is he the type who might slip and say something to somebody?"

Malcolm looked as if he were weighing his words. "Andrew is the baby of the family. He was our parents' favorite—like a puppy dog, ridiculously friendly. Even to store clerks. Takes 'love thy neighbor' too far, in my opinion."

Watching carefully, I waited. People inevitably gave away information with small facial movements or hesitations.

Malcolm sighed again. "To answer your question, it's possible he could have told his children. They could have told their playmates who blabbed to their parents at the dinner table. You know how fascinating hidden alcoves and passageways are to children."

I nodded. The Nancy Drew/Hardy Boys syndrome. "Tell me about Andrew's family."

"Andrew married a woman he met when he was a Rhodes Scholar in Paris. Noe. Roman Catholic. He's the first in several generations to step out of our family's Episcopal tradition, but he was smitten at first sight." Malcolm shook his head. "Lucky devil. He's still smitten. They have four children."

Good Catholics, like my parents. "How old?"

"Oldest one's eighteen, first year at Yale. The youngest one, Theresa, is five." Malcolm sighed again. "He'll never be without family around. By the time Theresa leaves home, he'll have a lapful of grandchildren. They're just one big happy family over there."

There was that streak of jealousy or competition again, almost but not quite hidden in his tone of voice. Malcolm must be feeling especially bitter today. Watching him, I felt another stab of sympathy. Though I'd never admit it out loud, I envied my brothers for having so many children. Those early holidays were almost unbearable with all the little ones running around.

Paul entered the dining room from the kitchen, wearing dark slacks and a tie tucked into a cashmere sweater. His right leg didn't seem as stiff today, but he still slightly favored the left one. "Thank you," I said to Malcolm.

"May I go make some phone calls?" he asked. "Gabby should be here any minute. I'll need to sit down with her."

I nodded. Malcolm walked like an automaton toward the kitchen. I heard the back door open. Then I heard Malcolm's voice in a low rumble, followed by a woman's crying sounds.

Paul sat down at the table in a seat next to the windows. This morning, his clean-skin smell included a whiff of delicate cologne. His face looked tanned in the morning sunrays sifting into the dining room through the front window—a healthy shade of bronze that contrasted with his light hair. Must be living in Texas, where both the sun and the stars shone brighter, at least according to the song.

Before I had a chance to ask, Paul volunteered, "Ask anything you want. All of us want to find out who's responsible."

<h1 style="text-align:center">4</h1>

Gabriel

Gabriel left New Haven on I-95. He pushed the speed limit as far as he dared on the way to Kennedy airport. The *Gospel of Judas* manuscripts from the safe last night were stowed in an overnight/laptop bag on the seat next to him.

Gabriel's skin couldn't contain the energy he felt. Pleroma had infused his body with power, a spiritual force exploding inside him. His knuckles turned white on the steering wheel with the vitality caged inside his body. Nothing short of death itself could give him such a spiritual high.

When he had knocked on Dr. Barnes' room at 7:00 this morning, she had already changed into her pajamas from her traveling clothes, getting ready to take a nap. Thanking him for the tea, she had smiled and had actually given him a tip. A *dollar*! She had paid him for killing her! Gabriel laughed out loud, remembering her corpse on the floor. Gabriel couldn't get over the fact that he had been the instrument of God, literally taking the breath of life from the enemy.

His only regret was that he couldn't leave a hatchet as his calling card. There was no way he could carry the tea and a hatchet. Even down his pants leg, too bulky—someone might have noticed, like the girl on the elevator going back down to the lobby.

Gabriel sped along, weaving in and out among the trucks and making sure he didn't go but four miles over the speed limit. He pretended that the Dodge Neon the American Patriarch had provided for him was a Maserati.

The traffic slowed and he caught sight of red and blue blinking lights ahead. Oh, no. He barely had time to make his flight as it was. He didn't need any hassles from the cops.

And for sure he didn't need a delay.

He slowed to a crawl. He'd asked the Patriarch to give him more time, but he said this flight was perfect. "The scheme has to play out like clockwork. We can't have you hanging around New Haven a moment longer than necessary."

He spotted two uniform cops waving the traffic down to two lanes. The traffic slowed, but didn't stop.

Gabriel smiled casually as he passed, though he'd sweated through both his shirt and the wool sweater. This morning had gone as smoothly as a dream. Gabriel wasn't about to miss his plane.

Gabriel's confidence grew with every mile he put between himself and New Haven. He wondered when someone would discover the late Dr. Bonnie Barnes.

5
Isabella

As I looked at Paul, I couldn't help noticing his gray-blue eyes matched the dove colored sweater he wore. And his cologne reminded me of a picnic under citrus trees on a spring day in Italy. "I mean it," he said. "Ask anything you need to."

"All right." I shut down the sensory input and decided to probe potentially delicate matters first. 'Tell me about your family relationships. Andrew and Malcolm are your uncles—" I crossed my legs and looked pointedly at my notebook instead of Paul's eyes.

"My mother is their middle sister—the buffer zone growing up. She went to Yale like everybody else except me, and moved to Dallas to marry my father, Charles St. Clair. Also a Yalie and an old Texas family."

"Buffer zone?" I glanced up, curious at his choice of words.

"My mother is referred to as 'the one who got away.'"

"I see." Actually, I didn't see. No one in my family could get away, and most of them wouldn't want to.

"One does, of course, keep up appearances. She used to visit Pappadad and Mims here in this house, and she'd bring me so I'd have something to do with my summers. I lost my tennis career when I had the accident. I was ranked first in the nation at seventeen, 160 in the world, and had already gone pro." Paul smiled wistfully. "But I was bookish, too, so everything worked out."

"Professional tennis? Like Federer and Roddick and that guy from Spain?"

His smile broadened. "I'd already beat number seventy-six in the world and had gotten to the quarter finals at Wimbledon."

My God. I wanted to ask him what it was like to grow up in a family that seemed to have everything—and then to lose so much in an accident. *Why was he not bitter?*

I pulled myself back on track. "How do your uncles get along?"

Paul's eyes met my eyes, as if testing the waters. "Let's put it this way, my mother will be here for Victoria's funeral. Victoria was her best friend. But I don't think she'll come back to New Haven often now that Victory is gone. She can't stand being around both Andrew and Malcolm at once."

"Do they fight?"

"Fight?" asked Paul. "They're both much too urbane to yell or cause a row of any kind. No, it's much more subtle and subterranean. I don't think Malcolm ever got over the fact that Mims and Pappadad doted on Andrew. He takes every opportunity to pour a little verbal acid on Andrew whenever he can."

"Has anyone in your family ever gotten violent?"

"Heaven forbid. Violence is bad manners."

I had spent the last year interviewing families from all walks of life. The Campus Killer had selected his victims indiscriminately. No one I interviewed had called violence "bad manners." I was way out of my social league here.

Paul continued, "The really galling thing for Uncle Malcolm is that Andrew doesn't seem to notice his little digs. Both my uncles have been good to me, but especially Malcolm. To tell you the truth, I think he sees me as the son he never had."

"I can see that."

"Pictures of Andrew as a baby show him laughing. On the other hand, Malcolm was a solemn little boy who turned into an even more serious adult. Losing his wife Mary and the child didn't improve his personality.

"Victory had finally made him laugh again." Paul shook his head. "Life isn't fair, is it? I accepted that long ago. Still, it's hard to watch people you love go through difficult things."

No, life was not fair. But I didn't understand Paul. His suffering had seemed to make him more compassionate and insightful, not angry. What was up with that? I took a deep breath and continued gathering information. "How does Andrew relate to Malcolm?"

"Andrew has accepted that life has handed him good things on a silver platter. I'm not saying he hasn't worked hard, he has. But he wants to make a contribution."

Paul paused for a moment before continuing. I could feel his trust level deepening. "If anything, Andrew feels inferior. Though he hides it pretty well, I think he suffers from the younger son complex. Feels he's never measured up to Malcolm's success." Paul sighed. "Outside his trust fund, Andrew's salary isn't very good, whereas Uncle Malcolm makes a fortune with the law firm."

I continued to write down the family background in my notebook.

"Last night was the most upset I've ever seen Uncle Andrew. He really wanted to present those documents. He *needed* to give them to Yale, to make his mark on the Divinity School—a legacy he could have no other way. He's plenty smart and he's famous, but he stopped publishing when he went into administration."

"What kind of dean is he?"

"Loved. People love Andrew—students, faculty, the Board of Directors. He actually invites all the students to his home for dinner. And he looks after his faculty. He's hired a couple of hotshots in their fields and has kept YDS at the top."

"Can you think of anyone who might know about the safe or the code?"

Paul thought for a moment. "The only non-family member who might know something—how much I haven't a clue—would be Uncle Winthrop."

"*Uncle* Winthrop? Winthrop Smythe? A brother-in-law?"

"No, no. We've just always called him 'uncle.' He's my godfather, and Malcolm is godfather to his son."

"Yes. Malcolm mentioned Winthrop and his godson. Jeeper."

"Jeeter. John Winthrop Smythe, Jr."

The doorbell rang. Malcolm came out from the kitchen, thudding and glowering down the marble hall. "I'll tell those so-and-so's they'll just have to wait until 10:30 like the rest of the press." I watched him fling open the door.

"Your mail." The police officer guarding the crime scene handed him a small stack of letters. "I wouldn't let anyone cross the line."

"Thank you," mumbled Malcolm. He closed the door and walked back down the hall, picking through the envelopes as he passed the open dining room. When he came even with Paul and me, he stopped and turned a post card over, back and forth a couple of times. "This is odd." He handed me the post card.

The picture on the post card showed a sculpted frieze in a half-moon shape. Semi-formed figures of men and women struggled from the stone void, as their arms reached out toward the sun.

I turned the post card over and read the fine print. "The picture is a sculpture from the National Cathedral in Washington, D.C." I paused. "'The creation of humanity over the west entrance, sculpted by Frederick Hart working under master carver Vincent Palumbo.'"

Malcolm said, "Yes, but read the message. Typed, not written. I don't know anyone who would send me something like that."

"Is it addressed to you?"

"Yes."

I read the message aloud. "Blessed are the merciless, for they shall see the truth."

Paul gasped.

"What is it? It sounds like some sort of warped beatitude," I said, recoiling.

"It's straight from the *Gospel of Judas*—one of the beatitudes Jesus supposedly told Judas in private. When Andrew and I translated them into English, we called them 'The Black Beatitudes.'"

"'The Black Beatitudes?' You mean like the beatitudes the Jesus Seminar voted down with black markers?" I recalled a group of theologians a decade or two ago who got together to decide which of Jesus' sayings were authentic and which were not.

"Yes. The Jesus Seminar voted red for what they believed Jesus said, and black for what He didn't say. Andrew and I didn't like what the Jesus Seminar did, but when it came to the *Gospel of Judas,* we felt that those Black Beatitudes were evil. There's no way Jesus said any of them."

"I see." I leaned toward him. "Can you explain a little more? Why would—"

"Yes," Malcolm interjected. "And please explain why would someone send me a Black Beatitude? It's merciless, all right. This post card is especially cruel after last night." Malcolm joined us, sitting down at the table.

I nodded in sympathy. *How could any belief system think that the merciless were blessed?*

Paul nodded. "Mercy is a weakness. It keeps you involved with your fellow earthly creatures instead of seeking the higher wisdom of God. Remember, Gnosticism caters to those who have the secret knowledge."

I nodded. "Yes. But—"

"The point is this. The *Gospel of Judas* makes it okay to use earthly means to get ahead spiritually."

"Like mercilessness. It's the mercilessness people who get what they want. I see."

"Right. The Black Beatitudes are tweaked and contorted versions of the originals. Like Judas as a hero."

"So we're back to Judas as the only one who got it right," I said.

"I think it's time to give Dr. Barnes a call," said Paul. "It's ten o'clock."

I agreed, but my mind had snagged on something as I continued to examine the post card. "Here's another peculiar thing. The card is postmarked from New Haven, not D.C."

"When?" asked Malcolm.

"Last night. At precisely 8:32 p.m."

"Last night?" echoed Malcolm. "I don't understand. What time did the coroner say the murder took place?"

"Between seven and eight."

"Then this was posted right after the murder," said Paul, adding in a quiet voice, "While we were at the club."

"Correct." I said, "Someone sent a post card of the Washington Cathedral from New Haven."

"It's definitely time to call Dr. Barnes," said Paul.

"I agree." I pulled out my cell and called Dr. Barnes' room at the Courtyard. No answer. The front desk said they'd given her an automated wake-up call five minutes ago, as requested. The front desk added, "The maid will be checking in shortly to see if she needs anything."

"Thank you." I turned to Paul. "She's probably in the shower."

"We'll call back," said Paul. "Andrew should be here soon. Maybe he found Dr. Barnes' movie version of the Sethian history."

"Good."

Maria and Bob stepped into the dining room, kits in hand. "Excuse us for interrupting," said Bob, "but we're ready to get back to the lab."

"One more item." I held the post card up by the edges, while Maria dug in her kit for a clean baggie.

My phone rang. "O'Leary." It was the Courtyard.

"Detective?" asked the voice at the front desk. "Are you the one who just called about Dr. Barnes?"

"Yes." My nerves went on alert.

"I'm afraid we have some bad news."

"Bad news? About Dr. Barnes?"

"Housekeeping went into Dr. Barnes' room to see if she wanted it cleaned."

"Yes?"

"The maid found her on the floor. We've called EMS, but I think it's too late."

"Block off the room and the corridor. I'll call the medical examiner and forensics. We'll be there immediately." I clicked my phone shut and felt my stomach tighten. "Body at the Courtyard. Identified as Dr. Bonnie Barnes."

Malcolm shot up out of his chair. "What?" Paul, too, was clearly stunned. He almost lost his balance as he tried to stand up. "She's dead? Andrew is going to have a fit. His conference is down the tubes."

Malcolm's pallor turned even grayer than before. "Now, we won't have the chance to ask her any questions."

In the last five minutes, the case had suddenly grown from a lizard into a dragon. What were the odds Dr. Barnes had simply choked on her breakfast, or had a stroke? Slim to none. I suspected her death had something to do with the documents stolen last night. But why would anyone kill Dr. Barnes?

Unless she was about to reveal something in her talk.

I had to get a copy of her speech. "Would you please call and ask

Andrew to meet me at the hotel room?" I asked Paul.

"We'll follow you," said Maria, zipping and marking the baggie.

"I gotta stop for a coffee," said Bob. "My system can't take another corpse without a shot."

"Fine." I stood up to gather my belongings.

"I'm coming, too," said Paul.

"No," I said automatically. "It's a crime scene."

"Yes. I understand," he contradicted politely. "But I need to be there."

I was accustomed to men trying to overpower me—but not with grace and finesse. I dropped my pen in my purse and clicked the clasp shut. I hesitated. He was a layman, ignorant about criminology. He'd be in the way. I didn't want any distractions.

"I'm not a Sethian expert, but I know more than Andrew. And more than almost anyone else in the field." Paul stood tall.

Grudgingly, I admitted to myself that the more brains we had on this case, the better. "Fine."

"Thank you."

I grabbed my topcoat. "Ride with me. You can call Andrew from the car. Tell him to postpone the 10:30 press conference until noon."

6
Isabella

A beat cop had already sequestered the maid in the hotel's hallway. Flustered and crying, a large black woman in a starched gray uniform said, "When I opened the door, she was just laying there. I took one look at her and screamed bloody murder. My supervisor called 911." She wrung her hands. "I never touched nothing, I promise."

"Hi, Ted. He's with me," I said as Paul and I walked past the police officer. "I'd like a copy of your statement when you're finished." Ted nodded.

Maria and Bob stepped out of another elevator and followed us down the hall. I turned around and said, "Hope you guys are up for staying out late this morning."

"I only need four hours of sleep a night," said Maria.

"Not me," said Bob, yawning. "My middle name is Van Winkle. But I'm pumped and ready to go." He held up a paper cup of coffee in a mock toast. "Here's to catching this dastardly murderer."

Dr. Bonnie Barnes' remains lay on the floor at the foot of a queen size bed, the sheets still rumpled from last night. I took a quick inventory. Standard issue hotel room. One inexpensive suitcase, worn around the corners, with a jumble of clothes bursting out over the sides and onto the floor. Had the killer tumbled her suitcase, or was the vic herself untidy?

I looked down at the corpse of a middle-aged woman who had died alone in a hotel room far away from home. Her face was purple and contorted. Paul took a sharp intake of breath. He began to lose his tan.

"Why don't you sit down?" The last thing I needed was a fainter.

Paul nodded and perched on the edge of the bed, looking the other way.

"What have we got, Jane?" I questioned the medical examiner, an older woman with soft curls and grayish red hair. Jane looked up from her kneeling position near the body. "Looks like she's been dead about three hours. It's 10:00 or so now. I'd guess she died somewhere close to 7:00, 7:30."

Jane lifted the vic's eyelids. "See her eyes? Dilated pupils. She was having convulsions. That much is clear. At first glance, I'd say she was poisoned."

"No way this is a natural or accidental death?"

"I don't think so. We'll know more when I get her on the slab." Jane closed the victim's eyes. "She left some scraps of breakfast on the plate. Be sure to get samples of everything she ate and drank. We'll see if we can match it with the stomach contents."

I saw a *USA Today* on the table next to dirty breakfast dishes.

"Two cups of tea," added Jane. "The British love their tea."

One empty cup next to the plate, and one with a bit left in the bottom on the dresser next to the bed near the vic's purse. Nothing else of a personal nature in the room. "What about the rest of her belongings?"

"The whole room is virgin soil," said Jane. "I just got here myself, right behind Ted, out in the hall talking with the maid who found her. Poor thing."

Jane stood up and closed her case. "I'm out of here. Send the body to the morgue. I'll be waiting."

I watched as Maria and Bob walked the grid. They picked up ten or twelve stray hairs, all from different heads. "Hotels are a gold mine for trace and fingerprints," said Bob.

"Too bad so much of it's from innocent people," I responded.

"Hey, if killers left business cards, we'd all be out of a job," said Bob.

"One of them did," said Maria. "Don't forget last night in the safe."

I sat down next to Paul on the bed and went through Dr. Barnes' purse. "Passport, stamped yesterday. Credit cards, lots of cash."

"Jeez. Why kill somebody if you don't take their cash? It's not stealing if they're already dead," said Bob.

Maria rolled her eyes at Bob. "Only a toothbrush in the bathroom. No cosmetics," she added.

Paul turned to me and said, "What about her briefcase—her speech, or her laptop?"

"What briefcase? What speech? What laptop?" said Bob.

"Exactly," I agreed, scanning the room and turning to Paul. "Her speech. What do you know about her speech tonight?"

"Only that she thought the Sethians were still active, that they hadn't died out in the third century as scholars thought. She wanted her findings to be a surprise, but she hinted she'd uncovered some pretty high powered individuals in this secret conclave."

"So we're back to the Sethians. Current Sethians," I said.

"Theologically, they tend to shun the world and the flesh, but—" ,

"For a group that's so spiritual, these Gnostics certainly are careless with other people's flesh."

Paul nodded.

"A bunch of theology doesn't help in the practical realm." My shoulders slumped. "And what about the picture of the creation frieze on the postcard? What's that about?"

"Creation is when the Christian path diverged from the 'true' belief. The beginning."

"The beginning of what?"

"For Sethians, the beginning of the Christian problem. Christians believe that Jesus was present from the beginning, as God, and thus also at creation."

I pondered for a moment as I thought of other, nastier implications. "I hate to be a theological party pooper, but with two deaths in two days, it could also be the beginning of a Sethian rampage of destruction and death."

7
Gabriel

Gabriel felt naked without his customary labret, the one he wore to deliver the tea to Dr. Barnes this morning, but he knew he needed to change his look. After he had driven slowly past the overturned eighteen-wheeler and the police officers helping the traffic flow, he had a smooth ride into Kennedy Airport. He parked the car and strode inside to check in for his overseas flight. Carrying only the documents in his overnight bag, he knew he wouldn't even have to change the time on his watch because he'd be back home in thirty-six hours.

When he arrived in London, he would hop the first flight to Glasgow, where a man with a green umbrella and a black overcoat would meet him and exchange laptop totes. He would then hop back to Heathrow, finding everything he needed for the next job in the traded bag—map, key, credentials, and a few items to make sure no one recognized him later. Then he'd take the train to Oxford and Dr. Barnes' place.

A cakewalk.

The Sethian faith had changed his life, doing what religion was supposed to do. God was supposed to give meaning to life on earth, with the promise of everlasting life for a job well-done. Gabriel's personality traits that Christianity had tried to squelch and make him feel guilty for—his penchant for action, his desire to destroy unnecessary objects, his need for power, his ability to serve the greater good—these things the Sethian Brotherhood honored. Gabriel had never been happier or more fulfilled.

He got his boarding pass at Kennedy and checked in for the plane to Heathrow. He sat down and waited, aware that the dye he'd used on his hair this morning was making his scalp itch. He'd picked up a true crime book in the airport bookstore and settled in to read.

8
Isabella

In the Courtyard hotel room, I said to Bob and Maria as they were leaving, "Call me if you find anything promising."

"Maybe we'll get a post card tomorrow with another clue," said Bob.

"We should be so lucky." I turned back to Paul. "Are there any other

Sethian documents besides the *Gospel of Judas*?"

He nodded. "A couple in the Nag Hammadi in Egypt. But not fresh news like the *Gospel of Judas*."

"Do these other documents portray the group as dangerous?"

Paul shook his head no.

The strands of this case were beginning to form a pattern. Andrew's conference on Ancient and Apocryphal Literature with the big manuscript debut tonight. Dr. Barnes' keynote speech. *Something had triggered a docile religious group into violence.*

"Okay," I said. "Let's review the facts. 1) Death is not a bad thing to Sethians, but a release. 2) Two people have already died over the *Gospel of Judas*. 3) Mercilessness is a virtue. 4) Judas is the example of good discipleship."

Paul said, "All true. The problem is, Dr. Barnes was the only one in the world who knew about current Sethianism activities."

"And she's gone."

"We have to find out what was in her speech tonight."

"Yes. Everything hinges on what she discovered. The problem is, we have no speech, no laptop, no briefcase, no notes." I felt frustrated and discouraged. Then I had a thought. "Did Dr. Barnes email a copy of her speech to your uncle Andrew?"

"No," said Andrew, stepping inside the room.

"Oh, good, you're here," I said.

"Only one step ahead of the body baggers." Andrew took one look at the body on the floor and said, "I can't do this twice. I just can't. Let's go downstairs to the coffee shop."

I stood up. "Sure."

Once we'd sat down with our coffee, I said, "This case is no longer an ordinary break-in, but an international incident. The FBI will be knocking at our door. I want to find out as much as we can before the press is clawing all over us, and we have to fight the feds for jurisdiction."

I turned to Andrew, whose hair was beginning to stick up in front from running his fingers through it. In the newspaper, he looked like a dashing public figure, but today he looked a little unkempt. He was obviously distracted.

Andrew said, "The feds?? They aren't investigators. They're a bunch of lawyers and accountants."

I shrugged. "Not all. But it will be a turf war."

Andrew took a swig of coffee. "Chief Crenshaw told me you're the best on the east coast. I want you to stay on the case."

"It's not up to me. We'll have to wait and see." I changed the subject. "I need to know everything you both know about Bonnie Barnes. Do you have the material she sent?"

Andrew tossed a packet toward me. "It tells the Sethian story, all right, but it's useless."

"Maybe not. Background is essential to every case." Paul and Andrew looked at each other bewildered and miserable, discussing *sotto voce* what they were going to do about the conference. Andrew's appearance differed from Paul's and Malcolm's. Malcolm's dark suit and white shirt was a formal, tasteful statement of grief, and Paul's softer sweater and dark slacks indicated an openness to help in a less formal role. Andrew looked—well—disheveled, not at all the dapper man on the front page of yesterday's paper. He wore the same shirt as yesterday (I recognized a stain under his tie), and his hair was beginning to get mussed from running his hands through it.

While they talked, I read the material.

Dr. Barnes had taken the Sethian creation story and turned it into a screenplay. Grade B, but captivating. "Voice-over the sun rising above a majestic mountain range: 'Adam and Eve's first two offspring proved disastrously ill-adjusted. Abel was dead, and Cain wandered the earth with the mark of a criminal on his forehead. The two original parents gave it another try and produced a third child, a divine child, named Seth. This is their story.'

"Captions explain as colors unfold in the background: 'God creating the spiritual universe.' Love is a misty blue, wisdom a vibrant red, goodness spring green, knowledge orange as pumpkins, and light as white as snow. Fade.

"Wagner playing as the aeons come into being, males and females in exotic costumes with hair of fire or gold or ivy. The most famous aeon, Sophia (wisdom) dressed in flowing purple robes trimmed with ermine."

"See what I mean?" Andrew interrupted.

"Don't be so hasty. This is the Sethian bible here. Don't forget, our current and dangerous group believes this to be true."

"I'm going to the men's room." He got up and walked away.

Paul said, "You'll have to excuse him. His world has just fallen apart." Paul added, "Keep reading. I know how important research is. You do have to understand their beliefs to figure out what they're doing."

"Thanks." I continued with the screenplay. "During Sophia's reign in heaven, she gets bored with her glory and brains. Scene: Sophia sitting in her royal chambers eating pomegranates and figs. She decides to spice up her life. She wants to take over God's function and do some creating of her own.

"Next scene: a dark and stormy night on the mountaintop. Thunder and lightning. Sophia wielding her scepter. The skies become quiet. Out of the valley creeps her creation, a half-god named Yaldabaoth, a serpent with a lion's head. Yaldabaoth is a rebel."

Isabella recognized these facts from her quick research this morning. Soon the Sethian creation story would begin to parallel the Judeo-Christian Bible.

With a few crucial differences.

Bonnie's play continued. "Yaldabaoth steals the scepter out of Sophia's hand and in turn he creates the earth and Adam and Eve. Instead of a scene from the traditional paradise, Yaldabaoth's earth is a dark forest. Adam and Eve cower behind the trees.

"Next scene: in all his slimy and terrifying monstrousness, Yaldabaoth stalks Eve because when he created her, she absorbed part of the power he stole from Sophia. Yaldabaoth wants the power back.

"Music reaches a crescendo. Yaldabaoth catches up with Eve. He throws her to the ground and tries to rape her."

This scene was very different from a wily serpent appealing to Eve's desire for knowledge. In Sethian belief, it was a violent attack by a monster holding a screaming woman to the ground.

"The struggle subsides. Yaldabaoth leaves in disgust. He realizes that the power he desired has been transplanted into the Tree of Knowledge. Slowly Eve arises, finds Adam. They eat the fruit of the tree. Final scene: the birth of Seth, divine precursor to Jesus."

Andrew returned and sat down just as I was finishing the script. "Violence was there from the first."

"Sethians have no concept of sin," added Paul. "The earth is a difficult and dangerous place because it was created by a flawed creature,

Yaldabaoth. The trick is to become one of the elect with special knowledge so you can escape the earth for the spiritual world of peace and eternal life."

"Was Dr. Barnes a Sethian?"

"No, no," said Andrew.

"I think she was plain vanilla Anglican," said Paul.

"How did she get so deep into this group? What tipped her off that they hadn't died out?"

"Bonnie knew the former Vice-Chancellor of Oxford, Master of her college, Christ Church College. She was a rising star in the academic community, and he had an interest in early Gnostic groups," said Paul.

"The Vice-Chancellor?"

Andrew responded, "Yes. Robert Cole." He paused. "The Vice-Chancellor is the one who runs the University."

Paul interjected, "The Chancellor is an honorary title, but the Vice-Chancellor is the head guy, serving a, what—four-year term—something like that—on a rotating basis."

"During Robert Cole's tenure, the Chancellor became ill. Cole actually took over the Chancellor's duties for almost a year and a half. A unique situation."

I tucked the information away. "Go on."

Andrew continued, "I met Bonnie in 2004 at the conference in Switzerland, when the first Judas fragments showed up. She told me she had met with Dr. Cole for supper. Somehow, she charmed, weaseled, or browbeat information out of him."

"What kind of information?"

"Apparently he told her that he was a member of some secret society, but was getting disenchanted with the direction they were going."

"Hinted," corrected Paul. "He didn't tell her outright."

"That's right," said Andrew. "She said Dr. Cole was very cryptic and dark. She wasn't sure it was dangerous, just secret." Andrew paused and ran his hand again through his tousled hair. "We didn't think it was dangerous either. After all, Yale has had secret clubs for centuries."

"Andrew and I organized the conference and invited her to speak." Paul sighed and shook his head. "Judas was in the air that year. It was all anybody talked about."

"This Dr. Cole, is he still the head of Oxford?"

"Oh, no," said Andrew. "Shortly after meeting with Bonnie, he was killed in a car wreck."

A car wreck. *Hmmm.* "What kind of information did he give her?" I asked.

"Mostly a warning," said Paul. "He tried to scare her off."

Andrew nodded thoughtfully. "She ignored him, of course."

"Why? Why is this group dangerous?" I was still trying to make the jump from a quiet, spiritual Gnostic religious sect to a violent, murdering terrorist group.

"We're talking in cosmic terms here. Eternal life is at stake," said Andrew.

"Is killing part of their theology, like Muslim men who get to sleep with a thousand virgins if they die for Allah?"

Paul thought for a moment. "If you take the Black Beatitudes to the max, the code of ethics that emerges is one of destruction. The Black Beatitudes encourage vengeance and hatred."

"Remember, not all Gnostics believe in the Black Beatitudes. Just the Sethians," said Andrew.

"I understand that," I agreed. "Not all Muslims are terrorists. Not all Christians are holed up in Montana, spawning people who blow up daycare centers in Oklahoma. The Sethians must be the Gnostic extremists."

"One thing Dr. Cole said made an impression on Bonnie," added Paul. "Cole wanted to tell her more, but was afraid. He said she alone would understand. That's what made her think he was talking about Sethians."

"I see. He gave her enough information to pique her interest." I paused. "Now they're both dead."

This investigation was not at all like the Campus Killer's. On that case, I'd known early that I was dealing with one individual, a sick human being taking out women one by one.

Actually, my dream this morning was not far off. This Sethian case was like grappling with an octopus in murky waters. I was afraid it would wrap its arms around me before I could wrap my mind around it. "What kind of a car accident was it?"

Both men shrugged.

"I'll get what I can from police records. In the meantime, I want to see a copy of the *Gospel of Judas.* You do have a copy?"

Andrew nodded. "We all have a copy. Bonnie would have been carrying hers with her, most likely."

"In English?" I asked, hoping to could read it right away.

"Paul and I collaborated on a translation. We're going to publish it with Yale Press in January." Andrew's face fell and he ran his fingers once again through his gray hair.

Paul reached over and patted his uncle's forearm. "It's still coming out. The experts have certified it. No matter what, it will be the definitive edition for the next century. The original was just a showpiece and a grand gesture."

"Yes, but it was *our* showpiece, and *our* gesture. We were robbed." He paused, tragically dramatic. "The whole world has been robbed."

The three of us sat looking at the dregs of our coffee. Andrew said, "Back to the feds. Let the FBI come and do what they want." He turned to me. "I'll talk to your boss, Richard. The Guildford family will fund you to go over to England. I want the Chief to get permission from Scotland Yard for you to go through Bonnie's place and ask questions over there."

It didn't happen often, but I had heard of special cases when a privately funded detective did special work for a victim's family. "Whatever is best." I looked evenly at Andrew, an icon of religious distinction, with a rumpled shirt and hair askew. I'd wager not many people had seen him like that.

It seemed to me that Andrew had an especially deep investment in the manuscripts.

<h2 style="text-align:center">9
Isabella</h2>

The three-story house on St. Ronan had the look of understated elegance, with dark almost maroon brick and white trim. "Turn the corner and go in the back," said Paul, when I approached it. A mob scene waited under the porte-cochere and on the front lawn. Ah, the press, again. A paradox. The press was one of America's greatest instruments of ferreting out the truth. It was also one of America's greatest means of distortion. Right now they were a serious pain in the neck.

"Hurry," I said. "Get in the back door." A few of the reporters spotted my car and were sprinting to catch me before Paul and I could get inside.

Malcolm, looking starched and funereal, greeted us in the kitchen. We gravitated toward the table in the dining room. With no shame, reporters and cameramen peered through the windows. In a disgusted motion, Andrew pulled the light blue silk draperies before sitting down.

"Short and to the point," I told Andrew. I knew from recent experience the feeding frenzy that could develop if the sharks were given any leads, hints, or openings. "Make them do their jobs. Don't give them anything you don't want the whole world to know. Don't imply there's more to the story.

"I know Chief Crenshaw wants to get this solved as quickly as possible. He'll make a statement soon." The members of the press were still licking their chops over the Campus Killer, more than eager for a new thrill today.

"Now, Andrew, are you ready?" Andrew had gone home and cleaned up nicely. He and Malcolm both looked sharp and ready.

Andrew said, "I'm going to offer a reward. How about one million?"

Malcolm looked doubtful. "It's worth six. The person who stole it would know that."

"But the thief will have to sell it on the black market for less. Besides," Andrew continued, "we're not only aiming at the thief, but at an accomplice. A million would make it worthwhile to rat out a partner."

"Maybe the Sethians hired a thief," I added while trying not to choke at the cool million the family was offering.

"Somebody who can be bought," said Andrew.

Malcolm nodded. "All right," he said. "I just want it back."

"Okay, let's go. I'll stand next to you both on the front steps, ready to cut off questions and hustle you back inside after Andrew finishes. Remember, stick with the facts, and whatever you do, don't mention Dr. Barnes. We want to be one step ahead in connecting the dots."

10

Isabella

Andrew handled himself well with the reporters, I thought. Malcolm didn't say a word. After the press conference, Andrew went back to his office at the Divinity School. As I collected my notes and prepared the next step in the investigation, I eyed Paul, wandering restlessly around the downstairs of Malcolm's house, jingling the keys and coins in his slacks pockets. Malcolm had disappeared into the bedroom.

"I have to speak with Winthrop Smythe," I said to Paul. "Do you have his phone num—"

"Let me come with you," Paul responded instantly.

This time, I didn't hesitate as long as before. "Okay."

Paul looked grateful to have something constructive to do. "I'll call and make sure he's home and not at the office."

The Smythes also lived on St. Ronan, two blocks away. Cozy. In spite of socio-economic differences, neighborhoods had one thing in common. Like kinds stuck together.

Winthrop Smythe opened the heavy mahogany door of his Mediterranean villa—sandy textured walls, balconies dripping with vines, and a red-tiled roof. He wore an Armani suit, but his hair and eyebrows were bushy and overgrown. Winthrop appeared to be a contradiction in terms: civilization competing with a streak of the wild. Culture winning, but not by much.

"Come on in," he said, reaching for my hand. "Winthrop Smythe. Just saw the press conference. You and Andrew did a good job."

"Thank you." Paul followed me inside.

"Do you think the reward will do any good?" Winthrop asked. "I'll up the ante if you think it will bring Victoria's killer to justice."

"We'll see," I said. Winthrop led us to a sitting room in a home done on the inside like a villa, too—casual and elegant at the same time. Huge abstract paintings in blues, sand, and ochre hung on the walls. He clapped Paul on the back and then pointed out two striped chairs across from the couch. "How can I help you?" he looked back and forth between us.

Paul deferred to me, motioning with his hand. I said, "I have a few questions to ask since you are such a close friend of the family."

"I know, I know. And to eliminate me as a suspect." He dug the heel of his tasseled loafer into an expensive twill carpet. "Trust me, I'll do anything to help catch the person who did this."

Maybe yes, maybe no. I watched him closely. "Tell me about your safe, the one the Guildfords copied when they remodeled."

"Yes. We were happy with the design and the company. Ours is hidden behind the bar. First you have to know it's there. Then you have to know the combination to get in. Double protection."

"Do you know Malcolm's combination?"

Winthrop hesitated just a brief second. "Strictly speaking, no."

I watched his eyes as they moved around his living room. His eyebrows twitched. "What, exactly, do you mean?"

Winthrop sighed. "Malcolm never told me the combination, but I know other combinations and passwords—for his computer at work, for an emergency bank account. He wanted me to know in case something happened to both him and Victoria. It's always either his initials, or the year he was born, or both. He's not very creative when it comes to security."

"Do you know anyone else who might know about the safe or the code?"

Winthrop shook his head no.

"What do you know about Malcolm's new intern, Clyde Sneed?"

"He works for both of us. Actually, I hired him. Found him in England. A bells and whistles recommendation from a firm of solicitors we've worked with in London. Also, I met his father, a barrister, when Malcolm and I were over there starting our firm's branch office twenty-five years ago. Clyde's been with us since this summer. Intelligent. Caught on quickly. Wants to stay over here and get his MBA."

Their stories matched. I made a second note to meet Clyde Sneed.

"Have you ever heard of the Sethian Brotherhood?" I asked.

"That rings a bell."

Paul nodded and interjected, "Right. We had a discussion that Christmas we found the manuscripts in the basement."

"At the club," agreed Winthrop. "But don't press me because I don't remember much. Some Gnostic group as I recall."

Winthrop was smooth. He spoke easily and his body language shouted "sincere" as he leaned forward, hands on his knees, eager to help.

"What can you tell me about Dr. Bonnie Barnes?"

Winthrop looked puzzled. "Dr. Bonnie Barnes? I'm sorry, I don't know who that person is."

I pressed on. "What were you doing between 7:00 and 8:00 last night?"

Paul looked as if he might say something but reined himself in. I noticed that he and Winthrop shared a glance.

"Paul can tell you. I saw him and Malcolm at the club. Must have been close to 9:30. I was having a late dinner. My wife was at a charity thing, and I took Clyde Sneed to the club."

Clyde Sneed again.

"Where were you before that?" I asked it gently, in deference to the family's friendship, but the answer was nonetheless important.

Winthrop looked down at the floor, again digging the heels of his loafers into the carpet. "My office. Clyde and I closed it down last night."

"What about Mr. Sneed? Where was he between 7:00 and 8:00?"

Once again, Paul and Winthrop shared a look.

"Clyde had depositions in Hartford for most of the day, into the evening," Winthrop said. He brought his eyes into direct contact with mine.

Winthrop Smythe had not directly answered my initial question. "You say you were at the office between 7:00 and 8:00. Can anyone vouch for you?"

"Paul will vouch for me. I would never, never kill Victoria. I would never steal the manuscript from two people who were like brothers to me. This was Andrew's big moment. No way I'd take that away from him."

Again, he had sidestepped the question. "So you were alone at the office until Clyde Sneed arrived back from Hartford. What time was that?"

The eyebrows started twitching again. "A little after 8:30."

"I see." Time enough to mail a post card. I wrote in my notebook for a minute, intentionally creating a silence, hoping he would jump in and give me more information. He didn't.

"All right," I continued. "Where is your son, Jeeter?"

"Ah, Jeeter," sighed Winthrop. "We put Jeeter on a plane to Arizona two days ago. He is at a drug rehabilitation center. We plan to go out there for Family Week between Thanksgiving and Christmas." He looked pained as he spoke of his son.

"I'm sorry." I closed my notebook and placed it in my purse. "Would you mind stopping by the station on your way back to your office and letting the forensics team get your fingerprints?"

"Absolutely. I'll give them DNA, too, if they want it."

"Thank you." Paul and I stood to leave.

I watched Paul hug his godfather. I sensed genuine affection on both sides, and a look from Paul that conveyed both sorrow and regret.

In my mind, though, the verdict was still out on Winthrop Smythe and Clyde Sneed.

11
Isabella

On the way to the police station, Paul said, "For what it's worth, I think he's telling the truth. He's never lied before; I don't know why he'd start now."

My experience told me that people started lying for all different reasons, but I didn't want to disillusion Paul. I asked, "What's his family like?"

"He has two kids, both boys, one my age, a lawyer in his and Uncle Malcolm's law firm. Jeeter is a few years behind me. He's a fun-loving, party kind of guy. Hilarious to be around, but parties a little too much sometimes." Paul paused, as if searching for the right words. "Let's just say he's taking his time finding himself. I don't see him a lot any more."

"Are they a religious family? What church do they attend?"

"Trinity on the Green. Episcopal. Same as Malcolm. If Winthrop has a flaw, it's that he's a workaholic. He skips church a lot to go to work." He paused. "To tell you the truth, I'm surprised he took a break last night at 9:30 to go the club for dinner. Often, he works straight through until midnight."

If Paul and Malcolm ran into him and Clyde at 9:30, that would have given either one of them ample time to swing by the Guildford house, get back to the office, and still make it to the club.

Paul and I approached the imposing, contemporary police station. I parked and we walked up the outside stairs and through the angular columns to the lobby. Upstairs in the lab's fingerprint room, Maria looked glum. Bob tried to stifle a yawn, but couldn't. He shook his bald head like a formerly shaggy dog trying to keep himself awake.

"We've got no news in the fingerprint department. All prints on the post card matched either postal workers', Malcolm's, or yours," Bob said to me.

"We also have no news on the boot print from last night," added Maria. "There were too many footprints in the hotel carpet this morning to isolate an indentation that might have matched the boot print in the library last night."

"And to make your day complete—it's official. Our new partners on the case are...." Bob pretended a drum roll, "The FBI."

I closed my eyes. "I knew it." No matter how cooperative they were (or weren't), the Feebs brought complications. I sighed but pressed on.

"Okay, let's rustle up some good news here. How about the poison? Have you isolated it?"

"Yes," said Bob. "Belladonna."

"Well, at least we know what we're working with."

"'Fair lady,'" said Paul. "I thought belladonna was a herb used for colic or asthma or something."

"Correct," said Maria. "But in a weak form. It's also called deadly nightshade—too much will kill you. And it's not a pretty death. First you feel feverish, pulse racing, skin flushed. Then your throat starts getting raw and burning and you lose your voice. You can't swallow, and your body starts convulsing from the hands and feet inward. Then you die. Doesn't take long."

The poor woman. Dr. Barnes probably had no clue what was happening to her. I changed the subject. "No hatchet at the crime scene this morning?" I hadn't seen one, but wanted to double check.

"No. It's still a mystery," said Bob.

"So. We're at a stalemate. Tell you what. Go home. Take a break. You two look a little frayed around the edges, and who knows how long it's going to take us—"

Just then, my phone rang.

12
Gabriel

On the flight to London, Gabriel enjoyed his meal and one glass of Chardonnay. One glass would help him sleep better on the plane, but not affect his judgment when he landed.

Gabriel had a feeling he knew who would meet him carrying a green umbrella with the snake handle. The Grand Patriarch. The old man wouldn't want anyone else touching the precious manuscripts. Gabriel knew the old guy was grooming him for something important, but he still reminded him of a bird of prey. Gabriel had never met someone so terrifying and mesmerizing at the same time.

Gabriel closed his book. Time to sleep. He leaned his seat back and closed his eyes.

Images of his first trip to Scotland rose like the mist from Brigadoon. It was his first flight alone (Sethians always traveled alone to their meetings). But his Sethian sponsor—the man in the bar—had bought his tickets and prepared him well. When Gabriel arrived in Glasgow, the rain poured out of the sky. A man with a green umbrella led him into a Rolls Royce driven by another man in an old-fashioned taxi driver's hat.

The old man rasped when he talked, as if he had something stuck in his throat. While they drove through the outskirts of Glasgow, he asked Gabriel questions on unrelated topics. Did he have a girlfriend? Which parts of the Bible were true? And—the young man's personal favorite— what was the most thrilling physical sensation he'd ever had? The old man had inched closer and closer in the backseat. He started to make Gabriel uncomfortable with the smell of old, damp wool and vinegar.

They drove about thirty minutes, through a small town. Then they pulled off the main highway onto a one-lane road leading back into the hills, the Lennox Hills, Gabriel found out later. By now it was dark. Gabriel did not recall seeing a sign of any sort.

After a mile or so through hilly country, Gabriel saw a castle in the distance, with candles gleaming from every window. At the time, he recalled a special vacation touring the United States. His parents had taken him to Excalibur in Las Vegas, arriving in the dark. He felt the same tingling awe.

Only this time it was the real deal.

The chauffeur pulled up under an enormous gray stone archway, probably hundreds of years old. Gabriel looked up several stories at the round turrets and the high gabled windows. *A real castle. He was walking into a dream too good to be true.* His whole body throbbed with exhilaration, and he wondered if the castle had a dungeon with instruments of torture.

The old man led him inside, where light from ancient candelabras reflected off the polished floor. In a small, round room to the right, the old man instructed him to hang his coat on a rack already filled with coats. He handed him a black robe and a hood made from soft black velvet that covered his face. The old man had arthritis and yellow fingernails, like talons. He patted him, claw-like, on the shoulder. "I like you," he said. "You'll do just fine." He paused and his eyes glittered. "I hope this is the beginning of a long and....fruitful....relationship."

The round room must have been inside one of the turrets. The old man told him to enter an elevator on the far wall, and go down to the basement. "Wait until the clock chimes 9:00." He pointed to an antique grandfather clock next to the clothes rack. Gabriel remembered sitting in a folding chair watching the minutes tick by, feeling almost sick with anticipation.

At 9:01, he had emerged downstairs from the elevator into a round wine cellar the same size as the waiting room. One of the wine racks had been moved to reveal an open door leading into the basement, a huge room. The dark space was lit by tapers in sconces along stone walls blackened over the centuries. Manacles dangled, left over from when the basement was a dungeon. The young man was so excited that he started to get an erection as he entered the hushed and holy space.

A group of fifty men dressed in black hooded robes formed a circle around one man, also dressed in black. The man in the middle wore a large emblem on a gold chain, a snake wrapped around a T-shaped cross. On top of the altar loomed a gold statue of the same emblem, making huge shadows.

"Welcome, my child," said the man in the center. The man had a raspy voice just like the man who'd picked him up. Had he sat in the car next to the Grand Patriarch himself?

The circle opened for him to join. The central figure began to dance and chant. "Glory to God, king of Pleroma."

The men in the circle said, "Amen."

The man in the center twirled with his arms outstretched. "I am Seth, your beloved son, present at creation, divine incarnation."

The men chanted, "Amen."

The central figure bent down, scooped his hands from the floor and lifted them up. "True son of Adam and Eve."

"Amen."

"I will be wounded and I will wound."

"Amen."

"I will be born and I will bear."

"Amen."

"I will be released and I will release."

"Amen."

Gabriel remembered the flowing motions of the Grand Patriarch as he danced and chanted, and the men responded in the flickering shadows.

"I will be united and I will unite."

"Amen."

"I am a mirror to you who perceive me."

"Amen."

"I will die and I will kill."

"Amen."

At this point, the Grand Patriarch swept around the circle, like a banshee, making stabbing motions at each man while dancing and turning and singing a haunting melody—five notes over and over in varying patterns. When he had made the circle completely, he stood in the center with his hands raised high.

The men fell on their faces before him, arms outstretched. The young man fell down, imitating the others.

The central figure chanted, "*I die, and I am alive forever.*"

"Amen."

After a moment of silence, the Grand Patriarch said, "You may rise. We will now induct our youngest member. He is 'The Messenger of Life.'" The Grand Patriarch gestured to Gabriel, beckoning him to join him in the center.

Gabriel had scrambled to his feet and nearly tripped over his robe. As he approached the altar, he still could not see the face of the Grand Patriarch.

The Grand Patriarch said, "Secretary, get the Book of Life." One of the hooded men turned behind him to an enormous wooden cabinet carved with faces of gargoyles. He brought out a large, leather-bound volume and carried it to the center of the circle. He held it for the Grand Patriarch, opened to a page where lines had been drawn and several signatures had already been written.

The Grand Patriarch faced the young man, indicating that he should kneel. Two candles on the altar flickered violently, spitting wax. "In each generation, the Sethian Brotherhood has fifty duties assigned to fifty members, and no more. This generation is the one that will establish Judas as the rightful heir to heaven. Do you understand your commitment?"

The young man nodded. "I do."

"Do you understand that you follow in a line two thousand years old, working to bring down the false Christ and destroy Christendom forever?"

The man nodded again. "I do."

"Do you solemnly promise to uphold your duties as The Messenger of Life, no matter what the cost to you or to others?"

"I do." The man's voice rose in pitch with his fervor.

"Do you promise to die before revealing the existence of the Brotherhood?"

Kneeling on the floor surrounded by fifty of the most powerful men in the world, Gabriel remembered being five years old. He had sneaked into the bedroom of a friend's baby brother. The baby lay asleep in his crib, and Gabriel had quietly stuck pins in his feet, just for fun. Caught and severely reprimanded, he had learned to keep most of his fantasies to himself.

As Gabriel pledged loyalty to his true family in the dark room, he knew all his dreams were about to be realized. He wouldn't have to limit himself to fantasies. There was, after all, a place for him in the universe. "I do."

"Then inscribe your name in the Book of Life."

The young man had written his name with a hand shaking from excitement, awe, and wonder.

"Stand," ordered the Grand Patriarch.

He stood. The Grand Patriarch gave him a three-fold hug and presented him to the Brotherhood. "The Messenger of Life has been inscribed in the Book of Life. He will join those in the Incorruptible Generation."

The Grand Patriarch then whispered into Gabriel's ear. "Like Judas, you will be condemned. Like Judas, men of the world will not understand your actions. But like Judas, you are the special one, the one who will live forever. In each generation, The Messenger of Life is chosen especially for his faith, fortitude, and obedience. Bless you, my child."

At that point the rest of the men had filed out and the Grand Patriarch had spoken to Gabriel alone. Then Gabriel had returned through the wine cellar to the elevator, gone up into the little room, and changed his clothes. Soon, another man had arrived with a green umbrella to escort him to the car. The same driver returned him to the airport. The trip home had been filled with images of the dark and holy chamber, where men of courage planned to save the world.

13
Isabella

"I'm going to England, thanks to your uncle," I said to Paul after hanging up from my conversation with Crenshaw. We sat at my desk in the detectives' room.

"Uncle Andrew is focused and persistent. He usually gets what he wants," said Paul, with a smile.

"I suspected as much." Paul obviously placed great trust in his Uncle Andrew. It crossed my mind, however, that Andrew might be sending me to England to get me out of the picture.

I rode with Paul down the elevator of the police station and through the front lobby crowded with people dealing with pending cases, parking tickets, and other legal problems.

Once we stepped outside, Paul said, "I'd like to take you to lunch. Are you hungry?"

One of my rules was that I never went to lunch with family members of a victim. I didn't want to risk losing perspective and missing something while the bodies piled up. Besides, too much about this case was hitting close to home. "I don't know if it would be best."

Paul opened the door for me. "All right. I'll catch a cab. Call me if you have any questions."

I started to drive away. What was I, nuts? Paul Guildford was the first man in a complete package I'd met since Ronny. Would socializing with him make me lose perspective? The scent of his cologne lingered in the front seat, and I made a snap decision. What the heck. I was so drained and brain-dead from the Campus Killer case, I'd probably already lost my professional edge.

Paul had turned toward the curb. I rolled down the window and called out, "Actually, I'm starved."

Paul buttoned his camel cashmere topcoat against a sudden gust of frigid wind. "Maybe you're right. Professional distance is good."

A city bus lumbered past on the way to Union Station. An available cab followed. After all the men I'd turned down in the past year, not to mention the past several years, I was astonished to find myself afraid he would hail the cab and disappear. Good grief. What was the matter with me?

Paul seemed to weigh the nuances of the situation. Then, he let himself into the passenger seat of my car. "How about Thai?"

"I love Thai." I would probably have agreed to go along, even if he had suggested eating fried rubber bands.

14
Isabella

"Spring rolls," I said. Spring rolls were like rolled up salad, and, even though my appetite had somewhat returned, I couldn't take the chance on trying to force down something heavier just to be polite.

"Pad Thai with shrimp," said Paul. The waiter collected our menus and left us in a room jutting out toward York Street, with windows on three sides. Students passed by, carrying backpacks and breathing white clouds that matched the floating wisps against an azure sky. *Was I ever that young and innocent?*

I watched Paul across the table, his manners gracious. He came from generations of gentlemen trained to smooth the rough ways of the world. The smile and nod at the waitress, how he placed his napkin in his lap. Paul was a sensitive and refined man, a refreshing novelty in my world.

"I want to talk about heaven," I said.

Paul laughed. "Come to West Texas. You can see it from there."

"No, seriously. What does heaven mean to the Sethians? Most Americans are concerned with this life, not the next. But the Muslim suicide bombers aren't—our culture doesn't get it. We think they're crazy. We can't comprehend religious zeal so passionate that we'd give up our cars and our big screen TV's—much less our lives."

Paul nodded slowly. "True. We want a faith that makes life easier, not a belief system that asks us to die."

"These Sethians, though. Something's in it for them. A heavenly reward?"

"In a way." Paul rubbed his forehead and thought for a minute. "All Gnostics believe most people die and turn to dust. Period. End of life. But those with *secret insider information* get to live forever."

"Okay."

"For Sethians, a chosen few have the spark of the divine. They get to live forever. They're called the 'incorruptible generation.'"

"How do you know if you're one of the ones with the divine spark?"

Paul smiled. "You know because of Sophia. Wisdom. She reveals it to you."

Personally, I didn't think Sophia was so wise. After all, she's the one who created the monster Yaldabaoth. "Where does Jesus fit in? He's a central figure in the *Gospel of Judas*."

"Jesus is the great moral teacher. But it's Sophia's secret knowledge that's at the heart of Gnosticism."

"I see. Christianity, on the other hand, is available to anyone who chooses it."

Paul sighed deeply. "And so is heaven." He stopped talking and looked out the window. An old man in a ratty overcoat walked past, clutching a notebook like a life preserver. "It's a consolation, actually. You know. When you lose someone."

The old man walked slowly out of sight, his head bent down. Suddenly, silence hung between us as Paul looked from the window and back at me. All I could think about was Ronny sailing off the bridge in despair and the church telling me he wasn't in heaven.

My heart started to hammer against my ribcage, defying explanation. This was getting much too personal. Lunch was a mistake. I twirled my water glass by its stubby stem as conversation sputtered, died, and rolled over on its back.

Fortunately, Paul had the social skills to redeem such moments. His full, sexy lips spread into a generous and inclusive smile. "Well, ever since last night, you know all our family secrets, and I don't know anything about you except what I've read in the paper. Do you have brothers and sisters? Where did you grow up?"

Gratefully, I returned his smile. I wasn't much good at small talk, but he was right—turn around was fair play. "I grew up here in New Haven. I have four brothers. In case you can't guess, I'm Irish Catholic on one side, and Italian Catholic on the other. I was pretty sheltered by my brothers."

(Sheltered, that is, until I grew up and my life fell apart one Thursday evening a week before Thanksgiving. But of course I wasn't about to talk about that. That was one rule I would never break.)

Fortunately, our food arrived. I bit into my spring rolls wrapped in bib lettuce.

"Where did you go to school?" Paul asked between bites.

"I got a full scholarship to Yale. Went to Catholic schools all the way up." I paused. "I was the first person in my family to graduate from college. My dad's a foreman at a granite company, where two of my brothers work. Another brother works for the city, and my baby brother drives a bus. Altogether, I have fourteen nieces and nephews."

Considering his background and education, Paul was probably bored with my family story, but I plowed on anyway. "After I spent a year at seminary, I got a Ph.D. in criminal psychology." I took another bite of spring rolls.

Paul put down his fork and ignored his food, focusing his clear, dove-gray eyes on my face. To my surprise, he didn't look bored, but he was probably just being courteous. "I'm impressed," he said. What was the subject of your dissertation?"

The next part was guaranteed to put him to sleep. I swallowed. "Brain-waves of the psychotic killer. Very technical. Brain scans can already tell a lot about personality, but the dissertation enters uncharted territory with chemical analysis as well."

He listened with intensity. "No wonder you're so good at what you do. What's your greatest challenge in criminal investigation?"

I laughed. "My greatest challenge is also my greatest asset. I'm a dual personality, which means I have two dominant sides of the brain. In investigative work, I depend both on scientific analysis as well as intuition. I can't afford to ignore the scientific evidence, but I also can't afford to ignore a hunch. As a result, I work every investigation going full steam on two tracks."

"I see," said Paul, wiping his mouth with his napkin. "Speaking of hunches, do you have any hunches about this case?"

I picked up another spring roll. "As a matter of fact, I do."

Paul waited for me to finish my bite, and then asked, "Do you ever tell your hunches to interested parties?"

"Almost never." It was true, but I was playing with him.

Paul looked disappointed.

"But I suppose I could make an exception this time." I smiled and leaned forward. "Here's what I think. Why would someone steal two high-profile manuscripts? Money? Not for re-sale. They're too widely known—Andrew's right. The thief would get a fraction of what they're worth on the black market. For getting money fast, an armored car heist would be more practical."

"What other motives?"

"Before Dr. Barnes' death this morning, I might have said ransom. I take your manuscripts, and you give me money to get them back."

"But you don't think that any more."

"No. I'm thinking now a collector. Someone who wanted the

manuscript for itself. In which case, offering a million dollars is a laugh. For this perp, it's not about money, but about a personal relationship with the stolen goods."

"But not just any collector," said Paul, finishing off his meal.

"No. You're right. When the top international specialist in the Sethian Gnostic Brotherhood is murdered right before she gives a talk unveiling its existence, I think the secret brotherhood wants to remain a secret. This group has some powerful members who can make that happen."

I took my last bite. "In short, I think we're up against something big and dangerous. They wanted that manuscript and they got it. They wanted Dr. Barnes silenced and they got it. The Sethian Brotherhood is used to getting what they want. Whatever their theology is, they've convinced themselves that the end justifies the means."

The waitress appeared and started clearing our plates.

"What about the FBI?" Paul handed the waitress his credit card.

"The FBI will come in and make a big splash, driving this group farther underground. What I'd like to do is to keep working on it from a different angle. We've got to find out—not just who the killer is—but who is behind the curtain. We can do it a couple of ways."

I knew I had his full attention. "Since I'm going to England to investigate Bonnie Barnes and any records she may have left behind, Chief Crenshaw has agreed make a big public statement about taking take me off the case. I'll be working under the radar."

"When are you leaving?"

"Tonight."

Paul's lips parted in a wistful smile. "Wish I could go with you. I have to step in for Dr. Barnes tonight."

Before I stopped to think, I said, "I wish I could hear your talk." The flutter from last night flickered again. I was rescued from a full body hot flash by my cell phone.

The waitress brought the ticket. While I listened on the phone, Paul calculated the tip and signed, returning the card to his pocket.

I clicked the phone shut. "You'll never guess what the coroner found inside the pocket of Dr. Barnes' suit jacket."

"I don't know."

"A post card. No fingerprints at all this time."

Paul's eyes widened. "Must have been hand delivered by the person who poisoned her. We didn't have to wait until tomorrow to receive it in the mail."

"We'll have to stop by the lab again. Do you mind? You can help me interpret the message."

15
Isabella

Back at the lab, Paul and I found Maria and Bob in the same clothes they'd been in all day and last night. "No rest for the wicked," said Bob.

"Here's the post card," said Maria. "This time it was hand-carried instead of mailed. The murderer probably slipped into the vic's pocket. Nobody's fingerprints were on it, even Dr. Barnes's."

The victim hadn't touched the post card. Maria was probably right.

I looked at the picture on the front. It was a photo of the War Memorial Chapel in the National Cathedral. The head of the suffering Christ was surrounded by thorns of cast aluminum suggesting barbed wire. The brass halo simulated cannon shells. The small print description told about the Honor Roll, many volumes of books to the right of the altar, containing the names of the thousands of men and women who died in the armed forces.

"Okay," I said, handing Paul the card. "This is the second murder and the second post card. Again, it's the Washington Cathedral."

"This time something to do with war," he said. "War. Let's see…Christian war…holy war…a memorial to bloodshed…honoring those who fought for right…. Some sort of battle, maybe between good and evil."

"When the roll is called up yonder, I'll be there," quoted Bob.

"Or maybe all of the above," I said.

Paul turned the post card over. "We also have a typed message on this post card, like the first one." He read aloud, "Blessed are those who value knowledge more than life, for they will be given secret wisdom."

I looked up at Paul. "Is it what I think it is?"

Paul nodded. "Another Black Beatitude."

I tried to ignore the shivers that shook my body. "Secret wisdom. What we were talking about at lunch." I rubbed my hands up and down my arms.

"What secret wisdom?" asked Bob.

"You get into heaven if you're a Sethian with secret wisdom," said Paul. "But the message is a little more complicated."

"Give me fingerprints any day. I don't understand this stuff," said Bob.

"The Beatitude states that knowledge is more important than life," said Paul.

"Okay," I agreed. "So if you want to get knowledge, you have to be willing to die. Once you die, you get the secret wisdom."

"And once you get the secret wisdom, you get eternal life," said Paul.

Something wasn't quite right. "Seems to me that I'd want a guarantee of getting the secret wisdom and eternal life if I'm willing to die for knowledge."

"That's where faith comes in." Paul was re-reading the message on the card.

"In light of Dr. Barnes' demise, it's clear that the murderer values knowledge above life. Bonnie's life, anyway," I said.

"Remember their theology. For the elect, death brings both wisdom and eternal life."

"Forgive me if I seem cynical, but I think Dr. Barnes was killed—not so she could *get* secret wisdom—but because she already *had* secret wisdom. The Sethians' secret knowledge, and they wanted to keep it secret."

Maria, Bob, and I watched Paul as he walked around the lab, holding the post card in its baggie. He said, "You may have a point, but we've got to tie the message with the photo on the front. War. History is filled with religious wars, justified by believers in one God or another."

"Like the terrorist war we're in now," said Maria.

"Do the Sethians believe that Dr. Barnes' death was part of a war of good vs. evil in the search for secret wisdom?" I asked. The question hung in the air like a limp helium balloon. No one spoke.

"Oh, dear." I felt goose bumps return, creeping up and down my arms. "What if this message is not just about Dr. Barnes? What if it's a declaration of holy war?"

16
Paul

Yale Divinity School looked the part: Georgian architecture, a courtyard surrounded with red brick buildings and white columns, and

Marquand Chapel majestically ruling over the quad. In this secular day and age, the Divinity School located at the crest of Prospect Street reminded the rest of the Yale campus that one of the world's greatest universities had been founded on the study of God.

Upstairs in the Common Room, Paul placed his briefcase against the wall and grazed the cocktail buffet, arrayed as enticingly as if nothing tragic had happened. It was loaded with shrimp and olives on toasted crackers, artichoke dip, star fruit, strawberries, and the *de rigueur* vegetable tray. Personnel from Yale's food company poured wine to a dispirited group of international scholars in shock and disbelief.

Paul looked around the room. The governor of Connecticut and the president of Yale stood in the corner next to Paul's briefcase, talking with Andrew and Malcolm. Personal friends of the Guildford family, they had apparently decided to come as a show of support. Winthrop Smythe, his godfather, had also arrived.

Paul headed over to greet them. He couldn't help noticing that they stood out from the room full of scholars, the way they dressed and carried themselves. Scholars as a breed would never conquer the world, thought Paul. But the world would be more difficult to interpret without them.

Paul's parents arrived late, straight from the airport. His mother Lindsey was a petite and attractive woman edging toward sixty, but looked ten years younger. She had Big Texas hair, blonde but not brassy, and almost lavender-gray eyes.

Paul's father stood taller than any of the Guildford men, his hair turning charcoal gray. For forty years he had remained on the outskirts of his in-laws' clan. Andrew spotted them and waved. "We're ready," he said, leading the group of scholars and guests to the Missionary Room, where the empty glass showcase awaited condolence speeches instead of victorious congratulations.

Paul went to retrieve his briefcase before leaving the room. At first, he couldn't find it, and his heart skipped a beat with anxiety. But he quickly discovered that someone had moved it closer to the corner. Thank goodness. This afternoon he'd hurriedly thrown together a speech to take Dr. Barnes' place, and he needed his notes.

Without Dr. Barnes' facts, Paul couldn't say much, but he could at least give a little background on Sethianism and mention the possibility of a current Brotherhood. The world deserved to know—and how much danger could he be in without any specific information?

Paul followed the crowd up the library's curved staircase to his favorite room at the Divinity School. Built and decorated like a Victorian library with a series of small alcoves and private desks, the Day library held several thousand books about missionaries who spread the Good News around the world.

No good news this evening, Paul thought wryly.

Nervous, Paul reviewed his major points in his mind while the governor, a handsome man entering his silver years still as attractive as an ad for Senior Centrum vitamins, thanked the Guildford family for everything they'd done for the state of Connecticut. "This family doesn't ask what it can do for its country; they just do it," he said, listing their contributions such as the new Hartford Center for the Arts and a Head Start building.

Next, the president of Yale expressed gratitude for the Guildfords' part in the recent restoration of YDS. The red bricked buildings with white trim now looked as authoritative and elegant as they did originally.

Photographers from several local and national newspapers, and cameras from the Hartford and New York televisions had a field day capturing the scene.

Andrew spoke briefly, ending on a hopeful note, with a prayer that God would turn the hearts of the thieves to return the manuscripts for the benefit of the greater good.

Then the group processed to Marquand Chapel for Paul's lecture.

After everyone was seated, Andrew began to introduce Paul. "Dr. St. Clair has graciously agreed to step in for the late Dr. Barnes."

During the introduction, Paul reached inside the briefcase for his speech. He groped around for the speech he'd placed on top. His fingers couldn't feel the folder in the main space, so he started feeling around in the side pockets. His heart started beating faster. Where was his speech? Placing the briefcase on his lap, he opened it wide.

The briefcase was empty, except for the small Book of Common Prayer he always carried. Paul froze as he watched his uncle in slow motion at the podium. He was sure he had placed the speech inside before he left the house. No speech. What was he going to do?

Andrew finished the introduction and the audience began to clap. Photographers started clicking as Paul rose mechanically from his chair. *Someone had stolen his lecture.*

He moved toward the podium, deciding what to do. As the applause died out, his family on the front row began to notice something wasn't quite right. His mother gave him a worried look.

Paul stood for a moment, surveying the audience, wondering who in the crowd was trying to silence him. Though anxiety began to send tremors through his body, he decided he would not be silenced. He would have to adlib, but he would not apologize and sit down.

He began to speak. "In the *Gospel of Judas*, Jesus says to Judas, 'Step away from the others and I shall tell you the mysteries of the Kingdom.' He gives Judas special information not available to anyone else. Jesus favors one disciple—Judas—giving him a leg-up into heaven."

Paul's mind raced as he wondered where to take his train of thought. He tried to remain calm and remember what he'd written earlier in the day. "In the *Gospel of Judas,* Jesus also instructs Judas to turn Him in. Obedience or betrayal? This question has been argued thoroughly since the 2004 discovery of the Judas fragments."

Paul placed his hands in his pockets to keep them from shaking. "This evening, I'd like to discuss some of the implications of what the *Gospel of Judas* tells us." He pictured Dr. Bonnie Barnes' body on the floor of the Courtyard. Then he forced the image out of his mind. He had to continue.

"The *Gospel of Judas* recognizes the problem of evil but puts a different spin on it. When Jesus pulls Judas aside and commands him to turn Him in to the authorities, He denies Judas the possibility of making a choice for himself between evil and good—thus negating the need for redemption. *What is evil thus becomes good.*

"Sethians blame evil on Yaldabaoth, a power-hungry monster, who created a flawed world because he himself was flawed. The *Gospel of Judas* makes it too easy on us. It's always easier to blame someone else for our actions. Even our own Bible illustrates that human tendency when Adam tried to blame Eve, and Eve blames the serpent."

Paul looked at his family. Responsible, God-fearing citizens. They had taught him well the lesson of taking responsibility for his actions.

He continued. "Christian belief hinges on choices—the choice to believe, or not to believe. The choice between good and evil. The choice between right and wrong. In the *Gospel of Judas,* Judas' actions are no longer betrayal, but obedience—a notion that creates a completely different scheme of salvation. Only those who have the special knowledge of

Judas' role can achieve eternal life. They are the 'incorruptible generation.'"

Paul paused. "The moral implications of this theology are staggering." He pictured his Aunt Victoria bludgeoned and lifeless in her own entryway because some Sethian was being obedient.

Taking a deep breath, Paul hoped he would have the courage to finish what he needed to say. He continued, "Dr. Barnes believed that Sethians are a current, secret, and powerful force. The empty case upstairs is an example of Sethian theology and obedience in action. Because the *Gospel of Judas* contained secret information, a certain group felt entitled to it and obtained it at the price of two human lives."

He concluded, "The rest of us who are not Sethians are thus excluded from true salvation and doomed to die."

A hushed silence fell over the chapel when Paul stopped speaking, followed by a thunderous applause.

Chapter Three
SATURDAY

1
Isabella

On the flight to England, I had plenty of time to wonder about the Campus Killer's lack of Internet privileges and to speculate on how fast the D.A. could get the trial underway. Then I fell asleep before the meal. I just wasn't hungry.

London in November was dreary, much like New Haven. I landed in the kind of gray rain that newscasters described as "soup" and hopped on the express train from Paddington Station to Oxford. I barely had enough time to meet Detective Inspector Timothy Higginbotham from Scotland Yard.

Tempted to doze off and on, I kept my eyes open, watching the people around me. British commuters stayed behind their newspapers, and two young children squirmed and asked questions of their parents. The landscape changed outside the window, from industrial factories, to suburban duplexes, to pastoral scenes—and, finally to the spires of Oxford ahead.

A middle-aged man had gotten on the train in London and seated himself behind me. He rustled his newspaper a lot and got up once, glancing at me out of the corner of his eye when he thought I wasn't looking. He followed me off the train in Oxford and entered the men's room carrying a green umbrella with a carved, knobby handle.

Detective Inspector Higginbotham was waiting for me at the Porter's Lodge near the entrance of Christ Church College. I paid the cabbie and looked around. The entrance archway looked like (and probably was) a prototype for the colleges at Yale. "Timothy Higginbotham, here," he extended his hand.

"Isabella O'Leary."

Detective Inspector Higginbotham was a lanky, beak-nosed Brit with an upper class accent and stooped shoulders.

Leaving the entrance portal, we stepped into another world, the hushed atmosphere of rarified learning. With gray stone and leaded windows, the old buildings were hidden from the street by walls protecting the students from the rest of life.

Apparently, Dr. Barnes was one of the few Fellows who actually lived at the college. As the porter led us to Dr. Barnes' rooms, Higginbotham pumped me for information about Bonnie Barnes' murder.

I'd never worked with Scotland Yard before, and I'd never been sent on a privately funded mission. I didn't even bring my piece on the flight. What kind of official status did I have with the law enforcement here? None. To get what I needed, I'd have to tread delicately.

Higginbotham was an affable, nerdy type. I figured he'd probably moved up rapidly in the ranks based on ability, not territory wars. I decided to set the tone by being agreeable and offer what I knew. "The poison turned out to be belladonna. The murderer spiked her tea."

"How dreadfully uncivilized. One should never alter someone's tea." Higginbotham shook his head. "One of the oldest poisons in the book. Probably made from roots. The most potent part, you know."

I nodded. "We questioned the hotel staff. Dr. Barnes arrived early and told the desk she didn't want to be disturbed until 10:00. She'd called ahead and breakfast was waiting in her room."

"What time are we talking about?"

"She got to her room a little before 7:00. One oddity we found was two cups of tea, one with a few drops of normal Earl Grey in the bottom, and one poisoned near her bed. We figured the poisoned one was delivered later."

"Who delivered her breakfast?"

"Room service staff. A young college student named Jennifer. Jennifer said she had two more deliveries on different floors between 7:00 and 7:15. She did remember a young man in the elevator when she got back on the sixth floor."

"Description?" asked Detective Inspector Higginbotham as they passed through the cloisters. He reminded me of a crane.

"In his late twenties, with dark hair, dressed in a hotel uniform. Had a silver labret."

"A what?"

I pointed to my chin below my lips. "A piercing here."

"Of course." Higginbotham looked embarrassed to be caught ignorant. He recouped quickly, though. "Part of the staff? Did she recognize him?"

"No. In fact, she thought it was odd that she hadn't met him. She thought she knew all the staff on her shift. He might have been somebody new. Or a guest who happened to wear a white shirt and black slacks. He didn't have a name badge."

"Anything she remembered about his features? Maybe a sketch artist—"

"Yes, we've got one on it. Dark hair, almost black. Medium build, medium height, medium weight. No distinguishing features, although she commented he was 'hot.'"

"Hot?"

"Sexy."

"Oh, that's a helpful clue," said Higginbotham. "One woman's meat is another one's poison." He paused. "Sorry. Bad choice of words."

The porter slowed down at an ancient oak door, with an iron knocker and handle from the Dark Ages. "Here we are." He started to unlock it with a key from a huge, jangling key ring, but the door swung open on its own. The porter said, "That's not a good sign, now is it?"

Higginbotham took control. "Here, allow me." He pushed open the door. The room had been tossed in total disarray. The porter took one look inside and eased himself out of the situation.

I sighed. "I was afraid of this. Still, I'd hoped to get here first."

Detective Inspector Higginbotham said, "Forensics is on the way. In the meantime…" He pulled out a pair of plastic gloves and put them on, snapping them at his wrists.

"Do you have an extra pair?" I wanted to participate as more than a spectator.

Higginbotham hesitated, and then said, "I suppose so." He eyed me as he handed over a clean pair of latex gloves.

The sitting room was furnished with a sofa from the fifties—cushions slashed—and a couple of antique chairs that had been hacked and broken. A massive desk and a credenza at a right angle had also suffered from unnecessary physical abuse.

The bedroom off to one side had received similar brutal treatment. It resembled the Guildfords' library. "If this murderer's trademark is destruction, it's the same person."

Higginbotham shrugged. "Sethians could have branches on both sides of the Atlantic. In which case, this one's a Brit."

"I don't think so." I shook my head, walking among the debris toward the desk. Every drawer had been emptied on the floor. File folders, papers, pens, paper clips, and other office supplies lay strewn around the room. Even a hooked rug had been overthrown, as if Dr. Barnes might have hidden something under it. "This damage looks familiar. Hack marks on the furniture."

"We'll see. One must not jump hastily to conclusions." Higginbotham folded his lean form and sat down cross-legged on the floor. I sighed to myself again and joined him. He established his authority in a voice louder than necessary. "Anything that mentions 'Sethianism' or 'Gnostic' is what we're looking for. Also, anything with Dr. Cole's name."

"Maybe if we tried to reconstruct her filing system."

In spite of his attempts to look in command, Higginbotham seemed adrift in a sea of paper. He picked up the nearest sheet. A list of names. "Students."

I offered a sheaf still clumped together. "Lecture notes, different years."

"Student essays."

"Good. Read the topics and see if the students might be regurgitating some of her own ideas back to her."

Higginbotham looked down his nose. "That sounds unpleasant."

"It's an American undergraduate habit—even in the best schools, we have to work on critical thinking skills."

"I'm sorry to hear that."

I decided to ignore his British snobbery and continued to sift and sort through the detritus of twenty years of serious and brilliant scholarship. After awhile, my backside started to go to sleep.

Nothing of substance to help our case.

Next we waded through the books. A library of over two thousand volumes had been dumped and lay in naked chaos, spines broken, pages flapping.

Again, nothing.

A "correspondence" file revealed professional letters on every topic except Sethianism. Dr. Barnes' personal correspondence was mostly chatty letters to friends, news to her elderly parents, and thank you notes she'd received for small but meaningful things she'd done for her students and friends.

"Whoever did this had plenty of time. He obviously slipped past the porter. Who's on night duty?" I asked.

"I'll make enquiries later. This bloke on dayshift didn't know anything."

We stood up in the middle of the room, reluctant to face a stalemate. Detective Inspector Higginbotham said, "Maybe forensics will find something."

I was not hopeful, but you never knew where breaks in a case would come from.

"I don't suppose she saved her work on a memory chip," said Higginbotham.

"I think that's one thing the person who preceded us was looking for." I tried a different tack. "Do the Fellows ever use the library computers? Maybe we could track her research if she had a carrel in the library?"

"I'll have the computer chap check. Fellows have particular codes and passwords, and he might be able to trace her sources if nothing else."

A cheery young man with a forensics kit appeared at the door. "Oh, my," he said, surveying the damage. "First hurricane of the season, I see."

Higginbotham introduced me to Robin and then unpeeled his gloves. "We'll leave it with you, Robin." He turned to me. "I'm going to talk with the computer chap. It's a massive system, and perhaps somewhere, somehow…" he trailed off.

"Good. I'm going to make a few cold calls, starting with the family and friends of Dr. Cole." I tried not to allow discouragement overtake me, but I realized I had placed high hopes on finding something in Dr. Barnes' apartment.

As we were leaving Dr. Barnes' apartment, my eye caught on something half-hidden behind the door. My pulse quickened. Was it what I hoped it was? "Wait," I said, pulling the door aside.

Lying against the floorboard was a small axe.

2
Paul

Before leaving New Haven, Isabella had asked Paul to keep on the lookout during Victoria's funeral. "Perps often attend funerals, lurking around. They try to get a secondary high from watching the effects of their handiwork on the family."

She paused, "I know it's hard because you're involved, but you've got to be my eyes and ears. The FBI will be there, but I'm hoping you'll catch things they might not. They won't know who's on the fringes. You will."

Paul had not called to tell her about his stolen speech. Maybe he would try to reach her after the funeral.

On Saturday afternoon at the old Episcopal Trinity Church on the Green, police officers directed overflow traffic to the nearby hotel parking lot with reserved spots for Trinity attendees.

Paul and his parents arrived in a limousine and strode to the front of the church with dry eyes and dignity. As the family slipped into the old wooden pews, Paul couldn't take his eyes off the newly renovated stained glass window, a glittering work of art that made the church feel like a large antique jewel-box.

Victoria's sister and aging mother sat on one side of Malcolm, Paul and his parents on the other. Andrew and his family sat in the pew behind them. Paul reflected on all the tears and joy the stone walls and wooden kneelers had absorbed in the century Trinity had stood on the corner of the Green.

The service was short and to the point, Anglican fashion. Cremated and placed on the altar covered with a pall, Victoria went out in style.

Afterward, Winthrop Smythe and his wife Elizabeth followed the family out to the limousine and to the country club for the reception. In the same room his parents had had their wedding reception, Paul watched his Uncle Malcolm suffer through hundreds of well-wishers and hand-shakers in dark suits. Paul stood nearby and eyeballed each guest, introducing himself to the ones he didn't know. Malcolm knew them all.

The governor said, "Coretta and I want to have you to the mansion for dinner sometime in the next month. We'll let you know." Paul knew that Malcolm could expect an engraved invitation within thirty days. The governor was as good as his word. He and Malcolm had gone to Yale together. The governor had built his administration on the foundation of good friends and promises kept.

The law firm was there in full force, with one exception. Clyde Sneed. Winthrop gave Malcolm an email Clyde had sent, expressing his condolences. An email for the death of the boss's wife! Not even a hand-written note. Paul had only met Clyde Sneed once, outside the club. He wondered what was so important that Clyde thought he could excuse himself from this occasion.

Even LeRoy from the country club had left his serving duties temporarily to show his respects at the funeral. Paul had spotted him at the back of the church.

At the club LeRoy approached Paul with a tray of wine—red, white, and rose. Paul took a glass of red. "Thank you for coming to the funeral."

LeRoy gave his customary half bow and seemed genuinely sad. "Mrs. Guildford was one of my favorites. She never said a cross word to me even once when I spilled coffee on her lap."

"She spoke highly of you, LeRoy. And I know my uncle appreciates your coming, too."

LeRoy bowed out and continued to circulate among the guests.

Paul scouted for two hours at what had turned into one of New Haven's elite social occasions, heavily laced with wine and an open bar. Paul overheard Elizabeth Smythe talking to his mother as everyone was leaving.

Elizabeth grasped Lindsey's hand and her eyes were filling with tears. She said, "We don't know. He's done this every time he's been in treatment, but we had hoped this time—" She shook her head.

Winthrop approached and took his wife by the arm. "Come on Elizabeth. Don't upset yourself." He turned to Paul. "It's Jeeter. This time we sent him to the Meadows in Arizona, out in the middle of nowhere. And we escorted him to the plane ourselves."

Paul said simply, "I'm sorry." Jeeter was so addicted to drugs that he had once spent six weeks on the streets of New York while his worried parents sent a private investigator to find him. He had run away from five treatment centers, six counting this latest one. Paul counted his blessings.

When only family was left, Pappadad tottered over to Malcolm, Andrew, and Lindsey. "That was fun," he said, his gaunt face curved into a smile. "But where was Victoria?"

His attendant pulled him toward the door. "I'll get him on back now."

Paul and his parents drove home with Malcolm. Paul would have to tell Isabella the funeral was a wash for suspects. Everyone who showed up belonged.

Except for Clyde Sneed, who was conspicuously absent.

3
Isabella

My taxi passed Tolkien's home several blocks beyond Oxford University near Banbury Cross Road. We continued to wind around residential streets until we reached a two-story brick house on a quiet lane. Cello music wafted from a room in the front of the house. I paid the driver and walked toward the music.

The street was empty except for a man walking a terrier, and another taxi that turned off a block away.

A woman with short frowsy hair and dewlaps under her chin answered the door. She held a cello bow in her hand and looked irritated at the interruption.

"Mrs. Cole?"

"Yes."

I introduced myself and asked if I could come in and ask a few questions about her late husband.

"I suppose you need to come in now because I suppose you are on a time schedule," she said. "The authorities always want to do things when it's convenient for them."

I put on my best manners. "It won't take long, and I apologize for the inconvenience. I'm in England for a short time."

"Well, it's not tea time, so we can dispense with that. I suppose you can come in for a minute or two."

I entered a sitting room from another era. Although I didn't know much about antiques, the room was stuffed with furniture probably worth a fortune. I sat down on a brocade couch. Mrs. Cole resumed her place on a spindle-legged chair in front of a brass music stand.

"We're looking into the murder of Dr. Bonnie Barnes. She was in the United States this week, and—"

"I heard about it. Can't say I'm too sorry. Bit of a strumpet in my books, but that's neither here nor there. Can't imagine why you want to ask me anything."

"Dr. Barnes had a significant conversation with your husband a couple of years ago. He implied that he was a member of a secret society—one he wanted to get out of, or was unhappy with. Do you know anything about a group he might have joined?"

Mrs. Cole's doughy face rested for a minute before her dewlaps shook no. "Can't say that I do. He wasn't a Mason or anything like that."

"Did he travel a lot?"

"Heavens, yes. Public relations for the University, especially when the Chancellor was ill. Speeches. Whatnot."

"Did you accompany him?"

"Not when I didn't have to. I did the 'stand by your man' thing for events in town, but I'm with the Oxford Symphony. And someone had to oversee the three wild offspring we managed to produce."

I got the feeling Mrs. Cole hadn't played the grieving widow for long. The fist of anger started to clench in my stomach. Some people couldn't appreciate what they'd lost. Summoning my professional resolve to overcome personal feelings, I forced myself to move on. "Can you tell me about his car wreck?"

"The car crash. Yes. I told him he was going to commit suicide in that old Bentley. Bad tyres, bad brakes. He didn't even get the oil changed on a regular basis. Tyre blew out coming back from London—a puncture. He skidded into a light post and died on impact." She sighed. "It was terribly inconvenient."

Inconvenient. For a moment, I was too stunned to say anything. This woman had just called her husband's death inconvenient. I had to struggle to keep my voice on an even keel. "Was there any question about whether the wreck was an accident?"

Mrs. Cole's eyes almost disappeared into her fleshy cheeks. "My dear, are you suggesting someone did him in? Who would possibly benefit from his death except me? He had no family money, and the only thing he left me was a skimpy insurance policy and this house."

People have killed for a lot less, but I didn't think Mrs. Cole would or could have arranged her husband's death. I didn't think she cared enough. "No, I was just wondering if the police had looked into the possibility someone may have tampered with his car."

"No, my dear. It was a tyre puncture. They found the nail. Bad luck that he skidded."

I nodded, thinking of a hundred ways Dr. Cole's car wreck could have been staged to look like an accident. But two years later, it would be difficult to prove. "Besides his business colleagues, can you think of any friends he saw on a regular basis?"

Mrs. Cole picked up the cello and began fingering the neck. "He didn't have time for friends. The only person he saw outside work was his brother, Allen, who lives in London."

"May I have his address? If it's not too much trouble."

Reluctantly, Mrs. Cole set her cello against her chair and went over to a desk with a hundred pigeonholes. She rummaged around in three or four of the cubbies. Then she pulled out an old address card.

"Is that everything?" she queried, sounding hopeful.

I copied down Allen's address and phone number. Looking around the room had given me an idea. "I know you'd like to get on with your practicing, but I was wondering if you saved Dr. Cole's papers, or his calendar, or his schedule of trips and contacts." It struck me that Mrs. Cole didn't throw much of anything away.

"Upstairs. First door to the right. Take anything you want." She sat down and picked up the cello. "And now, if you'll excuse me."

Behind the first door to the right, I found the grand prize. Every document from Dr. Cole's tenure had been preserved in ceiling to floor filing cabinets by a secretary who must have been frighteningly organized. It looked like everything had been transferred home from his office and abandoned. Mrs. Cole had obviously shut the door and never opened it again. Dust was so thick I could write my name in it.

First, I combed through the correspondence, even though I suspected that, if Dr. Cole had been killed by a group threatened by his discontent—or maybe a threat of disclosure—someone would have ditched the incriminating letters.

I was right. Nothing.

Next I moved to the filing cabinet with his trip itineraries. I found an entire drawer devoted to Dr. Cole's travel, especially heavy travel during 2002-4. Before long, I noticed a pattern. Interspersed with his trips to London and other universities, I discovered that he spent the first weekend of every January, March, June, and September in Glasgow. He took the same flight on Friday afternoon from Heathrow, returning Saturday afternoon. When I checked the other years, I discovered only two times when he didn't make the trip on the prescribed dates. I tucked the schedules and dates in my tote bag.

I spent another hour going through Dr. Cole's papers. The only interesting thing I found was a typed list of major cathedrals around the world: St. Paul's in London, St. Basil's in Moscow, Notre Dame in Paris, the Seville Cathedral, and the National Cathedral in Washington, D.C. Alphabetical order, according to cities. On impulse, I stowed the sheet in my purse and took it with me.

I called a taxi from my cell phone. When I went downstairs, Mrs. Cole was so deep into a piece by Bach that I let myself out the door.

4
Isabella

I hopped the train back to London, and had just enough time to get to my hotel before darkness descended in late afternoon. As I flagged down a cab at Paddington Station, I noticed a middle-aged man with a green umbrella get into the cab behind me. Was it the same man from this morning? I couldn't tell from a distance, but something about his green umbrella niggled at me.

The cab followed me all the way to my hotel. When I got out, the cab turned the corner and moved on down the street. I caught a brief glimpse of the man in a hat reading his newspaper.

The Guildfords had put me up in a nice, refurbished hotel on Tothill, not too far from Westminster and the new Scotland Yard. The Sanctuary House was a four story, four star hotel with thirty-four rooms. Upstairs, I stretched out on the bed and looked over the lights of London. My feet hurt. I'd only made a few trips overseas, but they threw off my body's timing for a week. In the bathroom mirror, I saw a tired woman looking back—the same brown eyes, brunette hair, and smooth skin. But tonight all I saw were dark circles under her eyes. The Campus Killer, and now this. Would I ever get my looks or my energy back?

I decided to order room service and go to bed. When I finished eating, it was only 4:45 London time. I didn't care. I slid into my travel negligee and removed what was left of my make-up. After flopping down on the bed, I called Higginbotham.

In a chipper voice, he asked, "And how did you find Mrs. Cole?"

"Musical."

He laughed. "Yes, to mix the orchestral metaphor, she plays to the beat of a different drummer. However, her participation in the symphony didn't seem to hurt her husband's career."

Treating Higginbotham as a team member rather than a turf opponent seemed to be working well. I told him about Dr. Cole's trips to Glasgow and his brother, Allen. "I'm calling on him early tomorrow morning, before he has the chance to escape from his house." I laid my head back and fought against nodding off. Falling dead asleep in the middle of the conversation could only hurt my cause. "What about the computers?"

Pause. Long pause. Perhaps Higginbotham was deciding whether or not to include her in his information loop. *Come on. I'm too tired to play these games.*

But the pause was simply leading up to a sneeze. "Excuse me. Rather a wash, I should say. Scholars these days tend to fall into two camps—those who love the feel of old books, and those who recognize the value of googling." He paused and sighed. "Dr. Barnes was the latter. But she was a one-computer woman in love with her laptop. Apparently, she used only her own computer and took it everywhere—had the latest wifi, etc."

"Ah, yes. The laptop that went down with the ship."

"Into the ocean of oblivion, so to speak." Higginbotham paused. "However, there is one bright spot. Dr. Barnes had a graduate assistant, I believe you call them."

I sat up straighter. "Yes?" Depending on the relationship Dr. Barnes had with her Research Assistant—well, I knew that some RA's handled a great deal of the work, to the point of writing drafts for speeches.

"Yes. And she's in the process now of downloading all the files Dr. Barnes sent her as well as the material she prepared for Dr. Barnes—any references to current Sethian activities."

"Wonderful." In spite of my tiredness, I felt relieved. Perhaps there was hope after all. I paused, debating whether to push the limits of my new colleague's willingness to cooperate. "Also, just for grins, could you pull the police report on Dr. Cole's accident? See what happened to the car, that sort of thing?"

"Do you suspect foul play?"

"I'm just curious."

"Consider it done."

"Great." Higginbotham was turning out to be as accommodating as I hoped.

Higginbotham cleared his throat. "To change the subject from business to pleasure, could I interest you in a bit of supper?"

Oh. Now I understood. He was going to hit on me. Lanky Timothy Higginbotham with the glasses that kept sliding down his nose. "How about lunch tomorrow?" I said with as much enthusiasm as I could muster. "I'm bushed and tonight I'm afraid I would fall asleep face first in the food."

No response. I closed my eyes. The last thing I wanted to do was offend this man. I needed him to help me with this investigation. "I'm so sorry. But by lunchtime, we can compare notes from the morning."

"Yes, quite. How about Rules? At noon."

"Sounds good." I added, "If there's an emergency, please tell the concierge to sound the fire alarm because nothing short of a blast in my ear will wake me for the next few hours."

"Of course. See you at Rules." He rang off.

I hung up and snuggled under the delicious down comforter. I barely had time to wonder whether Paul had seen anything suspicious at Victoria's funeral, before I sank into a profound sleep.

Little did I know how long it would be before I got to sleep again.

5
John

At Glenairie Castle, Mrs. Wallace knocked on the door, waking her employer up at 7:00 in the evening.

John McCullough groaned. Where was Rupert, his valet? Oh, yes. He had an errand in town.

John opened the door in his nightshirt, "Tell Rupert I'm not getting dressed this evening."

"Yes, sir."

"Oh, and Mrs. Wallace. The portraits." He pointed to the hallway lined with oil portraits, cracked and yellowed with age. He knew she didn't like the dour, life-size dead people staring down at her. She tended to avoid dusting the frames.

Most visitors to the castle thought the portraits were his ancestors. But no.

John McCullough had a more exalted heritage than mere Scottish aristocracy. John kept the document of his ancestry in the false bottom of an antique Egyptian tray on his desk, with current correspondence scattered over the hieroglyphics.

Out of the various housekeepers he'd employed over the years, Mrs. Wallace was the best. He liked her and gave her all sorts of perks. She understood his need for privacy. Four times a year, she cooked for his little house parties. She laid out the food and silver for fifty, and then left to visit her sister in Edinburgh on Friday. On Sunday, she returned, cleaned up, and changed bed linen in twenty-five bedrooms. She never asked a single question.

When she got too chatty with him (it couldn't be easy for her spending so much time out in the country), McCullough sent Rupert in the Rolls to take her to the community recreational center he built ten years ago in Cairnhill, the town twelve miles down the road from Glenairie. Had a big indoor swimming pool, three squash courts, a gym with fancy equipment that made your muscles hurt. To top it off, he'd built a pub inside, in the old style—dark wood, smell of beer.

The voters were most grateful; the community center ensured John McCullough's place in Parliament for as long as he lived.

He wrapped his robe around him and sat back down on the side of the bed. The mattress sagged with the impression of his body and that of his grandfather's before him. John looked around his lair. The walls were paneled in dark wood overlaid with centuries of varnish, and a polar bear rug by the side of the bed. He'd hung a tapestry of an Arcadian princess and a unicorn on the far wall, so he could revisit the sharp, pointed crown of the mythical horse every day when he woke up.

A satisfied man, McCullough rubbed his hands in anticipation of the culmination of his life's work. Only a few days to go.

In the study, John found an email from the American Patriarch: "Missions two and three accomplished. Subject number two dispatched, no complications. Post card planted. Laptop lifted. No evidence. Mission three: safe journey, papers delivered. Subject's apartment purged.

"P.S. Dr. St. Clair's replacement lecture was removed as instructed, but he spoke anyway. No damage worth mentioning, but he'll be watched carefully."

Good. Providence was with them. All exigencies were covered.

Leaning back in his chair, John McCullough warmed with love for Gabriel. From the moment he picked him up at the airport that first time, a missing piece of his life fell into place. John would never have children in the flesh, but he had a child in the spirit, someone to carry his precious burden into the next generation.

The young man's herbaceous smell from his shampoo, the way he worked his fingers when he spoke, his ardor—everything about the boy turned him on. Moxie most of all. When John asked him what his greatest physical sensation had been so far in his life, the boy had answered, "Watching the newscasts of 9-11, over and over. I couldn't get enough of seeing the airplanes blast those buildings. It was such an incredible statement of faith and courage."

The Grand Patriarch answered the American Patriarch. "Good work. Be sharp for Monday."

John checked in with his network of brothers. Spotter Four in America had hacked into the New Haven police computers and was keeping up from the inside. Good.

London Six had met Detective O'Leary at the airport and followed her movements to Oxford and back. Good.

He answered, "Sunday. Brown umbrellas for those directly involved."

Since his heart attack, time was of the essence. The doctors had insisted he quit smoking and take his medication, or he could die any day. McCullough followed the regimen carefully—he knew he would have enough time, if everything went according to plan.

Christendom was over. Islam wasn't the only powerful force in the world working for the destruction of the Western hegemony on life.

John McCullough's star would flash like a comet across the night sky.

John made sure Mrs. Wallace had left the kitchen and gone to her quarters for the night. Wearing a dark blue velvet smoking jacket and wrapping himself in his plaid afghan, he took the elevator down to the basement. There he pressed the button to unlock the door of the holy chamber. He moved through the dark, sacred space by torchlight. Inside, he lit the wall sconces one by one. At the back of the room, an enormous cabinet lined the eastern and most holy wall.

With reverence, he unlocked the holy of holies and took out the prize of the Sethian Brotherhood: the *Gospel of Judas*, translated and hand embellished with gold leaf—delivered only a few hours earlier. The Grand

Artist had engraved a fourteen carat gold box, with the crucified snake on the lid to hold the sacred document once it arrived.

John placed the document on the altar in the center of the room and lovingly ran his hands over the vellum. He opened his arms. "Oh, God, accept the gift of your servant."

Chapter Four
SUNDAY

1
Andrew

At the Sunday morning session of the Ancient and Apocryphal Literature Conference, attendance was abysmal. Harvard's Distinguished Professor Dr. Lytle spoke to seventeen scattered scholars in the RSV classroom at the Yale Divinity School. Andrew made it a point during breaks to speak with every scholar who'd stuck it out, giving his personal thanks for their participation.

Andrew found comfort in working the crowd. Harboring an introverted personality, Malcolm had once said that Andrew would have made a good cruise director on a party boat. Andrew suspected he'd meant it as an insult, but he didn't care. He'd rather be friendly than morose.

Bill Pepperling, the Associate Dean, had returned from his trip to Newport. He sidled up to Andrew, standing near the tray of doughnuts, croissants, and pastries. "Goodness, I don't believe I've ever attended a conference this disastrous. It must be terribly difficult for you."

"Hello, Bill. I see you're back. How are your parents?" Smarmy on his best days—toady and sly on his worst—Bill Pepperling had made a bid for the deanship that Andrew won. Bill was the one person on staff that Andrew had to pray daily for the forbearance not to strangle.

"Dad's not well. He had a hard week."

A hard week. Bill Pepperling's father was not the only one who had a hard week. Andrew stuffed his mouth with a large bite of a cheese Danish so he wouldn't say something he'd later regret. From behind pop bottle glass lenses, Bill watched him. Bill's eyes were swollen with ill-disguised delight that an international disaster had landed on the shoulders of the man whose job he lusted after.

After he'd chewed and swallowed the massive bite, Andrew replied, "I'm sorry you weren't here, Bill. You missed everything. Paul was brilliant."

Bill blinked a couple of times and said, "Yes, yes, I'm quite sure." His pockmarks left by acne scars seemed especially noticeable on his face today.

"God redeems everything for the faithful remnant," Andrew continued, pounding home his point.

"Quite true. Quite true. Still, one would wish for a happier ending," Bill said. He left Andrew and greased his way across the Common Room to spread his gloom around to others.

Bill's ass licking had only kicked up a notch when he lost the deanship. Andrew wondered the cost he paid in terms of keeping his ambition in check. He was a young man, in his late twenties. What was his hurry?

Bill had a mousy wife and two mousy children, but Andrew wouldn't have been surprised to find that he kept a stripper for a mistress, or had some other outlandish secret life outside his family. No one could be that unctuous in all aspects of his life. His father had been successful in the liquor business. Bill frequently visited his parents down the road in Newport. *What was he really doing when he left town?*

During the conference's last session after lunch, Andrew addressed the die-hard stragglers. "Many of you are going on to New York for the American Academy of Religion and the Society of Biblical Literature Conference. I wish you safe travel. Please spread the word around the AAR/SBL about the reward for the manuscripts. Perhaps someone has picked up some information without even knowing it. God bless."

After everyone had left and the custodians had cleaned up, the quadrangle was deserted. Most students had either gone home for Thanksgiving, or left for the huge national conference in New York. Andrew let himself into the darkened library and went up the stairs to the Missionary Room, where he stared desultorily at the empty case. He pictured Victoria on the floor of her home, frozen in death. Then, memories of Victoria at all stages of her life began to flood him from the past.

The summer of 1978, the Smythes, the Guildfords, and Victoria's family, the Birdwells, took a Mediterranean cruise together for a month. All the young people were in their twenties. They had toured Santorini, Rhodes, and Crete, drinking and dancing from Spain to Turkey.

When the ship docked in Alexandria, Andrew didn't feel like going ashore, so he stayed on the boat. So did Victoria, who had a headache.

They discovered each other by the pool around 2:00 in the afternoon, surprised the other one had stayed behind. Victoria was a tanned goddess two years older than Andrew. Her legs glistened from suntan oil as she lay resting in a deck chair in the sun. She had always taunted him, since they were children. "Bet I can beat you to the end of the pier," she'd say every summer at the beach, until Andrew outgrew her.

That summer, she glanced at him from underneath a large-brimmed hat with designer sunglasses. Her lips were moist and her bikini barely covered the essentials. "Bet I can drink more ouzo than you."

Not to be unmanned by his childhood competitor, Andrew said to the waiter, "Bring them on. In pairs."

Andrew and Victoria spent the next hour watching the blue of the Mediterranean and the shoreline of Alexandria become hazier and hazier. Finally Andrew stood up. "Will you excuse me? I think I'm going to be very ill very quickly." He made it to the deck rail and lost all the ouzo he'd ingested, before collapsing back into the deck chair.

The next thing Andrew remembered was waking up in Victoria's stateroom, lying in her bed with a cold compress on his head. "I win," she said from an armchair across the room, her golden, lean, and shapely legs crossed.

"No, I win," Andrew managed. "I'm in your bed, am I not?"

"Yes, you are. However, you're by yourself." Victoria eyed him coolly, but with interest. Her speech was slurred.

"Come here," Andrew patted the bed beside him.

"I make it a point never to kiss boys after they throw up." She held up her drink and toasted him from a distance.

Andrew leaned over to the nightstand as the room rocked gently in the quiet harbor. He dialed room service. "One toothbrush, please. Room 811."

For some reason, Victoria thought it hilarious and almost fell out of her chair laughing.

When Andrew weaved into the bathroom to brush his teeth, he also took a shower among all of Victoria and her sister's toiletries. He emerged totally naked, strode over to her chair, knelt, and began to lick her legs.

"Well, well. Malcolm's little brother, all grown up." Victoria set her drink down, took off her hat, her bra and bikini bottoms. She and Andrew landed on the floor rolling around underneath the coffee table. She pulled away and surveyed Andrew from head to toe—young, muscular, and ready to go. "Isn't this a nice surprise? The last time I saw you without clothes, you were five years old and peeing in the bushes."

Andrew stopped conversation with his lips on hers.

Thirty years later, Andrew stood in the library at the Yale Divinity School staring at the empty case. He saw Victoria instead, her long dark hair entangled in his arms—both of them lying in her stateroom all afternoon until the sunset rendered the clouds purple and tangerine, floating on the horizon out their balcony window.

Before the shore party came back on board, Andrew stood up and kissed her hand. He returned to his room, where he had spent the next twelve hours in bed. Asleep. Alone.

Neither one had ever mentioned the afternoon in Alexandria again.

Andrew stood in front of the empty case and wept.

2
Isabella

Where was I? Oh, yes.

London. Now I remembered. Quickly, I got dressed and went downstairs to grab a Continental breakfast. An older gentleman with wingtips and a brown umbrella stared alternately at my legs and a newspaper. Outside, there was only one taxi in sight. Good. No middle-aged man skulking around. I got in and gave the driver an address on the outskirts of London.

Bordering on seedy, the street looked like a neighborhood of mixed races, mixed income levels, and mixed ages. If homes were an indicator of success, Allen Cole hadn't done as well as his brother Robert. I rang the doorbell on the left side of a duplex half-bricked on the bottom with siding on the top.

I rang twice more and was just about to go back to my cab at the curb, when a man with whisker stubbles answered the door. "Mr. Cole?" I asked.

He rubbed his eyes and stared out at me from underneath a gray unibrow. "Who wants to know?"

"I'm Isabella O'Leary from the New Haven, Connecticut Police Department. I'd like to speak with you about your brother, Robert Cole."

"Connecticut?" He paused. "My brother, Robert?" A puzzled smile spread over his grizzled face. I guessed he was around sixty, and had been handsome at one time. But that was many late nights ago. He wore striped pajama bottoms and a wife beater.

"Let me see your badge." He squinted in the morning light. "I have to make sure it's not from a candy box."

I showed him my identification. Obviously the man was careful.

"All right," he said. "Looks legit. Besides, sweetheart, you've got me wondering what a beautiful young woman like yourself is doing on my doorstep on a Sunday morning, bringing up my dead brother. Come in."

I signaled for the taxi to stay and followed Allen inside, stepping into a room filled, not with beer cans and clutter as I'd expected, but with vivid canvases of abstract art—rich with color, and sophisticated. "These are gorgeous. Are you the artist?"

"Allen Cole." He extended his hand. "Getting ready for a show at the annual British Abstract Painters. Sorry about the mess. Here, love, have a seat." He moved a well-used palette gobbed with paint and gestured for me to sit down. "Tea?"

"No, thank you. I've got the taxi waiting, so I can't stay long."

The artist moved some oilcloths and brushes and sat down on a footstool used as a paint table. "What would you like to know about Robert? I can't imagine what has come up in New Haven that concerns my deceased brother."

I filled him in about Dr. Barnes' death and the conversation she had with Dr. Cole. "You see, we think he told her something about a secret group called the Sethian Brotherhood. Something that tipped her off and ultimately got her killed when she got too close." I paused. "Do you know anything about this group? Whether your brother was involved in any way?"

Allen sat thoughtfully amid his work and the smell of oil paint. At last, he said, "My brother and I were fraternal twins. He was the darling, and I was the slob. Suited me just fine. I never wanted the pressure that my parents put on him."

He gazed out the front window. I followed his eyes, surprised to see another cab slowing down in front of Allen's house. Allen interrupted himself, "Looks like I'm Mr. Popularity today." The cab stopped, then pulled away. There was the middle-aged man in the hat again. This was too much. I tried to get the tag number, but my own taxi blocked it from sight before the man's taxi sped away. I gritted my teeth.

Allen continued. "Anyway, when Robert went up to Oxford, he got in with a crowd way above our social standing. Father was a greengrocer in London, not far from here, in fact. We grew up in this house. In Oxford, Robert was suddenly hanging out with a bunch of rich swells."

"Did you keep up with him?"

"He rarely came home to visit. Hobnobbed about, going to house parties. Then, his promotions started coming thick and fast. Before you know it, he was Master of Christ Church, then Vice-Chancellor of Oxford, wining and dining with upper crust all over England."

"Yes, but isn't Vice-Chancellor the grunt job—committees, paperwork, day-to-day running of the University? Isn't the Chancellor the glamorous part?"

"True, but, you see, the Chancellor fell ill for a long time. Someone high up on the food chain decided Robert should do the honors in the interim. Seems irregular in retrospect."

I made a note. "Who were some of his cronies back then?"

Allen shrugged. "Oh, fellow by the name of Edward Hobbs. Owns a group of newspapers in the United Kingdom. Let me think, who else? Richard Banks, kind of a quiet fellow, a government official now, pretty high up in MI 5, I think, although you don't hear much about him."

"So the friends that he got in with are movers and shakers."

"Yes."

"What were your brother's religious views?"

"It's hard to say. When we were small, we went to the parish church, like most people. But then we both fell off, you know, like so many did. My brother was nominally Anglican—and a rather high Anglican at that. But personally, I'm not sure he believed much of anything."

"Can you think back to when he might have lost his faith?"

Allen cupped his stubbled chin in his hand. "Now that you mention it, the first Christmas he was home for holiday from Oxford. We were watching the telly—a car bomb in Ireland, Prots against the Catholics. He said, 'The Christians have it wrong. God has revealed a better way, but not to everyone.'

"We didn't discuss religion again until right before his car crash."

I felt my heartbeat quicken. "Really?"

"Yes. I'd done a commission for a church modernization. New

windows and so forth. They had me do a series of Holy Week banners with different scenes on them. You know, Jesus riding into Jerusalem on the donkey, and so on.

"Anyway, Robert stopped in front of the banner of Judas kissing Jesus on the cheek and out of nowhere said, 'Betrayal is betrayal, not obedience. Violence is a human choice.'"

I repeated, "Violence is a human choice?"

"Yes," said Allen. "He didn't talk in enigmatic terms very often. He was a practical man. I asked if he would like to put his comments in context, and he said, 'No. But I have some work to do.' Just like that, and walked out. I thought he had to get back to his office. A day or two later, he died."

"'I have some work to do,'" I repeated. "That's an odd thing to say after his first comment." I paused. "I need to tell you that, in light of other events, we are wondering whether your brother's death was an accident."

"You're joking."

"No. I'm not. From what I've learned in the last few days about the Sethian Brotherhood and their beliefs, they think Judas didn't betray Jesus, but rather acted on divine command. Your brother spoke with the leading Sethian expert in the world right before he died. He gave out enough information for her to spend the next two years uncovering what may be a powerful international organization—and violent."

"He never mentioned anything like that." Allen shook his head.

"It's highly secret, and it's a long story. Their beliefs are based on the *Gospel of Judas*, the document recently discovered before your brother died. As it turns out, an American family had another copy—complete in Greek and in a Latin translation—owned by the family since some monk in a monastery translated it."

"What? I don't understand—"

"I'm getting there. Last Thursday night, this manuscript was stolen from the family, right before they donated it to Yale."

"Yes. All right, yes. I remember seeing a news flash on the BBC or something. A cook was murdered on a game show."

"Not exactly, but that's the same story. The next day, Friday, Dr. Barnes, from Oxford—the leading Sethian specialist who talked to your brother—was found poisoned in her room in New Haven. All her notes and laptop disappeared. She was to give a keynote address at Yale on the Sethian Brotherhood."

"Oh, my. The plot is beginning to thicken. You are here because a conversation with my brother got Dr. Barnes started on her research, and my brother died shortly after he spoke with her. And now she's dead and no one knows squat about this Brotherhood." He rubbed his face stubble.

"That's it."

"Rather shaky, I have to say," said Allen.

"Yes, but two people are dead, an incredibly valuable manuscript is stolen, and it's my job to firm up shaky leads."

"I also have to say that Rob's comment about Judas and having work to do makes more sense after what you've told me. He may have been a part of this group, and then become disillusioned with them. Maybe his 'work' was to expose them, or get out of the organization. What do you suppose made him change his mind?"

"He also said, 'Violence is a human choice.'"

"Oh, God. What if he knew this group was turning violent?"

"Well, somebody has turned violent. We just need to find out who and why." I dug in my purse and pulled out a business card. "My cell phone number is on the back. Give me a call if you think of anything else."

3

Isabella

Apparently Rules was a famous lunch place, the oldest restaurant in London. I was reading about it in a guidebook I found in the back of the taxi when Allen caught me on my cell. "O'Leary."

"This is Allen Cole, with some interesting developments."

"Yes?"

"It never occurred to me that my brother hadn't run over a nail in his old Bentley. I don't even know how someone could rig a puncture that could kill someone. All along I suspected Rob was a member of a secret group. I thought it was a drinking club." Allen paused. "I don't think that any more."

"Why? What's happened?" I fished in my purse for my notebook, ready to take notes.

"Fifteen minutes after you left, somebody else knocked on the door. I looked out the window and saw a telephone van parked in front. I asked, 'Who is it?' A guy said, 'Dan. I'm from the telephone company. Somebody reported your phone out of order.'

"Blimey, I'm thinking. It's Sunday morning. You can't get the phone blokes out here on a workday if you call them ten times."

I was writing all this down as the taxi made its way through light London traffic. "I hope you didn't let him in."

"Not a chance. Told him, 'just a sec,' and used my cell to call the bobby at the station down the street. You should have seen Dan the phone man run the second he heard the siren."

"Quick thinking on your part.'

"The kicker is that the officer traced the van to a phone company van that went missing five minutes after you left."

Coincidence is one thing, but Allen's story tipped my cab theory over the edge. Someone was following me. "Have they found the van now?"

"Dumped about a mile from here by the side of the road. Wiped down. No sign of 'Dan.'"

"Probably had a car waiting. Anything in the van?"

I heard the police bobby talking in the background. Allen said, "Just phone equipment—probably planned to put a wire tap."

I wasn't sure. Whoever was running this show didn't need or want information. They wanted information stopped. "Allen, where and when is the art show you told me about?"

"Next Friday at Brighton."

"Can you transport your work there early—like now—and take a brief vacation at the beach until it opens?"

"No, I really think that's being a bit too, well—"

"Please reconsider." I used my firmest voice.

Allen stammered around a bit. "Well, I—I guess I could do. Bit brisk for a vacation, but I could find a well-lit room somewhere and finish up." He paused. "Do you think they'll try to come back?"

"Yes, I do. If they think you are giving me information, I'm not sure what they'll do. Can the policeman watch the house while you're gone?"

I heard him talking with the bobby. "Quite," said Allen. He paused. "I still think you're being a bit too—"

"Allen, did you see the photos of your brother's car wreck?"

Silence. Then, "Yes, I did."

"Do you want to live to do another show?"

"Point taken."

"I hope I'm mistaken, but these people aren't fooling around. They're not taking any chances. I worked on a case once with a woman who refused to leave her home, and she got her throat cut that night."

"All right. All right. I'm not really the adventuresome type anyway. I always sketched while Robert fought the dragons."

"Good." I hung up. The last thing I needed was another body.

4
Gabriel

The AAR/SBL conference hosted several thousand members, spread among five large hotels in Manhattan. The taxi carrying Gabriel wove in and out of traffic, swerving while the driver cursed in a foreign language. Gabriel disembarked and entered a lobby filled with professional, scholarly types, each one lugging a suitcase on wheels like a small caboose. He joined the line to check in at the desk.

Idly, he picked up a conference program. Dr. Henry Hawthorne—graduate of the University of Chicago Divinity School and recently appointed Associate Professor at Wheaton College—was scheduled to speak Monday morning at 10:00. His seminar was entitled "The Gospels Revisited: The Early Canon in the Twenty-first Century."

When Gabriel worked his way to the check-in counter, he asked casually, "One of my classmates is staying in this hotel. Could you give me his room number? Henry Hawthorne, from Wheaton."

A pretty Asian girl at the desk said, "I'm sorry, but we don't give out the room numbers of our guests."

A minor setback. "I understand completely." He had other ways of getting the information. He didn't want to press the issue and draw attention to himself.

After getting his own room number and key, the Gabriel rode a crowded elevator up to the eighteenth floor. In his room, he changed into a tweed jacket with leather elbow patches so he'd blend in with the ivory tower crowd.

At 5:30, he went downstairs to one of the conference rooms. The University of Chicago hosted a cocktail party for its graduates and faculty. He passed by the cheese table and spotted Dr. Hawthorne chatting it up with what must have been some of his old classmates.

Everyone was talking about the two murders in New Haven, and the theft of the *Gospel of Judas*. Who would do such dastardly deeds, and why? Smiling to himself, Gabriel moved on to the cantaloupe and pineapple tray. He relished the fact that everyone was talking indirectly about him.

He overheard Hawthorne saying, "If they're going after scholars now, then nobody's safe."

Hawthorne had no clue how right he was.

5
Isabella

Paul called me right before the cab arrived at Rules. "Hey, you're up early," I said.

"Couldn't sleep."

"How was the funeral?"

"I like Episcopal funerals. The emphasis is on the joy of resurrection." He paused. "Clyde Sneed missed it. He sent an email with a lame excuse."

"I'll have to check it out when I get back. Looks pretty suspicious. Anybody there who didn't belong?"

"Nope."

"What else is going on? How was your speech?"

Paul didn't answer immediately. "Paul?"

"Somebody stole the speech out of my briefcase during the reception. I put it over next to the wall where anyone could have gotten to it."

"Somebody stole your speech? To keep you from talking about the Sethian Brotherhood?" Oh, God. At least they didn't kill him. "What did you do?"

"I said what I was going to say. I didn't know any specifics about the Sethians, so I don't think I'll die over it, but—"

The cab pulled up to Rules, the meter ticking. "Listen to me, Paul. Let me call the chief and have the house watched."

"Absolutely not."

The cab driver was pointing to the meter and gesticulating for me to get out. "This is serious business."

"I know. But my dad is here. Malcolm's here. It's fine."

I pulled out a wad of colored money and thrust it toward the cabbie. "Watch your back, Paul. I mean it. I'll call you tonight."

The waiter led Higginbotham and me to a table in an alcove. Framed art from *Punch* and cartoons from the early *Tatler* decorated the walls.

I slid into my chair and placed my napkin in my lap, worried about Paul. What was he thinking? Dr. Barnes had just been murdered before she stood up in front of the same crowd and talked about the Sethians. Oh, no. Surely, Paul had more sense than to reveal the post cards. We were keeping the messages away from the press. I forced myself to look at the menu.

After analyzing the wine list, Higginbotham ordered a bottle of something I'd never heard of. Clearly, he took his wine seriously. When it arrived, the Detective Inspector started to pour me a glass. I held my hand up. "No, thank you. I'd hate to be tipsy in case I got into a chase scene with thugs." Smiling, "I need all my wits about me."

"Yes, quite," he said. Higginbotham had perfected the British art of remaining urbane under all circumstances. He helped himself to the wine.

After we ordered, I leaned back and noticed Higginbotham's fresh haircut and an extra dose of aftershave—an overpowering scent in contrast to Paul's understated one. Higginbotham's cologne reminded me of a crowded pick-up bar. "You go first," I said. "What do you have?"

"Yes. Indeed." He took a sip of wine, never taking his eye off me, as if I might get away from him. His glasses started their downward slide toward the end of his nose. "Spoke with the night porter at Christ Church. Affable fellow, seems to know everyone who comes and goes. The night in question, he did let someone into the college. A young man, a hippie type with rather long hair, dishwater blond, and a wispy beard. Said he was a chap from Univ—had a pass card, so he gave him the okay. Also had his laptop with him in a case, the porter noticed. Headed toward the library."

"Laptop case. That's how he got the hatchet through the gate, and got out the documents and whatnot." I paused. "Did the porter say how big he was? Body type?"

"Average. Wore ratty blue jeans and sandals with white socks. Other than the beard and hair, just your average studious type, a bit older than the undergrads. Took him for a serious grad student."

"Average size."

"Blonde hair and a beard. Wasn't the other fellow dark?"

"Yes, but hair can be changed. Size, weight, and height are harder.

Hmm. I don't suppose he had a labret."

"Chap didn't mention it. But, of course, labrets can be removed." Higginbotham took another sip of wine. "I'll get Robin to see if we can find where he bought the hatchet. Can't have brought it with him."

"This perp is very careful. You'll probably find it's a generic hatchet, bought outside Oxford," I said. "Not too many stores on the High Street sell hatchets." Maria and Bob had gotten nowhere with the hatchet.

A waiter brought our food, poached perch for me and escargots for Higginbotham. How could anybody eat snails? I asked, "What about Dr. Cole's car and the police reports?"

"We'll never know on that one, I'm afraid. The car was smashed in a compactor. The mechanic who signed off died last year. There's nothing in the records to indicate that the car had been tampered with. Cole filled up at a petrol station a mile or two before. Checked his tyres, seemed okay. Could have picked up the nail any time."

"Just think, a few yards more or less, and he wouldn't have gone flying into the post." The perch flaked on my fork, and I added a little lemon juice.

"Life's quirky that way."

"What if somebody shot a nail gun at that very moment?"

Higginbotham held his snail mid-bite in the air. "Never thought of that. Plenty of bushes around for good cover." He finished the bite and said, "You Yanks, always on the lookout for violent crime."

"Unfortunately, it's a way of life." I added, "Before I forget, would you mind checking travel dates for these two men: Edward Hobbs and Richard Banks."

Higginbotham apparently recognized the names. "And what, may I ask, do a newspaper magnate and a highly placed spy have to do with this case?"

"Perhaps nothing. However, Allen Cole told me that these men ran with his brother. In fact, they sort of scooped him up at Oxford to be in their crowd at university. An unlikely set of friends for the son of a small grocery store owner. His whole career was rather unlikely for a man of his background."

Higginbotham started to protest. "Now you mustn't think that everyone from a lower class background can't get to Oxford. We have good charity schools that feed scholarship students into—"

"You don't have to tell me how it is. I went to Yale, but I'll bet there are two Oxfords, just like there are two Yales. I sat in class with a senator's son. He never asked me to lunch or anything else."

"Yes, I see your point. I suppose it won't hurt to check the airlines. What times, exactly did you want me to check?" Higginbotham downed the rest of the first glass of wine and poured himself a hefty second glass. I hoped he held his wine well.

I put down my fork and fumbled around in my purse. "The only odd thing I found in Dr. Cole's travels was a pattern of flights to Glasgow that nothing explained in his files. Here it is. He left London on Friday of the first week of every January, March, June, and September, and returned the next afternoon."

"His trips to Glasgow could be totally unrelated."

"Yes, but if he's part of a secret group, they have to meet somewhere, don't they?"

"I suppose so, but not necessarily in the same place. Perhaps the group moves around from city to city."

"Maybe." Higginbotham seemed determined to deflect my request. I leaned forward. "But Dr. Cole was still doing something in Glasgow unexplained by his work documents, and not known to his wife." I cut the julienne carrot strips and green pepper on my plate and finished eating.

"Of course, his wife is a little vague."

"Yes, but still, it's worth a shot." I wasn't used to having my suggestions rebutted, and I was determined to get those records checked. I smiled sweetly and wiped my mouth with my napkin. "That was delicious."

Higginbotham watched me. "I suppose I can put someone on it." He finished off his escargots. "Now for the *piece de resistance*."

"Oh, no, I'm full."

"My dear, I meant the *piece de resistance* of the conversation, not the meal." He smiled and winked, leaning in toward me confidentially. For a moment I was afraid I was the *piece de resistance*. "I am trusting that we are truly working together." He looked at me meaningfully over his glasses.

This *tete a tete* was suddenly making me wary. Men. If I communicated my physical aversion to him, he could cut me off, and I'd be a professional pariah. I swallowed and smiled again. "Yes. And I think we make a good team."

He grinned broadly, his teeth crooked and slightly gray. "Good. Professor Barnes' graduate assistant Rachel copied every note, every scrap, every document Barnes gave her. Her room was a rat's nest. She handed me a box and said, 'Professor Barnes once told me I had an obsessive-compulsive disorder, but in the end I guess I was right to save everything.'"

"Oh, that is the *piece de resistance*. Excellent job, Timothy." I paused. "If I may call you Timothy."

He beamed. "Of course."

Surely some bit of information would come from the notes. Dr. Barnes' killer had gone to a lot of trouble to ensure nobody got even a breadcrumb of a clue from Dr. Barnes' work.

Suddenly, I had a frightening thought. "Say, do you know whether you've got a tail?"

"I hope I'm more evolved than that." He chuckled at his own joke and finished off the second glass of wine. "No, seriously, I don't think I do, but spotting tails is not my forte."

"The reason I'm asking is because I do." I told him about the man with the green umbrella and the man with the hat in the taxi at Allen Cole's, and the telephone van.

Higginbotham looked alarmed and poured himself a third glass of wine.

"My point is this. If someone knows you went to Dr. Barnes' assistant's rooms, then she could be in danger."

"Which is why I left Officer Jones at her place, just in case our ransacker returns. If we thought of Rachel, then you can bet sooner or later, this group will, too."

"Thank you." Higginbotham might be nerdy, but at least he knew his job. I asked, "What about the material in the box?"

He smiled. "It's now safely ensconced in my office, where I plan to comb over it this afternoon. Would you care to join me?"

Without missing a beat, I gave him a warm smile. "Yes, as a matter of fact, I would."

6

Isabella

The new Scotland Yard was an imposing glass building at 10 Broadway, where officers guarded entry with Heckler and Koch G36 assault rifles guaranteed to scare off curious tourists and deter terrorists.

Upstairs, I decided Detective Inspector Higginbotham's office resembled him. Clean cut and spare. Higginbotham followed me into the room. A sheaf of papers about four inches thick lay on his desk. He motioned to a standard issue chair in front for me to sit in. On his intercom, he called the pool. "Anybody there?"

A lone voice scratched back. "Yes, sir."

"Bernadette. Good, yes, I was wondering if you would mind bringing us some tea up from the fourth floor."

"Good idea, sir. I was just thinking it was about teatime."

I wasn't surprised to find people working at Scotland Yard at all hours. Criminals worked around the clock and so did the people who caught them.

"Let's see what we have," Higginbotham said, dividing the pile evenly and handing half to me.

Couldn't wait to get my hands on the notes Dr. Barnes had collected. The first few pages consisted of handwritten Internet sites—everything from sites of Nattvindens Grat's song "Sethian Seal," to occult groups that mentioned "Seth" or "Brotherhood." Dr. Barnes had X'ed out all of them. I recognized some from my own googling, and I mentally discarded all of them, too.

The Sethian Brotherhood would hardly keep an updated website on its current activities.

In a packet clamped together, I found a reference from an ancient source around the time of the Venerable Bede. As I looked through the packet, I noticed that the information had been arranged chronologically. The second reference was in the mid-sixteenth century. Here and there, Dr. Barnes had located a reference to the brotherhood, mostly in letters, diaries, marginalia—all of which she had photo copied and documented as to date, place, time, and source.

My friendliness toward Higginbotham, the lanky crane, was worth every smile. Sifting through the copies of old texts, I began to pull together the secret history of this group. No one except an ardent and devoted scholar could have culled so many references from so many sources all over the scholarship map.

Here was the first reference to what Paul had discovered in his grandfather's basement. "Sir Guildford, Member of Henry VIII's Privy Council, bequeaths his library to his son, Peabody Guildford, scholar of

Christ Church College." What followed was a list of documents and the provenance. Most had come from Stoneleigh Abbey, a monastery closed by Henry VIII. It was given to John Guildford, with a stipulation to include the library.

The specific references read: "Item: Ancient Greek manuscript, *Gospel of Judas*, verified by Brother Caedmon, Monk and Scriptor, discovered with papers brought back from the Holy Land by Sir Peregrine. Item: hand-embellished Latin translation translated and transcribed by Brother Caedmon, Monk and Scriptor."

"This is incredible," I said aloud. "This stuff goes so far back. No wonder the world got excited about the Guildford's basement discoveries."

Higginbotham laughed. "You Yanks are always impressed with old things. I happen to attend a church still standing from the Saxons."

I held up the sheet of paper. "This is a specific reference to the very same documents stolen Thursday night. The provenance is impeccable."

"Keep digging. Let's find the group that now holds those very same documents in their hot little murderous hands."

I skimmed over the list of items in the library bequeathed to Paul St. Clair's ancestor. Several documents I recognized. Others I didn't—but I assumed that Paul would know what they were. If even half these books still existed, the Guildfords could buy a small country with the proceeds of the sale.

Toward the end of the list, I found a reference that must have sent chills of excitement down the spine of Dr. Barnes. "Item: Members of the Sethian Brotherhood."

"Timothy," I said. "Look at this. At one time there *was* a list of members of the Brotherhood. Of course, it's been five hundred years, but if we could find that list, it would be a place to start. Memberships in the Yale clubs have been passed down for centuries. British families trace back a lot farther."

"Let's sift through the rest of this and then call Dr. St. Clair. See if Dr. Barnes contacted him about the possibility of a list being in his basement."

A brisk young woman wearing jeans walked in with a tray, which she set down on the corner of Inspector Higginbotham's desk. "There you are, sir."

"Bernadette, this is Detective O'Leary from the States," said Higginbotham. I nodded and smiled.

"What are you working on?" asked Higginbotham.

"Just finishing a face-match scan."

"It's Robin's day off. Would you mind checking some airline dates of travel for me?"

Good. Higginbotham was pulling through on the travel dates of Edward Hobbs and Richard Banks to Glasgow.

"I'll probably go home when the program finishes. I'll email you the results." As Bernadette walked out, Higginbotham poured fresh tea into two cups with saucers—a far cry from the coffee maker and Styrofoam cups at the New Haven police station. I said, "White, please," before he could ask. "And two lumps."

"I'm impressed. The lady knows how she likes her tea." He stood up and handed me the cup. "Now we're fortified. Onward."

"Thank you." I sipped the hot liquid. Once Higginbotham dropped his Casanova role, he was actually pleasant to work with. Sharp eyes, good sense of humor.

After a careful reading, I reached the end of my stack. We traded papers. "You'll need to read this," said Higginbotham. "Brings things into focus."

In Higginbotham's stack I discovered what he was referring to, a penciled version of Sethian history. Documented, no less. Dr. Barnes had written it out in longhand and made a copy for Rachel. I started to get chills up and down my arms.

Apparently, the Sethians had been a well-known Gnostic sect before the birth of Christ. Incorporating the new Christian religion into their previous beliefs, the Sethians believed Jesus was the reincarnation of Seth.

As orthodox Christology and beliefs became hammered out in the church councils during the first four centuries, mainstream Christianity became the official religion of the Roman Empire. Sethian Gnosticism seemed to die out.

But only seemed. Pockets of believers here and there in the Holy Land and in the desert of Egypt kept the Sethian tenets and myths alive. They also preserved ancient documents written concurrently with Biblical materials. Sethians lay dormant, like much of civilization, during the Dark Ages.

However, at some point—and no one knows when—a small group of Sethians migrated north to England, settling around the monastery of

Jarrow. Like many of the Germanic people, they became Christianized. However, they kept a few of their own beliefs. Their refusal to conform to Roman Catholic beliefs sent them underground.

Then came Richard I of England, also known as Richard the Lion-Heart. In 1189, Richard ascended the English throne after his father, Henry II. Only one year later, 1190, he set out on the Third Crusade. Along the way, he married Berengaria of Navarre and joined forces with Philip II of France to storm Acre.

This much I vaguely remembered from history. I remembered that Richard had remained in the Holy Land to sign a treaty with Saladin to allow Christians access to Jerusalem's holy sites, but I didn't remember that Philip II had returned to France to plot against his former ally.

On the way back to England, Leopold V of Austria captured Richard and imprisoned him. According to legend, Richard's favorite troubadour, a man named Blondel de Nesle, wandered through Germany singing a song only he and Richard knew. When Richard answered Blondel from his prison, Blondel was able to tell the English where their king was held captive.

Richard returned to England on the condition that he would raise ransom money to pay off the Holy Roman Emperor for his release. When he returned to France to fight Philip, he was killed. His brother John ascended the throne.

Richard's story intersected with the Sethians in an interesting way. Richard was gone from England during most of his reign. Two powerful men, Hubert Walter, Archbishop of Canterbury, and William of Long-champ, Bishop of Ely, administrated the realm for him, acting as head of both church and state at different times. Walter used a few un-clerical tactics. For example, Walter burned the Church of Mary-le-bow to drive out a rebel who'd taken sanctuary there. His actions caused many to call for his dismissal.

Instead, he gained in power, continuing as Chancellor under King John. A slender piece of evidence connected Walter to the Sethians. His brother, Thomas Walter, was a monk at Stoneleigh Abbey. In one of Hubert's letters to his brother, Hubert thanked Thomas for the support of the Sethian Brotherhood. The letter implied both funds and influence.

The next reference was to the Guildford's list of members. The Sethian Brotherhood had continued underground using hidden influence and money to steer the course of British history. The name had popped up here and there, once in reference to an appointment of a peer to Lord Chancellor, once in reference to an uprising at Canterbury Cathedral, and once in the death of a pious and influential member of the royal family. But only hints.

Though the trail went cold in the eighteenth century, Dr. Barnes had photocopied a recent piece of correspondence typed on a typewriter and dated 1938, addressed to someone at McCullough Steel Works from someone in Germany. The names of both the sender and the addressee had been torn off. Dr. Barnes had highlighted two sentences, near the end of what looked like a business sale of ironworks from McCullough to Krupp Industries. "We can both look forward to the inevitable conflagration as the foundations of Christendom are eroded. The great day of light will dawn for this generation, and a new era of the Brotherhood will emerge in Seth."

I looked up. Higginbotham was watching me. I asked, "Do you realize the implications of this?"

"Yes, actually, I do." He pulled a piece of paper from his neat stack on the corner of his desk. "Last night I cruised the Internet and found a line from the fragments of the *Gospel of Judas*. One piece stuck in my mind. Judas is asking Jesus when 'will the great day of light dawn for the generation?'"

My eyes widened. *What, exactly, was involved in this "great day of dawn?"* A conflagration? Bombs leapt to mind. Bombs as in war. I remembered the post card with the picture of the war memorial. "Where did Dr. Barnes get this?"

He shrugged. "I haven't the slightest idea."

"Who has the original?"

"Again, I haven't the slightest."

"What is McCullough Steel Works?"

"Ah, that I know. A leading producer of war materials for Britain during both world wars." Higginbotham leaned back in his chair and began tenting his fingertips. "Old Sir John is a famous Scottish success story. Like Andrew Carnegie, only Sir John came back home."

"Is he still around?"

"No," Higginbotham shook his head. "He was knighted after the second war for his contribution to the British war effort. He made millions, of course, and he invested well. Cagey old dodger. Just as industry was shifting away from iron and steel production, he created a new branch of his company called McCullough Electronics."

"Is McCullough Electronics still in business?"

"Oh, yes. Makes something like 60% of the hard drives for European computers. Small steel plant is still going—everything subsumed under 'McCullough Industries.'"

"So the old man was knighted for British war effort. Did the British government know about McCullough's relationship with Krupp? Do you suppose they were involved in secret traitorous activities?" I pressed him.

Higginbotham took a deep breath. "I've been thinking about that. Of course, we'll have to check with the spy fellows, but this letter seems to transcend mere loyalty to country. I think the German sender and the British receiver had a higher bond of solidarity. The letter was written before the war, and my guess is that records will show no further trade with Germany after the blitz on Poland in September 1939."

"So—"

"I surmise that both sender and receiver were members of the Sethian Brotherhood. They realized that war was inevitable (in spite of our dear Neville Chamberlain's head-in-the-sand efforts to avoid it). Finally, they sensed that the war, no matter who won or lost, would weaken the institution of Christianity in the wake of a global disaster."

"Which, of course, has happened. Postmodernism. Atheism. Materialism. And so on." I'd heard that the church in England had dwindled even more than the churches in the United States.

Higginbotham continued, "The goal of the Sethian Brotherhood seems to be the undermining of Christian belief. Perhaps accompanied by death in large numbers."

"Maybe they should team up with Al Qaida."

"Maybe they already have."

7
Paul

Paul allowed himself to luxuriate in the bubbles of the bathtub jets at Malcolm's guesthouse. His parents were staying in the other guest room apartments on the second floor of the main house. All doors were double-bolted, the alarms set.

His mother offered to fly Paul to New York on Monday so he could attend the conference. Paul had already arranged for a hotel suite. He had planned to travel with a colleague, Dr. Mark Bryson, but Mark had come down with the flu at the last minute.

As Paul sat in the tub, self-pity began a slow spiral inside of him. Most of the time, he considered himself lucky—to be alive if nothing else. But the events of the last days had taken their toll. Sadness for Malcolm overflowed into sadness for himself. Malcolm was alone again and Paul was feeling his own loneliness. He always thought he'd be married by now. But—but what?

Paul grabbed the scented soap and ran it over his body. Cucumber melon. After his accident, doctors had put him on antidepressants. He had lain in his hospital bed refusing to talk to anyone. What good was living if he couldn't play tennis?

Life had robbed him of his passion.

One day the Rev. Bobby Joe Shoemaker showed up, an Episcopal priest who wore cowboy boots and a collar. He walked in, took off his hat and sat in the chair next to the bed. He sat in total silence for thirty minutes, and then he got up and left.

Bobby Joe did that for three days before Paul finally asked him, "Aren't you going to say anything?"

"Not unless you want me to," said Bobby Joe.

Paul had closed his eyes and listened to his heart echoing in the dark hole he lay in. "Okay, answer me this. How could God love me and let this happen?"

"Beats me," said Bobby Joe. "But He does. Let me tell you a story."

"I don't want to hear a story. I want an answer."

Bobby Joe ignored him. "Too bad."

Trapped in a hospital bed, Paul couldn't leave the room, so he closed his eyes again to block Bobby Joe out. He would rather die right now and get it over with.

Bobby Joe started talking in a twanging Texas voice. "Old man one day took his kid out to teach him calf roping. Kid was five, maybe six.

"So he goes out and shows the kid how to rope a post. Then he shows him how to tie the calf's three legs together. They practice, and practice. Then the old man takes the kid to a far pasture to get a calf. Calf is a mean so and so, but the Daddy don't know how mean."

"Can't you hear me?" asked Paul. "I don't care about a kid calf-roping."

"Tough." Bobby Joe continued. "Long and the short, the calf runs the kid down and knocks him over. He falls and breaks his leg on a big rock. The kid is crying and screaming. The daddy scoops him up and carries his kid a mile back to the house. All the time whispering, "It's okay. I love you. It's okay. I love you.

"Doctor comes and fixes the kid's leg, but it doesn't heal right and he's got a gimp leg the rest of his life. Has to do something else besides be a cowboy like he'd always wanted."

Bobby Joe had stopped talking. Paul opened his eyes. "And?"

"Think about it," said Bobby Joe as he set his cowboy hat on his head. "That kid and his daddy got to be real close after that. The kid knew how much his daddy loved him. He figured out being loved was more important than being a cowboy."

Furious, Paul watched Bobby Joe limp out of the room.

After he got out of the hospital, Paul struggled with rehab for years and years and years. Just learning to walk again. While everyone else was dating and following their dreams, he strapped himself into machines, his muscles cramped in agony. Where was the good in what he'd gone through?

The first week that he was able to hobble without a walker, he made it to the street corner and back. He came home, sat down alone on his couch, and cried. For the first time, he felt like someone was carrying him in big, strong arms, rushing him to safety whispering, "It's all right. I love you."

Now, sitting in the tub as his fingertips turned to prunes, Paul reminded himself that good days were blessings, and you couldn't take blessings for granted. Too often bad stuff rained down on you like diarrhea. Faith was what kept you from drowning in it.

Paul's cell phone rang next to the soap dish. He turned off the noisy jets and answered it.

"I need you," said Isabella from very far away.

"Isabella? Is that you? I can barely hear you. Just a second. I'm in the tub. Let me get out and go into the bedroom. I'll get better reception." Setting the phone down, he hoisted himself out of the tub. He grabbed a towel and went into the bedroom. "How are you? Are you still in England?"

"That's better," Isabella answered. "I can hear you now."

"Good."

"Detective Inspector Higginbotham of Scotland Yard and I found copies of Dr. Barnes' notes she gave her Research Assistant. One was a reference to a list of the members of the Sethian Brotherhood. This list may have been in the box with the *Gospel of Judas* that you found in your grandfather's basement. Material that your Guildford ancestor brought over from England. Do you remember any of the other documents?"

Paul said, "Yes. In fact, I went back to the originals when Dr. Barnes called with the same question. Andrew, Malcolm, and I sorted through the documents together. We found a treatise by a little-known Scholastic; parts of a lading bill for a ship leaving Venice in 1350; notes from the journal of what appears to be an Augustinian monk from Egypt, date unknown; and a stack of Greek inventory for what looks like court records."

"Anything else dated in the sixteenth century? The Greek stuff is too old."

"Yes, I almost forgot. A poem by Thomas Wyatt. Nothing that resembles a list of names."

"What an odd list," said Isabella.

"Yes. The knights would pick up documents they thought might be valuable to sell in England. People don't realize many of the knights were practically illiterate. Often they didn't know what they were carrying home."

"Thomas Wyatt. Is he the one who supposedly had an affair with Anne Boleyn before she married Henry VIII?"

"One and the same. I checked up on him when we found the poem. He's known as one of the fathers of the English sonnet."

"I'd forgotten that."

"Wyatt also paraphrased some of the penitential psalms." Paul paused. "Come to think of it, what we had looked to be a paraphrase of one of the psalms."

"Do you still have it?"

"No. We gave it to the Beinecke. They couldn't guarantee its legitimacy. Something about the cadence, although the vocabulary and the carbon dating matched. Still, they have it stored for scholars who want to look at it."

"Do you have a copy?"

"Yes."

"Good. Can you fax it to me? Here's the number."

"Okay." Paul could feel her enthusiasm over the airwaves from half-way around the world.

"Also send the Scholastic document, if you don't mind."

"Why?" Then it hit him. "A code."

"Right. Some of the psalms are elaborate acrostics, and my money is on the poem by Thomas Wyatt being a code for the list of members' names. But I'll check out the Scholastic as well."

"Of course," said Paul. His small bout of self-pity was disappearing, replaced by excitement of a challenging word puzzle. "I'll work on it too, from here."

Isabella said, "Good thing the English keep such elaborate registrations for crests, property, etc. Maybe we can track the descendants."

"It's a lead, and any lead is good," said Paul. "I'll go down to Malcolm's library and get our copy of that document. What time is it there?"

"Creeping toward the wee hours, but we're still up and going."

"When are you coming home?" asked Paul.

"Not sure. There's plenty to do here, now that the case is widening—checking out McCullough Industries, for example. Dr. Barnes found a link that looks promising. But I think the Chief wants me back in New Haven soon to coordinate with the FBI." She paused. "Are you going back to Texas?"

Paul said, "I'm scheduled to go to New York to the AAR/SBL Conference tomorrow first thing, but I don't know yet. I might just go home. I go to this conference every year, and it wouldn't hurt to skip a year."

Unbidden, images of Isabella flooded Paul. Her flowing hair that she casually tossed over her shoulder during interviews, her smooth skin, eyes that danced, and slim legs offset by high heels.

He wanted to say, "Let's fly to Paris for Thanksgiving," but he didn't want to intrude on her independence or her professionalism. He also feared she'd turn him down. Instead, he said, "Well, if I don't see you, good luck with the case. You can always call me. I'll go downstairs now and fax that poem to you."

"Thank you," said Isabella. She paused. "Wish you were here, working with me."

Paul thought she sounded almost as if she meant it.

8
Isabella

After we received the fax from Paul, the inspector ran off several copies of the poem and the Scholastic document. "I'll get these to encryption first thing tomorrow morning."

"I need to get back to the hotel. I'm wiped out. This looks like a poem to me, not a code. I'm afraid my brain has shut down for the day."

"Good plan," said Higginbotham.

"I'll get a cab." I began gathering my coat and purse.

"Oh, no," said Higginbotham. "I'm not going to trust you to a cabbie. I'll run you by your hotel on my way home."

I was afraid he'd offer to give me a ride—and then offer to walk me to my room—and go one step further and offer to protect me through the night. "No, no. That's okay, I don't mind, really."

"I insist." Higginbotham stood rigid, a long steel pole of will power in the center of the room. "You are not getting hurt while I'm in charge." His tone suggested the machinery of power. This was a new side of the nice but nerdy man I'd been working with.

I knew when to fold my cards. "Thank you."

Higginbotham drove his Range Rover out of the parking garage like a truck. I bounced around on the seat wishing I were driving my Mini Cooper. Timothy drove with one eye in all the mirrors. Though the hotel was only a few blocks away, he wove around London for ten or fifteen minutes and I had a sightseeing tour of the Westminster area and Trafalgar Square. Finally satisfied no one was following, he pulled up to the front door, where "The Sanctuary" announced a safe haven in large gold letters. He leaned toward me as if he were going to kiss me.

I froze before I realized he was simply checking out the surroundings. Maybe I was narcissistic to think he was trying to put on the moves. The only car in sight was a parked Mercedes on the other side of the street. In the shadows, it looked empty.

"You've got my number," he said. "Call at any time."

As I opened the car door and turned back to thank him, I caught a hint of concealed desire in his expression.

He said, "I…would you…no. Never mind. I'll call you tomorrow."

I nodded, escaped from the car, and walked briskly through the lobby—deserted except for two businessmen still conversing over drinks. No man in a hat. No green umbrellas. Home free, for tonight anyway.

By the time I got off the elevator, I'd taken off my stiletto heels. One day soon I'd have to switch to the kind of shoes my mother wore, but not yet. My bunions still had a few good years left.

I checked up and down the hall. No one. Using my card key, I opened the door a crack and started to let myself into the room. Without warning, my heart skipped a beat. Someone besides the maid had been there. All my instincts went into overdrive as nerves prickled throughout my body.

Was that person still in my room?

If so, I couldn't let him know I suspected. As a cover up, I began to hum a carefree song, the first song that popped into my head, "London Bridge." If my visitor were lurking inside waiting, I had to make him think I was caught unaware.

At the same time, my eyesight, hearing, and sense of smell sharpened to catch the most infinitesimal give-away signs. Heart pounding, I scoured the room through the six-inch crack of the door, my senses picking over every detail.

Besides the room smell of fresh paint and clean linen, I caught a whiff of a sharp, unfamiliar cologne. A pair of my underwear hanging over the top of my open suitcase. I distinctly remembered leaving my clothes folded inside this morning. Still humming, I instinctively reached for my piece before I remembered I'd left it in New Haven. Richard had instructed me to leave my gun behind. Too much paperwork for a fact-finding mission funded by the private sector. Bobbies didn't carry guns, yadi yadi.

My pulse picked up speed. I refused to give in to panic, no matter how hard my heart raced. My shoe would have to do; I held my stiletto heel poised as a weapon. Then I eased the door open, scanned the whole room quickly as I'd done many times before when entering unknown scenarios.

No one was in plain sight—not that I'd expected to see someone standing in the middle of the room. Keeping my back to the wall, I ducked and checked under the bed. No one. Taking the same precautions, I checked behind the desk. No one there either.

In the corner of the room, an *en suite* bathroom had recently been re-done during the hotel's refurbishing. The closer I got to the bathroom, the sharper the cologne scent grew. I threw my purse on the bed, making as much noise as possible, and turned on the radio to cover up the sound of my movements.

The bathroom door was barely cracked, the light off inside. But the switch was located outside the door. I formulated a plan as the radio played a popular song from the United States about a woman who lost her man to a vamp. At the crescendo of the woman's emotional pain, I acted, doing several things at once.

I flicked on the light from outside the bath room, simultaneously glancing down, where two small shadows showed—a man's two shoes standing right behind the door. Quickly, I grabbed the door handle and slammed the door with all my strength into the hidden man's face. Someone behind the door groaned; but faster than I expected, the door swung open.

Terrified, but functioning on automatic pilot, I stepped back, armed with my high heel. My heart thudded as a man, dressed as a Fleet Street executive complete with a hat and umbrella, jumped out at me.

It was the man from the train.

I dodged him, eyeing his umbrella raised in the air. Using reflexes and practiced skills, I timed my move just as the knobby handle of the umbrella crashed down on the tray of water glasses on the side counter instead of my head. He raised the umbrella again and came after me.

I swerved, ducked, and turned. Getting my balance and bearings, I took aim and stabbed the intruder in the eye with the heel of my shoe. Bleeding, he dropped his weapon, clasped both hands over his face, and ran out of the room.

My heart still racing, I chased after him barefoot down the hall. He went through a fire door and locked it after him. He clattered down the stairs.

Damn. I raced toward the elevator, which, fortunately, hadn't moved since I'd gotten out. When it reached the ground floor, the doors opened and I ran face-to-face into Timothy Higginbotham.

"What? Excuse me—"

I grabbed his sleeve, yanking him toward the front door. "Get in your car. I see him. Quick." The man in a hat and a topcoat was running out the door, still holding his face, while blood dripped on the expensive carpet.

The concierge, a man with slicked back hair, wearing a gray uniform, stared. "Madam, shall I call the police?"

"I am the police," said Higginbotham, dashing ahead of me toward the man.

I remembered my shoe, which I'd dropped on the floor upstairs. And the umbrella. Evidence. "Call security and block off room 314! Don't touch anything." I chased after Higginbotham out the door.

"What she said," added Higginbotham.

Higginbotham's Range Rover was parked twenty feet away from the Mercedes now idling directly in front of the door. The man jumped in the back seat and the car pulled up Tothill Road before he had time to close the door. Higginbotham was too late to stop the Mercedes, but he ran to his own car and started it. I caught up with him, climbed into the front seat on the wrong side while he did a U-turn and sped after the Mercedes. This time I caught the license tag number.

Whatever happened to the British reserve? Every case presented something new, and this one almost offered death by umbrella.

9
Paul

Paul settled at the desk in his uncle's guest room, looking over the poem he had just faxed to Isabella. Having a task to do cheered him. His funk disappeared.

Paul had studied Psalm 119 in the original Hebrew, fascinated to see how the acrostic appeared. He looked at Wyatt's psalm now before him, examining it for form. Twelve verses.

Looking in the small Book of Common Prayer he carried in his brief case, he found the seven penitential psalms Wyatt had translated.

Labeled *"Dixit Injustus,"* the poem in front of him didn't match any of the other penitential seven. In fact, Wyatt's psalm actually dealt with *not* being penitential. Paul thumbed through the psalter until he found a poem that began *"dixit injustus"*—Psalm 36. Twelve verses.

Paul looked at the first two verses in his Book of Common Prayer:
"There is a voice of rebellion deep in the heart of the wicked;
there is no fear of God before his eyes.
He flatters himself in his own eyes
That his hateful sin will not be found out."

Being the good scholar he was, Paul went downstairs again into Malcolm's still shattered library and found the Amplified Version. It was the most complete version of the Bible he could find. The Amplified Version read:

"Transgression [like an oracle] speaks to the wicked deep in his heart.
There is no fear or dread of God before his eyes.
For he flatters and deceives himself in his own eyes
That his iniquity will not be found out and be hated."

Poring over Wyatt's copy, Paul didn't know much about symbolism and rhyme and all that. However, he knew that a paraphrase was going to be looser than any translation, and, because it was written by a poet, probably more flowery. He read Thomas Wyatt's version:

"Deep, underground wickedness reigns in once thankful hearts; emboldened sins, lust, evil yet speak in oracles;
They possess pride only, yet not thankfulness or fear of God.
They flatter themselves regarding iniquities grave or noisome evil, longing to deceive themselves;
Evil ones speak not about pride, even to themselves."

Wyatt's version was definitely expanded and ornate. But the subject matter was the same—how the wicked flatter and deceive themselves and don't fear God. Paul knew immediately that the list of names of the Sethian Brotherhood was not going to be found in the *meaning* of this psalm.

No, the monk who was a part of the Brotherhood and who translated the *Gospel of Judas* did not consider himself as wicked. He would have thought of himself as one of the righteous ones. Christians were the evil ones.

So the encryption had to be in the letters, rearranged to form a list of names. First, Paul tried a simple acrostic with the first four lines: D T T W….no. At least not in English. He tried what he could in Hebrew, and got nothing.

Then, he tried the first letters of each word for the first four lines:
D U W R I O T H E S L E Y S I O
T P P O Y N T O F O G
T F T R I G O N E L T D T
E O S N A P E T T

No, the code had to be more complicated than that. Perhaps the letters had a referent outside the poem. The only problem with that was that the letters all formed real words and made sense. The poem was an actual paraphrase of Psalm 36, from beginning to end. A code with an outside reference would read like jumbled letters.

Next, Paul considered anagrams from the first letter of each line, then from the first letter of each word.

Nothing.

Then he gave each letter of the alphabet a numeric symbol and worked through the first verses in a variety of ways, one after the other. Finally, his back started hurting from sitting in the antique chair for so long, and he looked at his watch. Almost midnight. He knew from experience that he needed to go to bed when he achieved this level of frustration. The Eureka principle worked only when the problem was temporarily abandoned.

Paul crawled into bed, where he tossed and turned, his mind churning and churning. When he finally drifted into an uneasy sleep, he dreamed about random clusters of letters thrown into the air like rose petals by Isabella, who floated down the aisle of Trinity on the Green dressed as a bride.

10
Isabella

The Range Rover careened left around the corner into a major thoroughfare, just missing a car heading toward us. Higginbotham's bony fingers gripped the wheel. I said, "You were at the elevator. How did you know—"

"After I let you off, two men came around the corner from the other side of the hotel. They got into the Mercedes and started it up, moving closer to the front door. Then they sat there, idling, waiting. Hold on."

I slammed against the door as Higginbotham turned another corner, the back lights of the Mercedes visible several cars ahead. Going sixty miles an hour on the wrong side of the street was terrifying. Westminster Abbey whizzed by on my right.

"I circled the block and came up on the other side of the corner behind them. Just a sec." The Mercedes' taillights turned, and turned again as the car sped around the roundabout in the center of Westminster. I held my stomach as Higginbotham circled, spinning the screeching Range Rover on two wheels as he went around the corners. Big Ben loomed overhead, tilting at a dangerous angle outside the window.

"To make a long story short, I got suspicious and walked inside to check on you."

"Where you met me at the elevator. I see."

The Mercedes was making almost a complete circle before heading up a street I thought was Whitehall. The traffic was heavier than you'd expect on a Sunday night, and cars honked and veered as Higginbotham left the Houses of Parliament in the distance.

We passed Downing Street on the left, Higginbotham trying to catch the red taillights of the Mercedes and ignoring all traffic signs as he ducked around anything in his way. At one point, he seemed to be gaining as the red lights grew larger. Then, a night postal delivery vehicle pulled out in front of him from nowhere. Higginbotham skipped the curb, grazed a lamppost, and nearly hit a small staircase with a railing.

He struggled to get back down off the curb and onto the street, but the taillights had grown smaller. "Heading toward Soho," he said, stepping on the gas.

Flying up Charing Cross Road, Higginbotham said, "So tell me, what happened to his face?"

I balanced myself with one hand on the dashboard. "He tried to knock me on the head with his umbrella, so I stabbed him in the eye with my high heel." I looked down at my bare feet and tattered stockings.

"Good God." Higginbotham followed the lights as we headed into another roundabout. He suddenly swerved in the opposite direction, going against the traffic pattern. He'd almost blocked the Mercedes, but at the last minute the car turned off to the right.

Higginbotham screeched around and followed. Again he had almost caught the taillights, when a delivery truck backed out of an alley and blocked the Range Rover completely. Higginbotham sat on the horn and the astonished driver stepped on the gas, moving the vehicle back into the alley. But the Mercedes had disappeared.

"Bugger," said Higginbotham under his breath as we stared down the rows of parked cars along a suddenly quiet avenue.

11
Isabella

Back in room 314 at the Sanctuary House—the hotel that had not lived up to its name—Higginbotham and I found a young man dressed in a hotel security uniform standing outside the door, talking with the concierge from downstairs. "Madam, I'm terribly sorry," he burst out as soon as he saw us get out of the elevator.

"Who is this man?" asked Higginbotham.

"Roy Smith. He booked a room on the same floor earlier this evening. I had no idea—"

"We'll check out his credentials later," said Higginbotham. "Probably phony."

"More than likely, the license tag is from a vehicle rented to John Doe," I added.

Higginbotham stepped past the two men and I followed him into the room avoiding broken glass from the umbrella's collision with the drinking glasses on the floor. Robin was already crouched down collecting samples. Higginbotham had called him at the end of the chase. New Scotland Yard was a lot closer than Charing Cross.

"He wore gloves," I said. "And a hat. He was a proper English gent in a topcoat. Wingtips, the whole bit."

"Did you notice his face?" asked Higginbotham.

"Yes, I did. He was between forty-five and fifty, slight crow's feet around the eyes. Blue, not Windex blue, more sky blue on a humid day. His lips were full and bowed and his nose was small in proportion to his other features."

"Height?"

"I'm 5'6" with no shoes, and he stood about four inches taller. It's hard to judge with the hat, but I'd say about 5'10". Medium build, although, again, he could have had a paunch or he could have been skinny. I couldn't tell because of his topcoat."

"Excellent," said Higginbotham. "We'll get you to a sketch artist. You too," he said to the concierge.

"Now what about this umbrella? Let's bag it and get it to your lab."

Higginbotham examined it closely, wearing gloves. "Brown. Heavy. The handle's got some lead in it, I'd wager. Not just carved wood. The damn thing's like a weapon."

"Just a minute. Let me see the handle that almost crushed my skull."

Higginbotham handed me the umbrella. "Devilish looking thing when you really look at it."

The handle resembled a carved T with a snake coiled around it. "The watermark! And the green umbrella!"

"Green? Um, looks, well, brown to me," said Higginbotham, appearing confused.

"No, no. The man who followed me yesterday carried a green umbrella just like this one." I knocked my hand to my forehead. "I've seen another umbrella like this, too. I just figured it out."

Higginbotham continued to look at me through his glasses and scratched the back of his neck.

"At Dr. Cole's house. In the stand by the door. Same size, same color of green. In the hallway, the handle looked like a piece of gnarled wood, but you just don't see too many green umbrellas that particular shade, or ones with handles like this."

"Umbrellas...why the different colors? A hierarchy? Function? Symbolism?"

"It gets better," I said, excitement coursing through my veins. "This snake thing was found as a watermark on a slip of paper left in the safe at the Guildford's house after the robbery. Our CSI techs found it under the microscope."

"Good God," said Higginbotham.

"Good grief," said Robin

Higginbotham turned the umbrella around in his hands, twirling it slowly, examining every grain of the wood. "Oh, my," he said. "Look here." He pointed to a small inscription at the base of the T-shaped cross. "S.B." He paused, and then whispered, "Sethian Brotherhood."

"We're getting close," I said. "Let's get the sketch artist now and get this perp's face out on the morning news."

Higginbotham looked at his watch and I looked at mine. It was 3:12 a.m. I couldn't believe it was so late. Or so early. My internal clock was severely skewed.

"Easy does it. We can assume the Sethians have the stolen documents. We've got Rachel covered, you covered—what else can they do?"

"But—" My policy had been to work a case until you dropped. But I was not on my home turf.

"I insist." Higginbotham turned to the concierge. "Get Ms. O'Leary a new room and post security outside the door." He turned to me. "Nothing's going to happen before tomorrow morning. I'll come around to fetch you at 9:00."

"Thank you."

Higginbotham hesitated and lowered his voice. "Or I could stay with you myself."

"No, no. You get some sleep. We need your mind sharp for tomorrow."

"I suppose so."

By the time I got to my new room next door, I had only a few hours until 9:00. It had been the longest day of my life.

Chapter Five
MONDAY

1
Gabriel

Monday dawned clear, bright, and cold in New York City. Gabriel woke up refreshed, ready to start the most meaningful week of his life. He hated New York City, especially Manhattan. It was a symbol of everything flawed on earth. Instead of the pure air of spiritual heaven, New York belched smog, and crowded bodies excreted filthy matter, further polluting this doomed and tainted planet. Thank God he was one of the elect.

This morning, he would be a hotel jockey again. He arose from bed and got busy. At one level, he found his job too easy. Nine-eleven had taught the average person nothing. Both Americans and Brits were gullible, willing to give away all kinds of information. A fake ID at Oxford had gotten him straight into Dr. Barnes' rooms, past the garrulous night porter who never suspected a thing.

Then, last night, he'd distracted the hotel staff in the linen room with a box of Godiva candy, ostensibly thanking them for the excellent service during the conference. They gushed in gratitude and crammed candy down their throats while he stole a uniform. When would people ever learn?

Most of humanity had missed the boat, including himself until a few short months ago. Without wisdom from Sophia, people were fundamentally stupid. That's why he couldn't believe that God had ever condescended to take on flesh of humanity. No respectable God would do that. The true God was a purely spiritual being. Those few called to rise above this cesspool called Earth would live forever without the encumbrance of a body of any kind.

For the second time, he thanked God he was one of the few.

This morning, he needed to dye his hair auburn. He had let his natural beard grow for three days. The only problem was that dye made his scalp itch, giving him dandruff.

Gabriel placed lifts in his heels to make himself taller. With the uniform, he'd blend right in. The hotel was so crowded that nobody would notice him. Nobody looked at the staff anyway at these conventions. They were too busy making contacts.

Dr. Henry Hawthorne was the first speaker at 10:00 this morning in Conference Room C downstairs.

After Gabriel had changed his appearance, inspected himself in the mirror to make sure he looked like the hotel staff, he took the service elevator downstairs at exactly 9:45. Inside Conference Room C, he placed a fresh glass of water for the speaker on the podium, then waited courteously outside the room with his pitcher of water on a round tray.

2
Gabriel

Conference Room C filled to capacity. With disdain, Gabriel looked over all the people eager to hear why the *Gospel of Judas* didn't measure up to the other gospels.

The tables, however, had started to turn.

The next phase was about to begin. Gabriel watched through the panel window of Conference Room C. First, the session chair introduced Dr. Henry Hawthorne, giving his credentials in glowing terms. Henry buttoned his jacket and walked up to the podium. He took several gulps of water before beginning. *Yes!*

The target started reading. He looked nervous, a typical academic reading his lousy paper. *Take another sip of water*, urged Gabriel silently.

He'd figured out from the schedule that the papers were supposed to last twenty minutes each. He wouldn't have long to wait. Dr. Hawthorne started out in a strong voice, as if he'd practiced reading the paper a hundred times. He seemed to gain momentum and confidence.

Just wait.

He was in the middle of doing the scholar's bit, making points one and two about the bunk he was spouting. "Third," he started, and then stopped for a moment. He started looking a little queasy and hot. Pausing, he took another drink of water. "Excuse me," he said and smiled to the audience. They began to give each other questioning looks.

"The third criterion is unquestionably the most important in the church fathers' decision concerning what to include in the canon. No favoritism among the disciples. The Gospel of John comes close, in referring to the 'Disciple Jesus loved,' but no special information was relayed to him to the exclusion of the other disciples. In fact, John and his brother James, who wanted special spots in the Kingdom, were quickly put in their place by Jesus."

The young waiter knew what was coming, and felt a rush of blood and excitement as he watched through the panel window. Suddenly, Dr. Hawthorne lost his voice. He coughed and sputtered, but the words came out as whispers. The young man smiled as he watched the good (and soon to be dead) professor reach toward the glass of water for another sip, to try to get his voice back.

"To continue—" he rasped. Before he could say another word, his hands and fingers began to twitch. "Excuse me," he whispered.

Gabriel felt an erection come on as he waited eagerly, watching Dr. Hawthorne's St. Vitus dance in front of his colleagues. Two women on the front row jumped out of their seats and approached him at the podium. "Are you all right?" he heard one of them ask.

No, he isn't, answered the waiter in his mind. *And it isn't over yet.*

Dr. Hawthorne's whole body began to convulse and he fell to the floor. "Water, water," he kept whispering. One of the women held the glass to his quaking lips, spilling it down Dr. Hawthorne's face.

The session chair jumped up and started running to the door. "I'm going for help. Somebody call 911! We've got a sick professor in Conference Room C."

Gabriel smiled, left the water pitcher on the large round tray outside the door, and made himself scarce before the session chair had the opportunity to spot him as he came rushing out the door.

Gabriel then went up to Dr. Henry Hawthorne's room, where he let himself in with a filched card key. He dropped a post card with good tidings, leaving quickly before someone found him.

3
Isabella

I had forgotten to set an alarm when I finally dropped into bed at almost 4:00 this morning. I was embarrassed when Detective Inspector Higginbotham knocked on my door right after 9:00, waking me up. I peeked out the peephole to see him fresh and perky standing next to the security guard.

I wasn't about to open the door and let him see me with wild hair and no lipstick. "I'm sorry. I overslept. Give me thirty minutes."

"I'll move on then. Robin will round you and the concierge up in just under an hour. He's running a wee bit behind this morning as well."

"Thank you." I jumped into the shower.

Once Robin, the concierge, and I arrived at Scotland Yard, we went straight to Higginbotham's office. We got the sketch done, and I was satisfied it was a good likeness.

"What's up with McCullough Industries?" I asked.

"We shipped a couple of blokes up there bright and early this morning, with search papers to look into old records. In the meantime, I've been doing a bit of browsing through what's already on file."

"Anything interesting?"

"Not so far. John McCullough started the steel company in 1910. Oldest son of a farmer near Dunfermline in Scotland. Same town where Andrew Carnegie was born, but McCullough was a generation younger. At age fourteen, McCullough hitched a ride to the new world on a transport, went to New York. Got a job with Carnegie, starting at the bottom."

"Didn't Carnegie start at the bottom, too?"

"Yes, Carnegie started as a bobbin boy, but by the time McCullough crossed paths with him, it was some time in the 1890's—Carnegie's heyday in steel. Carnegie sold his company in 1901."

"So what did McCullough do?"

"Young John McCullough was obviously a bright lad. Picked up Carnegie's methods. Focused on efficient business, first-rate lieutenants, and production rather than fiddling with stocks. He came home, where he repeated Carnegie's success on a smaller scale."

"And of course, World War I didn't hurt his prosperity, I'm quite sure," I said.

"Indeed, it didn't. Not to mention World War II a few years later."

"I see. Who's in charge of the business now?"

"It's gone public, but still run by one of the grandsons. Old John the grandfather lived until ninety, and had one son, John, late in life. John Junior had two sons, one John the third, who is a current Member of British Parliament, and his younger brother, James, who is the President and CEO of the entire operation."

"Who was in charge during World War II?"

"The old man. He was born in 1880. During WW II he was in his early sixties. John Junior was in the war, enlisted in the Royal Air Force at seventeen and survived the Battle of Britain. John Junior died fifteen years ago, after he helped his dad get the electronics off the ground."

"So that leaves—"

"The two grandsons, John the third and James, his younger brother," Higginbotham finished for me.

"What about the business with Krupp?"

"That's what I hope the team up in Glasgow finds out."

Hmmm. What had the old Sir John McCullough passed on to his son and grandsons? Was there a secret brotherhood in the legacy?

I said to Inspector Higginbotham, "If you catch them fast enough, they won't have time to destroy documents."

"That's what we're hoping."

"Good."

Higginbotham's phone rang. He said, "We've just barely started. Keep at it." He hung up. "Encryption has some new computer program it's trying on Wyatt's poem."

I laughed. "Do you think Thomas Wyatt envisioned his poetry being analyzed by a computer, picking apart his work syllable by syllable, letter by letter?" I shook my head and sighed. "Life was simpler then."

"Simpler, but not easier. I did my university work in the medieval period. Trust me, no one of any consequence survived Henry VIII's reign except the Archbishop of Canterbury, Thomas Cranmer. Being a courtier was a dangerous occupation."

My phone rang. "Excuse me. It's my Chief." I got up to walk out into the hall, where I listened in shock. Then, I came back into Higginbotham's office and said, "I've got to get back to New York. Another Biblical scholar has been poisoned at a conference. They've found another post card in his room."

4
Isabella

I called Paul right before I departed from Heathrow. "I hope you decided to go to the conference in New York," she said.

"Isabella! Where are you?"

"Sitting in my seat on the runway at Heathrow, ready to take off and go to your conference."

"Actually, I was planning to fly back to Dallas with my parents this afternoon. You sound upset. Why are you going to the conference?"

"You haven't heard."

"No, I've been up here in the guest house throwing myself against a brick wall with Wyatt's poem."

"A Biblical scholar from Wheaton was murdered."

"No." He paused, breathing hard. I could feel his tension over the phone. "Who?"

"Young professor named Dr. Henry Hawthorne. Got up to give his talk at 10:00 this morning, and keeled over dead."

"That's only two hours ago." I could tell Paul was having trouble taking this news in. "Are you sure it's a murder? Do you think it's related to the *Gospel of Judas*?"

"Symptoms of belladonna, same as Bonnie Barnes." I paused. "They found a post card from the National Cathedral in his room."

"Oh, Isabella. I'm starting to feel sick. What kind of monster did those manuscripts unleash? If we had only known, my family—we never would have—we should have burned the manuscripts the minute we found them."

I might have known he would feel responsible. "This scenario has been in play for two millennia. The manuscripts were the tip of the iceberg."

I wondered whether he had considered his own narrow escape. He could have been poisoned instead of merely having his speech stolen. I paused. "I'll be in around 9:00 this evening, your time. I have a favor to ask you."

"Ask anything. Nothing is worth the loss of three lives over a gospel that's heretical anyway."

Settled into my seat by the window, I knew the announcement to put away electronic devices would be coming on any minute. "Will you meet me at the conference?"

"No—I'll meet you at the plane. I can borrow Uncle Malcolm's extra car. Just give me the flight number and time."

I heard Paul writing down the information. "Where are you going to stay?" he asked.

"I don't know. I'll get a room somewhere."

"You won't get a room anywhere near the hotel. These conferences take up all room space for blocks. Trust me." After a long moment of silence, he added, "I already have a suite at the hotel booked and paid for, with an adjoining room. I was going to bring a colleague Mark Bryson, but he came down with the flu."

This was interesting. I blushed and turned away from the person in the seat next to me so he wouldn't see my flaming face.

Paul said, "A professional arrangement. I promise. It's better than staying at the Y."

Higginbotham and his corny advances was one thing. But what kind of breach of ethics was it to spend the night with a family member on a case? Paul was right about one thing, though. By staying at the hotel I'd be in the middle of the action. Otherwise, I might be stuck a mile or two away and miss something important. "Thanks. I accept."

My plane started rolling down the runway. I said, "See you in a few hours," and hung up, turning off the phone.

I watched out the window as the airplane taxied down the runway. Anger and determination had propelled me back into the land of the living after the tragedy of Ronny and the baby's death..

But what about the land of the loving? It had been a long time since I'd spent the night in close proximity to a man. Even in a separate room.

5
Gabriel

Gabriel had an hour to kill. For pure entertainment, he outfitted himself in his tweed jacket with patches at the elbows, affixed a dark moustache and beard to his upper lip and chin, and donned a pair of tortoise shell glasses with clear lenses. He bought a newspaper and settled in the lobby to watch.

At first the hotel tried to contain news of the professor's death, working with the conference chairs to keep the conference going. Word of mouth and cell phones, however, functioned like lit matches at a propane plant.

As he read the paper, he looked for articles about the deaths in New Haven. He caught the story about Dr. Paul St. Clair's speech and the empty showcase at Yale. The article gave no information about the current Sethian Brotherhood, because Gabriel had gotten to Dr. Barnes on time. Dr. St. Clair had mentioned the possibility that the group was alive and well, but the story sounded vague. Perfect.

One thing that was missing was any reference to the post cards. This was not good. The police were probably holding back the post card information to the press—which meant that people were not getting the messages. That had to change. People needed to know that this was not a series of random deaths, but spiritual warfare.

Gabriel knew from the conference bulletin that a plenary session was scheduled after lunch in the auditorium next door. He figured someone would make an announcement at that time. Sure enough. He got up and sauntered after a cluster of three men, one obviously the FBI Special Agent in Charge (SAC) and the other two officials—he figured the Presidents of the AAR and SBL. With his stolen conference badge, Gabriel walked right into the auditorium. He watched as the three men addressed thousands of members of the renowned, reputable—and suddenly vulnerable—academic institutions.

The SAC, an older, balding guy with a gut, had trouble quieting the crowd. When people stopped talking, he introduced himself. "I'm Stewart Williams, the FBI Special Agent in Charge of this case. You may have heard of the death of Dr. Hawthorne this morning. Everything is under control."

SAC Williams had not allowed media into the auditorium, but the cameras and reporters waited right out the set of double doors. Within fifteen minutes of this meeting, all America would know about the latest murder. Thousands of wives, husbands, and mothers would be worrying about their relatives at this conference.

Gabriel was getting a buzz from the panic spreading in the auditorium. He felt the warm rush of blood through his body.

"Please remain calm," the guy with the gut advised. "The conference will continue as scheduled. We <u>will</u> find the perpetrators."

Not if I can help it, thought Gabriel.

Stewart Williams had sweated through his shirt by the time he'd finished speaking. Gabriel noticed the dark rings with disdain as Williams walked off the podium with the conference chairs. The AAR President, Jasper Jones, was a younger man who looked like a business executive instead of a scholar. The SBL President, Samuel Tash, was a middle-aged gentleman wearing an ill-fitting suit off the rack. He looked the perfect image of someone who spent his time indoors, nose in a book.

They passed right by Gabriel on the back row as they left the auditorium. He could have reached out and touched them. Gabriel eased out of his seat along with several others, following the three men in charge.

Stewart Williams was giving the other two a little lecture as Gabriel lurked nearby. He said, "Keep the Information Booths staffed at all times. We'll feed you information as it becomes available. The only rooms off limits are Conference Room C, and the twenty-fourth floor of this building, where Hawthorne was staying."

"What about the media? They're right out there," said Tash, the wisps of his thinning hair beginning to curl from perspiration on his head. The men could hear and see the media murmuring restlessly, eager to cross the yellow tape.

"Gentlemen, comb your hair. We are about to give a press statement. Let me do the talking, please. Are you ready?"

Jasper Jones slicked his hair and tugged on his suit coat. The middle-aged man said, "But—"

"Practice saying, 'I have no comment at this time,' and follow me until we can get out of here."

Tash nodded.

Stewart Williams stepped into the fray, flanked by two New York police officers. He was immediately bombarded with questions from the horde of press in the lobby.

Gabriel made his way toward the door, lost in the milling crowd. Williams held up his hand. "Quiet, please." He waited, at least a dozen microphones thrust into his personal space. "A scholar from Wheaton College in Illinois was murdered this morning a little after 10:00. His name is Dr. Henry Hawthorne, and his next of kin have been notified."

Someone shouted, "The FBI were here in fifteen minutes. Does this death have any relation to Dr. Barnes' murder in New Haven?"

"Her death is still under investigation. We are currently looking for possible links. That is all the information I have." Williams spearheaded his way through the mob, and Gabriel could hear the professor behind him mumbling, "No further comment at this time" all the way back to the hotel.

Riding up the elevator, the young man toyed with his moustache and planned his disguise for tomorrow. He knew the old man in Scotland would be proud. He might even praise him in front of the whole group. Gabriel had at last found the parental approbation he had hungered after for so long.

In addition, thanks to the Sethian Brotherhood, Gabriel, like God, possessed the power over life and death. He shivered with excitement.

6
Bob and Maria

Bob and Maria reached the New York hotel before the Evidence Response Team had finished working Conference Room C and Hawthorne's hotel room. As a professional courtesy, Stewart Williams gave them permission to observe. "But the feds," he said, "Are running this show. Don't get in the way."

Bob took a deep, ominous breath and clenched his fists. Maria stepped in and said sweetly, "Thank you. I promise we won't hamper your investigation."

After Stewart walked away, Bob whispered, "What the—."

She whispered back, "Shut up. You know how these things go. Interstate case. End of story. Get your butt upstairs before he changes his mind."

"They may be the feebs, but *we're* going to be the ones who nail this sucker," Bob muttered back.

Maria went to Conference Room C, where she observed the witnesses making official statements. She asked a couple of the witnesses to repeat what they said. Dr. Hawthorne had stepped up to the podium, taken a drink of water, and started speaking. Within ten minutes had lost his voice and started convulsing. He was dead before the EMS arrived.

Only one person had noticed a hotel attendant with a pitcher of water standing outside the room. The attendee had come in late, and the waiter had turned away from her when she walked up. "Usually the hotel people are friendly," she told Maria. "At least they nod at you. It was like he didn't want me to see his face."

Maria examined the place where the hotel attendant had stood. Crouching on her knees, she discovered a few pieces of trace—a green string, a dyed red hair, and some white, flaky, powdery looking material. She bagged it all.

The glass of water on the podium and the pitcher had both been taken back to the New York lab. The ERT had combed the room for fibers, hairs, and other residue. The party was breaking up when Maria sneaked out her swab and ran it over a drop of water still glistening from where Hawthorne had spilled it as he started convulsing. She would run her own results.

Upstairs, Bob stood along the sidelines as the techs finished the room. After watching the team in action, he approached a petite blonde woman with a pixie haircut. He flashed her his badge and a big smile at the same time. "I don't want to cause any friction here, but can I just take a quick look-see at the post card?" He had heard the head of the team tell her, "We're gonna get all evidence to the lab ASAP." He had to see the post card before the feds whisked it away.

She looked him in the eye, then up and down.

"I'm official. Honest," said Bob. He added, "Your boss said we could watch. My partner and I ran the first two post cards in New Haven before the case got out of hand." He winked at her.

"Okay. I'm Shirley," she said. She handed him the baggie with the post card tucked inside.

"Thanks, Shirley." He gave her his biggest grin. "Mind if I copy down the message?"

"Be my guest." She handed him a pen and a piece of paper. The picture on the front showed the three-lancet stained glass window in the Maryland Bay of the National Cathedral. The fine print said that Rowan LeCompte had designed it, with the theme of religious toleration. The Maryland General Assembly had adopted the 1649 Act of Toleration, one of the early legal attempts to create religious harmony. Bob wrote down every word.

On the message side of the post card, Bob noted the same type and font as the others. This one said, "Blessed are those who challenge the world's authority, for they shall balance the scales of injustice."

Bob wrote slowly and double-checked his copy.

"Got it?" the pixie haired blonde asked him.

"Yeah." He handed the card back to her. "Thanks, Shirley. Betcha won't find any prints." He left and went downstairs to find Maria.

7
Paul

Paul headed down the stairs from Malcolm's guesthouse and into the garage. His father followed him. "You sure you want to do this?" his father asked.

"I do." Paul looked at his dad, a kind man, but also a tough man from a tough Texas family.

His father gave him a bear hug, and Paul instinctively knew his father understood: Paul wanted to help solve his aunt's murder. His skills and ability had already made a difference in tracking down the killer. This was his chance to prove himself.

"Remember, son, it's a deadly game."

"I know." Paul tossed his suitcase in the trunk of Malcolm's spare car. "Tell Mom to be careful flying home. I'll be back in Dallas for Thanksgiving."

Driving to New York, Paul re-analyzed the work he had done on the poem. Of all the word puzzles he'd ever tackled, this one was most confusing. The solution was staring him in the face. He was simply too close to see it.

He parked at the airport, and went inside to meet Isabella. Her plane was only a few minutes late. Paul stood in a cattle pen of people waiting to meet their friends and relatives from London. He spotted Isabella striding down the corridor. *She was the most beautiful woman he'd ever seen, from silky hair to legs that could conquer the world.* Paul noticed that several other men spotted her, too, looking her up and down, eyes resting on the spectacular legs.

Suddenly, he remembered Mary Sue Blankenship his sophomore year in college. She stood at the bottom of the curving staircase inside her sorority house, staring at his walker. After a lifetime of hospital and rehab, a friend had set Paul up on his first date in years, and Paul was nervous.

Mary Sue Blankenship had flipped back her golden hair and said,

"I'm so sorry, Paul, but I feel like I'm getting a stomach virus. It's nice to meet you, though."

"Did you tell her about the accident and my leg?" Paul had asked his friend as they left the sorority house.

"Well, no, not exactly." Paul's friend had fallen all over himself with apologies. Paul had returned home and gotten plastered. Took him two more years to get up the nerve to ask someone out again.

Paul stood taller as Isabella approached. He'd come a long way since Mary Sue, but he still felt like a pauper looking at a queen.

8
Isabella

I spotted Paul in the crowd, a beacon of light in his camel cashmere topcoat. He greeted me with a smile and took my bag. "Thank you. I'm exhausted."

On the way to the hotel, Paul said, "I found out Clyde Sneed couldn't come to Victoria's funeral because he's on vacation in Canada."

"Canada? Did he leave a number where he could be reached?"

Paul shook his head no.

"Interesting." Hmmm. I'd still have to do more checking into Clyde Sneed's visit to Canada.

"Tell me more about your trip," said Paul.

I told him about the man with the umbrella in my room and the chase in Higginbotham's Range Rover. Paul took a sharp breath. "Are you all right? Did anyone else try to follow you?"

"Inspector Higginbotham escorted me everywhere after that."

Paul scoured the cars around us and behind. He checked all the mirrors. I smiled at his earnestness, but doubted he could spot a tail. "I think we're okay."

Paul navigated his way out of the airport traffic. His face showed its strong bone structure as different angles of light played in the darkness of the car. He looked worried. "Did anybody strange get on the plane with you?"

"Yes," I answered with mock seriousness. "There were all sorts of strange people on my flight. There always are." I smiled. "Just kidding."

"Well, I'm serious," said Paul, his eyes still focused on the traffic going into the city.

I was touched that he wanted to protect me. "I don't think so. Inspector Higginbotham escorted me to the plane. He ran the passenger manifest through the computers, and there wasn't a single criminal in the bunch."

"There wouldn't be," said Paul. "None of this crowd has ever been caught."

"True, I suppose," I said, yawning in spite of myself. "Sorry. How's the poem coming along?"

"It's at the tip of my fingertips," he answered. "The code is either simpler or more complicated than anything I've ever worked with."

"Tell you what. When we get to the hotel, let's fax your notes to Timothy Higginbotham. He's got a new code-cracking program. He'll be thrilled."

"Ah. Timothy Higginbotham, the good Inspector," said Paul.

"Yes. He was quite solicitous and helpful, actually." I realized that I had mentioned him three times since I'd gotten in the car. All three times in a favorable light.

"I see," said Paul. "What kind of a person is this Detective Inspector?"

Was a bare hint of jealousy creeping into Paul's voice? He continued, "Is he smart? Is he going to help catch this group?"

As I looked at Paul, I felt a pang of –what? I wasn't sure, but whatever it was shot through my abdomen, exciting me and scaring me at the same time. And it didn't go away, even when I looked out the window.

It was a feeling I hadn't had in a long, long time, not since I first met Ronny O'Shaunessey. But someone with Paul's classy background would never be interested in a woman from my side of town. And barren as well, I thought bitterly.

"Detective Inspector Higginbotham is a thorough man, doing his job," I replied.

"Good."

Paul and I sat in silence as we entered the tunnel to Manhattan.

9
John

John McCullough had spent a busy evening in his castle. He reviewed his emails before he erased them from his hard drive. By the time Paul and Isabella reached the hotel, it was 3:30 a.m. in Scotland.

London Four had botched his assignment in the London hotel room. How hard was it to catch a woman by surprise and bop her on the head? He wasn't supposed to kill her. That was a job for Gabriel, the Messenger of Life. Just a warning. But not only did she get a good look at him, she blinded him in one eye. And then the ridiculous chase in the car. None of that should have happened.

The Grand Patriarch had to send him to Morocco until the storm blew over. John McCullough was not pleased.

The evening paper Mrs. Wallace brought him featured a sketch of London Four on the front page. Fortunately, John had planned for any and all unhappy eventualities. Foresight was why the Grand Patriarch was in charge. Even London Four's family had no idea where he was.

Outside of that incident, however, the master plan was proceeding well. The Messenger of Life had emailed the American Patriarch, who forwarded the good news to John that the Monday project in Conference Room C had gone swimmingly. Gabriel was ready for tomorrow.

The Grand Patriarch thought about the Messenger of Life. John considered Gabriel a special angel, sent by Pleroma to fulfill the master plan.

Within months, John McCullough would probably die and become part of the incorruptible generation. He had no children and he despised his brother and his family. Who would inherit his legacy?

John answered the email with lavish praise and asked that the American Patriarch forward his response to Gabriel. Everyone needed a person from the next generation to pour their soul into, someone who would carry on their work, who would worship them.

Gabriel was John McCullough's personal Messenger of Life.

The third email was from John's brother, James. Scotland Yard had shown up on his doorstep with search papers, and had torn the company files apart. They wouldn't tell him what they were looking for. "They carted off a bunch of records from the war, when Granddad was still running the Steel Works. Can you tell me what the hell is going on?"

John had written back, "Don't have the slightest notion. Just give them whatever they want."

James, James, James. James was perfect to run the company. A scruffy Scot, born and raised to make and save money. Too bad James wasn't the first child. He would have gotten the castle and the real inheritance as well.

Scotland Yard would find nothing. John had made sure of that when his father died, making a clean sweep himself through all the company's records. He had placed all pertinent and incriminating documents in the castle's basement in the archives section.

The last email was from the Washington Patriarch, Felix Darrington, a retired architect and an indispensable part of the plan. Darrington wrote: "Tell the Messenger of Life that the crux of the National Cathedral's structure is the Joseph of Arimathaea Chapel."

The Joseph of Arimathaea Chapel! What an incredible coincidence. John rubbed his hands together with happiness. No, not coincidence. *His plan of destruction could not possibly fail now.* The stars were with him.

He brought the Egyptian tray closer, placing it on his lap. First, he fondled the gold inlay, running his fingers over the hieroglyphics. Then he slid the precious parchment out of the false bottom. He stroked the smooth vellum, mottled with age and soaked with patches of maroon and brown dried blood.

Pleroma, providence, God—all were on his side. His legacy would be fulfilled before he died.

John sat in his chair, his afghan wrapped around him in the dark. Despite the day's victories—and the incredible coincidence at the Cathedral—something bothered him.

How had Scotland Yard known to go looking for papers from the old McCullough Steel Works?

When one of the lookouts had overheard a conversation between Dr. Robert Cole, Vice-Chancellor of Oxford, and that fat, ugly Dr. Barnes, he had taken care of the problem before Dr. Cole could have the chance to betray the brotherhood. Then he had taken every single scrap of evidence from Dr. Barnes' home and computer. What could he have missed?

Cole had given himself away at his last meeting of the officers. Once a year, in January, the leaders, the Circle of Five, stayed behind the general meeting to conduct the business of the brotherhood. The Grand Patriarch, the American Patriarch, the Secretary, the Treasurer, and the General Overseer were the only ones who knew each others' names—and even they didn't know the names of the other members.

The Grand Patriarch was the only brother who knew everyone.

The Secretary, Dr. Cole, had begun to object as discussions for the upcoming holocaust began. "Let the Muslim terrorists bring down the

Christian faith. We can just sit back and let it happen. Give them more money. The state of Christianity in Britain is almost nil, and it's dying fast in America, too."

The Grand Patriarch had sniffed the first wind of dissension among his inner circle. "Brother Cole. Can you be more specific in your objections? Have you had a religious experience of a Christian sort?"

Dr. Cole's hood had completely covered his face as he looked down. "No. It's just that I don't want the deaths of so many people on my hands."

"Not even for the sake of your eternal life?"

Dr. Cole couldn't answer and had remained silent for the rest of the meeting. The Grand Patriarch had had him followed by London Four, who happened to overhear parts of the conversation with Dr. Barnes.

Cole was dead within the week, and all documents had been sent to his widow's upper room. London Four went through them in the guise of a grieving friend and colleague while the widow played her cello downstairs.

The Grand Patriarch had let her keep Cole's umbrella, but nothing else from the brotherhood.

What could he have overlooked from McCullough Steel Works? John McCullough arose from the chair in his study and gazed out over the bleak near-winter landscape. Located in a hollow, the castle was surrounded by the Lennox hills, beautiful in the summer, but stark in the winter. He longed for the sun and the sand of the desert.

James was not the leak. Poor, dull James. James thought he was having a pleasant life, with his American California wife and two spoiled children. He never knew what he was missing by remaining a staunch Presbyterian.

Granddad, the old wizened man with the look of a lean panther, had called his two grandchildren into this very study once. "Boys," he said, crooking a gnarled finger at them and patting his lap. He wanted one on each knee. John was ten and James was six. John had allowed himself to be hoisted on the bony leg, but kept one eye on his grandfather's face. James started crying for his mommy and ran from the room.

John had watched his grandfather's gaunt cheeks harden and the look in his eyes become even colder. Within minutes, their mother carried James in, snuffling in her arms. She plopped him on his grandfather's knee. "There, James. Be nice. Your grandfather doesn't see you very often. He thinks you are a fine boy."

James had continued to wail until his mother took him out of the room, lacquering the old man with apologies. "I don't know what's gotten into him. Perhaps he's coming down with something."

The old man cranked out a laugh. "Then it's best he doesn't come around and infect the rest of us." His grandfather reached into the desk drawer and handed John a bag of candy—his favorite, chocolate and caramel. Spontaneously, John hugged the old man.

After that day, the bond between John and his grandfather was sealed. Bit by bit over the years, the grandfather had told him the stories of Seth and Yaldabaoth and how the world was created. He always left him with the feeling there was more, something really special he would find out one day.

As the old man approached ninety, John was matriculating from the University of Glasgow. That Christmas holiday, old Sir John called the family together. He set the enormous table in the dining room with fine china, silver, crystal, and imported flowers. John knew something was up. His grandfather had become deaf and so gnarled that his head barely showed above the top of his wheel chair.

Rupert, young then and his grandfather's new valet, had poured the finest light champagne. His grandfather made a toast, "May we all die well." Thus began the feast of roast duck, potatoes Gruyere, asparagus hollandaise, and trifle.

Between bites, Rupert had wiped the old man's mouth. His false teeth clacked when he chewed and food tended to spew onto the napkin tucked into his collar. When he'd finished the meal, he said, "Don't get up." Then he dismissed Rupert.

"Here's what's going to happen when I die."

John's mother had started to protest, but her father-in-law wouldn't have any of it.

"I'll be nine bloody decades old in a month, and I'm too tired and cranky to live much longer. I'm telling you now what's in my will, so nobody fights when I'm gone." He paused for a wheezy breath.

"Nobody gets the title, of course. It dies with me. You'll have to earn your own titles." Sir John had glared at the group, challenging them to live up to his standard. He continued, "It's my steel company, and I'm leaving it to John, my only son, RAF hero. When he dies, the company goes to his son James. Not John, my grandson. No arguments."

No one had said a word, but John the grandson remembered feeling stung, wondering why his little brother got the company and not him.

Granddad had continued, "It's my castle. I bought it. I'm not leaving it to my son, but to young John my grandson, along with twenty percent of the company's stock."

John the grandson had looked around the table, where his parents caught each others' eyes. This bequest was highly irregular. Old Sir John knew they had expected to move into the castle soon. Instead, their son had bagged the prize a generation ahead of schedule.

The grandfather had turned his wrinkled face toward his son. "You get the townhouse in Glasgow. It's ten thousand square feet and should be adequate. Besides, you already live there. I don't care who you leave it to when you die."

Young John the grandson had been the first to speak. "Thank you, Grandfather. I hope you don't die for a long time." The others chimed in, "Yes, yes. Thank you." John realized that he had come out very well. He would never have to work to earn a living.

"I'm going to bed. Rupert! Come get me." Rupert had appeared from the kitchen and wheeled the old man into the elevator and upstairs into his bedroom.

In the middle of the night, Rupert had awakened young John, the grandson, asleep in his favorite guest room. Young John loved the green room with silk draperies and an enormous portrait, a solemn and anonymous family from two hundred years ago, painted against a dark background.

Rupert had had to shake him a second time. "Your grandfather is calling for you." Groggy, John wrapped his robe around him and stepped into fleece slippers. He followed Rupert down the hall. The old man was seated in the wheelchair, wide awake, and said, "I want to show you something." He coughed. "Rupert, you wait here."

John had wheeled his grandfather to the elevator, one of John and James' favorite parts of the old castle. They used to ride up and down the five stories, getting out in the elevator rooms on each floor, where a different round sitting area greeted them on the upper levels and a wine cellar in the basement.

John had pushed his grandfather into the lift and his grandfather's bony finger pressed B. So they were going to the wine cellar. Why at this ungodly hour? When the elevator stopped, young John wheeled his grandfather out. "Turn me around," he said.

On the outside panel of the elevator, he inserted a small key at the top and pushed another button below the other buttons. James and John had always wondered what that button was for, but nothing had ever happened when they pressed it.

Behind John and his grandfather, the far wine cellar wall turned, revealing a dark, cave-like room. "Candles are on the walls, matches in the alcove. Go light the room," ordered his grandfather.

John had felt a tingling in his groin that spread throughout his whole body. He'd never expected this room. He thought he'd gone over every nook and cranny of the castle as a child, hoping for a magic wardrobe that would lead him into another world.

Now he'd found it.

After he had lit the candles in sconces along the wall, he returned and wheeled his grandfather into the center of the room. They stopped in front of a stone altar with a giant solid gold statue on it. His grandfather said, "This is your true inheritance, my son. It's my legacy to you."

Speechless, John had waited for him to explain.

"I am the Grand Patriarch of an organization two thousand years old, and the inner circle has voted you to replace me when I die." He had gone on to explain the Sethian Brotherhood and its role in ending the Christian era. When he finished, he said, "I must know if you are willing to accept its responsibilities."

So this is what his grandfather had been preparing him for. John whispered, "Do you need an answer now?" He was testing the waters. What would happen if he said no?

"Before we leave this room."

John walked around the dark basement, inhaling the scents of smoke, incense, and energy.

His grandfather interrupted his thoughts. "You can stand for Parliament on the side. You will be in a position to lead all of Britain."

Young John's life's purpose and meaning, his goals and dreams, had coalesced at that moment. He bent down and hugged the old man. "Thank you, Grandfather."

"God—Pleroma—is the one you should thank. He gave you openness to the true faith and obedience, unlike your father and brother. You are his true descendant, and mine. Now let me show you the archives. And a special document that tells you who you are."

10
Isabella

Paul and I entered the New York hotel, a plush lobby with chandeliers, oriental rugs, and massive, tapestry-covered furniture, a room as big as a high-end furniture show room. When we checked in at the desk, I asked about the day's events. A young Asian woman wearing teardrop earrings filled me in.

A bellhop with a gleaming brass cart carried our bags up to the top floor. "You do travel in style," I said. My room in London had been clean, decorated in soft dusky pink and brown colors, with a touch of elegance. Here I walked into a huge, luxurious suite with a king-size bed and sitting area decorated in blacks, grays, and glass. I saw another bedroom off to the side, smaller but no less luxurious, and automatically headed for the smaller room.

"No, this one's yours," said Paul, tipping the porter. He carried his bag to the smaller room.

"No way," I said. It was bad enough he was paying for what should have been a business expense in the first place—but I couldn't run him out of his room.

"Yes, way. That's final." He shut the door between us.

I'd never been in a penthouse suite. I sat down on the bed, turned down with a white satin comforter and a bank of pillows, all down feathers. There were no less than eleven pillows in an array of shapes. Fluffy heaven. I would sleep well tonight.

But not yet. First I called the lab in New Haven. Bob answered, "Road Kill Café, can I help you?"

I shook my head at Bob's antics, but was grateful for the smile he coaxed out of me. "What if I had let the inspector at Scotland Yard borrow my cell phone?"

Bob said, "Then I would have said 'Oops, wrong number. This is the morgue.'"

"You are hopeless."

"Hey, it's late, and we've been on this case five days now without a break in sight. Someone has to lighten the situation."

In the background, Maria said, "Give me that phone. Hello? Isabella? Are you back safely? Are you in New York? I've got the poison from this morning. It's belladonna, same as last time."

"Belladonna. Where do you get belladonna?" I asked. "Not medicinal herbs, but a supply concentrated enough to kill someone in ten to fifteen minutes?"

"You grow it and use the roots. You'd need to know a bit about chemistry to dry it and mix it into a deadly dose, but it can be done."

I heard Bob in the background, "My turn, my turn. Hello? I have all the post card information, in case the jerky feebs—excuse me, I mean our esteemed colleagues—won't let you see it. Got a pencil? Okay—" He proceeded to give me the information on the post card.

"Blessed are those who challenge the world's authority, for they shall balance the scales of injustice." Once again, I felt chill bumps up and down my arms. "I'll talk with Paul about this. He'll know how to interpret the message. Thanks, guys."

Though I didn't understand the meaning, I couldn't miss the intent.

11
John

The archives. John McCullough remembered his grandfather and the night they spent in the basement together before he died. A huge, carved mahogany cabinet, like a sideboard with drawers and storage compartments decorated the east wall. "No one is allowed access to the archives except the Circle of Five, but you must know everything in here," his grandfather had told him.

Sir John had ordered his grandson to take out the wooden boxes, each with a carved lid. Inside the first, he found lists of every generation of Sethians going back over five hundred years. A new generation started when the old Grand Patriarch died and a new Patriarch took over. The lists were done in calligraphy and illuminated like the medieval work done by monks. "I am the only one who has a key to this box, and you will inherit the key when I die. No one else will know these names, except you."

John had been shocked to recognize names of the most powerful men in the world on the list.

The second box held minutes of the annual meetings of the Circle of Five, beginning in the sixteenth century, although the documents were sketchy until the nineteenth century.

John had asked his grandfather, "How are the new members selected?"

"A current member is responsible for replacing himself. He selects a relative or a close friend, usually in the next generation. He watches them, testing them to see whether they might have the ability and the desire to carry on. Then, when the brother is sure of the man he's selected, he reveals the secrets."

"What if the person says no, after learning all the secrets?"

"That's why the selection and preparation are so important. The brotherhood can't afford to have people running around knowing our secrets. It's only happened twice in my reign, but those people are quieted."

John's skin had burned. The question had hammered at the door of his heart, and yet he knew he would never ask: "What would you have done if I had said no?" He had said yes, so he would never have to face the thought that his own grandfather might have overseen his extinction.

The third box held the Book of Life that all members signed at initiation.

John's grandfather had said, "Each member is given a role, and that is their name in the brotherhood. The brothers know each other by these names."

"How can you keep them from running into each other out in the world, especially if they happen to come to Glasgow on the same plane?"

"You can't, entirely. Yet every brother knows never, never to refer to brotherhood business in public, and never to refer to their brotherhood name outside brotherhood business."

The fourth box had held originals of copies of every Sethian document ever discovered. "When documents come available, we obtain them," said his grandfather. "*Whatever the cost*." His grandfather's blue eyes, blurred with cataracts, had lasered into John's to make sure he understood the meaning.

John had nodded. "I'm to keep on the lookout for new documents discovered."

"That's right," said his grandfather.

The other boxes had contained miscellaneous papers and references to the brotherhood. Before computers, it was necessary to communicate through written documents. These had been carefully preserved and ordered according to date. "Only members of the Circle of Five have access to any of these."

Now years later, as John sat in his study after the events of Monday, he wondered if Robert Cole, the former Sethian Secretary and Vice-Chancellor of Oxford, had managed to steal one of the documents and give it to someone.

Wrapping himself tightly in his afghan, his feet bundled in slippers with wool socks, John stole out into the corridor. First, he made sure Mrs. Wallace and Rupert were asleep. Then he took the elevator down to the holy room.

He pressed the button under the panel and watched as the wine cellar door opened. The moment never failed to thrill him. He lit the sconces on the east wall, and pulled out the box with documents he'd retrieved from McCullough Steel Works. He knew all seventy-six by heart, having spent many nights down here learning the history.

He thumbed through the correspondence between his grandfather and the European Patriarch, a German high up in the Krupp industries. Names but not dates had been removed. Sorting through the stack, he didn't notice anything missing at first. So he counted the items of correspondence from the beginning of the company until the use of computers. Seventy-five.

He counted again. Seventy-five.

Cole had taken one of the letters. John felt bile pour into his veins and his heart pumped the black blood of anger through his body. It only took him a few mintues to figure out which letter was missing.

12
Isabella

I knocked gently on Paul's door in the New York hotel. The noise sounded muffled, but I thought he said, "Come in," so I opened his door.

Paul stood in the adjoining bathroom, naked, with a towel covering his privates. He took one look at me and his whole body blushed.

His build took my breath away. Tall and muscular, he had blond hair on his chest and legs like a surfer. From the back, you couldn't tell one of his legs had undergone so many surgeries. Both his arms and shoulders were buff and his torso had a six-pack.

"I am so sorry," I said and quickly shut the door, my heart beating too loudly. I had not expected—well, I wasn't sure what I had expected. I knew expensive clothes covered a multitude of flaws, and I figured Paul looked passable underneath his clothes. But he was so…so sculpted. I hadn't seen a nude male for a long time. And I'd never seen a male body so….well, he looked like the statue of David my friends and I had giggled over in their high school art class before any of us had seen a real naked man.

I stood on my side of the door without a clue what to do. Pretend it never happened?

Paul opened the door, clothed in a workout T-shirt and shorts. "Well, now you've seen me in my pajamas," he joked, obviously nervous and trying to make light of an awkward situation. "Come on in."

I sat down in a chair, averting my eyes toward an etching of a water lily hung in a gilt frame on the wall next to the bed.

Oh, God. The few men I'd gone to dinner with in the last couple of years barely bothered to make conversation with me. They were eager to get on to other things, which, to their surprise, didn't happen the way they thought. Now here was Paul.

Time to get back to business. Compartmentalize. I said, "Well, I need your help again with the post card they found in Henry Hawthorne's room, with a Black Beatitude on it."

"What was on the front of the post card?"

"A window at the National Cathedral honoring a Maryland act of religious toleration. Apparently it was the first official Act of Toleration in America."

"Religious toleration. Hmm."

Then I quoted what Bob had told me: "Blessed are those who challenge the world's authority, for they shall balance the scales of injustice."

"I remember this one. It's talking about the scales of *injustice*, not the scales of justice."

"What's up with that?"

"When I first read it, I remember thinking that in order to balance the scales of justice, you have to assume an unjust world. Good people work to tip the balance from injustice to justice.

"As the scales become equal, one side increases in justice, but the other side decreases and feels like the world is getting more and more unjust for them. For other people to get equality, some people have to give up something. The people who get justice feel good, but the others feel they're getting cheated."

"Yes, but picture the statue of Lady Law with the scales. As the scales tip and become even, then you have neither justice nor injustice, but equality," I said.

"But it doesn't feel that way if you've given up something so someone else can have more. Especially if you wanted to keep the upper hand, or stay on top."

"Okay. Let's assume that the Sethians view the world as a just place, not an unjust place—"

"They can't view the world that way. It goes against their theology. The earth is a flawed and terrible place."

"Unless you're one of the elect. Then the earth is just because everybody else is getting what they deserve." I closed my eyes. "I hope you know I'm getting lost here."

"Stay with me," said Paul. "In Sethian thought, to tip the scales of injustice means to reach equality through letting the bad guys get what they deserve. The Sethian cup of justice fills up as everybody else's gets emptied."

"Challenging the world's authority then is a good thing for them."

"Yes. Basically, this beatitude justifies what they are doing."

I sat piecing together the threads of thought. "What about the picture, the Maryland window and the Act of Toleration?"

"Hmm," said Paul, sinking his chin into the palm of his hand. "Whether your worldview is just or unjust, the history of the West has been a movement toward the establishment of equality. But it hasn't been easy."

"That's an understatement."

"The Maryland Act of Toleration was an attempt in the New World to allow all religious groups freedom—"

"Away from the established church in England, where church and state were still attached."

"But the Sethians weren't included in the Act."

"That's because no one knew they still existed! They would have been included if they'd been a public religion."

"Doesn't matter. Apparently it didn't stop them from feeling that the world owed them something. I guess they feel that they've been second-class citizens in the world of religion."

I nodded. "So now they are going to challenge authority—"

"By killing Christians—"

"So that they can balance the 'injustice' they think they've suffered from."

I stared at Paul and he stared back. "How twisted can you get?" I asked.

Paul sat on the side of the bed and I leaned forward in an overstuffed chair done in wild black and white geometric shapes. The heater kicked on. Paul said, "Poor Dr. Hawthorne. I wonder what his great sin was. What was the topic of his paper?"

"I don't remember." I got up to retrieve a copy of the program in my room. I'd left it on the bar in the kitchenette.

Paul called after me, "I'll bet fifty dollars it has something to do with tolerance or prejudice."

I came back in reading aloud from the bulletin: "Bingo. 'The Gospels Re-visited: The Early Canon in the Twenty-first Century.'"

"What does the abstract say?"

Thumbing to the back of the program, I read for a moment. "Here it is. 'A variety of early gospels were rejected from the canon because they did not meet the criteria of sacred literature.'"

"Rejected. The *Gospel of Judas* was rejected from the Bible."

"Yes. Dr. Hawthorne has written a book on the subject."

"A book that put him on the Sethian hit list," said Paul.

"God help us all," I said. It was the closest thing to a prayer I'd said in years.

Chapter Six
TUESDAY

1
Isabella

Tuesday morning in the hotel's business center, I called Detective Inspector Higginbotham. Paul stood by, ready to feed his thwarted attempts to unravel the poem's code into the fax machine. Last night I'd gone back to my room after my discussion, but I couldn't get Paul's naked body out of my mind. As he stood next to me, I smelled his warm body mixed with the scent of aftershave.

"Inspector, this is Detective O'Leary. I've forgotten your fax number, and wanted to send you Dr. Paul St. Clair's notes. He's working with me on the case. Has your computer come up with anything?"

"Good morning, Detective O'Leary." Higginbotham seemed cheery. "No, we haven't got anything yet. Here's the fax number."

I read aloud the multi-digit number to Paul and he started sending the fax. I said to Higginbotham, "What about McCullough Industries?"

"We're still working on that, too. Caught them off guard, though. Took a haul of documents to the local station in Glasgow. My team will spend the rest of today and tomorrow weeding through them." He paused. "I'm getting the fax."

"Good." I nodded to Paul.

"You'll never guess the mystery man who attacked you in your hotel room," said Higginbotham. "We plastered the papers with his sketch, and I got a confidential call straight to my line. Two distinguished visitors showed up in my office early this morning."

"Who?"

"Edward Hobbs' wife and lawyer."

"Edward Hobbs. Wasn't he—"

"Yes. British newspaper magnate. Funny thing. Turns out he's gone missing. Never came home after his little encounter with you the other night."

He was probably at the hospital tending to his eye.

Higginbotham continued. "He called his wife and told her he was going overseas on business, but she knows better. He never leaves without his medications, so she smells the proverbial rat."

"I'll bet she does."

"The wife and lawyer spent all day trying to keep his absence quiet to his employees, his secretary. Then—presto! The evening paper arrived, and they found themselves staring at his likeness."

"Sort of ironic that his mug shot was spread throughout the British Isles in one of his very own newspapers." I knew I shouldn't delight quite so much in another's misfortune, but I was pleased that the man who attacked me had been hoisted on his own petard.

"Hadn't thought of that." Higginbotham laughed. "There's a certain justice in it after all. However, he seems to have vanished off the planet."

"This group is good. They're scary, they're so good."

"We have taken the opportunity to send a team to Hobbs' house to see if we can uncover any emails, documents, mistakes he might have made in communicating with the master planner of this week's events." Higginbotham interrupted himself. "Oh, wait. The fax is finished."

"Did you get it all?"

"Ha!"

"I'll take that as a yes."

"Ha! Tell Paul he's got it. Right here on the first page."

"You're kidding. Paul didn't see anything on the first page. I didn't see anything on the first page." I whispered to Paul, "He says you've got it."

Paul shook head. "Impossible. The letters didn't form names."

I retrieved the first page and stared at it, perplexed. I said to the inspector, "I'm going to let you talk to Paul. It still looks like random letters to me." I clicked on the speakerphone.

"Brilliant, old boy," said Higginbotham in a tinny voice from the phone. "You've beat our new equipment. The computer has been struggling with a new program, and you got it right off the bat."

"I hate to be dense," said Paul, "but the letters don't look like names to me."

"That's because you don't have a background in Medieval and Renaissance England. Look at the page with me."

We saw:

DUWRIOTHESLEYSIO
TPPOYNTOFOG
TFTRIGONELTDT
EOSNAPETT

"Follow me," said Higginbotham. "These are all common names five hundred years ago. In the first line, "Wriothesley" jumps right out. First initials, D.U. Second line, we have T.P. Poynt. Third line, T.F. Trigonel, and finally E.O. Snape. Extra letters added in each line to fill out the poem."

I stood next to Paul staring at his paper. Neither one of us had recognized the names, and they had shouted from the page.

Still looking dumbfounded, Paul said, "This code was as simple as the one I designed in fifth grade to write notes to a girl I liked." He laughed out loud. "Whatever happened to 'Smith' and 'Jones'?"

Higginbotham joined in the laughter.

Paul said, "I wonder if the monk who translated the Greek *Gospel of Judas* is the same one who encoded the names of his brothers. I feel like I know him personally. I translated his Latin work into English. He did an excellent job."

"Likely. He's probably the one who embellished the manuscript as well." Higginbotham paused. "Well, thank you, Dr. St. Clair. Isabella, I plan to attack this list and get back with you."

"Good." I hoped that the list of sixteenth-century Sethians would yield at least one current legacy.

2
Gabriel

Gabriel had successfully released three people in the last six days. He ordered room service for breakfast around 11:00 a.m. Yesterday, he had stayed in his room during the rest of the uproar, finished his true crime book, and watched television.

Now, before his fourth murder, he planned to enjoy Belgian waffles, loaded with whipped cream and syrup. He would then get ready for this afternoon's activity, followed by a flight to Washington, D.C.

He would need to age himself thirty years before he left the hotel room.

Dr. Reginald Bloome's talk was scheduled for 5:00 Tuesday evening in the auditorium. Bloome's exalted reputation, plus the fact that this was his last AAR conference, gave him the honor of being a plenary speaker. Gabriel figured that even people who disagreed with him would want to hear what he had to say.

The room would be packed with scholars waiting for a speaker who would never arrive.

Gabriel knew that Dr. Bloome had signed up for the tour of the Museum of Modern Art at 2:00. While he was gone, Gabriel planned to enter his room and plant poisoned strawberries with a thank you note from the President of the AAR, Dr. Jasper Jones himself.

That should give the authorities something to ponder. Gabriel would return fifteen minutes later with the post card. This time he would bring his hatchet for a little extra pleasure.

After the Belgian waffles, Gabriel changed his appearance and admired his handiwork in the mirror. Yes, he looked at least thirty years older, with bushy gray eyebrows and skin that actually looked saggy and old. The wig made his dandruff itch, but he'd just have to endure it. He slumped, as if he had bad posture or a calcium deficiency. Perfect.

The room was wiped down, and his bag was ready to go. Gabriel's new hatchet lay next to his bag. Too bad he hadn't been able to leave a hatchet near Dr. Hawthorne's body. Too many witnesses. And he didn't have time in Hawthorne's room.

The compensation had been getting to stick around outside the door of Conference Room C almost long enough to see Dr. Hawthorne die.

Balancing the small tray with the hotel's card that read, "Congratulations on your distinguished career, AAR President, Jasper Jones," Gabriel backed out his own door and down the hall to Dr. Reginald Bloome's room. He was just letting himself in with a stolen card key, when the old man himself came around the corner. Startled, Gabriel felt the sudden press of his bladder.

Dr. Bloome hailed him and said, "Excuse me. That's my room."

Gabriel had not expected Dr. Bloome to return so quickly. He stood paralyzed for a brief moment. *Pull it together*, he told himself.

"Ah," said Gabriel. "Are you Dr. Bloome?" he asked, knowing full well who he was. He'd studied the pictures of this man for several days.

"Yes, can I help you?" As Dr. Bloome approached, he craned his neck at the chocolate covered strawberries.

The young man held out the tray. "These are for you, sir. Compliments of the AAR and the hotel."

Dr. Bloome read the card. "How nice to be remembered."

"Shall I put these in your room?" Gabriel couldn't wait to unload the tray, hoping the old professor wouldn't notice the white gloves he wore and think it was unusual.

Dr. Bloome opened the door himself. "No, thank you. I'll keep the card and show it to my wife, but I'm allergic to strawberries, and chocolate upsets my stomach."

Just then, another member of the AAR turned the corner and headed toward the room past Dr. Bloome's, a young woman with a long, flowing skirt and a blue velveteen hat. Dr. Bloome hailed her. Gabriel watched as he read her identification badge. "Charity. Here, my dear. These have just been brought up to my room by the hotel, and I can't eat them. Do you care for chocolate covered strawberries?"

Gabriel again stood paralyzed, this time for longer. If he withdrew the tray, he would draw attention to himself. On the other hand, if he let this young woman take a strawberry, he would poison the wrong person. He had no time to decide. Either way he was screwed.

The girl's face brightened. "Oh, they're my favorite!" She picked up a plump, juicy strawberry and put it in her mouth. As she smiled, she noticed Dr. Bloome's identification tag. "Oh! Dr. Bloome!" she said when she swallowed her bite. "What a pleasure to meet you. I've read two of your books. My name is Charity Collins. I'm just finishing my degree at Duke Divinity School."

Dr. Bloome extended his hand and shook hers. As the two made small talk, Gabriel coughed. "Excuse me, shall I take these away? What would you like me to do with the rest?"

Dr. Bloome said to Charity, "They're all yours, my dear. May you have a long and illustrious career. Now, if you'll excuse me, I need to lie down and rest before my talk this evening."

Charity relieved the young man of the tray. "Oh, thank you so much." To Dr. Bloome she said, "I'll see you in a couple of hours at your talk."

Gabriel hastened toward the stairwell where he hid, waiting until the hallway was empty to go back to his room.

Once inside, he removed his disguise and scratched his head—his dandruff itched like fury. He had fifteen minutes to wait before he was sure the poison would work. He cursed and ranted to himself. How could he have been so stupid? He should have checked to see if the old man had any allergies.

This time the American Patriarch was going to kill him. Or worse, ban him from the Brotherhood. Just when he was becoming somebody important. He felt no exhilaration, only despair at his mistake. Shame spread through him like a fever. *Maybe his father was right. Maybe he was a failure. Maybe he would always be a failure.*

Gabriel looked on the program, desperately trying to find Charity Collins listed as one of the speakers. No. She would look like a random victim—which she was, he thought ironically—instead of the intended victim, whose speech topic was an affront to the Brotherhood. Dr. Bloome's work on Christian orthodoxy was the reason he'd been hand selected. Holy hell. Now the messages wouldn't match.

Gabriel slipped the hatchet into his bag. He would work out his emotions on the furniture.

Double-checking to make sure he had left no fingerprints or evidence—he wasn't too upset to be careless—he checked the hallway to make sure it was clear, and let himself out. Three doors down, he entered Charity's room. He planned to drop the post card on the body, hack up the furniture, and hightail it out of there.

Charity lay on the bed, as if she were resting. Her hands were folded neatly on her chest. Gabriel slid the card under her clasped hands and took out his hatchet.

Just as he raised it above the chest of drawers, the body groaned and Charity's eyes flickered open. "Who is it?" she said weakly.

Electrified with surprise, Gabriel dropped the hatchet, grabbed his bag, and bolted out the door. He ran down the empty hall, where he caught the elevator down eighteen floors. Once in the lobby, he forced himself to amble and not sprint out into the city.

How had he messed this one up *twice?*

3
Isabella

I sat high up in the hotel's penthouse suite at my computer, willing it to yield information about the case. When my cell phone rang, Paul popped his head around the door from the adjoining room, with a look of curiosity. The young Asian desk clerk said, "You asked me to call if anything out of the ordinary happened? Well, there seems to be a problem in Room 1819."

"Thank you," I said. "We'll be right there." *Oh, please, not another death.* I motioned to Paul to follow me.

Paul and I knocked on Charity's open door. Inside, I discovered an FBI tech with a pixie haircut sniffing green leaves and stems from eaten strawberries on a tray. She put a small piece in a test tube and turned to the doctor leaning over a young woman on the bed, listening to her heart with a stethoscope. He said, "Same symptoms as yesterday. Administer magnesia and get her some strong coffee."

A middle-aged man with a beach ball paunch and wearing an FBI jacket tried to stop Paul and me from entering the room. "It's a crime scene," he said brusquely.

I read his nametag, "Stewart Williams," as I flashed my badge. "Isabella O'Leary, New Haven Police Department. If I'm not mistaken, you found a post card on or near the body."

Williams looked me over. "Yeah," he said, grudging and more than a little suspicious. "Is that a lucky guess, or do you read minds?"

Old school, die-hards like Williams who still mistrusted women in the field had been around for most of my career, although they were getting fewer and fewer. I said with authority, "I'm the first detective on the case, from New Haven—originally my jurisdiction. I've just returned from Scotland Yard. If you let me observe, I might shed some light on this incident."

Williams looked me over again, this time like a piece of meat. Out of the corner of my eye, I saw Paul's jaw set as he started to step forward and say something. Then Williams nodded curtly, letting us in the room.

"He's my assistant," I nodded at Paul. Paul narrowed his eyes at Williams and barely nodded. Williams ignored Paul. I sighed silently. Clearly, Williams was territorial. I hoped he wouldn't be rude.

After a few minutes, Charity was able to sit up and relate what happened. She had taken the strawberries into her room and eaten every single one of them. She hung her head. "I've worked so hard to lose a hundred pounds over the last year. Now I struggle with bulimia. But I just couldn't resist the strawberries. So after I finished, I went into the bathroom and made myself throw up."

I patted Charity's shoulder. "I hate to say this, but it looks like bulimia saved your life."

Charity nodded. "There was one weird thing. When the young man came into my room and put the post card under my hands, he had a hatchet in his hand. I may have been hallucinating."

"No," I said. "You weren't. Where was he standing with the hatchet?"

Charity pointed across the room near the chest of drawers. I walked over and looked behind the chest. "Sure enough." I motioned for the pixie-haired tech to come and bag a small new hatchet with red paint on the blunt end of the blade.

I smiled at Williams, gloating just a little. He was clearly furious that I had pre-empted him with my discovery. He pulled me aside and said, "Follow my lead. Here's how we're going to do this. I'm going next door to get Bloome and question him before he gets over here. You call the hotel manager and the AAR guy, Jasper Jones, and get them up to the room pronto. Line them up along the bed. Tight formation."

He pulled up his pants, sagging at the back. "From here, I'll ask the questions."

Great. A Type A personality. When I interrogated people, I preferred to let the conversation lead me to vital information rather than lining suspects up and grilling them. It took a long time, but that's how I'd trapped the Campus Killer.

I nodded at the FBI agent, even though he was getting under my skin. Fine if he wanted to run the show like a Marine boot camp. I sat down next to Charity and made the phone calls.

A few minutes later, Williams led in Dr. Bloome, who went straight to Charity and burst out, "I'm so sorry. You poor girl. I had no idea about the strawberries. I would never have offered them to you. Are you going to be all right?"

Charity extended her hand. "I know you didn't do it."

Dr. Bloome started to sit down next to me on the bed, when Williams said, "Over here." Just then, Dr. Jasper Jones entered the room and

Williams pointed out his seat. He was followed by the hotel manager, an efficient-looking woman around forty, wearing a red suit.

"Is everybody here?" asked Williams. He pulled up a chair at the end of the narrow space between the two beds.

"We can use my office, if you like," said the manager crossing her legs and tucking in her hem. She was obviously uncomfortable with us all crammed in together on the sides of the beds.

"No," said Williams, in an uncivil tone of voice. Okay, so he was rude. And a control freak. Probably figured he wouldn't be in control in the hotel manager's office—it was somebody else's territory. He continued, "Dr. Bloome verified Charity's story. Dr. Bloome left the MoMA tour early because of indigestion. As he approached his hotel room, he saw an attendant with a tray of strawberries using a card key to enter his room."

Dr. Bloome nodded.

I took notes while Williams carried on. "Dr. Bloome declined the strawberries but took the note card from the tray. Then, Charity walked up and Dr. Bloome offered her a strawberry. They spoke for a few minutes. The attendant asked what to do with the strawberries. Dr. Bloome gave them to Charity, and she took them back to her room. The attendant disappeared."

He paused. "Charity ate all the strawberries, and then threw them up again. She lay down to rest because she started feeling strange. Next thing she knew, a young man entered her room and placed a post card under her hands. When she opened her eyes, he ran away. She called the front desk."

I said, "Sounds as if Dr. Bloome was the intended target."

"Me?" asked Dr. Bloome. "Why would anybody want to kill me?"

I leaned forward and asked, "Just out of curiosity, what is the topic for your paper tonight? Doesn't it have to do with Christian orthodoxy?" I remembered seeing his name on the schedule of events I'd scanned earlier.

"Yes. It's entitled 'The Importance of Christian Orthodoxy in an Inclusive World.'"

"Have you been vocal in any of your work about the dangers of sects or cults or New Age theology?"

Dr. Bloome adjusted his glasses, "Yes, as a matter of fact I have. I wrote an article for *Christian Century* that warned against straying from Scripture into quasi-Christian thought."

188 Leslie Winfield Williams

"Then they were probably after you." I saw another piece plunk into place. The Sethian's plan had been to steal the manuscript, then follow up with a series of murders and messages. First, was Dr. Barnes, the leading authority who might reveal them to the world. Next were leading Christian opponents from the two largest academic groups in the United States.

The Sethians didn't just want these scholars dead. They wanted murders that shouted "We're out to get you!"

"Hmmm. Two dead scholars at a religious conference."

"I'll take it from here," interrupted Williams. "It doesn't matter."

But it did matter. Where had I heard of that before? I must have looked puzzled because Paul leaned over and whispered, his breath warm and minty. "The Chicago debates, 2005. The two Christian scholars against two Judas defenders."

It clicked as I remembered the headlines from the Chicago *Tribune*. "Yes. A fire destroyed their hotel room."

"One of the scholars smoked, and everyone thought the fire was an accident," whispered Paul while Williams was talking.

Paul and I again stared at each other. "Was it?" I asked.

"Are you two finished?" Sarcasm dripped from every syllable. Williams was getting red in the face and rubbing his pants legs with impatience. "Let's get back to the program at hand."

Keeping my voice civil was taking a toll on my nervous system. Williams was exactly the sort of man that turned my blood hot, and I wasn't used to being railroaded. I gave him my best smile, ignored him, and said, "Just one more question. Dr. Bloome, "What denomination are you?"

"Methodist."

"What was Dr. Hawthorne?"

Paul said, "I think the program said he was Baptist."

"Dr. Barnes was Anglican. They are going for ecumenism, not specific denominations—Christians as a group. It's possible a Lutheran is next. Or maybe a Catholic."

Williams interrupted in a booming voice, much louder than necessary. "This is my investigation. You're observing as a courtesy. One more interruption, and you're out of here. Now, I'd like to get the facts on this attempted murder before we start speculating."

Damn it. Why did he have to be such a jerk? We were all on the same side here. "As you wish."

Not only was he a jerk, but he was ugly. He had nose hairs sticking out, and his gut reminded me of my pregnant stomach. I thought FBI agents had to stay in shape. Damn the Sethians. Damn this FBI control freak.

As I sat hemmed in tight formation on the bed, I wanted to give a wordless, soundless scream. Itchy skin, pumping heart, tight stomach—the symptoms of an upcoming potential short circuit in my nervous system if I didn't get out of here pretty soon.

I forced myself to calm down as Williams pressed on. "So the hotel attendant at Dr. Barnes' door was a middle-aged guy going on sixty. That right?" Both Charity and Dr. Bloome nodded.

"And the other one was in his late twenties? You sure about that?" Williams asked Charity.

"I was really groggy, but I know for certain he didn't have gray hair and his face looked smoother," said Charity. "I could be wrong, but I don't think so. He had one of those thingies below his lip. A piercing."

A labret. I looked at Paul meaningfully. I remembered the description of the hotel assistant who brought Bonnie Barnes her tea. He wore a labret. Williams asked, "Is there any chance that the man in the hall could have been wearing a disguise? A gray wig? False eyebrows?"

"He looked pretty authentic to me," said Dr. Bloome, "but then again, I wear trifocals."

Charity shook her head. "I wasn't looking at him. I was looking at Dr. Bloome."

I re-crossed my legs in the small space, feeling my spirits sinking lower and lower. At least Williams was asking pertinent questions, even if his tone resembled a drill sergeant's.

Williams asked, "Did either of you notice anything unusual about the hotel attendant? Did he wear a name badge?"

Dr. Bloome said, "You know, I don't recall that he did."

Charity closed her eyes, and took deep breaths. "Let me think. He wore white gloves. I remember that."

Williams turned to the hotel manager. "Do your people wear white gloves when they deliver?"

"No," she said. "On occasion they wear latex, but not cloth."

He asked, "Was either one of these men tall or short? What about their builds?"

Dr. Bloome said, "The attendant was medium to short, with a hunched back, like he was starting to get osteoporosis."

Charity said, "Right. I don't have a clue about the man who entered my room. I was lying down and couldn't get an angle on his height. He was medium build. Kind of reddish hair. That's all I know."

Medium. There it was again. The man who held the water pitcher yesterday was described as taller than average, but one can always make oneself taller with lifts in the shoes. Getting shorter was the trick—and hunching over would do it. But reddish hair.

Medium height, weight, and build. Same as in New Haven, only with dark hair. Hair could be dyed. Had the same man committed all four crimes? I caught Paul's eye and he nodded.

"Excuse me," I said. "May I ask—"

"No." Williams stared me down.

It was all I could do not to stand up and smack him, the sweaty, ugly jerk. I knew more than he did about this case, and what he didn't realize was that I would find out what I needed to know *no matter what*. I must be really, really tired. With tears of fury and depression welling up, I steeled myself, refusing to let him think I was upset at all.

Williams held up the bag with the card from the strawberry tray, showing it to Jasper Jones. "Have you ever seen this?" he demanded.

Dr. Jones looked flustered in spite of his neat appearance. In fact, I thought he looked appalled as he realized the implications. "No, of course not."

"It's from you."

"I can see that." He stared at Williams. "However, I did not sign this card, nor did I send it. You can check with a handwriting analyst."

Williams showed it to the hotel manager. "Where do your people get these cards?"

"Customer service has them. The sales reps have them in their desks. They're scattered around. Anyone could have picked one up."

Dr. Jones said, "I give you my word, I had nothing to do with this. I have been in meetings all morning. You can check my whereabouts for the last two days. Any number of people can vouch for me at any given moment."

I didn't have the heart to tell him that it wasn't any good to protest. He'd be checked out, just like everybody else. Someone had masterminded this whole operation. By his position in the AAR, he proved he had the organizational skills to pull off a sophisticated series of murders

"Shirley!" Williams yelled. The pixie-haired tech poked her head in the door. "Dust for fingerprints on the card and tray." He gave her the bag and continued. "So we've got two men—maybe one—who posed as a hotel attendant both yesterday when he poisoned Dr. Hawthorne's water, then today with the strawberries. Where did he go?"

We all sat there for a minute before Paul spoke up after clearing his throat. "He's probably staying at the hotel as a guest." Duh. Good for Paul.

"He probably is." Williams turned to the hotel manager. "Here's what I need from you in the next thirty minutes. Talk to your people and find out who ordered the strawberries. Get me a list of everyone staying here the last two nights and tonight, and credit card numbers."

Paul added, "And you might check to see if any of the hotel personnel has had a card key stolen or lost."

Dr. Jones said, "What about the conference? We could limp through the rest of the events with one murder. But if word gets out about Dr. Bloome, well—"

"Not to mention another potential victim tomorrow," said the hotel manager, probably already calculating how bad another death would be for business.

Williams scratched his balding head. "Close it down."

"What about my final speech?" asked Dr. Bloome. "I'm scheduled in less than an hour. It's a plenary session. Perhaps you could make the announcement after I've given the speech." Dr. Bloome sat up straight and pushed his glasses back up his nose with authority. "To tell you the truth, I'm outraged that someone would try to stop me from making this speech."

He continued, his face getting redder and redder. "And to think he tried to poison this young lady, a totally innocent victim. It just burns me up." He stood up. "It just galls my socks off!"

Everyone in the room applauded.

"You got it," said Williams. "Jasper and Tash and I'll make the announcement after your speech, Dr. Bloome. Go get 'em."

Williams continued, "In the meantime, we'll go room to room, starting with this floor. We can't contain the guests, but nobody in this room goes home until we're finished." Williams looked around the room. "Okay. Everybody's dismissed after Shirley gets your fingerprints. No offense ladies and gentlemen, but we don't take anybody's word for anything."

After the room cleared, I stood up, having squelched the urge to cry and replaced it with steely resolve. I addressed Williams. "Nice job, Special Agent." I took a deep breath. "Now. We need to see the post card, please." I wasn't asking. I was demanding.

4

Isabella

Paul stood up very close to Williams, where he had a good two inches on him. "I think that's a very good idea."

"Fine." Williams handed over the postcard to Paul, bagged and ready to go to the lab. Paul and I examined the post card while Williams spoke with the lab tech in the hall outside the door. He must be hell to work with.

The picture on the front of the post card featured the chancel and sanctuary of the National Cathedral in Washington, D.C. I studied it a long time before turning the card over.

Paul looked over my shoulder. On the back, the fine print explained that the Jerusalem Altar had been made of stones from the quarries outside Jerusalem, the same quarries that King Solomon's temple came from. The massive stone bishop's chair was carved out of rock from Glastonbury Abbey in England, where the abbot died under Henry VIII for refusing to shut the place down. The communion rail featured eleven carvings of eleven apostles. And a blank wooden block for Judas.

"Look. Judas was left out," said Paul.

Williams came back into the hotel room, and stomped over to us. "So?" he said impatiently. I ignored him and said to Paul, "Exactly. There were twelve disciples counting Judas, but the National Cathedral only included carvings of the other eleven."

"It's an insult to the Sethians to leave out their hero."

"The National Cathedral seems specially designed to insult this group. What's the Black Beatitude?"

"Black Beatitude? What the heck— Let me have that." Williams grabbed the card away and read it to himself. I watched him start pacing in frustration. He muttered, "I'm one month before retirement, hoping to go out on a slam-dunk. Then I get stuck with the humdinger of the decade."

Williams was clearly out of his element with the postcards. He glowered. "Why? What do these religious fanatics want?"

Paul's and my silence could have knocked him over with courtesy as we waited for him to let us see the post card again. Sometimes getting what you want required pandering and patience, rather than a show of control—although I still felt like kicking him as he blustered around, doing battle with his tough-guy-who-never-asks-for-help persona.

Finally, Williams stopped stomping back and forth and said, "Okay okay. I've looked at all the messages and all I see is America's national religious monument on the front of these post cards, and cryptic, crappy perversions of the Bible on the back." He stuck the card at me without looking at my face.

Paul and I smiled at each other, but didn't let him see. I knew what it cost a guy like him to ask for help.

"The message is a Black Beatitude, from the *Gospel of Judas*," I said, reading aloud: "Blessed are the proud, for they shall sit at the right hand of God."

"See? It's a bunch of crap," said Williams.

"Not for the Sethians," said Paul. "Pride in their elite status is important. The world honors pride, too, but Jesus didn't."

"You got that right," said Williams.

"But the *Gospel of Judas*. That's a different story," said Paul.

Williams was frowning again. "Somebody tell me what's going on with this group."

"The *Gospel of Judas* is a Sethian document," said Paul. "According to the Sethians, Jesus marked Judas out as special but warned him that the world wouldn't understand his actions. The world would revile him until his moment of glory."

"I pretty much revile the Sethians right now." Stewart Williams looked impatient.

I continued, "This latest post card builds on the last one. Judas is left out of America's national monument. Judas is the Sethian's hero, and to give him a blank spot among the other disciples is an insult of the highest order."

"In the Sethian system, Judas will have the last word. He alone will sit with God, whereas the other eleven are not part of the incorruptible generation, and won't go to heaven. As the Black Beatitude says, pride is good. Elite spiritual status is good. The Sethians are special and they want the world to know it."

"Sheesh." Williams rolled his eyes and fumed. "The world is crazy. We got Muslim terrorists who hate America. Their conservatives are as narrow as ours, except they kill large numbers of people when they get mad."

He paused and rubbed his head. "Now we got another religious group with their panties in a wad. These Sethians. They give out hints, *but what are these people trying to communicate?*"

"Well, the Sethians certainly aren't trying to win converts," I said.

"That's because Sethian Gnostics are a secret group," said Paul. "Christianity, Judaism, and Islam are both available to anyone who chooses to believe."

"I get it," said Williams. "What fun is it if anybody can join?" He laughed.

Paul nodded

"My question is," said Williams, "what's next? Are they going to keep going after Christian leaders who don't agree with them, picking them off one by one and leaving post cards?"

"That's what we don't know," said Paul. "One of the post cards suggested a holy war."

Paul and I continued to sit on the bed, analyzing and pulling together what we knew so far, while Stewart stormed around the room, as if his movements would stir up the answer.

"We know that the Sethian Brotherhood's initial act was to steal the *Gospel of Judas*," I said.

"We also know that they've murdered or tried to murder three scholars and my Aunt Victoria, who was probably in the wrong place at the wrong time," Paul added.

"The Black Beatitudes are giving us the character of the Sethian faith, by telling us what they considered 'blessed.'" A feeling of dread spread through my body as I pondered the implications of the post card messages. "This group wants to stay secret, but also wants to fight a war. Who does that remind you of?"

"Al Qaida."

"Exactly. My money is on some serious and violent terrorism," I said. "A big statement like 9-11 with lots of dead bodies."

5
Isabella

I made a quick call to the New Haven forensics lab. "What have you got on Hawthorne's death?" I asked Maria.

"I think our killer has dandruff."

"Dandruff?"

"I'm not sure it's his dandruff, of course, but there was some microscopic trace on the floor near the round tray where the hotel attendant supposedly stood. It's dandruff. We'll run the DNA."

"Good."

Maria added, "He also has dyed red hair. Recently dyed."

Dyed hair was no surprise. "Thanks."

I found the maid in the hallway outside Charity's room. She was young blonde woman smacking gum and wearing five nose rings. I approached her. "Do you remember a guest on this floor, a man fairly young, medium height and build? He may have been a part of the conference, but not necessarily."

The maid answered, "Yes. I saw two men who fit that description. One in here." She pointed to a room down the corridor. "He had a roommate, very tall and fat."

"No, he probably had the room by himself."

"Okay. A young man alone stayed in here." She pointed to a room three doors down from Charity's room. She smacked her gum.

"Can you let us in?" Maybe he was still there, but I doubted it.

The maid let us into an abandoned room. "Do you want me to clean the room?"

"No, no, not right now."

Paul turned to the maid and said, "Your card. Is this your only key?"

The maid looked embarrassed. Her jaw stopped working on the gum. "No. Somebody stole my card yesterday. I was here early, getting the cart ready, and when I turned around, my card was stolen. This key is Sandra's."

I picked up on Paul's line of questions and asked, "Did you report it to your supervisor?"

The maid shook her head in shame.

"It's okay, but I'm going to have to call and report it missing." I felt sorry for the young maid. I hoped she wouldn't lose her job.

I called Williams. He stepped off the elevator a few minutes later and joined us in the room.

"A young man who fits the description stayed here," I said. "And look." I pointed to almost imperceptible flakes on the floor in front of the vanity mirror. "Dandruff."

"Dandruff?" asked Williams. He looked at me like I was crazy.

"One of our techs picked up trace where the hotel attendant stood outside Conference Room C. Dandruff. Now here's this dandruff. Let's see if the DNA matches."

Williams flipped open his phone. "Shirley, get back up here. We got some dandruff for you to bag."

6
Isabella

I was on my way back up to the penthouse with Paul when my phone rang. It was Detective Inspector Higginbotham. After I filled him in on the latest events, he said, "Met with James McCullough at McCullough Industries this morning."

"James McCullough, the head man?"

"Yes."

"Good. Did you find anything?"

"Not really, no, but his office was big enough for a megalomaniac. Said it was his grandfather's office, the old Sir John. Outside of that, here's what we learned: First, James didn't think anybody in his family was a member of a secret group. Not his brother, John McCullough the British MP, or his father or grandfather."

"Do you think James was telling the truth?"

"Chap seemed straightforward. Thing is, I don't know how close James and his brother are."

"What do you mean?" I asked.

"Said he only visits the brother once a year at Christmas, for dinner. Also said that old Sir John and James' brother John were 'thick as thieves.' James actually shivered when he talked about his grandfather. Said the old man reminded him of a vulture."

"A vulture! That's pretty harsh for a grandchild to say about his grandfather."

"Here's another interesting bit. The old man left the castle to his grandson, the current John McCullough, Member of Parliament. Skipped right over his own son. Left James the company, but left John the castle and enough shares so he'd never have to work."

"What are you saying?"

"I'm saying that over here, it's peculiar to skip a generation like that. We're still tied by the vestiges of primogeniture." Higginbotham paused.

Why would the old man skip over his own son?

"What was even more intriguing was my visit to John McCullough's place. Hold on, my other line is ringing. I'll have to call you back."

7

Isabella

"Working so hard on a case makes me forget to eat or drink. Lost a dress size with the Campus Killer." I added, "And the longer it goes on, the more my stomach cramps." Paul and I walked into the suite.

"One of the less popular diets, I assume," said Paul. "Here." Paul stopped at the private bar, a large black granite slab, with a large basket of complimentary fruit and snacks on top. "Help yourself. Oranges, bananas, apples, nuts, energy bars, cheese, crackers, and look, here's a jar of marinated artichoke hearts."

I selected a bottle of water and a bag of peanuts. Paul picked a Dr. Pepper and an energy bar.

As I opened the peanuts, I felt my nerves tightening. No matter how fast we uncovered facts or decoded the post cards, Paul and I were still a step behind a highly organized killer.

I ate two peanuts and couldn't eat any more. After this afternoon with Williams, I knew my inner reserves were fraying. Two major cases back to back. My nerve glands were pumping overtime. Although my hands had started to shake with small tremors of stress, I was determined to keep pressing on.

My phone rang. "O'Leary."

"Higginbotham here."

"Good." I took a swig of water. At least I could keep myself hydrated.

"Back to this morning," said Higginbotham. "After leaving Glasgow, I drove three members of my team to the home of John McCullough, about a mile off the road to Cairnhill. 'Home' is hardly the word I'd use. As one of my team said, 'Blimey, it's a friggin' castle.'"

"You drove right up? No gate?"

"Scotland is owned by the Scots. No fences allowed, except for game. You may own the property, but anybody is allowed on it. Keeps the Queen's guards busy at Balmoral."

"I didn't know that. What about the castle?"

"A bona fide castle, several centuries old. And kept up well, too. Most families have had to sell their castles or let in visitors to pay the taxes."

"McCullough Industries must have done well since the war. What was this Member of Parliament like?"

"John McCullough looked just like his pictures in the newspapers and on the telly. Pointy-nose, raspy voice. He was wearing a velvet smoking jacket and bedroom slippers. Looked as if he'd just gotten out of bed."

"Did you catch him off guard?"

"I don't think so. His housekeeper had tea ready when we arrived. We sat in a little round receiving room, with an elevator in it. I asked McCullough if he or anyone in his family were members of any secret religious organizations."

"I'm sure he denied it," I said.

"Yes, but you can still gain information from how they answer."

"True," I liked to think I was well-schooled in observing body language.

"McCullough was smooth. Said his grandfather had belonged to a professional ironworker's guild, left over from the medieval times, but not a religious organization. I couldn't figure out his tell—no facial tics or anything—but I think he is a practiced liar."

"Or maybe he's just a politician."

Higginbotham laughed wryly. "A definite possibility. Then, after tea, he asked if we wanted a tour."

"Good. You didn't have to get a search warrant."

"Yes, but the offer made me suspicious. I figured he'd probably already hidden anything of interest."

"Could be," I said.

"The tour took over three hours. John stuck to us like rubber cement. In every room, he pointed out the tapestries, the arms on the wall, the portraits, while my team opened all the drawers and cabinets. McCullough's study was the National Gallery of Pedophilia—nude male statues, paintings, etchings, some in quite compromising positions."

"He's a government official. I'm surprised his porn gallery hasn't been exposed by the press."

"I suppose that if a naked picture costs over a thousand pounds, it isn't porn—it's Art with a capital 'A.' Anyway, I personally checked out his office, searching the desk for a false bottom or a hiding place. His blotter was from the last world war—vintage—and he had an authentic Egyptian tray covered with hieroglyphics. I checked his correspondence in the tray and it was all legitimate."

"So you found nothing in the office?"

"No, but McCullough seemed to take delight in watching us rifle through his belongings. As if he knew we wouldn't find anything." Higginbotham paused. "But the wine cellar held possibilities."

"What do you mean?"

"The wine cellar revealed a stock of singularly ordinary wine. I'm a bit of a wine connoisseur—" (I remembered his careful choice of wine at Rules) "and all McCullough had were a few racks of cheap and common labels. Most of them already gone bad. I said, 'Nothing special here, I see,' and he said, 'I prefer Scotch,' which didn't explain why he kept such a pitiable wine cellar at all."

"Maybe he feels it's his duty as a high muckety muck to have a wine cellar," I said. "Keeper of the castle and all that."

"But it got stranger," continued Higginbotham. "When McCullough pressed the button to go back upstairs, I noticed another button beneath the panel for the other floors. "Is there another floor beneath this one?' I asked.

"'No, no,' he said. 'It's a call button. There are no steps up and down to the wine cellar. The button alerts Mrs. Wallace or Rupert in case the lift is broken.' Then, he pointed to the ceiling and to a mechanical switch on the wall next to a painting of Italy. 'This switch opens a trap door, with a rope ladder.'

"I thought the whole arrangement a bit irregular and said, 'Too bad if no one is here to respond to the button.'

"'I am never here alone,' said McCullough. "I suffered a myocardial infarction last year and someone is with me at all times."

Higginbotham continued, "I remembered reading about his heart attack. But before he could stop me, I reached over and pressed the button. Nothing happened. Sir John smiled a most crafty, obsequious smile. 'You see, it only works when the lift is out of order,' he said."

"Creepy."

"That man is hiding something," said Higginbotham with conviction.

8
Isabella

After I hung up, I sat with Paul in the penthouse's black leather chairs, watching darkness descend on the city of New York.

"I'm starving," said Paul. "Would you like to go out to eat?"

"Can I take a rain check? We can do up the town after this nightmare is over. Let's stay up here this evening and keep working the facts we have."

"To tell you the truth, it's fine with me. I'll order room service." He smiled, the warm smile with slight creases in the cheeks. "What do you want?"

"I'll take a salad. Any salad. Surprise me." I still wasn't hungry. I couldn't even finish my peanuts. My stomach had tightened to the size of a golf ball, but I knew I needed to try to eat something.

While Paul called room service, I had a flash of insight and dialed Higginbotham back on my cell.

"Higginbotham."

"Isabella. Here's a thought. If the castle is, indeed, the meeting place for the brotherhood, maybe the housekeeper would be willing to have a private conversation with you. Surely she would notice if a large group of men descended on the place several times a year." I paused. "John McCullough couldn't feed or house that many men without a staff of some sort."

Higginbotham paused for what seemed like a long time, as if weighing my suggestion. "Now there's an idea. I'll ring her up tomorrow morning."

"By the way, have you checked the travel records of Edward Hobbs or that other fellow?"

"I'm sure the report is on my desk. I'll check first thing tomorrow."

9
John

John McCullough toasted his victory over Scotland Yard. He sat alone in his study with a bottle of Scotch brought by Mrs. Wallace along with her delicious tomato curry soup. "That's all for the night," he told her as she left the room.

He sipped the Scotch neat, limiting himself because of his heart condition. Savoring the moment, he re-played the tall, gawky inspector's expression when he pushed the button in the wine cellar. Ha! John had locked the button before his arrival. Detective Inspector Timothy Higginbotham could press the button all he wanted and the door would never open for him. He was a mere bureaucrat, not Aladdin.

McCullough knew exactly who was coming, and what they'd be looking for. The papers he kept in the holy room. Minus one, of course—the paper that had led them to the castle.

Maybe it was because he was getting older and had suffered a heart attack, but McCullough had felt spiritually awakened through the events of the last several days. He couldn't imagine that heaven would feel more uplifting than the spiritual high he was on. And yet, typical of the flawed scheme of earthly life, things had gone wrong, marring the purity of the experience. When he died and ascended, the heavenly spirituality would make this earthly spirituality—wonderful as it was—seem like making mud pies in a slum.

Higginbotham was a worthy adversary, along with that woman from America. Higginbotham had figured out there was more to the wine cellar than met the eye. Must be a wine connoisseur. For decades, McCullough had sent Rupert down on occasion for wine, and Rupert didn't suspect a thing. Then, too, the American detective had outsmarted one of his most trusted brothers in her hotel room. Winning over stupid people was no fun, but worthy adversaries were a pleasure.

He would figure out what to do with them after Thursday.

McCullough finished the soup and placed the dishes on the floor outside the door of his study. Now for more good news. He would check his emails and hear about the demise of Dr. Reginald Bloome.

Instead, his email from the American Patriarch read: "There's been a bit of trouble. Subject escaped. Messenger of Life has contacted me, but I'll be handling the situation tomorrow in person. Plan still on target."

202 Leslie Winfield Williams

McCullough felt his good spirits sink. He took the bottle of Scotch and poured it directly into his mouth, not bothering with a glass. The Scotch curdled in his stomach. *The plan must succeed. It must, even if he died trying.*

From here on out, everything had to move without a hitch. Otherwise, he would die another heart attack victim (a mere statistic)—and his soul would be lost in the blackness of the universe instead of shining like a comet throughout eternity.

He put the Scotch away and took a pill.

10

Isabella

After eating in the penthouse by the twinkling lights of New York City, I said, "I've got to get home tomorrow. The conference is closed, and the two suits I took to England have wilted."

"I'll drive you back to New Haven. Then I'll hop a flight to Dallas for Thanksgiving at home." Paul paused. "No. On second thought, I think I'll stay and spend Thanksgiving with Malcolm and Andrew. This Thanksgiving will be a hard one for Malcolm."

"That would be nice," I said, thinking of how lonely Malcolm would be this holiday season.

Personally, I dreaded the stretch from Thanksgiving to Christmas. My mother always over-decorated the house and yard, as if turkey pictures or Christmas ornaments would help my depression.

I picked at the soggy remains of my salad.

When Paul went back to his room, I turned on the television to catch the news. I got the tail end of Stewart Williams closing down the conference.

Then, to my shock and anger, I heard the reporter informing all of New York and the rest of America about the post cards. I couldn't believe it. *Somebody had leaked that information to the press.* Was it Williams? I felt like I was going to have the dry heaves.

The following story featured a pregnant woman run down by a car on Long Island.

I closed my eyes. I snapped off the television, clinging to the remote control. The young woman had lain on the sidewalk while camera crews hovered over her like predators, getting shots of the blood, the astonished look of pain on her face. The image imprinted itself on the inner screen of my mind. When I closed my eyes, headlights rushed at me in the dark.

I had to get home. My stress symptoms were maxxing out. I had seen too much in the last few days. I had pushed my mind too hard. Starting this afternoon with that Class-A jerk Williams, emotion had started to build up inside. My protective membrane was getting thinner and thinner, and I feared I would explode from the pressure of this case.

Between my own memories, the approaching holiday season, the Campus Killer, and this twisted and complicated investigation, I felt that life was a water hose stuffed into the mouth of a highly stretched balloon. I was the balloon.

The newscast with the pregnant woman had taken me back to the place of raw pain.

I stood up and took a long shower, washed my hair, and rinsed out my underwear in the marble bathroom. Then, I dried my hair, slipping into my nightie and the hotel's soft, fluffy robe, and crawled into bed. I would take deep breaths until I fell asleep. I would hold on just one more night, then I'd be at home in my own bed.

Just then, I heard a crash and Paul said, "Ow," and groaned.

I jumped up and knocked at his door. "Are you all right?"

Silence, then "Yeah. I conked my head on the corner of the glass table in here."

"Do you need some help?"

"No, I'm okay. I just—well, yes. Can you bring me some ice from the ice maker at the bar?"

I gathered a washrag filled with ice and entered Paul's room. He was sitting in his bathrobe on the edge of the bed. He held his hand to his forehead, which was dribbling blood through a soaked tissue.

Blood poured down his face and dripped off his chin. I rushed over to him and applied the washrag with ice.

Paul looked embarrassed. "Thanks. I'm okay. Head wounds bleed a lot."

"What happened?" I asked, seated next to him pressing gently on his gash to stop the blood.

"Oh, when I get tired, my leg cramps up. I tripped and caught my forehead on the corner of the table. It doesn't happen a lot."

I sat with him until the bleeding stopped, then went into his bathroom and got a fresh, damp washrag and cleaned up his face. "There. Now let me see your leg."

Paul leaned back on the bed and showed me his leg, still stiff.

"Roll over." I took Paul's calf in my hands and worked the muscle until it began to relax. I had a sudden impulse to massage the rest of him, those glorious buttocks and shoulders, but I stopped myself. He rolled back over and patted the bed next to him for me to sit down.

Cautiously, almost primly, I sat down and leaned back against the pillow bank, making sure my robe covered my legs.

Paul rolled away from me on his side, propping himself up with his elbow so he could see me. After a moment, he said, "You're a woman of many talents."

"Thank you," I said, feeling as fragile as a cracked egg. Maybe I should go back to my own room.

"Tell me about how you decided to become a detective. You're very good at what you do."

I knew Paul meant well. I knew he was making it clear that he was not going to take advantage of the situation and come on to me. I also sensed he was genuinely interested.

However, I could feel myself blushing. My pulse beginning to throb. I wanted to say, "I became a detective because I lost my family one Thursday night." Tears sprang up in my eyes.

Instantly sensitive to my mood, Paul said, "I apologize. I didn't mean to intrude." He looked distraught that he had said the wrong thing.

His kindness was the pinprick that burst me wide open. I didn't trust myself to respond. I lay next to him and felt the quivering start with my eyes and mouth and spread down my body. Like the tumultuous waves in the storm at the shoreline of the Olde Branford Inn, emotions begin to fling themselves at me, washing over me—wave after wave of sadness so deep I felt like I was drowning.

Flashes of memory—standing at the shoreline while cold rain pummeled my face, sprinkling the ashes of my baby.

Ronny's face when he proposed.

The priest who refused to give him a funeral.

My mother trying to make it better by hanging garlands of Christmas tinsel all over the house.

Before I knew it, my face was wet and my shoulders were shaking. I couldn't control myself. Eight years of tears came pouring forth. I turned on my stomach and sobbed into the pillow next to Paul.

"I was married once, but he committed suicide after a car wreck that killed our baby. I can't have any children. I'll never be able to have children."

I continued to sob. Paul stroked my hair in silence. I wept through eight years of isolation. I wept through eight years of keeping my condition bottled up inside myself, never telling anyone. I wept until I was so tired I couldn't move, and lay limp next to a man I barely knew.

Paul never said a word, but held me in his arms until I fell asleep.

Chapter Seven
WEDNESDAY

1
Gabriel

Early Wednesday morning, Gabriel loitered at the secluded spot along Rock Creek Parkway, waiting for the Washington Patriarch, Felix Darrington, to arrive. As instructed, Gabriel used his binoculars to look around among the trees and bushes. Sure enough, right on time, here came the old man, plodding up the trail. Gabriel turned his back so the yellow warbler sticker on his backpack showed and so he wouldn't see Darrington's face. Sethian secrecy. The Grand Patriarch insisted on it, and Gabriel could appreciate how the arcane discipline of silence had guaranteed the Brotherhood's secret safety for over a thousand years.

However, Gabriel had made it his own business to discover Darrington's identity. That way, he had something on the old man in case the plans went to hell. Yesterday had reminded him that everything on the earth was far from perfect. As much as he loved the Brotherhood and felt grateful for being one of the chosen ones, he would not be taking any potential fall alone.

The old man huffed and puffed as he approached Gabriel. When he caught his breath, he gave the signal. "Is the flock ready to head south?"

"They take off tomorrow," said Gabriel. The old man dropped his backpack and walked back down the path and out of sight.

Gabriel had arrived in Washington, D.C. yesterday after the disaster at the hotel. He collected the van rented for him under an assumed name and made his way to an address in the Adams Morgan area of the city. The Brotherhood had rented an apartment there, under a different assumed name.

Inside the closet in the bedroom, Gabriel had found four boxes of Prayer Books and Hymnals. They were gutted and rigged—almost ready for the Thanksgiving Day service. Only one ingredient was missing.

After the allotted time, Gabriel picked up the backpack and went back to his apartment.

Now he had the C-4.

2
Malcolm

Malcolm walked from room to room in his lonely house. He had started to clear out the library, but couldn't face the task by himself, finally called a trash company. They came and hauled away all the smashed furniture and wrecked knickknacks.

Wednesday morning, he stood with his briefcase staring at the empty, book-lined room. Victoria would have already bought and arranged new furniture by now. She had worked with a decorator when they refinished the house, but she had spearheaded most of the plans herself. She had a flair for the artistic.

Malcolm had called the decorator on Monday afternoon and given her carte blanche to re-do the library. "Anything. Just get something in here." He didn't think he could bear the empty room until the furniture came on Friday after Thanksgiving Day.

When he arrived in his office Wednesday morning, he returned his brother Andrew's call.

"Hey, Malcolm," said Andrew. "How are you?" Last Thanksgiving, Victoria had outdone herself for the family dinner with wild turkeys, duck, pheasant, and quail. The St. Clairs had even flown up for the holiday weekend.

"I'll be there," said Malcolm. "I'll bring some wine."

"No, no. Just bring yourself." Andrew, again trying to be nice, but beginning to grate on Malcolm's nerves.

"No, I'd like to bring the wine, if you don't mind," said Malcolm. He didn't want to be pandered to. Truth told, he'd rather spend Thanksgiving dinner at the country club, but he knew he needed to show up at Andrew's.

"Fine, great," said Andrew. "Paul's decided to come over here instead of flying back to Dallas. He's been in New York, but he's on his way back to New Haven today. You two can come together."

"I know. He called me." Malcolm hung up, then got out of his chair and closed the door to his corner office. New Haven was gray today, gray from the sky to the buildings to the streets. The gray was permeating through the window into Malcolm's spirit.

He recalled a day, what, fifty some years ago? A day as colorful as this day was drab. It was Malcolm's eighth birthday party. Hedges of hollyhocks, freesias, azaleas and daisies bloomed in a riot of color in their groomed back yard. Malcolm's mother had invited all her friends over, young matrons who had children near Malcolm's age, including Winthrop and Victoria—he still remembered Victoria in a new pink dress, soaked with chocolate sauce down the front by the end of the party.

Malcolm wore a miniature suit, with shorts, long socks, saddle oxfords, and a jacket. His mother hired a party coordinator who ran the party while the women drank mimosas on the terrace. The children ran screaming around the back yard, chased by the party coordinator.

At the end of the party, Malcolm, like a good little host, stood in attendance along with his brother and sister and said goodbye to the guests. Andrew, at age three, looked like a butterball angel. All of the mothers exclaimed how adorable he looked as he stood next to Malcolm and played to the crowd. "What a doll," said Winthrop's mother.

Malcolm was ignored.

When everyone left, stoic little Malcolm went up to his room and cried. It was *his* birthday. Andrew, his stupid younger brother, had stolen the show. He heard his parents outside his locked door, "Malcolm? Malcolm? Please let us in. What's the matter?"

His mother whispered to his father, "I don't have any idea. It was a lovely party." Finally, they left and went back downstairs.

For three miserable years at summer camp Malcolm excelled at nothing. Andrew won the archery competition, Andrew got the best camper award, Andrew beat him in the tennis tournament in the first round.

Their good friend Winthrop asked Andrew, not Malcolm, to be his best man. That blow was softened when Malcolm became godfather to Jeeter. But the only reason Winthrop asked him was because Andrew had turned Catholic by then. Winthrop wanted Episcopalians.

Jeeter and his nephew Paul were the only children Malcolm had, and they were both borrowed.

Now, on Thanksgiving Day—a day he had little to be thankful for—Malcolm would have to go to Andrew's house alone. He would watch the Happy Family laughing and interacting and having fun.

He couldn't bear the thought.

3
Isabella

I woke up alone in Paul's bed. Then I remembered the night before and gingerly touched my puffy eyes. It was late, almost 10:00. Last night had been an inexcusable display of emotion. Paul had already packed. He'd probably gotten away from me as fast as he could. I couldn't blame him.

I hurried back to my room, where I found a note from Paul taped to the bathroom mirror. "You are the most beautiful woman I have ever met. I'm downstairs in the coffee shop."

My heart skipped a beat. Maybe I hadn't made such a terrible fool of myself after all. I generously applied makeup to my eyes and packed my own bag. As I closed the door to the penthouse suite, I looked out the window. What a view. The skyline of New York City and a sun struggling to come out from behind a bank of clouds.

Maybe there wouldn't be a murder today.

In the coffee shop, I spied Paul reading the newspaper with a few crumbs of a croissant left on a plate in front of him. He stood up when he saw me. Shyly, I walked up to him and embraced him lightly. "Thank you."

He kissed the top of my head. "Let's get you a bite to eat before we head back to New Haven."

After Paul let me out in front of the police station, I stopped by the forensic lab to talk with Bob and Maria. I said, "You two look terrible." Bob had bags under his eyes, and Maria's face was pale.

"Well, you don't," said Bob. "You look like the cat that ate the canary. You have no right to glow after crossing the Atlantic twice, dashing to New York, then driving here."

"I got a good night's sleep," I said, hoping my face wasn't turning red. "Now, what's up here?"

"Dandruff from the hotel attendant who poisoned Hawthorne matches the DNA we got from the hotel room yesterday," said Maria.

"We knew it would," said Bob.

"Okay. So pull it together for me."

Maria jumped in. "We've got somebody, late twenties hired to bump off a series of victims. Two in New Haven, two in New York."

Bob said, "We don't think Victoria was part of the plan. She'd obviously just walked in the door—her suitcase was next to her shoes. Malcolm said she wasn't supposed to be home until the next day. We're thinking she interrupted the guy who was hacking up her library and stealing the manuscript."

"I agree." I followed along, skimming my own notes in my notebook. "Next murder. Dr. Barnes. We know this one is intentional. The murderer enters Dr. Barnes' hotel room, bringing her a cup of tea laced with belladonna and exits. He's unnoticed except for another hotel employee who thinks he's hot."

"Hot," said Maria, "which could mean anything. But he had a medium build."

"Yes, and the next day, I discover a hatchet in Dr. Barnes' apartment in England, linking Victoria's murder to Dr. Barnes'," I said. "Question: Did the same person kill Victoria, kill Dr. Barnes, and then fly to England, or are we dealing here with more than one hatchet-lover?"

"My money's on two people. Why would this Sethian group fly a murderer over to England, just to get to Barnes' flash drive and hack up her place? Seems like they could get local talent and save a lot of money and trouble," said Bob.

"Maybe another Sethian symbol is the hatchet."

"Yes, but—" Just then, my phone rang.

4
Isabella

I took the call from Timothy Higginbotham. "News," he said.

"We've tracked some of the old families from Wyatt's poem—well, not Wyatt, of course—but the monk's list of sixteenth-century members of the Sethian Brotherhood. Most of the families have died out. Or produced girls, and can't be traced by name."

"Tell me you found one name, just one—"

"Precisely. One name, and one name only. But it's a winner. Hobbs. Edward Hobbs' family can be traced directly back to the sixteenth century, living around the area of Stoneleigh. Small landowner, cousin who was a monk."

"Hobbs. Edward Hobbs. Wasn't he the man who attacked me?" I remembered clearly his face—and his shock when I punctured his eye.

"Precisely," Higginbotham repeated. "One and the same. We've been at his house and his office all day, searching through his records."

"I presume he's still missing."

"Yes. I don't know whether he was done in with a belladonna cocktail for letting you get the best of him—and a good look as well. Or whether he was spirited away to keep him from talking."

"Did you find anything of interest at Hobbs' house?" I asked.

"Edward Hobbs apparently has relatives in Scotland, and visits them from time to time, according to his wife."

"Did you contact them?" I asked.

"Yes, Hobbs takes a motor car and tootles on up to Glasgow several times a year. The relatives say he comes usually the first part of the month, three or four times a year. It varies from year to year."

"Glasgow."

"Right. Not Edinburgh, not the highlands." Higginbotham paused. "Here's the interesting part. He apparently arrives at his relatives' house Saturday afternoon and leaves on Monday."

I couldn't resist asking, "Did his wife say when he leaves home?"

I could almost feel Higginbotham smiling in triumph. "Early Friday."

"Got him." I felt a surge of excitement. "Now we just have to find a way to break the MP, John McCullough. Too many trails lead to that castle." I thought for a moment. "Did you have an opportunity to speak with the housekeeper?"

"Rupert the valet answered the phone. It's Mrs. Wallace's day off today. I pretended I was a sales person with a random call. I'll call for her again tomorrow. It's not a holiday for us over here. I know you'll be feasting on turkey, but some of us will be hard at work."

"My heart breaks for you. Trust me. I'll be back in the office after lunch with my family."

"I'll talk with you then. Have a happy holiday." Higginbotham paused.

"By the way, we haven't had a murder yet today. Maybe the Sethians have made their point and are retiring from the death business."

"We can only hope," I said.

5

LeRoy

For the last time, LeRoy hung up the waiter's uniform in his locker at the New Haven Country Club. He had just finished serving lunch to the mayor and his wife. Afterward he set all the tables for dinner, although the club did not expect a large crowd the evening before Thanksgiving.

LeRoy's long-awaited opportunity to open his own restaurant had finally arrived. He had received a call from an anonymous gentleman, a member of the country club. The gentleman had offered to give him $100,000 and send him to Cordon Bleu in Paris. The donor wanted to remain anonymous, just as the Christmas bonus he received was always anonymous.

LeRoy had jumped at the opportunity. There were only two conditions.

He'd fulfilled the first condition on Monday. LeRoy had flown to Washington, D.C. with two large suitcases filled with Prayer Books and hymnals. He had left the books in the closet of the bedroom in an apartment in the area of Adams Morgan. He had stayed in the apartment overnight, as instructed, and flown home Tuesday evening.

The donor was as good as his word. LeRoy had found his plane tickets waiting for him at the airport, as planned. This morning, he checked on the $50,000 wired to his savings account, as promised.

The second part of the adventure was easier than the first. LeRoy had been instructed to call a specific telephone number with a specific message. Ten minutes later he was to deliver a post card. LeRoy's benefactor had left a throwaway phone and a post card in his locker at the club.

LeRoy closed his locker door. He'd enjoyed serving at the country club, but nothing could beat owning his own kitchen. He'd packed his bag this morning, said goodbye to his mother. Just now he told the club manager he was quitting.

LeRoy grabbed his bag, the phone, and the post card—and left.

6
Andrew

The dean's house stood next to the seminary. It was an old, rambling Victorian-style home, re-done in muted colors, trimmed in white, with a porch and a gracious feel of days gone by. Late Wednesday afternoon, Andrew was in the kitchen with his wife Noe, a slight, attractive French woman. Noe had bobbed red-gold hair and a stomach flat even after giving birth to four healthy babies and two still-born infants. The two younger children watched a movie in the living room, eating popcorn. The older ones were upstairs taking a nap.

In spite of being French, Noe was not a chef. "The stuffing, it goes in this place here, yes?" She pointed to the turkey's gaping cavity.

"I think so," said Andrew, re-reading the recipe. "And what's left over goes in a pan." He took off his reading glasses and pulled her close to him. "Honey, let's get the club to bring the dinner. I'll call LeRoy, and they can deliver the whole thing tomorrow morning. I don't want to make you go through this."

Noe stood on tiptoe and kissed the end of his nose. "All these years I've been in America now. Never once I have cooked a Thanksgiving dinner all by myself. We went to your parents always until your father went to the nurse's home. The next year we went to Texas. Last year Victoria's, but never here. It's my turn. Poor Malcolm will need to be with his family. We will make it as happy as we can for him."

Noe's delicate features and thin lips drew downward in sincere sympathy with Andrew's brother.

Standing in the cluttered kitchen, Andrew knew all over again why he had married her. Brisk, efficient, quick thinking, she was also big-hearted. And sexy. She rubbed up against him. "Andre. Please let me fix the meal?"

Andrew warmed all over and snuggled back against her. "Why don't we take a little break upstairs so I can think about it?" He nuzzled and kissed her neck.

She pulled away and flirted with her eyes. "No. After the dressing, we have the sauce of cranberries. Then the pies, pumpkin and pecan."

Andrew knew why they had so many children. Besides practicing the old-fashioned Roman Catholic style rhythm method of birth control—which didn't always work—he couldn't keep his hands off his wife. "Okay."

The phone rang in the kitchen and Andrew pulled himself away to answer it. A voice said, "I know where it is."

Andrew looked at the caller ID. He didn't recognize the number. "Hello? Who is this?" The voice sounded familiar, but strange, too—as if the caller were trying to disguise his identity.

Silence. Then the message was repeated.

"Are you talking about the manuscript?" Andrew's heart skipped a beat. His blood surged with hope and exhilaration. Money. The caller was responding to the offer of a reward.

Noe heard him talking. She crossed the kitchen to stand close by, her face a map of excitement. Andrew said, "Do you want the reward? Do you have the manuscript with you? Do you know who has it?"

The caller said, "I will meet you in your office in two minutes. Go through the north door near the bookstore. Leave it unlocked. Go into your office and close the door."

"Close the door?" Why close the door? Andrew wondered. It didn't matter. He would do as instructed.

"Yes. Close the door."

"Two minutes. I'll be there. Let me call Malcolm, and—"

"NO!" shouted the caller. "Alone. No cops. No family. No friends. Or you will never see the manuscript again."

"Okay, okay, " said Andrew. This call was strange, but how dangerous could it be? "Are you coming alone?"

Silence. Then, "Yes." More silence. "The meeting will take an hour. If anyone interrupts, that's the end. The manuscript is gone."

"An hour?" An hour seemed like a long time.

Silence. Then, "Yes, an hour."

"I guess you'll be wanting me to make arrangements for the money."

"Two minutes." Click.

Andrew turned to Noe, "Someone called about the reward money! He's got information about the manuscript."

"I'll go with you," Noe said, starting to untie her apron.

"No," Andrew shook his head. His thoughts were still spinning. "I have to go by myself."

Noe cried, "But what if there's danger? How do you know this man is telling the truth?"

"I don't, but I'll be careful. I promise." Excited, Andrew wiped his hands on the dishtowel. He was desperate to get the manuscript back.

"Andrew, I don't feel good about this. Are you sure?"

"I'm sure. I recognized his voice. It sounded a little like LeRoy at the club." Nothing would stop him from making contact.

With fear and worry in her eyes, Noe reached up and gave him a big kiss on the lips. "I love you. Be careful."

"See you in an hour." Andrew dashed out the door without his coat. He hurried across the parking lot to the north entrance.

7
LeRoy

LeRoy looked toward the dean's house. The north entrance was too far back for anyone looking out the windows to see. Good. He crept up to the door and found it unlocked. As quietly as possible, he opened the outer door, then the inner door, and slid inside. Tiptoeing down the hall, he went upstairs to the office area. The dean's office door was closed. Hoping he wouldn't sneeze or trip, he crept down the hall and dropped the post card in the clear plastic box by the dean's door. He hastened back the way he came.

Moving toward downtown he made it to Union Station in record time. His train arrived on schedule. He relaxed as the lights from the scenery rolled by on the way to New York City.

LeRoy could expect another $50,000 in his savings account on the Friday after Thanksgiving. He had already received word that the Cordon Bleu was expecting him.

Rich people were a strange bunch. LeRoy just wished he knew whom to thank.

8
Andrew

Andrew sat in his office looking at his wall of family pictures, photos, and drawings his children had made for him. He went through the stack of paper in his in box. He could do some work if he weren't so nervous.

His watch said 5:20, ten full minutes after he'd received the phone call. Maybe this arrangement was a mistake. Maybe he shouldn't have jumped so quickly. Maybe Andrew ought to call campus security.

Yet the caller had given him no choice. He said two minutes and come alone.

He thought he heard someone approaching. No. His ears were playing tricks on him.

He was just about to call Noe, when someone knocked at the door. "Come in," he said, jumping to his feet.

Andrew was startled to see his brother Malcolm walk in. He wore a dark suit, and must have come straight from the office. "Oh, hello, Malcolm," said Andrew. "I was expecting someone else. Have a seat." He motioned to one of the chairs across from his desk. Would Malcolm's arrival jeopardize the caller's plan? "You can't stay too long. I have an appointment."

"Don't worry." Malcolm carried two cups of coffee from Andrew's favorite coffee shop. "Here. I brought Mocha." He set one of the cups down in front of Andrew on the desk.

Andrew loved Mocha. "Thank you." He was surprised at his brother's thoughtfulness. Maybe Victoria's death had made him a little more sensitive and kind toward his family members. Suffering did that sometimes.

Andrew took a swig and said excitedly, "I'm expecting someone any minute. I got a call from an anonymous person who knows something about the manuscript. I expect he's looking for the reward."

"Really?" said Malcolm as he settled himself in one of the two bargello chairs in Andrew's office. "So offering the reward money worked? Did he say where he had taken the manuscript?"

"No. He didn't actually say he had it in his possession. He said he knew where it was." Andrew sipped the coffee. "What brings you over here?" Come to think of it, Andrew couldn't remember the last time his brother had been in his office.

"I wanted to talk to you." Malcolm looked at Andrew. Andrew looked back. He saw a bitter man whose face looked older than his years. Trim, yes, but haggard. As if he'd been stuffed with tar and brambles instead of the usual organs, and his body was wasting away from the inside out.

Andrew had never really understood his older brother. Malcolm had shut him out of his life years ago, remaining a stilted and sad enigma. When Andrew was little, he used to beg Malcolm to come outside and play with him and Winthrop. But Malcolm holed himself up in his room studying.

At summer camp, they both took tennis lessons. One year they got placed in direct competition with each other. Andrew tried as hard as he could to let Malcolm win, but Malcolm had the natural athleticism of a bent twig. He spent most of his time in the weight room, whereas Andrew loved to be outdoors, or among people.

"What's up?" asked Andrew to his older brother, while keeping one eye on the door. Malcolm sat austere and solemn across his desk.

"I need to tell you something." Malcolm's face darkened. At the same time, his mouth formed the shape of a smile. "I know where the manuscript is."

Andrew almost choked on the coffee. "What? You know where the manuscript—what? I mean—"

Malcolm calmly sipped his beverage. "I know where the manuscript is."

Andrew felt as if Malcolm had hit him in the gut. "Okay. Why don't you tell me what you mean." Nervous, he eyed his brother, remembering the tennis match. As the two of them had hit the ball back and forth, Malcolm seemed to sink lower and lower into an emotional bottomless pit of depression.

Today, Malcolm's face wore an odd sheen of victory.

"It's in a place where it belongs. The manuscript didn't belong here in your little kingdom. You didn't need another feather in your cap. You've always gotten everything you wanted in life. The manuscript was mine."

Andrew pulled his chair up closer to his desk, stunned.

"The *Gospel of Judas* belongs with the true believers, not with the rag-tag remnants of a two-thousand year old scam."

Andrew's mind whirled, trying to keep up with his brother. "Are you saying that the manuscript is with the Sethian Brotherhood?"

Malcolm nodded smugly. "Finally, I know something you don't. I've waited a long time for this."

"And how, exactly, do you know this?" Where was the caller? Was he going to show up at all? Or was—? Oh, no.

Malcolm continued. "I know this because I set up the whole scheme. I am the American Patriarch of the Sethian Brotherhood. I am one of the chosen."

Andrew was beginning to feel hot and strange. He took deep breaths and tried to focus on what his brother was saying. "The chosen?" He took another sip of coffee.

"Yes. Only selected ones from the human race are part of the incorruptible generation. Christians are not among those who will achieve eternal life. Turns out, little brother, that although you may have gotten everything you wanted in this life, I will have everything in the next."

In spite of his uncomfortable physical condition, Andrew felt a stab of sympathy for his brother. "Oh, Malcolm. You've made such a terrible mistake. But it's not too late. You can still repent." He wiped his face with a tissue from the box on his desk.

Malcolm's face hardened. Hatred had calcified his features.

As his fingers began to shake, Andrew realized that Malcolm was beyond reach. Malcolm had sailed away from the continent of his family and landed on an island in an unknown part of the world.

Andrew took a deep breath, "Okay, so you arranged for someone to rob the safe?" The back of his throat felt dry and he had trouble swallowing. This news was really affecting him badly.

"Yes, as a matter of fact, I did. And I've also arranged for LeRoy from the club to take the fall. He is the patsy." Malcolm's face wore a gargoyle-grimace of a smile. He continued, "The manuscript is in Scotland in the sacred room of the Sethian Brotherhood. It lies in a special box designed by one of the brothers when I first told them about the treasure we stumbled on in our basement."

"So all this time, you've planned—" Andrew couldn't finish the sentence his voice was so weak.

"Yes," said Malcolm, leaning forward to watch Andrew. "And it's been delicious, every moment."

Malcolm, Malcolm. Where and when did he become so lost? Andrew managed to whisper, "But what about Victoria?"

Malcolm continued to talk, in a liquid smooth voice. "Victoria was not supposed to be there. She was collateral damage."

How could Malcolm sit across the desk from him and call his wife "collateral damage"? This news was upsetting Andrew worse than anything else in his entire life. His whole body began to shake.

Malcolm continued in a triumphant voice. "But you know, I really don't care. You see, before she left for her last taping in New York, she ended two years of happiness. After all those long years of being alone, I finally achieved what I deserved—a woman who loved me."

Andrew could barely hear him. Malcolm continued. "She shut me out with one little word. We were making love, and she slipped and called me 'Andrew.' I stopped caressing her and she looked puzzled. She didn't realize her mistake.

"I lay awake a long time listening to the softness of her breath as she slept. I remembered all the summer vacations. Especially the summer of the Mediterranean cruise."

Andrew began to convulse. Malcolm stood up and came around to Andrew's side of the desk. "I'd courted her through the Greek Islands. I was going to pop the question to her as we pulled into the New York harbor."

Malcolm's voice remained calm. "Then, after the last stop in Alexandria, she turned her cheek when I tried to kiss her. Started going to bed early, leaving the card table just as I got there."

Andrew closed his eyes, willing himself not to lose consciousness.

"A month after we got back, she became engaged to the animal who abused her and drank himself to death."

Malcolm said wistfully, "She was the love of my life." His voice hardened. "Remember the afternoon in Alexandria when only two people stayed on the boat? You and Victoria."

Andrew thought *I'm going to die, right here on my office floor.* He whispered, "Oh, my God. You've poisoned me." He looked up at his older brother, standing over him. He was smiling and happier than Andrew had ever seen him.

"Yes," said Malcolm, "I have."

Andrew lost consciousness and fell off his chair onto the floor.

9
Noe

After an hour, Noe couldn't contain herself any longer. She'd been peering out the window for the last forty-five minutes, trying to see something, someone. Nothing. She couldn't remember which door Paul had mentioned, but she'd watched him go over the hump at the back of the house toward the bookstore entrance. She headed straight there. Locked.

Just in case she'd been mistaken, she tried the north door next to the Office of Sacred Music. Locked. Getting worried, she ran around the quad, trying all the doors. Andrew, of course, had taken his keycard with him.

She arrived back in her kitchen both sweating and chilled at the same time. She debated for about five seconds whether she should call campus security. She didn't care if she became known as the batty French wife of the dean—she had already called them once for a false alarm. She dialed and waited at the outside door closest to Andrew's office.

A young woman in uniform with her hair in a bun drove up and parked near Noe. She unlocked the door. Noe ran upstairs and down the hall to her husband's office. It was locked too, but a strange smell came from under the door. The security officer unlocked the door. Noe saw her husband's foot sticking out from behind his desk. "*Mon dieu!*" She rushed over and took in the scene with her husband's white face and the eyes rolled to the back of his head. She knelt down and cradled his head in her lap. "Wake up! Andre, wake up, please wake up!"

"Ma'am, excuse me," said the officer. She knelt down, too, and felt his pulse. She shook her head and closed his eyes. "I'm sorry, ma'am."

"No!" cried Noe in anguish. "No, no, this cannot be!" She continued to hold him close to her, rocking back and forth and sobbing.

The police officer called her dispatcher on her phone. She lowered her voice. "We've got another body here. It's Dean Guildford. This poor family"

10
Isabella

I had just hung up from the New York television station that had spilled the beans about the post cards. Apparently, it was an anonymous tip dropped off in a manila envelope by a courier service. Photocopies of the post cards, front and back.

The Sethians were definitely sending a message with their actions, sort of like the videos of Osama Bin Ladin. They didn't want the world to wonder who or why. At the same time, they didn't want to be found. Cowards.

I flicked off the lights in the detectives' bullpen. I was ready to go home and change out of one of the drooping suits I'd lived in the last few days.

The phone at my desk rang. I answered it, "O'Leary."

Chief Crenshaw said, "Yale Divinity School. ASAP. Andrew Guildford is the latest victim."

Andrew Guildford. I stood speechless for a moment. At one time, I had considered him a suspect.

"Detective O'Leary? Are you there?"

"Yes, Chief. It's just, I'm stunned. I didn't think—I mean, the last two attempts seemed random. This one seems personal. As if the Guildford family is being singled out. Like the manuscript is evil, some sort of terrible bad luck charm."

"It's grim. I'll meet you over there. Andrew's wife already called his brother."

On the way out the door, I caught Bob and Maria before they left. "Get your kits. This time Andrew Guildford is the vic."

I approached the Divinity School, my stomach churning. The stately quadrangle had surrounded nothing but disappointment for me during my year there. Now a murder. When I arrived, I couldn't get up the driveway for all the media and cop cars. I wished it were against the law for media to listen in on police monitors. I parked in the dean's driveway next door and shouldered my way through.

I knew exactly where the dean's office was. Outside the door, Malcolm and Paul were consoling Noe. Noe's grief couldn't be contained in the stream of French she wailed as she thrashed her arms. Paul was saying, "Do you have her? I'll go tell the children." He turned to Malcolm, "I'll call the doctor, too. We've got to get something to calm her down."

I touched Paul's arm. "I'm so sorry." He looked at me with eyes overflowing with anguish.

At that instant, I realized that I didn't have the sole rights to human suffering. Suffering, I realized, was an unavoidable part of the shared human condition.

"I'm glad you're here," he said. "See if you can calm her down. The cops kept the children at the house so they wouldn't have to see their father like this. Somebody has to go tell them."

Malcolm looked miserable, lost, not knowing what to do. I gently took the weeping woman in my arms and held her. Then I led her to a seating area close by, placing Noe next to me on a small couch.

Finally, Noe collapsed against my shoulder. She shuddered, hiccupping with grief. When she could talk, I gradually drew the story out of her.

"Andrew said the voice was familiar?"

Noe nodded, her swollen face saturated with tears. A river ran out her nose. "He said it sounded a little like LeRoy at the club." I would check the phone luds and call the club.

222 Leslie Winfield Williams

A middle-aged man approached, carrying a bag like the doctors did on re-runs of old TV shows when doctors made house calls. Noe saw him and started crying again. "Dr. Devon."

"My dear one." He pulled out a stethoscope and listened. He clasped Noe's hand in his and said, "I'm going to take you to your house now. Can you stand up?"

I helped her to her feet. "There. Good," said the doctor. "We'll walk slowly and I'm going to give you a little something so you can rest. Maybe Malcolm can come over, and help with the children."

"Paul's over there now," I said.

"Oh, Paul is in New Haven? This is good, very good." He led Noe down the corridor to the elevator.

I joined Bob and Maria in Andrew's office. Malcolm hovered in the corner, wringing his hands. "Can we step outside for a moment?" I asked Malcolm.

He had to step over Andrew's legs to get out. He took one last look at his brother, holding his gaze on Andrew's face. I couldn't read his expression. When we got outside the office, I said, "I'm so sorry for your loss." The customary phrase sounded so empty, but I meant it.

Malcolm tightened his lips and clenched his fists. He couldn't speak. I sympathized with him, aching at the thought of what he must be going through. I waited a moment for him to collect himself. "Tell me what happened."

Malcolm took a deep breath and said slowly, "I had just arrived home from my office when Noe called me talking about LeRoy at the club. She was incoherent. Some woman police officer got on the phone and told me what happened. I rushed down here. That's all I know. Noe was too hysterical."

"LeRoy?"

"At the New Haven Country Club."

As he was speaking, my eye caught on the clear plastic in-box hanging on the wall outside Andrew's office door. "Just a second." I moved closer, peering at the only object in the box, a post card with a split picture on the front showing through the plastic. The National Cathedral. On the right side of the front, an aerial view of the entire structure. On the left, a shot of one of the chapels.

"Excuse me a minute, Mr. Guildford." I called to the techs inside the office. "Bob! Maria! Come here a sec!"

Maria rushed out, gloves on. I pointed to the post card in the plastic tray. "No wonder we didn't find it on the body," she said. "It was the first thing we looked for."

Bob said, "Let me dust it for prints. You never know. Maybe the fifth time's a charm." He took the card out and carried it into the office, where he laid it on a sheet of plastic spread on Andrew's desk. He swirled the dusting brush over the card. "Hey. Look what we've got here. It's a beaut of a print."

Maria handed him a piece of sticky tape so he could lift the print. I said, "Run it as soon as you get back. Then go to the country club and try to get a print off of an employee named LeRoy. I'll call the manager in a minute and tell him what's up."

Malcolm, who'd been standing in the shadows, rigid as an automaton, said, "May I leave? I'd like to check on Noe and Paul at the house, and then I want to go home."

"Sure." Poor man. I understood only too well that he needed to be alone in his grief.

While Bob and Maria finished working the crime scene, I made several phone calls. First, I called Stewart Williams to make sure he'd been notified. He'd never forgive me for being first on the scene, and I made a big deal that he was the first person I called. He was on the way.

Next, I called Detective Inspector Higginbotham. I knew it was late, but also felt he deserved to hear about Andrew's death from me, and not in the London morning newspapers.

"Good God!" he said when I told him the news. "Dean of Yale Divinity School. Sounds like they're shifting a bit with this one. Christian scholars and theologians have been the targets from the first. Thinkers of the faith. Not the figureheads like the pope or the Archbishop of Canterbury, or other power players."

"What are you saying?"

"I'm just thinking aloud here. Dr. Guildford is a bit of a figurehead as well as being a scholar."

"Okay, I agree. So far, the Sethians' murders have made a statement against Christians' beliefs and theology."

"Yes. I suppose there are two ways to make a point. If you attack the Christian power structure, faith springs up again and again and again."

I saw where he was going. "But if you attack the faith itself, then the institutions topple because they can't support an empty belief."

"History has proved that point." He paused, "But something has intensified here. They went for the jugular with Dr. Guildford. He's a not only a scholar, but he's head of one of the leading religious institutions in America."

I thought for a moment. "You think they're stepping it up? Like the serial killer that gets increasingly violent?"

"At first blush here, I'd say they're stepping it up, yes."

"I still don't know what message the card said. Let me call you after I talk with Paul." I added, "If it's not too late for you."

"Don't worry. I'll be awake."

11
LeRoy

LeRoy disembarked at Grand Central Station during rush hour. The enormous, cavernous hub pulsated with people jostling, pushing, pressing against him.

Outside in the melee of stalled traffic, blaring horns, and people shouting, he finally discovered a line of sorts and got the attention of a cab driver. He slid in the back seat, escaping into the relative quiet—though smelly—interior of a cab. Old hamburgers and the body odor of the previous occupants.

LeRoy watched out the window as the cab driver maneuvered through traffic, honking and muttering in Indian, or Pakistani, or something LeRoy had never heard before. He didn't like New York City. He'd never even climbed the Statue of Liberty. After Paris, he would return to New Haven, a small town in many ways, but a place where he felt comfortable.

He leaned back and tried to relax. He wondered what happened with Dr. Andrew Guildford in his office. How long did he wait before he thought to check the in-box outside his door? LeRoy had no idea what the message on the post card meant, but the church on the front was beautiful.

LeRoy had followed his instructions to the letter. He hoped the post card was helpful for the Dean. He'd always liked the Guildford family.

Pretty soon, he started seeing signs for LaGuardia Airport. Good. Now all he had to do was get on the flight, enjoy the movie, and land in

Paris tomorrow. He wished everything he did were this easy.

12
Isabella

I called the manager at the country club and explained the situation. "Dean Guildford? Oh, my. I'm so sorry. Very sorry."

"What can you tell me about an employee named LeRoy?"

"Yes. LeRoy Gautonierre. Funny you should ask. He's been a waiter here for a number of years, but today, he quit. Just like that. Came into my office a couple of hours ago. Said he'd gotten an opportunity to attend Cordon Bleu in Paris and was going to open his own restaurant."

Instantly, I went on the alert. "He quit today?"

"This afternoon."

"What kind of employee has he been over the years?"

"Friendly. Members like him. But this past week, he's been a little spotty about showing up."

"Spotty? What do you mean?"

"Well, he asked for time off on Monday and Tuesday, but came back this morning."

Monday and Tuesday. *Dr. Hawthorne was killed on Monday, and Dr. Bloome's murder was attempted on Tuesday.* "I need to ask you about Thursday, Friday, and Saturday of last week."

"Just a moment. I'll get my calendar."

I heard him rustling papers before he came back on the line. "Let's see. His normal shift begins at 11:00 and ends at 11:00 four days a week, Monday through Friday. His day off is Thursday, but he comes in sometimes on the weekends. For instance, he requested to work the funeral reception for Mrs. Malcolm Guildford."

Quickly, I figured out that LeRoy was not accounted for at work during Victoria's and Dr. Barnes' murders. On the other hand, he was in New Haven and not Oxford when I was in England. So the Oxford job at Dr. Barnes' flat must have been a Brit.

"Can you give me his address and the names of family members, please?"

"You don't think that LeRoy—"

"We're just following leads right now. LeRoy may have some

information we need," I said, determined to be non-committal. "A forensics team is on the way to lift fingerprints off anything LeRoy might have touched before he left."

"Of course. Whatever we can do to help."

"I'd appreciate your confidentiality."

I heard him swallow. Then he repeated, "Of course."

Outside the Divinity School, I fought my way to the dean's house. A mass of journalists with cameras, microphones, and equipment as the now-familiar news reporters tried to get a word from me. I knocked on the front door. Paul cracked it open and let me squeeze through. Andrew's four children stood around him in various stages of disintegration. The two older ones were trying not to cry, but the young ones clung to Paul's trouser legs. "No comment," he said to the press, and closed the door.

"Any way to get rid of these people?" he asked. "The phone's been ringing nonstop. I finally took it off the hook."

"When Stewart Williams—FBI's SAC—gets here, he can give them a statement. One of the perks of being in charge," I said, glad I didn't have to do the honors. "Is Malcolm here?"

"He went home to Pappadad's house," said the youngest child, Theresa. She looked about five years old. "What happened to my daddy? Why are all these people here?"

I bent down and embraced the two youngest children. "I'm so sorry. Your mommy's here and she's going to be all right. Your cousin Paul is here, too."

Paul asked the oldest cousin to order pizza, then sat down with me in the front room. I couldn't help noticing the difference between Malcolm's showplace on St. Ronan and this homey house. This house looked lived in, messy with toys, pillows, stacks of papers. This house revealed evidence of children and love.

I showed Paul the post card. He looked at the front with the cathedral spires, bell towers and hand-carved detail in every nook and cranny. The fine print on the back announced that the first stone of the cathedral had been laid on September 29, 1907. "Over a hundred years," murmured Paul.

"What chapel is on the other side of the picture?" asked Isabella.

"Joseph of Arimathaea."

"He's the one that brought the faith to England, right?"

"So legend has it," said Paul. "It was his tomb that Jesus rose from. According to the fine print, the chapel is on the lower level under the crossing, almost the dead center of the cathedral. The pillars that hold up the whole structure are twenty-seven feet in diameter at this point."

"Okay, so we have a picture of the whole thing, and a picture of the heart of the cathedral's structure." *Why two pictures this time?*

"If Joseph of Arimathaea brought Christianity to England," Paul paused for a moment. "I wonder who brought Sethianism to England?"

I had no clue. "You know, Inspector Higginbotham thinks that the killers have ratcheted up the stakes a notch by going after your uncle."

Paul patted the head of Theresa, snuggling against him on the couch. "I can see that. He's a bit of a hotshot in theology, and internationally known."

"Up until now, the post cards have shown only separate parts of the cathedral. There's got to be a reason that this one has the split picture."

"They could be saying that the spread of Christianity to the West is Joseph's fault. And the National Cathedral is the symbol of everything they hate."

Made sense to me.

Paul turned the post card over. "Looks like we have a two for one special on this one. More than one message." He read aloud, "'In the tenth hour of Paradise, after the destruction on earth, Heaven will rejoice in a day of thanksgiving when the true believers triumph.'" He read it again silently. "It's a direct quote from the *Gospel of Judas*."

"It is?" I felt a flash of hope, but then sighed. "All apocalyptic literature speaks of earth's destruction."

"But the tenth hour is significant. In the *Gospel of Judas*, time is divided into ten hours of preparation for Paradise. The tenth hour is the final hour of triumph. The incorruptible generation ascends into Pleroma. It's like the rapture."

The rapture. The ecstatic moment when Christian believers are transported from earth to heaven. Huge in certain Christian circles. I just stared at Paul. Implications of this post card worked their way into my conscious mind.

Something big was going to happen soon.

"They're taunting us," I said.

"Maybe they're like the millennialists before 2000 rolled around.

Nervous that the world was going to end."

"Higginbotham is getting closer in Scotland, but…." I trailed off. "What shall I tell him the card means?"

Paul shook his head. "I don't know. Some sort of triumph over Christianity. Tomorrow is Thanksgiving—maybe they think heaven will have thanksgiving at the same time. Earth will be destroyed and the Sethians will be taken up. The rest of us poor sods are stuck eating turkey and turning into dust. Or ashes."

The message was too vague, too far out of my reach. "What does the Black Beatitude say?"

"Blessed are those who do not mourn, for they shall fear nothing."

I caught my breath. "Those who do *not* mourn." Oh, God. How did one not mourn? This message must be especially painful for Paul and his family today.

Paul closed his eyes. "This message is clear. It's the world's unvarnished truth. People who don't love, don't mourn. People who don't love, don't fear. They have nothing to lose."

"People who don't love, don't mourn. Or fear." Paul was right, right in a terrible way. "It also implies that people aren't worth mourning for. Regrets and sentiment can cripple you," a fact I knew only too well.

Paul continued. "In the real Beatitudes, the people who mourn are the ones who receive comfort in the end."

I thought Paul was going to cry. He whispered, "Love is always more powerful than fear." Theresa crawled up on his lap with her torn and bedraggled blanky. She sucked her thumb. He patted her hair until she closed her eyes. "I love you, Paulie," she said.

Paul was so choked up he couldn't answer.

How could God allow so much suffering to innocent people? Paul gathered the small child in his strong arms. She hugged his neck. He finally spoke. "I'm going to take Theresa up to Noe. You're welcome to stay and have pizza with us."

"I can't. I've got to get home. And you need to be with your family right now."

"Paulie, will you come upstairs and snuggle up with us?" asked Theresa. He nuzzled her. "You bet."

I watched Paul carry his little cousin upstairs.

13
Isabella

Had it been only five days since I last pulled out of my driveway? It would be good to get home, if only for long enough to change clothes. On the way, I called Detective Inspector Higginbotham and re-played Paul's ideas about the post card's messages.

"Hmm," he responded. "I'll have to sleep on it. Destruction of earth and triumph in Heaven. Immediate destruction? I fear they've given just enough information to confuse us."

As soon as I hung up, my cell rang again. It was Bob. "We won the grand prize on the lovely, luscious finger print we got from the post card."

"Wow, that was fast. Let me guess. It matched LeRoy Gautonierre's from the country club."

"You get a bonus prize for the correct answer. We got a match off his locker where he kept his uniform." Bob paused. "He's flown the coop. Nobody knows where he is, not even his ailing mother."

The excitement of the chase was heating up, like the moment I realized Harold Spicer III had to be the Campus Killer. At last we had a specific suspect. "He may be heading to Paris. Cordon Bleu."

I looked at my watch. "Let's check with Stewart Williams. See if we can get a picture out in the tri-state area on the news. We've got enough time if we hurry."

As I pulled into my driveway, my phone rang again, from the recesses of my purse. "O'Leary."

"We've got LeRoy's face all over the eastern seaboard," said Williams. "He can't leave by air, bus, or train. If you turn on the TV, you'll see his mug at the end of the evening news. And by the morning edition, his face will be in every newspaper." Williams sounded elated, almost as if we were members of the same team.

"Good."

14
LeRoy

LeRoy paid the cab driver and hustled into the lobby of LaGuardia Airport. Lines of people at the ticket counters zigzagged through mazes set up with black strips and chrome posts. He checked his watch, 7:20. His plane left at 8:40, so that gave him enough time, if the line didn't delay him. He found American Airlines and got behind a family going to St. Louis for Thanksgiving. A pre-teen girl with braces on her teeth and too much lipstick kept talking about her Aunt Lettie's dry Thanksgiving dressing.

Of course, Thanksgiving. That's why the airport was so crowded.

Idly, he watched the TV monitors, strategically placed so people waiting in line could view them.

Suddenly, he heard his name called out loud. At first he thought he was being paged over the loud speaker. Then his eye caught his very own picture on the television screen, a picture taken at the club with the manager. "LeRoy Gautonierre. Wanted for the murders of Victoria Guildford, Bonnie Barnes, and a third murder tonight in New Haven. If you see this man, please call the authorities. A phone number flashed across the bottom of the screen."

Every nerve in LeRoy's body tightened. It felt like his body temperature went up five degrees. *That was <u>him</u> on the news.* He hadn't murdered anybody. What was going on?

The newscaster continued, calling the three deaths the "Manuscript Murders." LeRoy did not wait to hear any more. *He had to get out of here.* His heart felt like a pulsating fist. *What do I do?*

Fight or flight. If he turned himself in, who would believe that an anonymous donor had given a mere waiter $100,000 out of the goodness of his heart? Oh, no. He'd been set up. He had to get out of there.

Staring at the floor, LeRoy shuffled out of the line. Most of the people waiting near him were talking with their fellow passengers, not watching the television. But the young pre-teen girl looked straight at him. She tugged on her mother's sleeve. They both stared as he crossed the crowded lobby, hoping to disappear into the crowd.

He ducked into a men's room and entered a stall. He had no time to decide what to do.

Someone had implicated him in the terrible murders the last few days. Who?

The newscaster had said three murders. Victoria last Thursday, then that scholar-lady from Oxford. Who was the third?

As LeRoy sat in the toilet stall, he remembered the post card that was supposed to give Dean Guildford a hint about getting his stolen goods back. What if Dean Guildford was the third murder?

Who had double-crossed him? LeRoy thought hard. *Who had set him up to take someone else's fall?*

What was he going to do? Blood was rushing so fast to his head, he could barely think. His vision started to blur. He wanted to scream. A plan, a plan. He had to have a plan.

LeRoy sat down on the john, and ran his hands through his hair. He knew he couldn't fly out of here. In fact, the tickets at the counter probably had his name all over them.

Whatever he did, he'd better do it fast.

Inside his bag, he had a hoodie. That would help. He put it on and pulled the hood down over his face. Keeping his eyes to the floor, he walked out of the men's room in the opposite direction from the family going to St. Louis. If he could make it to the exit fifty feet away, he could catch a cab and find a cheap hotel—with no televisions in the lobby.

LeRoy knew he had to get out of this airport fast. Ten more yards. Then he saw a uniform cop approach the door and begin to stop and question everyone leaving.

Same with the exit farther down. Without breaking his stride, LeRoy turned down a third passageway and headed toward another men's room, where he holed up in the corner stall. *He was trapped like a rat.*

15
Isabella

I answered the phone while changing clothes in my bedroom. "O'Leary."

"Stewart Williams here. Someone spotted a man who looks like LeRoy at LaGuardia. It's swarming with teams of FBI and locals at every gate and every exit. His name turned up on a flight to Paris at 8:40."

My watch said almost 8:40. "Are you sure it's him?"

"He was ID'd by a twelve-year-old girl ahead of him in line. Corroborated by her mother. He was in an American Airlines ticket line—his tickets waiting for him. Pretty convincing to me."

"Good. Call me when you get him." I hung up.

16
LeRoy

In the corner stall, LeRoy pulled out his razor and shaved his head. Saving some of the clumps of hair, he used his deodorant stick to apply them to his top lip. Then he bulked up his frame with tee shirts, trying to look heavier than he was. He'd swagger out the door like he owned the place. He watched cop shows all the time and always wondered what he would do in an emergency.

Now he had the chance to find out.

LeRoy left his duffel bag on the back of the toilet, after removing his ID and nametag. As he passed a man and a three-year-old going in, the little boy told his daddy, "I have to poop."

Brazenly, LeRoy strode toward the exit, closing in. He pretended that he was fishing for something in his pocket, turning his head the opposite direction from the police officer. He had almost made it out the circular door, when the man and the little boy came running after him. "Hey! You forgot your suitcase!"

Alerted, the police officer looked at LeRoy. LeRoy froze for one second, then panicked and started to run. He made it through the revolving door and elbowed his way through a crowd at the curb. He ripped the handle of a cab right out of a woman's hand. "The nerve," he heard her say.

He slammed the cab's door behind him, the fist of his heart pounding. "Anywhere," he told the cabbie, looking over his shoulder. "Triple pay if you get me out of here fast."

The cabbie stepped on the gas, but the traffic was grid locked. After inching through twenty yards, the cab couldn't move. Three officers thundered toward him on the sidewalk next to the cab.

LeRoy slid across the seat, and jerked open the door on the other side. Dodging cabs, pedestrians, and shuttle buses, he darted toward what he thought was the way out. He was faster than the cops. He was also in better shape, and he was running for his life.

Behind him, he saw all three cops falling farther behind. His adrenaline kicked in a second time. What he didn't see as he looked behind him, was a concrete pillar and another cop coming from the side. He ran face first into the pillar.

He never saw, heard, or felt four officers cuffing him and dragging him across the pavement to the police car.

17
Isabella

I parked in a Visitor's slot at the seminary, a few yards from Andrew's driveway. The officer moved the tape to let me onto the grounds. Stewart Williams was being miked on Andrew's porch. He was surrounded by the press, buzzing and clamoring.

When I saw him, he shouted, "Got him!"

"Yes!" My heart was pumping with exhilaration. Success had apparently made Williams friendly. I shot him a thumbs up. As I knew from just a few days ago, there was no high like catching a killer.

Paul came out the side door to stand beside me. "Way to go!" He gave me a high five, but then his face darkened. "The rat. LeRoy must be a superb actor. I thought he liked our family."

"Let's go hear the details," I said and moved closer to Williams.

We worked our way to the front. The quaint house with its picket fence porch and a rocking chair was the picture of peaceful and safe American life. It was also a stark contrast to the news Williams was about to give. Paul and I listened as Williams gave the world the details of LeRoy's capture. He concluded with, "We'll interrogate him when he arrives in New Haven, and will keep the press informed. Thank you."

After he'd taken off the mikes, I said to Williams, "So he's coming here."

Stewart replied, "On his way. Should be booked in an hour, ready for questioning."

"May we join you?"

Williams hesitated a moment, then said gruffly, "Yeah sure. Why not?"

18
LeRoy

LeRoy regained consciousness in the back of a police car careening down a highway. Sirens and lights were going full steam. He touched his forehead, caked with dried blood. He had a goose egg the size of the empire state building—on a head with no hair. And what was the stuff on his upper lip?

He closed his eyes and tried to remember what had happened. Why was he in the cage of a cop car hurtling through the night?

Then he remembered. The airport. He was running, getting away from some cops chasing him. He must have run into something.

Then he remembered the television with his picture.

He churned with fear. What could he say that could convince the police officers that he hadn't killed anyone? Who could he call for help? The anonymous benefactor from the country club had betrayed him and set him up. There were so many wealthy and powerful members at the club that he didn't even know where to start looking for the person who had done this.

The cop in the front passenger seat turned around and said, "Well, looky, looky. Sleeping Beauty just woke up."

LeRoy turned his head toward the window. He was not rising to the bait. He was not going to say another word until he got a lawyer. He'd seen too many of those cop shows. They lied, they threatened, they tried every way they could to make you confess to something you didn't do.

The cop from the passenger's seat continued. "Boy, I know a lot of people who're gonna be real happy to see you in about an hour."

LeRoy remembered now. He could have outrun those cops to California if he hadn't hit that fricking post.

LeRoy didn't open his mouth the whole trip. He didn't care if he never talked again. By the time they pulled up to the New Haven police station, he'd made a decision. He'd use his phone call to contact Malcolm Guildford. He was the one person LeRoy could trust to believe he was innocent.

19
Isabella

The crowd of news reporters began to disperse to get ready for the next newscast. I said to Paul, "We've got almost an hour before LeRoy gets here. Let's go to Malcolm's and see what he can tell us."

When we arrived at the house on St. Ronan, Malcolm was already in a plaid robe and slipper scuffs. He had folded the newspaper his lap and placed a scotch on the table beside his reading chair. We knocked on the door of his bedroom/sitting area. Malcolm sat alone staring at nothing. I couldn't see his chest rising and falling and feared for a moment that he had died in his chair.

Malcolm turned when he heard the knock. "Oh, let me get you something to drink. Wine? Scotch? Cranberry juice?"

"No thanks," said Paul.

"I'm not thirsty," I said.

Malcolm gestured toward the love seat across from him. "Please, sit down."

Almost before he got to the love seat, Paul said, "They've got LeRoy from the club in custody. He was trying to leave the country and they caught him at LaGuardia."

Malcolm's face showed surprise. "LeRoy Gautonierre? That LeRoy?"

Paul nodded.

Malcolm's face took on a puzzled look. "Are you telling me that LeRoy is the one who has committed these murders? But why?" Then Malcolm's face paled with the look of anger, grief, and despair I recognized from the first night after Victoria died. "Victoria. That son of a bitch killed my Victory, and now my brother!" He grabbed his heart and struggled to stand up. "I'll kill him myself."

"Sit down, Uncle Malcolm," said Paul, gently setting his uncle back down in the chair.

Malcolm turned to me. "Are they bringing him to New Haven?"

I nodded. "He'll be here in about half an hour."

"We're going down to question him," said Paul. "We'll nail him, I promise."

"Can you tell us a little bit about LeRoy's personality?" I asked. "Was he sneaky? Honest? Did he have any quirks you noticed? I don't suppose anyone in your family did something to make him angry."

"Absolutely not," said Malcolm. "I always gave him a large Christmas bonus, and got our friends to contribute too." His voice gained in intensity and anger. "And to think he repays our generosity like this!"

"Do you know whether he belonged to a secret group, or went to a Gnostic church?"

"He doesn't go to our church, I know that. The only time I've seen him at Trinity on the Green is at Victoria's funeral. The hypocrite. Showing up for the funeral of the woman he murdered in cold blood."

"LeRoy told the club manager he was going to Paris to Cordon Bleu. He was going to open his own restaurant. What was that all about?"

Paul looked confused at my statement. "Wait. When Malcolm and I saw LeRoy last Thursday, he said he had to spend all his savings on medical bills for his mother."

"Cordon Bleu!" said Malcolm. "He's out of his mind. He has no clue what it takes to get into a place like that." Malcolm looked close to collapse. He downed the last of his drink. "I'm going to bed now. I'm very weary." He brushed a tear from the corner of his eye. "I can't stand any more."

Paul helped him to the edge of his bed and pulled down the ironed, monogrammed sheets. Malcolm looked his nephew in the eye and said, "Just make sure they get him."

20
Gabriel

In Washington, D.C., Gabriel watched television in the apartment that the Sethians had rented near Adams Morgan. He flicked the remote control constantly with impatience, not really watching anything. At midnight, he loaded the four boxes of hymnals and Prayer Books into the rented mini-van. For security reasons, the Washington Patriarch had provided a van with the logo for the Church Publishing Company painted it on the side. Gabriel had further altered the license plates, just for good measure. Authenticity was the key to a successful job. And after botching Dr. Bloome's murder, Gabriel really needed success on this one.

Winding around the District until he reached Wisconsin Avenue, he turned into the cathedral grounds. At night, the cathedral seemed even bigger, larger than life, and illuminated with spotlights highlighting its status as the monument it was. He couldn't help feeling overwhelmed. He hoped the bomb technician had given him enough C-four to do the trick.

Gabriel followed signs to the Chapel of the Good Shepard, the only part of the cathedral open twenty-four seven. He'd researched the cathedral's command post with all the security staff and skirted that area. For extra good measure, he wore a baseball cap with a brim that hid his face. He was taking no chances in case they had a surveillance video.

Gabriel found the chapel and toted in the boxes, one by one. He left them stacked along the inside wall near the door. He'd put a few real hymnals and Prayer Books on the top in every box, so if someone discovered them in the wee hours, they wouldn't suspect anything. Not likely, but you never knew. Tomorrow he'd come back as a tourist for the big event and place the boxes in the Joseph of Arimathaea Chapel, right before the service.

In case he was being taped, he knelt down in the pew and prayed, "God, please let me pull this off."

Then he went back to apartment to catch a few winks before the big day.

21
Isabella

I stood with Paul outside the one-way mirror of the interrogation room. A woman named Meg Tyler was the FBI Special Agent in Charge for the state of Connecticut, but she had flown to California a few hours earlier.

LeRoy was marched into a sparse room with a table and a couple of chairs. LeRoy looked straight at Paul through the open door before he entered the interrogation room.

"It's him," said Paul. "He's shaved his head, and has some fuzz or dirt or something on his upper lip. It also looks like he ran into a post."

"That's exactly what he did. Don't tell my boss, but a pillar at La-Guardia gets credit for the collar." Stewart Williams buttoned his suit coat getting ready to talk to LeRoy.

Stewart addressed Paul. "His phone call was to your uncle, who refused to talk with him. Imagine the nerve, killing two family members and asking the survivor to represent him. Came up with some cockamamie story about an anonymous benefactor funding cooking school. Showed us a fake letter from Cordon Bleu that supposedly admitted him."

"At least he's consistent with his story," I said. "That's what he told the club manager."

Paul shook his head. "Two-faced son-of-a—. How could he—" Paul slammed his fist in the palm of his other hand. "He duped us all."

Williams hitched up his belt before he sat down across from LeRoy. A guard took his place in the corner of the interrogation room. Paul stood next to me watching through the glass, his eyes transfixed on the scene behind the glass.

"I can't help it," said Paul. "I just want to beat the bloody pulp out of him." I placed my hand on his arm as he stood rigid with fury.

"What's your name?" asked Stewart.

Silence. LeRoy stared straight ahead.

"Okay, Mr. Smartstuff. Why were you running at LaGuardia? Your plane late?"

Leroy ignored the sarcasm and said nothing.

Stewart walked around to the other side of the table. He shouted, "Hey, you. I'm talking to you here. Are you going to pretend you don't hear me, you murdering dick?"

Silence.

Stewart Williams continued to pummel him with questions, but LeRoy stonewalled him. LeRoy wouldn't give his name, wouldn't look him in the eye, simply stared through Williams at his own reflection—which meant he was staring straight at Paul and me.

LeRoy was a very different suspect from Harold Spicer III, whose smooth talk went on for hours.

The questioning continued. Stewart got louder and more agitated, at one point lifting the table and letting it drop back down with a crash on the floor. I whispered to Paul, "You okay?" I asked.

"No. I've never been so angry in my life. I want to batter his face in. I have to remind myself over and over and over—this man is innocent until proven guilty." I noticed his hand balled into a white fist.

Williams continued to badger and threaten LeRoy, to no avail. He even tried sweet-talking him to get him to say something, anything.

"The worst part is," continued Paul, his facial muscles tightening. "If my family is ever going to heal from this week from hell, we've got to find a way to forgive him."

Forgive? How could he speak of forgiveness at a time like this? I stared at him in disbelief. He was serious.

Williams got up and stood behind LeRoy. He leaned down near his ear, probably whispering what would happen to him if he didn't talk. Then he shouted. LeRoy jumped, as if he'd burst an eardrum. But he still wouldn't look at him, or speak.

After a long time of total silence on LeRoy's part, Williams left the room. "Horse's ass," he said, red-faced with frustration. "We'll leave him alone for awhile. Pretty soon he'll have to ask for a restroom. We'll tell him 'no.' Maybe then he'll start talking."

Williams paced the hall. I settled into a chair to wait him out. Suddenly LeRoy—looking straight at the mirror—said, "I want to talk to Paul St. Clair."

With a rush of adrenaline. I sat up straight and looked over at Paul. Was this a good idea?

"What do you think?" I asked Stewart. Then I turned back to Paul. "You want me to go in there with you?"

"Yeah. Okay. No," said Stewart. Then, "Let's send Paul in alone and see how he does. LeRoy can't attack him; he's cuffed to the table."

Paul stood up.

Williams nodded. "Go on, soldier. Show your stuff."

I hoped Paul would handle the situation well. I doubt he knew either the rigors or the unwritten rules of the box, but sometimes innocence could do the job when hardness and persistence failed.

Paul hesitated, probably debating where to sit. He took a seat at an angle, glancing briefly at the window to make sure I had a clear view.

As soon as Paul entered the room, LeRoy's demeanor changed. "Dr. St. Clair, I didn't do this. I didn't murder nobody. You've got to believe me." LeRoy's eyes lost their glaze of coldness, and he appeared desperate as he pled with Paul.

Paul shook his head. "LeRoy, there's too much evidence against you." Paul gave no clue of the turmoil and anger he must be feeling.

"I'm being framed, man." He looked like a hunted animal.

"And who would be framing you, LeRoy?" Paul stared at him with a look that combined disdain and skepticism.

Good try, I thought.

"Someone at the club," said LeRoy.

Paul said evenly, "I don't believe you."

"You've got to believe me. It's the truth. The Guildfords have always been a stand-up family, but now your uncle won't even talk to me."

"And you're surprised? Victoria and Andrew are dead."

"Not by me. I've got to talk to someone who'll trust me." LeRoy's eyes begged. "Please, just listen."

Paul's face began to flush. "Make it quick."

LeRoy looked earnestly at Paul. "Somebody at the club is setting me up for this. I swear to God." He told Paul about the chain of events. "Somebody wired me fifty grand to help me start the restaurant. You can check my bank account."

At this point, Paul leaned into LeRoy's face and said, "If we find fifty grand in your bank account, we can assume that someone hired you to commit the murders. You better give up the name of who contracted you. Otherwise, you're taking the fall alone."

LeRoy begged, "You've gotta hear me out. All I did was deliver a post card to your uncle's office. I thought it gave a clue where the manuscript was."

"Look me in the eye and tell me you didn't kill my Aunt Victoria or my Uncle Andrew."

I held my breath. Was LeRoy going to lie? LeRoy looked squarely at Paul. "I did not kill anybody."

I almost believed him. I knew there had to be at least one other person out there, a mastermind. In England, someone—not LeRoy—had destroyed Bonnie Barnes' room. Edward Hobbs—not LeRoy—had assaulted me. Whether LeRoy committed the murders in the United States or not, others had to be involved.

Was it possible LeRoy had been framed to keep the group secret?

Possible...but how likely?

Paul continued. "What about Dr. Barnes? Did you kill Dr. Barnes?"

"No, sir, I did not," pleaded LeRoy.

"How do you account for the fact that you have no alibi for the time of her murder?"

LeRoy looked baffled. "How do you know I don't have an alibi? What time was she killed?"

"Friday around 7:30 in the morning."

LeRoy looked away.

"So where were you?" asked Paul.

"I was asleep, same as every morning. I don't get up until 9:00 because my shift doesn't start until later."

"You know your fingerprints were all over the card found outside the door of my uncle's office."

"Of course they were! I delivered the card myself. I thought the card was some sort of code to get the manuscript back."

"It's a code all right. A code of death."

"I swear to God—"

"Don't bring God into this," said Paul. He stood up to leave the interrogation room. I thought for a split second that he was going to strike LeRoy across the face. Then his innate urbanity won. Instead, he strode out, slamming the door.

The guard hoisted LeRoy up from his seat. "Let's get him out of here."

"Someone is getting away with murder!" shouted LeRoy.

22
Isabella

I patted Paul on his back when he came out of the interrogation room. "You did well."

"All criminals say they didn't do it. We'll crack him yet," added Williams. "We've got a team interviewing his neighbors, his friends, everyone who ever said hello to him in the grocery store." He wiped his brow with a handkerchief.

I felt drained, but I was too wired to quit. I turned to Paul. "Would you be willing to go over everything we have from the post cards one more time before we call it a night?"

"Yes. Let's go back to Malcolm's. He and Victoria have an industrial strength coffee maker with the best beans from all over the world."

"We won't disturb your uncle?"

"No way. The doctor put him on sleeping pills last week."

We entered Malcolm's home through the front door into a hallway glowing faintly from a light still on in the kitchen. Walking past the living room on one side and the open dining area on the right, I thought the house looked like a Broadway stage set before the lights went on.

I whispered, "I've always thought these houses along St. Ronan were beautiful and wanted to see one inside. But this is not the kind of tour I had in mind. Paul, I'm so sorry about your family and what you've been through."

Paul's jaw line tensed. "We can't quit until we get the whole group. Leroy is probably just the tip of the iceberg." He flicked the light on in the kitchen. "Let me get the coffee started, then I'll show you the upstairs. How about 'Jamaican Java'?"

"Great," I said. "But I didn't mean a literal house tour."

"No, it's good." Paul ground the beans and started the coffee maker.

"We have to wait for the coffee anyway. It would be a tribute to Victoria if you saw her home. She put her heart and soul into making this old house a welcoming place." I thought I heard Paul's voice catch as he spoke of his aunt.

"I would love to see the upstairs."

After he started the coffee, Paul took me up the grand staircase near the dining area, not the smaller stairs I'd seen off the kitchen. The left side of the second floor contained two bedroom suites, each done in different color variations of the same theme, floral. The right side of the second floor held a small ballroom with a kitchen behind it, off to the side. "Malcolm and Victoria had started having parties again," Paul said sadly.

We climbed another set of stairs to the third floor, where a hallway led to two doors at the end, one on the left and one on the right. Paul opened the left door. "The attic." I saw a storage room as big as my whole house, filled with enough Christmas ornaments to decorate my entire block. The room had no windows.

The door on the right was an office, with a huge desk and dusty bookshelves. "This was my grandfather Pappadad's escape. He kept mysteries in here, his 'trash' reading, he called it."

Stars shone brightly through a small garret window.

"Looks smaller than I remember," said Paul. "But I haven't been up here in twenty years." Paul ran his fingers over the dust on the desk, leaving a fingerprint.

As I watched him, something clicked in my mind. "You know, the only fingerprints on the post card were LeRoy's. None of the other post cards left at the crime scenes had any fingerprints at all. Doesn't that seem strange to you?"

Paul closed the door to the office. "What do you mean?"

"Well, it's very convenient to have someone locked up for all the crimes committed last week. Think. If someone put the post card in LeRoy's locker at the club for him to deliver, and if everything were legitimate—"

Paul caught on. "Then someone else's fingerprints would have been on the card too. The person who bought the card. The person who typed the messages. The person who wanted the post card delivered."

"Right." I paused. "Maybe LeRoy really is being set up."

Back in the kitchen, I accepted Irish whiskey in my coffee, along with heavy cream. Paul poured more whiskey than coffee in his cup. I fished in my purse for my notebook. "Let's go back over the messages one by one."

"Calling cards," said Paul. "The calling cards of death."

I examined the messages and my notes. "First was the message in the safe. Then, each death produced another post card with a twisted clue."

"Each message matches the picture on the front. Each card gives us more information."

"The Sethians must really despise the National Cathedral," I said.

"Let's go back to the first clue. We knew the group responsible because of the anagram in the safe. The Sethian Brotherhood. Death: Hero on this orb."

"Some hero. I guess they really aren't afraid to die."

"Or kill people." Paul sipped his coffee. "Then the first post card had a picture of creation. Taking it back to the beginning."

"Like their creation story is the real one, not the Bible. Yaldabaoth and the flawed world over and against pure spirit. Seth as the divine one, the forerunner of Jesus."

Paul nodded. "And the first Black Beatitude—mercilessness is blessed."

I let the warm liquid warm my throat. "They're warning us that they will have no mercy, so watch out."

"Okay, then the second card with the picture of the war chapel."

"They think they're in a holy war. They're letting us know that they are the spiritual elite, who will live in heaven while the rest of us turn back to dust."

Paul picked up the train of thought. "Then the third post card, with that business about toleration and balancing the scales of injustice. They wanted to make the point that Dr. Hawthorne's speech was prejudicial— the *Gospel of Judas* was rejected in the early days, and Hawthorne was saying that the decision was right. Even today."

I nodded. "Followed by post card number four and the blank statue of Judas as an insult to the Brotherhood. And the Black Beatitude about pride."

"They're saying that they're proud of being followers of Judas because Jesus told Judas he was going to win in the long run."

We sat a moment in silence, reflecting and sipping the coffee.

"The question on the last card is Joseph of Arimathaea. Is it the borrowed tomb? Is it that he was the one who supposedly brought Christianity to England?" I asked.

"I don't know. But for some reason, the Sethians are making a connection with Joseph of Arimathaea."

Paul continued. "Then, there's the double message. Thanksgiving in heaven at the tenth hour."

"And the Black Beatitude, about not mourning."

Paul reflected for a moment, holding his coffee cup cupped in both hands. "You know, the other disciples mourned the death of Jesus. They were sad and lost up there in that upper room. Judas was the one who went out and killed himself." He paused. "It's just occurred to me that Judas suicide wasn't in mourning Jesus' death. Judas wasn't even regretting what he'd done. He was simply taking the most expedient way to get to heaven, where he would bask in the pure spirit of heaven as the only obedient follower."

"Judas didn't fear anything."

"And neither do the Sethians."

"Oh, great. But there's one thing I still don't get. After hundreds of years of silence and secrecy, what has triggered them into taking action? Public action. They had to leak their own post cards to the press to make sure the world was getting the message."

Paul quoted, "'The tenth hour of Paradise. Destruction of the earth. Heaven will give thanksgiving. True believers triumph.'" He paused. "It can't be a coincidence that tomorrow is Thanksgiving."

"I agree. But their venue for death is closed—no conferences. All scholars will be eating turkey with their families."

"Something's going to happen tomorrow. I can feel it in my bones," said Paul.

23
Isabella

Depression began to take root as I felt my spirits go flat again. I sat quietly with Paul at the kitchen nook with a bay window looking out over a garden. Spreading my notes in front of me, I searched them for what they could tell me. The notes stared back in silence.

Looking out the window, I said, "My mother loves to garden. She grows vegetables."

"Victoria always used fresh herbs. She grew her own. Rather, Malcolm grew them for her. She hated gardening, but Malcolm loves puttering around in his yard." Paul sighed.

Getting toward the end of the coffee, I began to feel smothered, as if the hot blanket of all the world's sadness, including my own, were draped over my shoulders.

I had known the Guildford family less than a week, but I felt connected to them in a way that defied reason. I identified with Malcolm's loss, knowing what it was like to lose a spouse. Paul had not scorned me when I unburdened my secrets to him. He had understood, beyond words.

Sitting in Victoria Guildford's kitchen, I sensed I was on the verge of another crisis, this one spiritual. After this case, I couldn't go back to an empty faith. Yet I was scared of what lay ahead. "I need to ask you something," I said to Paul.

"Sure."

"The Sethians are willing to kill and to die for their belief in Pleroma and the triumph of Judas. I need you to tell me why the Christian God is better than Pleroma."

Paul hugged the coffee mug with his hands. I knew he'd give me an honest answer and not some spiritual claptrap. After a moment, he said, "A purely spiritual God is tempting, isn't it?" said Paul. "Bodies are such a burden, so vulnerable. So pathetically easy to destroy. Probably took Andrew just ten minutes to lose fifty years of life." Paul took a big slug of his coffee and Irish whiskey. "Matter is definitely flawed."

Paul's gaze drifted out the window to Malcolm's garden, tended and proper. No weeds or undesirable elements growing out of place. I sipped my coffee and watched him. He had no idea how much his words mattered.

"The difference is with the Christian God, it's personal. God loves *me*. God loves *you*. When you die as a Christian, you go to a place God has prepared especially for you. Pleroma is a pleasant concept, but vague and impersonal."

He paused. "And God is a gentleman. He never forces Himself on people."

"What do you mean?"

"Is it a love affair if the other person is forced to love you?"

A love affair? I caught my breath. Love? Theology wasn't about love. It was about feeling miserably guilty for your sins. It was trying to figure out what you'd done to deserve losing your baby and your husband. A love affair? Between God and His creatures?

"Okay, then explain suffering. How—" I couldn't finish.

The way Paul looked at me, I knew he'd spent time a fair amount of time in the same hellhole of doubt as I had.

"I don't know that I have an answer. Because suffering brings us closer to God? I know that's true. Because this life isn't the end of the story? Because He always turns things around in the end? Because—well—there are just some things nobody can understand." He paused. "Or explain." He paused again, this time for longer. "But once you've felt it, you can't ever go back."

"I see," I whispered. But I wasn't sure I did.

We sat for a long time, looking out the bay window at the back yard, with lights placed strategically here and there to highlight the terraced gardens.

As I was about to leave, Paul said, "The post card's message keeps going through my head. The tenth hour. Destruction of the earth. Triumph in Heaven."

"Wait," I said. "It wasn't the destruction *of* earth. It was destruction *on* earth."

"You're right," said Paul. "I've been thinking of global destruction, an atomic bomb. What if the destruction is smaller, or symbolic?"

"Or localized?" I paused. "I wonder what difference one preposition makes?"

Chapter Eight
THANKSGIVING DAY

1
John

Five hours ahead of American Eastern Standard time, John McCullough shut off his computer and went to eat breakfast at 7:00 in the morning. Mrs. Wallace bustled about in the medieval-sized kitchen with a roaring fire that reflected off modern chrome appliances.

"There you are, Mr. McCullough." She set a plate of fried toast, mushrooms, and eggs in front of him. "And your orange juice and tea, just like you like it."

"Thank you, Mrs. Wallace. It's going to be a splendid day. You know the Americans are eating turkey today. For supper I'd like a meal in honor of their Thanksgiving. Do you think you can arrange that? Turkey and dressing and cranberry sauce." He would have his own private thanksgiving feast for dinner.

"Yes, sir. I'm quite sure I have recipes, and I have to make a trip to town this morning anyway. Anything else?"

"Yes. Don't forget the green beans, steamed with a little butter." He paused. "I'll be going on to bed in a few minutes. This is important. Do not let Rupert wake me until 2:30. Is that clear? But tell him not to wake me any later, either. I'll be watching a national cricket match at 3:00." A cricket match that would be interrupted with a most delectable news flash.

John ate his toast and mushrooms. Nothing had ever tasted so good.

2
Isabella

I couldn't sleep. I got up at 5:15, dressed, and went to my desk at the police station. There I found a detailed email from Higginbotham, giving a blow-by-blow description of the conversation he had with Mrs. Wallace, the housekeeper at John McCullough's castle.

When he called the castle, Mrs. Wallace had indeed remembered the pleasant Detective Inspector. In fact, she said, "Yes, sir. Mr. McCullough was in a lovely mood after you left." She went on to commend her employer. "You know," she said, "he's a Member of Parliament. Takes his job serious, too."

Higginbotham apparently saw his opportunity and jumped in. "It's always encouraging to hear that our elected officials are working in Britain's best interests. Does Mr. McCullough ever have any fellow Members to visit him at the castle? To talk over business, or maybe for house parties on the weekends? You know how the queen has guests at Balmoral. Hunting and whatnot."

"Yes," Mrs. Wallace had told him. "Four times a year, he has—" Then she stopped. She cleared her throat. "I mean, well, no, not exactly," she said. (Higginbotham had pegged her as a gossip. I could practically see his delight at her chatty slip.)

Higginbotham had waited her out for a pretty long silence. Finally, she said, "Mr. McCullough has instructed me….well, this is not a good question right now, really."

Higginbotham tried again in his best chummy voice. "Surely, he must have guests. Government officials always do."

Again, silence. Then Mrs. Wallace said, "Mr. McCullough enjoys his solitude." She added, "And his privacy."

"He never has company?"

"No. Well, his brother and his family come once a year, but that's all."

"Are you sure?"

I smiled to myself, picturing Higginbotham patiently waiting out the garrulous housekeeper.

Higginbotham gleefully ended his email with Mrs. Wallace's final comment. "I'll tell you what, if you call back after 2:30 this afternoon, he can tell you all about his guests. Yes, that would be best."

Gotcha, I said aloud.

3
Paul

On Thanksgiving morning, Paul got out of bed at Malcolm's house and showered. His parents had flown in again last night in their private plane, a quick and miserable turn-around from Texas. They were still asleep in their suite in the main house.

Paul walked into the kitchen and made fresh coffee, this time Hazelnut. It was early, around 7:15. Malcolm was also still asleep.

Paul retrieved the paper from the driveway and settled into the breakfast nook. As expected, the headlines featured a picture of Stewart Williams standing on the steps of Uncle Andrew's house.

What a way to start Thanksgiving Day. Only when he saw the picture did he remember that the family's Thanksgiving dinner had been lost in the tragedy and chaos last night. He made an executive decision. He would order dinner from the club for tonight. At Malcolm's again. His mother could coordinate it. They could bring Pappadad, Paul's grandfather, who was still in blissful ignorance about Andrew. Noe and the children could come.

Depending on how things went today, he might even get up the nerve to see if Isabella would join them. She said something yesterday about having Thanksgiving at noon with her family. She'd be free in the evening.

Paul was depressed just thinking about Thanksgiving. No. He would not allow himself to sink into the slough of despondency. Grief was proper, but not right now. Today was Thanksgiving, a day set aside centuries ago by our forefathers under a different set of bleak circumstances. He was determined to give thanks.

If life had taught him only one thing, it was to look for the blessings. They were always there.

He took a swig of coffee and flipped the paper to national news. Big headlines: "American Presiding Bishop and Archbishop of Canterbury Celebrate at special Thanksgiving Service, Washington Cathedral."

Every national Christian leader would be there—Methodists, Lutherans, Presbyterians, the Catholic Bishop of Washington, even a couple of Baptists—in an ecumenical show of support. He read on. The Vice-President of the United States was also coming. The place would be packed.

It hit him. Washington Cathedral filled with Christian leaders. What time was the service? *Ten o'clock.* The tenth hour. Destruction on earth.

Yes, that would do it. What else could this week be leading up to?

He dropped the paper, and then dropped his phone trying to extricate it from his pocket. He fumbled Isabella's number before he finally got it. She was already downtown.

"Washington Cathedral," he said, his heart pumping. "The murders so far have all been warm-up exercises. The big bash—the Sethian triumph—is at 10:00 in a special service with our Presiding Bishop and the Archbishop of Canterbury and everybody who's anybody and a lot of other innocent people." He paused. "Has to be. All the clues point toward it."

"Calm down," said Isabella.

"Communion wine. Poison in the Communion wine. Can you think of a better way to kill a thousand people with no one suspecting?"

"I'll tell Stewart. Gotta go. I've got another call on the line. How fast can you get over here?"

"See you in ten minutes."

4
Isabella

I stabbed the call-waiting button on my phone. Before I had a chance to identify myself, Detective Inspector Higginbotham said, "Did you get my email? John McCullough has guests four times a year."

"Yes. Good work."

Higginbotham continued, "What about LeRoy, your suspect? Has he ever been to Glasgow?"

"FBI is still gathering information. Listen—" I stood up and started pacing in front of my desk. "Paul's come up with an idea here, too. Do you remember saying how something obvious was staring us in the face?"

"Yes, not in those terms precisely, but—"

"We may have been blind." I told him about the service at the National Cathedral in less than three hours.

He said, "Oh, my. Let's not jump to conclusions."

"Today is Thanksgiving. The latest post card message mentions destruction on earth, and giving thanks in heaven when true believers triumph."

"Yes, but—"

I added, "The tenth hour. The service is at 10:00. A little poison in the wine, and presto—you've got a church filled with dead people."

"Just a second." I heard the rustle of a newspaper. "Here it is in the London *Times*. 'Archbishop of Canterbury joins American Presiding Bishop and other Christian leaders in a rapprochement Thanksgiving Day service. A symbol of Christian unity, the service hopes to repair relations within the Anglican Communion."

I thought of something else. "The pictures of the National Cathedral on the post cards weren't just hints. They were the vehicle for a larger message." I couldn't stop pacing, my blood pounding. *The National Cathedral was the scene of the showdown...less than three hours from now.* "It's got to be the National Cathedral."

Higginbotham caught his breath, "It's a definite possibility." He continued, "Might I suggest that the FBI prepare a team to investigate?"

"I'm on it." Thanksgiving or not, I couldn't call Stewart fast enough.

5
Gabriel

Thanksgiving morning, Gabriel wore the Brooks Brother's suit he found hanging in the closet of the apartment in the Adams Morgan section of Washington, D.C. The Washington Patriarch had also left a tie, shirt, and shoes, all carefully selected so he'd blend in with the privileged crowd at the cathedral.

Finding a parking spot was already difficult, but he finally found a place several blocks away. He had trouble parallel parking the van. A sign down the street said, "No Parking," but he figured it was okay on a holiday. Three other cars had parked there.

Gabriel entered the cathedral from the west, staring again at its towering magnificence. He felt proud to be a part of this scheme. Not only would his actions guarantee him a place in the eternal bliss of heaven, the event this morning would make national and international history. It probably took a hundred years to build this monument, and it would be destroyed in a mere second, with one push of the button by Gabriel himself, the Messenger of Life. Such was the destiny of matter.

When he walked up to the cathedral door, a young girl was already handing out maps and service bulletins. Gabriel found the stairs and made his way down to the Chapel of the Good Shepherd. His book boxes were lined up, just as he left them. He tucked the brochure in his lapel pocket, then he carried the four boxes to the Joseph of Arimathaea Chapel, placing each box at the base of the pillars, out of the way so that nobody would notice them.

The pillars were massive. Once again, he hoped Darrington had done his homework and given him enough C-4 to blow the cathedral to smithereens.

He checked his watch. A little less than two hours. He'd distribute the books in the pew racks while few people were around. After that, he'd give himself a formal tour of the doomed cathedral, and then leave right before the service started.

All going according to plan. And Gabriel really needed the plan to work.

6
Isabella

I stood with Stewart in the detectives' room waiting for Paul. "I've got a chopper on the way," said Stewart, when Paul joined us. "We're going to D.C."

"I hope I'm not crazy—" Paul said.

"No," I interrupted. "It's got to be what the whole week has been leading up to."

"Even if it's not, we can at least check the situation out." Stewart spun around to Paul. "Communion wine. Good call."

"Can't think of a faster way to wipe out two Anglican bigwigs, leaders from at least five other denominations, and a thousand believers in a national monument to Christianity," I said.

"And the Vice-President, don't forget." Stewart was all over his phone. He put it on speaker so Paul and I could hear. "This the Cathedral? Give me the head of security." He tapped his foot. "Hello, this is Special Agent Williams, FBI, in charge of the Manuscript Murders. We have reason to suspect that the final target is the special service at Washington Cathedral this morning. We need to call off the service."

An officious voice on the other end said, "Excuse me? Call off the service? What do you mean 'final target'?"

"Have you been following the series of murders this week in New

Haven and New York?"

"Yes, but what does that have to do with the cathedral? This is Washington, not New York or New Haven. Do you think someone will die here this morning? Why?"

"No, I think it's more than that. An international cult-group is behind the murders. We think that they've targeted the National Cathedral for something big."

"And what information are you basing this conclusion on?"

I interjected, "We've deciphered coded messages from post cards left at the scene of the murders this week."

"What, specifically, do the cards say? Have you received, for example, a bomb threat?"

Stewart said, "Who the hell are you? Don't you realize the implications if –"

"Your evidence seems pretty thin to call off the service. Sir."

I couldn't believe the resistance we were getting from someone who was supposed to guard the security of a national monument. I interjected again, "Sir, this is Isabella O'Leary, from the New Haven Police Department. We found in the files a list of cathedrals—"

"Are you the one who caught the Campus Killer?"

"Yes, I am." At least I had his attention. I just hoped he would listen.

"That was a pretty cagey catch. I was reading about it—"

I cut in. "Thank you. However, we may have an international incident on our hands soon. Considering all the evidence combined, we need to—"

"With all due respect, Ma'am, I know you did a great job on that New Haven fellow, but this is different. We can't call off this morning's service based on clues from a post card. People have already started arriving to get seats."

Stewart joined in. "Hey—"

"I'm sorry. This is my cathedral, and I haven't seen a ripple. The Secret Service are here and more will be surrounding the Vice-President when he arrives. They checked out the cathedral yesterday and didn't find anything."

"Fine. I'll call my boss in Washington, and she'll talk to you. We'll be there in an hour." Stewart hung up. "Idiots," he exploded.

I balled my fists in frustration, my fingernails cutting into my flesh. "We've got to get there ASAP. The Secret Service won't be looking for poisoned wine."

"Right," said Stewart. "I'm out of the FBI in a few months." He hitched up his pants. "I'd rather look like an overprotective fool guarding a bunch of religious hot dogs than be remembered as the fool who couldn't read the tea leaves."

"I'm with you," agreed Paul.

"This disaster ain't happening on my watch." Stewart patted his gut and checked his watch one more time.

I said, "If we arrive by 9:00, that will give us an hour to check things out before the service starts."

7
Paul

While the three of them raced to the airport in the FBI car, Paul took a call from Malcolm on his cell. "How are you this morning? Did you get any sleep?" asked his uncle, sounding groggy.

"Yes," said Paul.

Malcolm asked, "Where are you? I looked in the guest room, and you weren't there."

Paul said, "We're on the way to D.C. When I read the paper this morning, I realized that the group behind the murders is going out with a big one this time. We think they've targeted the National Cathedral's special service."

Silence on the other end. "Hogwash. That doesn't make any sense. They've been poisoning individuals. Scholars. Why would they go after the National Cathedral? There aren't any scholars there today."

"We don't know what's going on. They may be trying to kill the two primate bishops and the Vice-President of the United States, or poison the congregation, or blow up the place. Maybe nothing, but don't worry. The FBI's on it, and we'll be there in a little less than an hour."

"Don't go, Paul. Why do you have to go? We need you here. Your parents are here."

"Don't worry, Uncle Malcolm. We'll be back in time for Thanksgiving dinner. I've ordered it to be delivered from the club. Mother can handle things. You two can go ahead and get started with Noe on the funeral arrangements."

"I beg you to reconsider. This whole thing is preposterous."

What was with his uncle? Malcolm was on the verge of whining. Paul tried another approach, appeasement. "Plus, we're not completely sure of LeRoy. Even if he did the murders, he's probably just the front man. We have to go check this out, we just have to."

"Please come home, Andrew—"

The car pulled into New Haven Regional Airport, where the helicopter was ready to fly. Paul said, "I've got to go."

He heard his uncle muttering something before the roar of the blades cut him off.

8
Malcolm

Malcolm hung up, furious. John McCullough had been determined to taunt the authorities as well as give out information. Months ago, Malcolm had told John that the last message on the post card gave too much away. "Our FBI is smarter than you think."

Ironically, John had been right. The FBI probably couldn't have figured it out. It was his nephew. He hadn't counted on the Guildford brains working against him on the other side.

Malcolm dialed the number he had never had to call before. He'd committed the number to memory over eight years ago, when he'd been promoted to American Patriarch, in the Circle of Five. He knew the Grand Patriarch would be at home today, waiting as eagerly as Malcolm.

"Hello," answered a female voice, probably the housekeeper.

"Yes, I need to speak with John McCullough."

"I'm sorry, Mr. McCullough is asleep. Can you call back at 2:30?"

"Two-thirty?" Malcolm gasped. Then he remembered the time change. Two-thirty was about an hour and thirty minutes away. "No, I can't. I'm calling from the United States. Could you please wake him now?"

"I'm terribly sorry, sir," said the housekeeper. "He gave me strict instructions not to wake him until 2:30."

Malcolm was ready to boil. "You wake him now and tell him I've lost my umbrella."

The housekeeper didn't say anything for a minute. Then, in a kind voice she said, "I'm sorry you've lost your umbrella, sir. But that's even less of a reason to wake Mr. McCullough." She paused. "You'll have to call back later." She hung up.

Malcolm dialed back immediately.

"Hello?" the housekeeper answered.

"Let me speak to John's valet." Malcolm had trouble keeping his voice civil.

"Is this the gentleman with the lost umbrella?"

"Yes it is. Forget the umbrella. Get the valet." Rupert would know the umbrella code. Obviously, John kept his housekeeper in the dark.

"I'm sorry, he's out on the grounds."

Malcolm could not believe this was happening. "Can you reach him?"

"No, sir. He's out in the Hummer."

"Can you go out and track him down?"

"I'm sorry, sir. I've got a special dinner to prepare, and there's no telling where he is."

Malcolm nearly threw the phone across the room in frustration. "Go wake him and tell him it's an emergency."

"An emergency in the States, sir? I don't know what he could do about it from here."

"JUST WAKE HIM UP, DO YOU HEAR ME?"

Silence. "I'm sorry, sir, there's no need to scream. I've been given orders, and I want to keep my job. You'll just have to call back later." She hung up.

Everything was going down the toilet because of a stupid housekeeper. The Grand Patriarch was the only one who knew the name and number of the Washington Look Out, and he was asleep.

Germany lost the war because no one would wake Hitler the morning of the Normandy Invasion. All Malcolm could do was sit at home and watch the Brotherhood's careful planning go down the drain.

Almost as bad, one of the few people he cared about on the face of the earth—Paul—was headed toward the thick of it. If he got caught in the crossfire and died, then where would Malcolm be?

9
Isabella

In the helicopter, I listened to Stewart shout into the phone to his boss in Washington. "We're going to land on the cathedral grounds!

Meet us there!"

"It will probably take them as long to get to the cathedral as it will for us," said Stewart.

I checked my watch. "It's 8:45."

Stewart nudged the pilot, who shouted back over his shoulder. "Touchdown in twenty minutes!"

That would give us almost an hour before the service started.

10
Gabriel

Gabriel loved the cathedral's gift shop. The one thing he liked about Christmas was decorating. He couldn't get enough of the ornaments. The cathedral had already put out baskets and baskets of little wreaths, bells, stars, and angels. As Gabriel wandered around, he spotted a book about the cathedral and its history, filled with beautiful colored pictures. He had to have one to mark this historic occasion.

Pleased with his purchase, he walked out of the bookstore and back to the Joseph of Arimathaea Chapel. Several people had paused to pray. Others strolled around in and out as they explored the crypt.

His books looked as if they belonged right next to the authentic hymnals and Prayer Books. He decided to go to the restrooms in the north cloister, adjacent to the security offices. He'd hang around, pretending to read his book and listen in to make sure it was business as usual.

11
Isabella

The helicopter set down near the Peace Cross. Stewart, Paul, and I ducked and ran out from under the thundering blades. We dashed toward the cathedral.

I had never seen the Washington Cathedral in person. It took my breath away, towering against the sky. The light gray stone and the architecture recalled the cathedrals of Europe hundreds of years old, where people had worshiped for centuries. How could anyone in their right mind kill people in such a place of beauty?

That was the point, of course. These people weren't in their right minds.

Stewart pointed to the entrance facing Wisconsin Avenue. "Security

Office is downstairs in the underground parking garage." All three of them jogged past people streaming onto the property and into the cathedral.

I noticed a black limousine parking in a special spot close to the entrance, and pointed to Paul. "Look."

"It's Archbishop Parker Rhodes and Presiding Bishop Elizabeth Regent. I recognize them from their pictures," said Paul. The pair emerged from the limo, along with a muscular hulk of a man who hovered around the Archbishop of Canterbury, obviously a bodyguard. "What should we do?"

"Just a sec," said Stewart, "I'll handle this." He hailed them. Paul and I followed him to the car, where the dignitaries were unloading hang-up carry bags. Stewart said, "FBI," and introduced himself. He asked, "Have you been following the series of murders this past week? Christian scholars."

"Yes. Dr. Bonnie Barnes of Oxford. And the stolen manuscript," said the Archbishop.

Elizabeth nodded. "As I recall, the AAR/SBL had to close down early." She paused. "And wasn't there another murder just last night? The dean at Yale."

"My uncle, Andrew Guildford," said Paul.

"I'm so sorry. This has been a terrible siege," said Elizabeth.

"We think the worst is just beginning," said Stewart. "Would you mind coming with us to the Security Office?"

Archbishop Rhodes and Presiding Bishop Regent looked at each other. The bodyguard said, "What are we waiting for?"

Their driver said, "I'll take your vestments to the sacristy." He loaded their clothes bags over his arm. They followed Stewart Williams.

12
Gabriel

Something was amiss. The first clue Gabriel had was the sound of a helicopter's wings beating over the cathedral and stopping. Not moving past. He stepped out the north entrance, but couldn't see anything. Maybe there was a hospital nearby. Maybe his nerves were just a little more finely tuned than usual.

The next clue came when six people hurried around heading to the underground garage—including a man and a woman dressed in purple shirts and clerical collars. He followed them, loitering as close as he could get without arousing suspicion. He pretended to read the book he had bought.

Gabriel couldn't hear what anyone was saying. From the excitement generated, he wondered if someone had caught on to the plan. He thought he recognized the lady cop from the newscast in New Haven, but he'd have to wait and see what to do.

Another man and a woman dressed in FBI jackets entered the Security Office.

This did not look good. Gabriel decided to go on downstairs and check on his books. There was no plan B. Unless he heard otherwise, he was ordered to execute the original plan no matter what.

13
Isabella

I watched Stewart as he introduced his D.C. colleague, Marietta Brookstone. Marietta had waist-length blonde hair pulled back, and no make-up—around forty. She looked sensible and smart. I hoped she lived up to her first impressions, since we were now in her territory.

"Tell me again why we should abort this service," said Marietta. "The service has been getting lots of press. It involves major Christian leaders and we heard last week that the Vice-President decided to attend. We need to have something firm to go on before we cancel."

I read between the lines. Marietta was concerned about her own press if she canceled a major public event and nothing happened.

Stewart pulled out the post cards and walked her through them from the beginning. Paul made interpretations. "The last one is only a suggestion, but it ties Thanksgiving Day at the National Cathedral with thanksgiving in heaven when this group triumphs. In the tenth hour. That's what time the service starts."

"Every post card has had a picture of the National Cathedral," I added. "This last one had an aerial view and talked about destruction on earth."

Marietta looked at Stewart, her eyes doubtful. "Yes, but—"

"Of course," exclaimed the Presiding Bishop. "Communion wine. We'd have a Jim Jones-style Christian Guyana."

The Archbishop interjected, "But we're not having Communion."

"Oh," she said. "That's right."

The group stood and stared at each other. The Head of Cathedral Security began to look smug.

"Then I don't see how we can stop—" started Marietta.

"But all the puzzle pieces fit," insisted Stewart.

The Head of Cathedral Security said, "That's that. We're not calling off the service." He turned around and headed back inside the office.

I whispered to Stewart. "Remember Victoria, her skull crushed. Not poison. This group has other talents."

Marietta shook her head. "I don't know."

Stewart huddled with Isabella. "What do you think?"

"My gut says something is going to happen. Snipers, a bomb. Even poison gas. The cards were a trail that led us here. A taunt. This group is just dying to get the best of us."

"Okay," demanded Stewart. "If we can't cancel the show, we can at least protect these people and cover our own asses."

"I'm sure the Archbishop and Presiding Bishop would appreciate that," I added.

The bodyguard said, "You bet your royal bum they would."

Marietta looked at her watch. "You've got a deal. We have thirty minutes. I'll get a team out here in plain clothes. And a bomb squad with dogs."

"That's not enough time to scout for snipers and bombs," said Stewart.

"They're on the way. I already contacted them," Marietta admitted with a grin. "Better safe than sorry." She whispered to Stewart, "It's my backside, too, if this service goes south. I just wanted to see if you agreed."

"We can start the service late if we have to," offered the Presiding Bishop.

The Archbishop asked, "Should we vest? Continue on?"

Marietta said to her assistant and to me, "Yes. Get them some armor underneath their vestments. We don't want to take any chances. They may be after the two of you."

I said, "Somebody needs to catch the Vice-President's people and alert him."

"Yes, I will." Marietta added, "Security, Paul, and Stewart can patrol the aisles now, scanning for bulges or suspicious characters."

Stewart told the head security officer. "Get your whole staff here. Now. We're going to post people at all the entrances. Surely you can't object to giving us some extra eyes."

Marietta said, "Hurry. We don't have much time."

14
Malcolm

At exactly 9:30 Eastern Standard Time, Malcolm dialed Scotland again. This time, the housekeeper was only too happy to get her employer out of bed.

"Yes," said John, picking up another extension. "Thank you, Mrs. Wallace. If you'll go hang up the other line in the kitchen."

Malcolm waited until he heard the click. "Circle of Five, American Patriarch. An emergency."

"Go on." McCullough's raspy voice sounded instantly alarmed.

"The FBI is onto the plan. They're going to try to stop it. I don't know how much they know. The feds from New Haven took a helicopter an hour ago to Washington."

"Why didn't you alert me earlier?" demanded John.

"I did," returned Malcolm. "Rupert was out on the grounds, and Mrs. Wallace wouldn't wake you. She didn't know the code. She thought I was someone who lost my umbrella."

"Bloody hell. Let me contact the Washington Patriarch. He's supposed to be on the spot, leaving the premises ten minutes before the service starts. That will clear him from the blast. We may have to step up the timetable."

Still torn between loyalty to Paul and loyalty to the brotherhood, Malcolm asked, "Should we abort?" He paused.

"No. Even if the bomb goes off early, enough people will die to make our point."

Malcolm hesitated. "My nephew is on site. He's the one who figured it out."

"Then you should have recruited him for the brotherhood. Sacrifices must be made. I'm sorry."

Malcolm hung up. He was in danger of losing another family member—someone he'd grown rather fond of over the years. If he called Paul and warned him to get out of there, he would be giving away the brotherhood. He would also be giving away his own part in the plans.

If he didn't call Paul, he could kiss him goodbye.

He would have preferred it another way, but the Grand Patriarch was right. Sacrifices had to be made.

15
Isabella

I helped Elizabeth put on a bulletproof vest under her robe. The Presiding Bishop said, "Once the place is crawling with the FBI team and bomb dogs, what is the congregation going to do? What if they're in danger, too?"

"Maybe we should make an announcement," added the Archbishop.

"The FBI team is dressed in plain clothes, like Secret Service," I said. "They'll be placed every few pews. People will see them, but we hope they'll think we are just taking extra precaution for the two of you and the Vice-President."

Marietta popped her head in the door. "We're going to close the bookstore now and get everyone upstairs. When we're sure no one is in the crypt, we'll send in the dogs to sniff the downstairs chapels. For maximum damage, it makes sense that a bomb would be on the lower level anyway. We'll play it by ear from there."

"I'm getting dry mouth from nerves. This hasn't happened since my consecration," said the Archbishop.

"Don't even think about drinking anything," said Marietta. "I'm going out to check on the dogs."

16
Gabriel

Gabriel spotted Felix Darrington milling with the crowd in the narthex. He was surprised to hear Darrington's cell phone ring. Felix looked alarmed at hearing his phone. He moved outside to a relatively isolated spot on the grass and answered it. "Hello." Then, Gabriel overheard him say, "Washington Patriarch."

Gabriel stood undetected behind a pillar, Darrington within earshot. He studied the program for the upcoming service, while keeping his ear trained to Darrington's conversation. Fifteen minutes to go. This phone call was another bad sign.

"Yes," said Darrington, moving even farther away from the crowds. Gabriel could no longer hear him, but watched his face. Darrington looked around. Then he shook his head no. Gabriel was tempted to approach him, but personal contact was a direct violation of orders. Gabriel wasn't supposed to know who he was.

Gabriel kept his distance, his heart thudding with anxiety. Darrington broke off his conversation, concealed his phone in his hand, and walked closer to Gabriel. He approached the young woman giving out programs at the main entrance. "Can you tell me whether a helicopter landed this morning on the grounds?" he inquired off-handedly.

"Yes," she said, her eyes lighting up excitedly. "It was awesome."

"Can you tell me about it?" asked Darrington.

"It had FBI on the side. It landed and then it flew off again a few minutes later. You know, the Archbishop of Canterbury and the Presiding Bishop are here, and the Vice-President, too. The FBI probably wanted to make sure security is good." She paused and handed out a program to a man behind Darrington. "It's so exciting, isn't it?"

"Thank you, my dear," said Darrington and walked back outside into an isolated space to continue his phone conversation.

Gabriel edged closer and strained to hear. He was sure Darrington was talking about the FBI helicopter. Just then Darrington stopped talking and peered over his glasses at the entrance off Wisconsin Avenue. A train of black SUVs entered going faster than the speed limit. Darrington walked around the Cathedral, following them to the gift shop entrance.

Gabriel followed him. He saw fifteen or so men and women in dark suits and ear wires hop out and enter the cathedral. This scene was very, very bad news.

The final vehicle, more like a security van, stopped behind the others and waited.

Gabriel heard Darrington say, "I'm not sure, but I think they've brought some bomb dogs."

Darrington hung up and started walking away from the cathedral. Gabriel blended into the crowd, heading straight for the Joseph of Arimathaea Chapel. He also checked the throwaway phone provided for him in the pocket of his suit coat, to make sure it was on. He had a feeling he'd soon be receiving a call himself.

17
Gabriel

The Security Officers closed all entrances on the main and lower floors, except the west entrance. Once he got downstairs, Gabriel double-checked the Joseph of Arimathaea Chapel. Hymnals and Prayer Books were still in place, undisturbed.

Lingering close to his goods, Gabriel saw several men in dark suits herding everyone out of the crypt. "The service will start in fifteen minutes. We'd like everyone upstairs, please," one man told him.

Gabriel complied. No need to draw attention to himself. Halfway up the stairs his phone rang. No surprise. "Yo," he said, moving quickly up the stairs and toward the only entrance left open, which was also his only way out.

"Plans have changed. Get out now. Press the button as soon as you're safe."

"Got it." Gabriel snapped his phone shut. With a confident gait, he sauntered out the door against the stream of people entering. He skipped across the lawn, and headed down the sidewalk to Wisconsin Avenue.

He had parked six blocks away down Massachusetts Avenue. Counting stop lights and traffic, he figured it would take seven minutes to get to his van, right at 10:57, if he didn't run. That would put the blast thirteen minutes ahead of schedule.

Whistling to himself, Gabriel crossed Wisconsin Avenue and headed toward his van. His heart was racing with the thrill of taking down such a monument. All his other adventures paled in comparison with an explosion like this one.

It was the chance of a lifetime.

18
Isabella

I saw the SUVs, and walked toward Marietta, who was directing her team as they helped clear the crypt and close the gift store. I stood by as Marietta motioned the driver of the last vehicle to pull up behind the cathedral. She had decided to let the dogs enter the undercroft through the Way of Peace entrance on the south side, to cause as little commotion as possible. Eagerly two hounds on leashes leapt out and scampered down the stairs, sniffing their way around the crypt.

The dogs covered the Bethlehem Chapel first. They nosed their way into every crack and crevice. Then they split up, one checking out the men's restroom on the north side, and the other the women's restroom on the south. From the restrooms the dogs came west toward the Joseph of Arimathaea Chapel. They entered from both the north and south sides. Once they got to the chapel, the dogs went crazy. They pulled their human accomplices toward the chairs with bookracks on the back. "What?" asked Marietta.

She pulled up a prayer book and opened it, thumbing through the pages. "Looks okay. But something's up." I pulled out a hymnal that one of the dogs looked prepared to eat. This time, I couldn't get it open. Both covers and all the pages had been glued together. I tried another one across the aisle. Same thing. I showed it to Marietta, who had also discovered a faulty hymnal.

"The post card said the Joseph of Arimathaea Chapel!" I said.

"Evacuate immediately!" Marietta shouted.

I looked at my watch. It was 10:55.

19
Isabella

"The Thanksgiving service has been cancelled. We've been asked to evacuate the building, which will happen in an orderly fashion. Please remain in your seats until the ushers reach your row. Thank you for your cooperation." As the message came over the loud speaker, the FBI team and security started at the back of the cathedral, freeing the congregation row by row, moving up the aisles.

I stood on the far left end of a row of chairs, and Paul stood at the other end. I directed the person in the end chair to lead the row to the rear of the church down the center aisle. Paul did the same thing on the far side to hasten the stream of people escaping through the aisles of the cathedral.

Paul was cool and collected under stress. He encouraged each person, calming down the frightened ones. One older woman in a fur and flamboyant hat said, "Well, I guess it proves the Bible right. The last shall be first and the first last. I was late this morning, but I'm one of the first to leave."

I watched as Paul patted the shoulders of the coifed and elegant crowd and steered them to the door. The Vice-President had been hustled out already by Secret Service. I'd seen crowds on television in situations like this, panicking, screaming, and trampling over people to get out alive. This congregation did not react like that. They murmured among themselves, surprised, but most stayed in place when they saw that the system would work faster than a mob scene.

Another voice came on over the loud speaker, Elizabeth, the Presiding Bishop. She began, "Our father, who art in heaven…" The congregation joined in as the first few rows escaped the building. Paul and I moved up the aisles, freeing the congregation.

20
Gabriel

Five blocks away from the cathedral, Gabriel spotted his van up ahead, with the detonator in the glove compartment. Good. Almost there. One minute to go. He presumed the old guy Darrington had gotten out in time. Whether he did or not really wasn't Gabriel's problem.

Gabriel did, however, have another problem. As he crossed the street, he saw two cars parked behind him, each with an orange boot contraption on their wheels—and a ticket cop booting his van with the same orange contraption that wouldn't let him move his car until he'd paid the parking ticket. Oh, no. Gabriel had heard about the obsession that D.C. cops had with parking tickets. Where he came from, it was okay to park in "No Parking" spots on weekends and holidays. He kicked himself.

Slowing down, he brainstormed. Okay, how should he play this? *He had to get the detonator from the glove compartment.* He could not fail this job.

On the other hand, he couldn't let himself get caught. As he walked slowly toward the van, he conceived a plan. He would bluff his way. He would approach the ticket cop, acting the epitome of polite manners. He would express regrets and willingly sign the ticket.

Let's see. What name was the van rented in? LeRoy Gaulf. No, LeRoy's last name was longer than that. Gabriel wished he'd paid more attention. LeRoy Gaulfinerre? It was French, he remembered that.

Oh, well, he'd write it sloppy so they couldn't read it.

After he'd handled business, he would reach into the glove compartment and casually remove the detonator when the ticket cop left. Then he'd walk several blocks away, and blow up the cathedral. He would disappear. The cops would never link him with the blast.

Gabriel wished the Washington Patriarch had hired someone who could make a detonator look like a cell phone. This detonator looked like a detonator and was too big to fit in a pocket. That's why he had to leave it in the van.

"Hello, officer!" Gabriel approached a surly looking black man with a face like Mt. Rushmore. He was going to be tough to charm. "I see that I've parked here by mistake."

"Yeah. Read the sign." The officer continued applying the boot.

"I thought it was all right to park here on a holiday."

The cop looked up at him like he was stupid.

"I'm from out of town."

"And I care because…?"

Gabriel tried a different tack. "I hope we can get this problem cleared up quickly. If you'll write up the ticket, I'm happy to sign it. And I'll be on my way."

"I don't care what you do. But you're not going anywhere until you pay the city."

"Not a problem." Gabriel opened his wallet and pulled out a couple of hundred dollar bills. "What is the fine? I'll pay you right now."

The cop stood up. "No you won't. You got another problem, buddy. Something wrong with your license plate. See, somebody put tape, making a 3 into a 8 and turning D's and P's into B's."

"Gosh, I don't know how that happened. Somebody must have fooled with my van while I was at church this morning." Gabriel felt his insides tighten and begin to cramp.

The ticket cop strode up and stood in Gabriel's face. "Tell me more, sonny. Guess what. There's no minivan registered to the 'Church Publishing Company.' This minivan is rented to a Mr. LeRoy Gotonierri."

"I see." Gabriel stalled for time. His heart pumped hard, and he felt like he was going to need a bathroom very soon. "There must be some mistake." Gabriel pulled out several more hundreds, making sure the officer saw him. "Maybe we can work out something."

"Too late. My friends on the way. They has a few questions for you

268   Leslie Winfield Williams

down at the station."

Horrified, Gabriel watched as a marked police car approached with sirens on, six blocks away, coming from the direction of the cathedral. "Just let me get my cell phone out of the glove compartment." Even with a few seconds' lead, he could grab the detonator, disable the ticket cop, and dart down an alley too narrow for a car.

Trying to hide his shaking hands, Gabriel pulled out his key and started to unlock the van. *Hurry. Hurry. Hurry.* He fumbled the key in the lock, but finally turned it and opened the door.

Just then, the ticket cop's walkie-talkie went off. Gabriel heard a message, probably from the cop car approaching. "Hold him. Don't let him get away."

"I don't think so, buddy," said the ticket cop. He grabbed Gabriel's right hand and pulled it behind Gabriel's back. He grabbed at Gabriel's left hand to render him unable to move. "What you got in that glove compartment that's so important?"

Gabriel struggled to free his right hand, but the ticket cop was stronger than he looked. The cop car was now only three blocks away. Gabriel had a split second to seize the detonator. Getting away would take more strength and adrenalin than he thought he had.

No. He had to find the strength. *He had to prove himself to the brotherhood.* Gabriel tensed every muscle in his body and prepared for the fight of his life.

With a ferocious yell, Gabriel wrenched his right hand free. With one fluid motion, he elbowed the ticket cop in the throat, sending him to the ground. The cop grabbed his neck, moaning and trying to get up.

Gabriel lunged inside the van, jerking open the glove compartment.

21
Isabella

It was taking longer than planned to evacuate everyone from the cathedral grounds. Officers stopped traffic on Wisconsin to allow people to flee across the street. Bullhorns warned residents and passersby on Wisconsin to vacate the premises immediately. Paul and I led the front and final row of the congregation to the exit.

As soon as everyone was out the doors, Paul grabbed my hand and started to run down the grassy slopes through the gardens.

"Just a second." I bent down to take off my heels. It was the second time in a week I had run for my life in stocking feet. I took Paul's hand again. We made it to Garfield Street, out of the Cathedral Close.

When we finally stopped to catch our breath, Paul said, "You're pretty fast for a girl."

"And you're pretty great, for a guy. Think how many people's lives you just saved by being smart."

We looked up at the cathedral spires, dominating the landscape even from a distance. Any second now I expected to see the cathedral go up in a blast, disappearing before our eyes. "She's such a beauty," I whispered.

Paul turned to me. "So are you," he whispered back.

I avoided looking at Paul while I put my shoes back on. When I glanced up, I noticed that today his gray-blue eyes matched the sky behind him in a strip between the clouds and the horizon. "What a week."

"That's an understatement." Paul nodded.

Suddenly, Paul drew me close to him. I caught a whiff of his scent as his lips—those sensuous, full lips—closed in on my astonished mouth.

22
Gabriel

At that moment, Gabriel snatched the detonator and ran. Sprinting parallel to the cathedral, Gabriel took advantage of the crowds appearing on the sidewalk. People rushed out of their apartments to see what the ruckus was about. Gabriel managed a two-block lead before he heard the police officers shouting, "Stop!" Their feet pounded the pavement after him.

Gabriel ducked through an alley. He pushed aside two old ladies wearing robes and slippers. He couldn't detonate the building while he was running. He would have to stop for a second to get the code right. Over his shoulder, he saw the two old ladies pointing in his direction as the police officers rounded the corner.

Just then, he saw a man in a jogging suit unlocking his car. Moving quicker than he thought possible, Gabriel shoved him aside and grabbed his key. The man fought back. He jostled Gabriel, making him lose his balance and almost drop the key. Gabriel knocked him a punch in the jaw, but the man was tenacious. He swung at Gabriel and hit his solar plexus. As Gabriel doubled over, he dropped the detonator.

The cops were half a block away.

There was no time to retrieve the detonator, but he could still get away. Gabriel kicked the man in the balls, jumped in the car, and slammed the door. He ran over the man's foot as he got away.

In his rearview mirror, Gabriel saw one of the police officers talking frantically on his walkie-talkie, while the other one retrieved the detonator.

23
Isabella

Paul's kiss felt as soft, as pliant, as strong as I had known it would. He explored my face gently with his lips. A light snow had begun to fall, and flakes drifted into my hair. I felt caught in my own world, my own snow bubble, where the figures live happily ever after. For so many years, I thought I'd never feel this way again. I wanted to stand on this street corner, kissing Paul until I died.

My phone rang. I ignored it. "Don't stop."

Paul smiled, pulling gently away. "Considering the circumstances, you might want to get that."

I sighed. "Of course." I flipped open my cell. "Hello, Agent Williams." I watched Paul as he gazed at the cathedral high above through the snowflakes. "You're kidding!" I gave Paul a thumbs-up. "Fantastic. We'll start walking back."

This time, I kissed Paul. "They got the detonator!"

"Great! What the—how? Who? Did they catch—"

"A young man dressed in a nice suit stole a car. The detonator fell out of his hand."

"Who is the man? Did they catch him? He's got to be one of the Sethians."

"I think he got away, but the cops have put out an APB for the car."

"Well, this one's not on LeRoy, we know that much."

Paul and I held hands as we walked back to the cathedral through the snow flurries. If I hadn't seen with my own eyes the cathedral towering above me, I might have wondered for a brief moment whether I'd been killed in the blast after all. Heaven, whatever that meant, couldn't be any better than this.

However, someone evil was still at large.

24
John

John McCullough paced in front of the telly in his bedroom watching the bloody cricket match. He didn't care about cricket, of course. He knew the channel that carried it always interrupted their shows for major news events. It was now 3:30, and all he'd seen was cricket.

With no cable out in the Scottish hills, he had three channels to choose from, all BBC. He flipped the channels at the station break. After advertisements for teeth whitener, a compact car, and a sports drink, a talking head came on. "We're sorry to interrupt your program..."

There. He grabbed his afghan and sat down. He felt every nerve in his body on fire. The news anchor continued. "In breaking news, the American FBI uncovered a plot to blow up the National Cathedral this morning during a special Thanksgiving Day service."

John's veins turned to ice water. He stared at the news picture of the cathedral, intact, bells ringing joyously. The newscaster continued, citing as heroes a Paul Guildford—probably the nephew of the American Patriarch—and Isabella O'Leary. Damned if it wasn't that woman who outsmarted Hobbs. *Heroes.*

No! He, John, was the hero! Like Judas was the hero. Judas was the role model for true discipleship. McCullough had been loyal and faithful, like Judas.

And failed.

He sat still until the cricket match returned. He didn't hear the newscaster giving out the rest of the details. All he could hear were those damn bells. Even after he turned off the telly, the victory bells clanged in his head, pealing, gonging, driving him mad.

The Sethians had been defeated.

"NO! NO! NO!" he screamed, clasping his head in anguish. He couldn't get the pealing to stop, clanging over and over. The bells pounded failure into the cells of his brain.

Mrs. Wallace came to the door. "Are you all right, sir?" she asked, a look of concern in her face.

"YOU'RE FIRED!" he screamed. "Get your things out by tonight. I never want to see you again."

Her face crumpled. "Is it something I've done?" she asked.

"Get out! Get out before I kill you!"

He could hear her sniffling as she turned around and went back to the kitchen and her room to pack.

"RUPERT!" he screamed. Rupert appeared a moment later. He carried a glass of water and McCullough's heart medication.

"Yes, sir. I figured you'd need this, sir."

John took the pill, and handed the glass back. "I've dismissed Mrs. Wallace. When she's ready, take her into town."

"I see, sir."

"No you don't see. She's a stupid, stupid fool." She hadn't waked him up in time. She was the reason the plot had failed.

"Yes, sir." Rupert prepared to bow out and take the glass back to the kitchen.

"And take the night off yourself. I wish to be alone."

Rupert hesitated. "Are you quite sure you wish to be alone tonight? Your policy about not sleeping alone in the house—"

John glared at his servant.

"Yes, sir. I'll be gone."

For the first time, John thought of the Messenger of Life, the tender young man who had worked so valiantly for the cause. All right, he made a few mistakes in New York, but he must be devastated as John himself.

McCullough forced himself to calm down. Another heart attack would kill him. He wouldn't have time to plan another bombing. He wouldn't have time to establish Gabriel as the heir apparent. *If he had a heart attack, his legacy would remain unfulfilled.*

One bright spot in this terrible debacle. He knew he could count on the young man's loyalty.

Otherwise, he would have to kill him, and John wasn't certain he could bear the thought.

25
Gabriel

After the mess-up with Dr. Bloome in New York, Gabriel had spent the following twenty-four hours analyzing what had gone wrong. He'd planned ahead for potential disasters on the National Cathedral mission.

He thought he'd covered all his tracks—the disguised the license plate, the logo on the van, avoiding the security cameras, the throwaway phone. A stupid parking error.

Yet his last contingency plan was still possible. Gabriel knew how to disappear. He had once spent six weeks invisible on the streets of New York.

Once he left the Cathedral area, he sped through the light traffic—most people were getting ready to eat turkey with family. While driving, he peeled off his Brooks Brother's suit to reveal a tattered and filthy sweat suit and socks with holes. He took out a piece of charcoal from a baggie in his pocket and smeared his face. Then he rubbed black ink from an old-fashioned fountain pen in his hair. He pulled up in front of a drunk weaving down the street. He turned the car off and got out.

"Hey!" he slurred, catching the drunk's attention and pointing to the car. "Wanna ride?" he said, feigning an inebriated state. "S'all yours. Free car." Gabriel tossed the drunk the keys. Then he pretended to pass out on the sidewalk.

The drunk took the bait. "Hey, man, a free car. Whadda you know?" It took him a minute to start the car. Gabriel watched from the ground, hoped no one driving past had noticed the scene. When the drunk finally lurched off straddling two lanes, Gabriel got up and walked, drunk-like, to the nearest subway station. He bought a ticket to the bus station.

On the way back to New Haven, despair and shame slammed into him. He knew what he had to do first when he got back. He couldn't help himself.

26
Malcolm

Malcolm answered Paul's excited call from Washington, D.C. He pretended as much enthusiasm as he could muster. He focused on the fact that Paul was still alive—a slim consolation for the miserable, unspeakable failure of the Sethian Brotherhood.

"Your parents have planned the family meal around for 7:00," said Malcolm.

A family meal was the last thing Malcolm wanted. Andrew's sniveling widow and children. Malcolm's father who probably wouldn't know where he was or what had happened to the favored child. Paul, excited about the aborted bombing. Icing on the deluxe, multi-layered cake of the evening would be his sister and her husband from Dallas. He was certain Charles St. Clair had always hated him.

Malcolm called Winthrop Smythe. "Can you come over tonight for dinner? I need a friend."

"I would if I could. I'm trapped at Elizabeth's mother's. It's just the three of us without Jeeter and his brother."

"I understand." Malcolm would have to go it alone. As he had for most of his life.

After he hung up, Malcolm made another phone call. "Come to my house," he told the Messenger of Life. "I'll protect you until this blows over and we can send you back to England."

27
Isabella

Paul, Stewart, and I sat in the FBI waiting room. Washington D.C. had lost all traces of the suspect, and found no fingerprints on the detonator. He had worn gloves, which was no surprise because everyone was wearing gloves in the freezing weather. The snow flurries had become a storm that threatened to shut down the city.

The police had found the stolen car, driven into a post, with a drunk passed out at the wheel. They had also found the suit and topcoat worn by the suspect who had dropped the detonator. But the suspect had gotten away.

I looked at my watch. "It's almost 5:00. Paul, why don't you have one more go at LeRoy. Tell him what happened today and see if you can get any more information out of him."

"Go ahead. Got nothing to lose," said Stewart. "I'll go down and get him to the box." Stewart left the room.

Paul nodded, "All right. But then I've got to get back to Malcolm's. We're having a family dinner tonight." He lowered his voice. "Sort of like supper at the Addams Family."

"Oh, Paul. It can't be that bad, can it?" I watched him shake his head yes.

Paul pulled me close. "I'm sorry you missed your own family's dinner at lunchtime."

I laughed, "It was a zoo with all my brothers and their children. When I called Mama, she was already in bed." I paused. "Anyway, holidays can be hard."

He traced the outline of my face. "Can you come to Malcolm's house tonight? It should be a pretty miserable experience, but I'd really like it if you could come."

I smiled. "I've never been invited to a miserable experience in advance before. Some invitations have turned out that way—but maybe it won't be as bad as you fear."

"If you come, I know it won't be so miserable. At least for me."

"I'd love to. I'm into miserable experiences."

Paul whispered, "Thank you."

"Let's go," called Stewart from the hall. "My wife has kept the turkey warm all afternoon. She says if we wait much longer, we'll all get salmonella."

28
Isabella

I watched Paul as he waited for LeRoy in the same interview room as last night. Stewart stood beside me watching from the other side of the glass.

After a few minutes, LeRoy shuffled in wearing feet chains and handcuffs in front of him. His head was still bald, but no longer shiny. He had a five o'clock shadow all over his scalp and face, making him look like a dangerous convict instead of a harmless waiter at an elite country club.

"Good evening," said Paul, when LeRoy sat down. The guard left, but refused to un-cuff him. "I guess you've heard about this morning. I was wondering if you had any connection to the man who was prepared to blow up the National Cathedral. Or if you had prior knowledge of the bomb plot."

LeRoy shook his head. "No, sir. I swear. This is some serious bad dream. All I know is that I was supposed to get to go to Paris." He added, "Nobody said anything about people getting whacked or blown up."

I bit my lip. I would have sworn LeRoy was telling the truth. Paul stared at him.

"I'm sorry, sir." LeRoy looked down at his cuffed hands in his lap. "I shouldn't have been so greedy. I should have demanded to know the identity of my benefactor. But you know, I get a big bonus every year from club members, and it's always anonymous. I just thought someone who liked me was giving me a break and didn't want any attention or credit for doing a nice thing."

"I know, LeRoy. My Uncle Malcolm is the one who gets up your Christmas bonus every year. His friends all chip in."

"I don't know why he wouldn't talk to me yesterday. I thought he'd trust me. I would never kill his family. I'd never kill anyone."

At this point, Stewart nodded at me to join him in the interrogation room with Paul. He sat down and said, "The FBI traced your phone to a throw away cell phone."

"See, that right there tells you somebody else is involved," Leroy pleaded.

"We know someone else is involved. We just need to find out who," said Stewart. "Go over yesterday again."

"I waited until 5:00. Then I came up the back way to the seminary and called Dean Guildford, just like I was supposed to. He went from his house to his office and shut the door. Then I slipped in and put the post card in the letter box outside the door."

"You didn't see Andrew in his office?"

"No. Did they find my fingerprints in his office?"

"No," said Stewart. I watched LeRoy carefully. Again, I thought he was either one of the best liars I'd seen, or he was telling the truth.

"See. I was never in the office. I never saw your uncle. Do you think I'd leave my fingerprints all over the card and not in the office?" LeRoy had bags under his eyes, but he had energy. "I thought the plan was some-thing different. I thought the post card was some kind of message, like the manuscript was hidden at that chapel in the cathedral or something. It said something about not mourning, man. I thought it was telling your uncle Andrew it was going to turn out all right. You got to believe me."

I said in an aside to Stewart, "You know, if you didn't know the rest of the story, I suppose the post card could be interpreted like that."

Stewart grunted in response. "You're still young."

Paul continued, "After you dropped off the post card, then what did you do?"

"Went to the train station. The benefactor gave me train tickets and told me plane tickets were waiting for me at the counter at New York."

"What about the money?" asked Paul.

"He was supposed to wire it to my bank. Like he wired the other money."

"What other money?" asked Stewart and I at the same time. Paul, too, looked puzzled. "There was other money? For what?"

"When I took two suitcases full of books to Washington, D.C. on Monday. Bunch of Prayer Books and Hymnals. They told me to stay until Tuesday and fly back that night. That's why I missed work those days."

I sat stunned. This man had carried the books that were later stuffed with C-four to blow up the cathedral. "Where did you go in Washington, D.C.?"

"An apartment in a cool section of town, Adams Morgan. After I dropped the books off, I spent the rest of the time going to restaurants, getting ideas and talking to the managers. When I got back, somebody had wired the money to my bank account just like they said they would."

I realized that LeRoy's actions could be corroborated. The police could take his photo around to the restaurants in Adams Morgan and verify his alibi during the times of Hawthorne's murder and Dr. Bloome's attempted murder.

LeRoy put his head down on the table and sobbed. "I just wanted to get ahead. This was my big chance to make some money, but I never killed anybody."

I stared at LeRoy, numb. LeRoy was a dead end. Paul put his hand on his forehead. "I need to call it quits for today. I'm starting to get the mother of all headaches."

"Fine with me," said Stewart. "I gotta go eat turkey and bounce grandkids on my knee. Don't have a lot of horsy rides in me today, but I've got to give it a shot, or I'll never hear the end of it."

Paul rubbed his temple and got up to leave the room. "LeRoy has been framed. Didn't you tell me the van in D.C. was registered in his name? He wasn't anywhere close to the cathedral this morning." He paused. "Someone from the Sethian Brotherhood is pulling all our strings."

"Yes," I agreed. "The puppeteer from hell."

Paul took my hand. "Let's go. Can't vouch for a pleasant atmosphere, but I can guarantee the food will be terrific."

29
Isabella

As I pulled up to the Guildford home, my phone rang. It was Higginbotham. "The computer has come up with some very interesting information."

"Good." I sat in my Mini Cooper on St. Ronan waiting for Paul to arrive.

"Eleven names of UK men who have flown in and out of Glasgow on the target dates the last few years. Plus nine men from the continent, two from Paris, three from Geneva, one from Berlin, two from Rome, one from Portugal. Like clockwork."

"Great!"

"Further, no less than seventeen men from the United States, flights originating from Dallas, L.A., Chicago, Denver, Washington, D.C., and New York. One from Toronto, one from Sydney, Australia, and one from Morocco."

I felt chills running up and down my arms and legs. We were getting closer. "Any names you recognize?"

"Almost all of the Brits. Wealthy men in positions of power, without exception. I'll get my team on the others first thing tomorrow."

"Excellent work, Timothy."

Paul drove up and parked under the porte-cochere. I hung up my phone, crossed the street, and walked with Paul into the Guildford home. At a glance, no one would have known anything was wrong. The library was blocked off, but the dining room across the hall was set for a banquet, with crystal, china, and more silver utensils than I knew what to do with. I would have to watch Paul carefully to know which to use.

A feminine version of Malcolm and Andrew walked toward me, smiling. "Lindsey St. Clair. We're delighted to have you with us, Isabella," she said. "Today is Thanksgiving, and we are counting our blessings. Having you on our case, and having you here for dinner are two blessings we can add. Come on in."

I could see where Paul got his determined optimism. My own mother wouldn't have stopped wailing for days if her brother and her best friend had just been killed. Apparently, upper class WASPs kept a stiff upper lip.

Lindsey St. Clair's courtesy, too, was flawless. I decided I'd had met my first steel magnolia. And it would take steel to get through this meal.

"We're dispensing with cocktails," continued Lindsey. "Alcohol is a depressant, and we certainly don't need anything to enhance the dominant mood this evening." She paused, and then said firmly, "Dinner is served."

Lindsey proceeded to place everyone around the table, with Malcolm at the head and herself at the foot. Noe sat at her left, Lindsey's husband Charles at her right, the children scattered on either side of an old man, Paul's grandfather. Paul and Isabella side by side in the middle.

After everyone was seated, she said, "Paul, would you return thanks, please?"

Malcolm glowered at her. "I don't know what we have to be thankful for."

"That's enough, Malcolm. Your job is to carve the turkey. If you can't be agreeable, perhaps it would be better if you kept your own company."

I wasn't sure, but I thought that Malcolm had just been warned he was being sent to his room if he didn't behave. I had never encountered the kind of civility like this that could withstand tidal waves of emotion under the surface.

Paul began the prayer. "Heavenly Father, we thank you for the many gifts you have bestowed upon us, including the gift of family. Bless those family members who have gone before us to be with you."

I heard Noe crying beside me.

Paul continued, "We thank you for this food. Keep us ever mindful of the needs of others. Amen."

I added silently, *Whoever you are, God, please let us catch the people who have created so much suffering.*

Without speaking, Malcolm began to carve the turkey. Paul's grandfather sat directly across from me. I smiled at him. He stared at me through his glasses. "You're not Victoria," he said. "Where's Victoria?"

"She couldn't be here tonight, Daddy," said Paul's mother.

He continued. "We're missing someone else, too, but I can't remember who." Malcolm handed him a plate of turkey.

"Here, Daddy," said Lindsey. "Let me get you some stuffing. It's special wild rice stuffing."

Malcolm sent a plate down to Andrew and Noe's youngest child, Theresa. She held her blanky up to her face and sucked her thumb. "I don't want anything but cranberries. My stomach hurts."

When everyone was served, Paul's mother picked up her fork and began eating. That was the signal. I didn't take my eyes off Paul the rest of the meal. He was subtly showing me how to navigate among the range of silverware—as well as his family's landmines.

An unreal absence of human feeling reigned at the table as Paul and his parents tried to make conversation with Andrew's children. Noe was the only one who couldn't keep her tears from rolling down her face and dripping off her chin.

After dessert and coffee, Paul's mother dotted her lips, placed her napkin on the table in front of her, and rose from her chair. "I've rented a special movie for the children while Noe, Malcolm, and I meet in Malcolm's sitting room to make funeral arrangements. The minister is coming tomorrow, and we want to be prepared. Paul," she said, "You may do what you please."

I didn't know whether I should ask to help clean up the dishes or not. After big meals in my family, all the women chipped in. But this wasn't my family. Not by a long shot.

My question was answered when Paul's mother said, "Leave everything as it is. Gabby will be here first thing tomorrow."

"I need to go," I whispered to Paul. He nodded. I approached Paul's mother and shook her hand. "Thank you for including me. None of this is easy, but you've made it—" I stumbled for words. "You've made it bearable." I added, "With grace."

Paul's mother looked at me with a lavender shade of the same gray-blue eyes that she'd given Paul. She added her other hand to my clasp. "Thank you, my dear. You are a blessing to our family." I felt the warmth creeping up my arm from this woman's hand before Paul's mother let go.

In the silence as we approached the front door, I heard a distinct thunk and a muffled laugh from the upper floors of the house.

Lindsey and Paul must have heard it, too because all three of us looked up.

Malcolm started up the stairs, apologizing. "I must have left the television on upstairs."

I thought, *why would Malcolm be watching television upstairs when he had a video/movie theater right next to his bedroom?* I was too tired to press the issue tonight, and I didn't want to offend the host who'd been through so much lately. Maybe he didn't want to spend time in the bedroom he had shared so recently with his late wife.

Paul walked me through the porte-cochere and across the front lawn to my car parked on the other side of the street. "Your mother's something else," I said.

"She liked you," said Paul as clouds came out of his mouth.

I blushed. "How do you know? I'll bet she's as polite to everybody she meets."

"She is," responded Paul. "But she only does the double hand thing to people she honest to goodness likes."

"Good. I liked her, too." I paused. "But not as much as I like you." I looked at Paul as he bent down and kissed me. This time, we both kept our eyes open and watched each other a moment before melting into a long and hungry embrace.

I was a different person from the woman who had been at the Olde Branford Inn a week ago.

Pulling reluctantly away from him, I said, "You need to be with your family." Paul opened my car door. I paused a second looking at Malcolm's house. "You know, I can't get a feel for that house. It's a beautiful home—it isn't that. The décor is perfect. But the feel. I think if I'd first seen it when Victoria was alive—"

"It would have been a warmer place. Victoria had a quality like my mother that makes people feel at home. They were best friends forever."

I looked over the front of the house, the brick, and the rambling but interesting architectural design. Something hit me. "You know, what, Paul?"

"What?" He was looking at me, not the house.

"See those two little windows up there on the third floor, the ones with gables?"

He turned his glance to the house. "Yes." He paused. "I see them."

"*Two* little windows, not one. Are those the only two windows on the third floor?"

"Yes," said Paul.

"I saw only one little window in the office last night. There was no window in the attic." I paused. "Where is the other window?"

He stared at the two little windows blinking at us like two eyes from the top of the house. Paul was shaking his head. "I'm not sure I follow you."

"The remodeling. Malcolm created a safe out of the dumb waiter shaft when they remodeled the house, right?" I paused and then dropped the bomb. "Maybe he made some other structural changes as well."

Paul closed his eyes, as if to keep out any new insights that might wreck what was left of this Thanksgiving Day. "Yes," he said. "I remember two windows in Pappadad's study. We decorated them with candles at Christmas when I was a child. Two windows."

"Are you thinking what I'm thinking?"

"Let's go," said Paul.

29
John

It was 2:00 in the morning, and nothing on the Internet could cheer up John McCullough. He heard the rumblings of thunder in the distance, and turned off his computer. He'd lost a modem once in a thunderstorm. He didn't want to take the chance of suffering Internet withdrawal if a thunderbolt hit near the castle.

He still heard the ringing of the changes at Washington Cathedral in his head. Victory, victory, victory, they chimed. Even when he had opened the home page on the computer, MSN news featured the damn place with the bells ringing. He could hear those bells clanging from across the ocean.

He hated Christians with a bloody passion.

No one had fixed John's supper. Rupert had taken Mrs. Wallace away and gone pubbing, no doubt. He was probably spending the night at his brother's house. John had been reduced to scrambling some eggs and eating an apple with cheese.

Now, he was hungry again, but his bile was too high to swallow anything except bicarbonate of soda tablets. He had to plan for the next move. He would never give up. If his grandfather's life had taught him anything, it was that persistence paid off in the long run.

His heart had finally settled into a normal pace. He pulled out his files on the structure of St. Paul's Cathedral. *He refused to die until his legacy was complete.*

30
Isabella

Paul let me go ahead of him through the front door, then he led the way up the private stairs to the second floor. Everyone else was back in Malcolm's bedroom suite. I instinctively began moving with stealth when we reached the steps leading up to the third floor. When we got to the top and looked down the hallway, we both stood silent and stared at the opposing doors.

I took over, motioning Paul to stand guard at the attic door on the left. I reached in my purse and pulled out a Glock. Moving like a cat, I opened the attic door, searched the dark room, and whispered, "Clear. No windows."

Then I turned to the door on the left side of the hall. The door to the room we'd seen last night, Pappadad's study. Again, I entered, Glock ready. Inside, I found no one, but I heard a sound from the other side of the wall, opposite the attic.

I got my bearings. The attic was on the back side of the house. The office was on the front. In Pappadad's study, I looked up at one of the two garret windows I had viewed from the street. I motioned for Paul to follow me inside the room.

"Where is the other window? It's not in the attic, and it's not in here," I whispered. I guessed that it should have been located on the right—the side from where I'd heard the noise.

Paul sighed and shrugged. "I don't know," he mouthed.

I spotted a tiny door in the corner behind the desk. Quietly, I made my way to the door with an antique knob shaped like a heart. Crouched down, I motioned Paul to stand clear while I quickly opened the door.

Inside, I found myself in a tiny bedroom. On my knees with my heart pounding, I pointed my gun straight at a young man with dyed hair, a blotchy black and red. He was lying on a twin bed, obviously strung out on drugs.

When he saw me, he laughed. Then he blinked and looked again. "Hey, don't shoot! It's a party." His eyes danced with a bloodshot glassy look that I was only too familiar with among criminals I apprehended.

Paul rushed to the door and crawled inside. "Jeeter!" he exclaimed. "What are you doing here?"

The three of us formed an unmoving tableau. "Oh, Jeeter." Paul's shoulders drooped as his whole body sagged. The realization must have hit him at the same time it hit me. "It's you and Uncle Malcolm, isn't it?"

Jeeter tried to sit up. I said, "Don't move." I held my weapon steady.

So this was Winthrop Smythe's son. He was medium height, medium weight, and he wore a silver labret.

"I'm not saying a word until I get a lawyer. Not even to you, not to anybody."

"Do you want me to call your father?" asked Paul.

Jeeter laughed, sounding like a crow. "I'll take a public defender before him." Jeeter's eyes darted around the room. He couldn't focus on anything, least of all Paul. "No, I take it back. I want to talk to Malcolm. He can defend me. Malcolm, yes, Malcolm." Jeeter continued to raise himself slowly, while talking like a freight train. "Not my father. Get me Malcolm." He started getting petulant. "Malcolm is my best friend, the only one who cares about me."

"That's not true," said Paul.

I said to Paul, "Get my cell phone out of my purse and call Stewart now. I'm not moving until he gets here." I lowered my voice, "After you make the call, keep him talking."

I closed in while Paul made the call. "It's not LeRoy. It's my uncle and a friend I grew up with. Malcolm's godson." Paul could barely talk. "Come in the front door and go straight up the stairs to the third floor. Isabella's got him at gunpoint."

Paul moved closer and sat in the chair. Jeeter continued to talk. "Black robes, man. And you don't know what you're missing. You have a poker up your ass all the time. Is it hot in Texas this time of year? I actually had turkey out of a can today, can you believe that? Canned turkey, but this is the good old US of A and it's Thanksgiving, so I'm going to eat turkey, by damn."

I noticed a half-empty can of turkey on the floor, jacked open with a jagged blade. "How's your Turkey Day been, old buddy? I picked up a little party stuff on my way back from—hey, I'm not going to tell you where I've been. You'll tell my parents and they'll incarcerate me again. Put me away like a dog."

Paul said, "Jeeter, I don't understand any of this."

"You can put your hands down," I said. "But don't make any fast moves." I kept the gun trained on him.

Jeeter leaned against the wall, sitting up in the disheveled bed. "My niche, you idiot," he said. "Malcolm helped me find my niche. Come on, Paul, can't you see? You know me. I hate prison and my house was a prison.

Then school was a prison, and work after that. Dad couldn't understand because he loved work. He was always at work."

"I'm not sure I do understand," said Paul. "My parents were as strict as yours."

Jeeter rolled his bloodshot eyes. "You don't know anything."

"What went wrong? That's all I want to know."

"Hey, man. Nothing went wrong! It all went right. It started when Malcolm bailed me out of jail that first time. Dad walked away. Told me I needed consequences for my choices. Tough love, he said."

I never moved, while Paul sat silent. He listened to his long-time friend talk, letting the cocaine or speed or whatever reveal his wounded nature, the nature his parents had tried so hard to heal. "Malcolm the brick. He said, 'I'm not taking you home. Your parents don't understand you.'" Jeeter leaned back and closed his eyes.

"Malcolm asked me if I'd ever thought about eternal life. I told him, 'Hell, no.' I was just trying to make it through high school. But Malcolm started talking to me about important things."

Jeeter opened his eyes and started to get up. I said, "Keep your seat."

"Okay, okay. I don't want to talk anymore anyway, especially to you or her or anybody. You were one of the ones who didn't give a rat's ass."

Paul looked up at me. I motioned for him to keep talking.

"So Malcolm told you about the Sethian Brotherhood?"

"Life was boring. B-O-R-I-N-G. Girls were boring. They all gave in too fast. No chase. No romance. The brothers were cool. They were *chosen*. Special. I was special. Do you hear? You wouldn't know."

Jeeter flopped back down on the bed. "I'm the Messenger of Life. All I had to do was slip a little something into people's food and water. That woman from Oxford and the other professor." Jeeter started laughing. "And I just walked away."

Paul asked, "Why did you kill Victoria?"

"Victoria? Because she recognized me. I didn't kill Andrew, though. Malcolm did that one himself."

Paul shuddered. He said, "Oh, Jeeter, oh Jeeter. I'm so sorry. None of us saw this coming. We could have helped you."

Jeeter's eyes were still darting and glassy. "Help? I don't need your help!! Can't you see? I'm happy, very, very happy." Without warning, he reached under the pillow behind him and pulled out a small hatchet.

286   Leslie Winfield Williams

Paul froze. I said, "Drop the hatchet. Now."

Jeeter's eyes danced at Paul.

I shouted, "Now! Or I'll shoot."

Jeeter laughed. "I'm going to get you, Paul. After all these years. Paul, the big tennis star, Paul the brave survivor. Paul, Paul, Paul, why can't you be more like Paul?"

Jeeter lunged.

I pulled the trigger releasing a round. Paul sprang up from where he was sitting. The hatchet crashed into the chair, lodging in the seat.

I motioned for Paul to edge away, out of range.

"No!" screamed Jeeter, clutching his shoulder, where a red stain was growing. He struggled to free the hatchet from the chair. "My new hatchet!"

"Sit down now, or I will shoot you again." I kept my weapon trained on Jeeter, now holding his shoulder and moaning incoherently. I asked, "Paul, are you all right?"

With quick reflexes, Paul had jerked himself away from Jeeter, but I could tell his heart was pounding. "Yes." He grabbed the hatchet and pulled it out of Jeeter's reach.

"The wound should be a through and through in the deltoid muscle. He'll be fine." I paused and said pointedly. "But I'll kill him if he attacks you again."

With relief, I heard footsteps on the stairs. "In here."

Stewart ducked into the little room, his weapon ready. He trained it on Jeeter. "So, who've we got?"

I dropped my arms down. "The man who's just confessed to killing a number of people."

His voice heavy with sadness, Paul said, "His name is John Winthrop Smythe, Jr. Also known as Jeeter."

Stewart handed me a pair of handcuffs while he kept his gun on Jeeter. "Cuff him." I read him his rights.

"What's next?" asked Paul.

"I'll call a bus," said Stewart.

"We'll have to go downstairs," I said softly. "I'm so sorry, Paul. I can't even imagine how awful this is."

Paul seemed to struggle for something to say. "Let's just get the next part over with."

"Come with me," said Stewart, jerking Jeeter to an upright position.

"What about my wound?" cried Jeeter. "I'm dying and nobody cares. I have to finish my canned turkey."

I bound his shoulders with strips from a pillowcase. "There. The ambulance is on its way."

"Did you see my uncle Malcolm on the way in?" Paul asked Stewart.

"Didn't see anybody."

"Good. We've got to get downstairs before Malcolm realizes we know. He's got a gun cabinet in the bedroom, and there's no telling what he'll do. He's not the uncle I grew up with, that's for sure."

31
John

Thunder increased, adding a bass note to the chimes in John McCullough's head. He knew the only way to get rid of the victory bells was to go downstairs, where he could handle the manuscripts.

The Christians could take away his triumph today, but they couldn't take away the sacred manuscripts he'd retrieved for the Brotherhood after five hundred years. The *Gospel of Judas* was his.

He left his study and walked down the hall to the anteroom and the elevator. How many men had come through this room, one by one, since his grandfather had installed the elevator? Men replacing themselves, perpetuating the Brotherhood through at least two generations of Grand Patriarchs in this castle.

The elevator hummed on its way down to the basement. It landed with a jar on the bottom floor. He emerged into the wine cellar. All he could think about was getting into the holy space, where he would once again feel peace... and where the God of the Universe would give him another plan.

He unlocked the system and pressed the button at the bottom of the panel. He experienced the accustomed thrill as the wine cellar wall disappeared, revealing the cave of deep, dark, holy space. He entered. He was the high priest of the true faith. Not even death could take that away.

His heart felt strong, the beats regular. Pleroma would give him another opportunity. Next time, the plan would succeed.

32
Malcolm

Malcolm looked up when Stewart led Jeeter into his bedroom, cuffed. Rage shot through his body, but he remained seated in his chair. How had they found Jeeter? What had tipped them off?

Malcolm thought of his rifles, in a case only ten paces away. He could hold the whole group hostage while he escaped. Paul caught him as he started to jump up, placing his hand like iron on his shoulder. His touch burned through Malcolm's suit. Without saying anything, he tried to remove Paul's hand.

Paul had betrayed him. Paul was dead to him. He had only the brothers. No matter how they tortured him, Malcolm would never give away the Brotherhood. Considering Jeeter's condition, however, he had little hope that Jeeter had lived up to his vow to die before telling any of the secrets.

Malcolm said calmly, "I presume you have come for me." Quickly, he assessed whether he could make it to the gun cabinet before the pot-bellied man or the woman detective shot him. He couldn't. It didn't matter. He wouldn't give them the satisfaction anyway.

Stewart nodded. "Sorry, sir. You are under arrest for the murder of Andrew Guildford. Anything you say may be used against you in a court of law—"

"I know the drill." Malcolm cut him off. As Stewart approached with a pair of handcuffs, Malcolm said with disdain. "I'm a gentleman. I'm a lawyer. I have too much dignity to try to escape. Take those bracelets away."

"What?" said Lindsey. "Would somebody please explain? Why are you arresting Malcolm?" She turned to Isabella.

Isabella sat down on the loveseat next to her and took both Lindsey's hands in hers. "It grieves me to have to tell you this, but your brother Malcolm killed your other brother, Andrew. We're not sure of the details, but—"

Paul's mother looked at Paul. "Tell me it isn't so." Paul shook his head. "She's right."

"Malcolm! Look at me. You didn't kill Andrew. I know you didn't. It was that waiter, that man they caught at the airport. You couldn't have killed Andrew. It's not in you to kill your own brother."

Malcolm refused to meet her eyes.

Paul's mother looked at her husband, who started gathering wind like a norther. Charles St. Clair stood up out of his chair, lumbered over to Malcolm, and towered over him. "You...you...." He seemed to be unable to find words strong enough, but looked like he was going to knock the stuffing out of him.

Malcolm sat still in his chair. "I always knew you didn't like me."

"That's enough," said Stewart, stepping in between.

Noe collapsed on the bed, burying her face in the comforter, sobbing. Paul squeezed onto the loveseat on the other side of his mother, who grasped Isabella with one hand and Paul with the other. He leaned against her, holding her shoulders. She didn't cry, she didn't wail, she didn't say anything except, "Malcolm, you will pay for this. On earth and in heaven."

If Malcolm could wrest any pleasure from this situation, it was because of his faith. He said, "That's where you're wrong. I may be punished on earth, but not in heaven."

Paul said, "You're right. God can forgive even you. But only if you're sorry."

Malcolm gloated. "I'm not sorry. I don't need forgiveness. I'll be one of the heroes in eternity while the rest of you are going to rot. Look at Judas. He's been misunderstood for two thousand years. But he's the only one who ascended in the end."

Paul's mother gasped. "You're not in that cult!"

Malcolm replied, satisfied in his own justification. "It's not a cult. It's the true faith. I'm part of the incorruptible generation, and we have important work to do on earth. We will triumph yet. Wait and watch."

Paul stared at him. "To think you stole our manuscripts. Right out from our noses."

"I didn't steal the manuscripts. Technically, Jeeter did. Although he was acting on my orders."

Everyone turned to Jeeter, standing in the background. "I'm shot," said Jeeter. "I want to file a lawsuit. Police harassment."

"Police harassment?" Lindsey Guildford could barely speak.

"Mrs. St. Clair, I'm sorry," said Isabella. "He was coming after Paul with a hatchet. He didn't stop, so I had to shoot him."

Lindsey St. Clair's breath caught in her throat, and her hands flew to her chest. "No! Coming after Paul with a hatchet?"

"I aimed for his shoulder, so he'd drop the hatchet. I didn't want to kill him."

Speechless, Lindsey Guildford St. Clair stared at Jeeter. Then she sat down again next to Paul, patting his back. "Thank God for Isabella. I might have lost my son as well as my brother and my best friend."

Paul continued, "So Jeeter did all the jobs?"

Jeeter nodded, his eyes still bloodshot, his hand gripping his wounded shoulder.

"We'll match the DNA to his dandruff," said Stewart.

Paul turned to his uncle. "And you had Victoria killed?"

"No, I did not kill Victoria, although she deserved what she got. She was collateral damage."

Paul's mother gasped again. "How can you say that about Victoria?" She turned back to Jeeter. "And how could you kill her?" She covered her mouth with both hands.

Paul sat up stiffly. "Where are the manuscripts? We have to get them back."

Malcolm observed his nephew. What had he ever seen in him all those years? No, he had picked the right one to groom for the brotherhood. Paul's faith was too strong. He was too self-righteous. "They will stay where they belong."

Isabella interjected with authority. "You do know that Scotland Yard will get to the bottom of this organization. They are very close." She stared him down. "Mr. Guildford, if you help us, you can help yourself."

Malcolm said, "I don't need help. I'd rather die." In fact, he was already prepared. He kept a miniature baggie of herbs from his garden in his change pocket. He did not intend to suffer humiliation one instant longer than necessary.

Another tiny pleasure from this past week was knowing that he had grown the belladonna himself, right in his own garden. All the brothers grew belladonna, just in case. Like Judas' death, suicide was not a sin if you were one of the elect.

Paul said, "I think you owe us, Malcolm. I can't wake up tomorrow and the next day and try to make sense of what you did. You don't have to give away your precious secrets, but you need to tell us how you ever got mixed up with the Sethians in the first place."

Malcolm sat smug, watching these people tied to him by genetics only, but with no spiritual connection. He almost felt sorry for them. "Only now are you interested." He laughed. "I'm happy to tell you. After Mary died, Dad sent Winthrop and me to London to start the law office over there. I've never been so close to despair in my life. Then, Jeeter was born in England. I used to hold him and sing to him. We had a special bond."

Malcolm continued, "I had a case with an important British official as a witness, and we got to know each other. He took me to his club. Like me, he had no wife or children."

Malcolm thought back to when he had first met the Grand Patriarch, young and dapper in an understated way, a shock of black hair, and a nose that made his face interesting. Within a year after drinks in a smoky alcove of his London club, John had recruited Malcolm.

Paul said, "You must have been an easy mark. Lonely, away from home—"

"I was not a mark!" said Malcolm. "It was the best decision of my life! These people are my true brothers." He looked once more around the room at the faces that resembled his. Even Andrew's children had the Guildford square jaw line to a greater or lesser degree.

He stood up. "I'm ready to go now. I don't owe anything more to any of you."

Lindsey stood tall. "Where's Victoria's jewelry? You had no right to give that away, too. I don't care what you did with the rest of the stuff in your safe, but her family deserves her heirlooms."

"I don't care about her jewelry. Give it to her family. Everything is back in the safe." He paused. "Everything except the house is left to the Sethian Brotherhood when I die." He spit out, "And I would have left them the house if it didn't still belong to Dad."

The wail of an emergency vehicle grew louder as it approached the house. Stewart led Jeeter to the ambulance. Isabella led Malcolm out the front door and into the backseat of Stewart's car.

Paul put his arm around his mother. "At least there's no press," he said. "That's something we can be grateful for."

"Call me," Isabella mouthed to Paul.

33
John

John McCullough put on his robe. Then he lit the two candles on the altar. Reverently, he circled the room lighting the sconces. Candle by

292 Leslie Winfield Williams

candle, the room came alive, as the flickering light defined the shadows.

John loved everything about this room. He loved the rough feel of the stone walls, unearthed from the Scottish hills. He loved the smooth floors, worn by centuries of feet coming and going in what was once a dungeon, and since his grandfather's time, feet dancing in holy ritual.

First, he bowed. Then he retrieved the manuscripts from their treasure box in the cabinet. He fondled every page of the vellum translation. He examined the "I" with vines and gold leaf that started the gospel, "In the beginning." The ancient Greek manuscript was too fragile to handle, but not the Latin one. He and only he was allowed to feel the holy book, to run his fingers over the hand-created letters.

He read the whole thing aloud in Latin, all sixty pages. He'd never forgotten the Latin he'd learned as a student. One of the first things he planned to do after tonight was to make his own translation into English. Then he would own the gospel inside and out. The truth would become part of his brain waves and his very body.

He heard distant rumbles as the storm raged outside. He was safe in his basement. Deep, dark safe.

Carefully, he replaced the documents. He stood up and bowed at the altar, taking one candle in each hand. Slowly, he began to dance, reciting the ritual he knew and loved by heart. He knew God would inspire him with another plan. Round and around he whirled.

"Glory to God, king of Pleroma."

He scooped his hands to the ground and raised them in adoration. "I am Seth, your beloved son, present at creation, divine incarnation."

Faster and faster and faster he went. He began to see a vision of the righteous ones, rising like wraiths over St. Paul's Cathedral in London. They floated into the sky, turning into clouds.

St. Paul's. Right here in his own commonwealth. He would have more control over the next attempt, when his vision would become a reality, and the bells would no longer peal.

As he whirled like a dervish, Sir John tripped on a stone's edge and fell to the ground. For a moment, everything turned black, but he began to see light, lots of light very close to him.

He had caught his gown on fire. He jumped up. When he did, the hangings on the altar with the insignia of the crucified snake started to burn. "No!" he screamed. He pulled the manuscripts away from the licking flames. He clutched them to his chest. He ran toward the wine cellar, but, in his frenzy, tripped again, crashing into a stack of wine, scattering glass and wine and fumes of alcohol around him. The manuscript flew from his arms as the room burst into a holocaust.

In the middle of the fire, his precious manuscripts began to curl at the edges as fire consumed the pages of the only truth John knew.

No! No! Not the manuscripts! He reached for them, burning his fingers. He couldn't hold onto them and they fell, burning, out of his hands.

John looked around, desperate. He couldn't die here. Not now. Not like this. *He had to live to carry on the Brotherhood.*

John screamed for his life before he remembered that he was alone. No one could hear him. He had to make it to the elevator panel. He staggered under the weight of his flaming cloak. He pressed the button and the doors started to open. Then he heard a crash of thunder from the storm outside.

The elevator doors stopped, leaving a crack about three inches wide. Simultaneously, the lights in the wine cellar went out, leaving only the candles in the basement and the bonfire. Flames licked at his legs, his robe.

He would not die here. He refused. His heart began skipping beats.

John pressed the mechanical lever to release the rope ladder. Nothing happened. He pressed again.

This time, the ladder fell halfway down but got caught on the picture of Italy on the wall underneath the trap door.

John jumped up and grabbed one corner of the rope, but the other part remained snagged. He jumped again. And again. The fourth time, he managed to work the ladder loose, but by now the flames had encircled the bottom of his cloak and threatened to ignite the bottom of the rope ladder.

Struggling against the fire and the fumes, he shed his robe, screaming in pain. He scrambled into the waiting room near the elevator on the first floor. Flames ate up the ladder and caught the rug in the waiting room on fire.

Still screaming even though he knew no one could hear him, John hobbled as fast as he could to his study and the antique Egyptian tray with the false bottom. He snatched the letter from its hiding place. He escaped down the hall to the kitchen, where he let himself out the door into the night air wearing only his long johns.

After he had started staggering up the road to the highway, he began to notice his feet and legs below the knees were seared and charred from the flames. His heart began fibrillating and he felt his chest contract in excruciating pain. He collapsed to the ground.

34
Timothy

Inspector Higginbotham arrived in Glasgow mid-morning. He rented a car, and headed out toward Cairnhill and the castle, passing through countryside soaked from last night's storm. He loved the smell of the country after a good, cleansing rain.

When he reached the turn-off to the castle, he thought he smelled fire. As he wound around the hills, the smell of smoke grew stronger. When he was almost in sight of the castle, a fire lorry passed him going back to town.

He sped up and turned the corner, stunned to see what had once been the castle. The turrets and walls were still standing, but the central part was gutted and charred. Slowly, he pulled up and parked among the official vehicles, including two more fire lorries and several officer vehicles. He got out and moved toward the hole where the entrance had been. The stench was overpowering. He pulled out his handkerchief and placed it over his mouth.

"Detective Inspector Higginbotham here, Scotland Yard," he said to a man who looked in charge. He flashed his identification.

"Diarmid McBride. Fire brigade from Cairnhill down the road." They shook hands. McBride continued, "How'd you get here so fast? Just a bit ago I notified the Yard when the fire brigade found McCullough over near the grove of trees. Him being an MP and all. Thought you'd want to know."

"I was already on my way from London. Working a case. Can you tell me what happened?" asked Higginbotham.

"Yeh. Apparently, the valet came home this morning around 10:00 after a night out. Said his old man fired the housekeeper and gave him the night off. No reason. Said Mr. McCullough wasn't himself. Threw a bit of a fit yesterday and wanted to be alone. Couldna say what teed him off like that."

Higginbotham thought, *I'd bet my pension I know what teed him off.*

"Valet said he broke his own rule about not staying at the castle alone.

The old man had a heart condition. Must have been a whopper made him change his mind. Now he's gone, dead underneath that grove of trees."

"It was a whopper all right." I didn't mention the foiled plot to blow up America's National Cathedral.

McBride shrugged. "Valet called us immediately. Flames were still lapping when we arrived. Lot of old, dry wood in that place. Portraits on the walls, tapestries." He shook his head.

"Thought the fire might have started in the cellar. Don't ask me what he was doing in the wine cellar in the middle of the night. All the bottles busted."

"What started the fire?"

"We've got chaps on it now. Valet said there was a room in the basement he didn't know about. Iron sconces on the wall. Must have gone down there last night. Electricity went out, we know that. Maybe the old man lit some candles to see with, and the place caught fire."

"You said McCullough made it out of the burning house?"

"Yeh. Coroner's down there. It's roped off."

"I'll go take a look, if you don't mind."

McBride nodded.

Higginbotham picked his way through the tall grass to the body. John McCullough's legs and feet were burned into black stumps. He lay contorted and sideways, clutching a large envelope. Higginbotham reached down and slipped the envelope out of the dead man's hands.

"Scotland Yard. I'm taking this," he told the coroner. He would examine it later. "Please keep me up to speed. Scotland Yard has been investigating him for another case."

"Will do, sir."

Higginbotham made his way back to the castle. He found McBride, "Do you mind if I go down to the basement and check around a bit?"

"Get some boots. You can't go by yourself. I'll go with you. Still smoldering in places."

After pulling on boots and a fireproof poncho over his suit, Higginbotham walked backwards down the ladder leading to the cavity in the ground where the wine cellar once stood. He saw the elevator shaft—fireproof—and got his bearings. Yes, another room had existed beyond the wine cellar. His instincts had been correct.

The only thing left was a stone altar standing in the center, and the remnants of relics. One enormous gold lump suggested the design of a crucified snake. Using heavy gloves, he lifted what remained of a box. Most of the contents had turned to ash, but he found one page at the bottom, curled up with a few words in Latin.

"May I take this?" he asked McBride, who stood at the base of the ladder, watching him. "I think it pertains to the case we're working on."

"Be my guest," said McBride.

Higginbotham would show it to Paul, Isabella's assistant. He would know if it was part of the *Gospel of Judas* stolen from the Guildford's residence.

Slowly, he climbed up the ladder out of the charred hole, ready to put his feet on the earth again. He looked up. The sky was blue and clear.

Chapter Nine
FRIDAY

Isabella

I was getting ready to leave my office at the end of a long, weary day. I had overseen the release of LeRoy Gautonierre, who—as it turned out—had been guilty of nothing more than a desire to own his own restaurant. Paul and his mother Lindsey felt so bad about the way Malcolm had used him, that they gave him a check for seed money so he could fulfill his dream.

Last night, Malcolm had died as soon as he arrived at the police station. He started convulsing in the police car, but didn't collapse until he got inside. Two cuffed prostitutes and a thug stopped talking to watch him die. He had poisoned himself with belladonna from his own garden.

I was right to be wary of becoming over-involved with the Guildford family. However, I'd been nervous about the wrong member. My identification with Malcolm's loss had blinded me.

Just as I was getting ready to turn off the light and lock up, my phone rang. *What now?*

"I'm toasting you at this moment," said the cheery but slightly slurred voice of Timothy Higginbotham. "A celebratory white wine from my cellar. Here's to your good work."

"Thank you, Timothy." It had to be close to midnight in London. "Are you still at your office?"

"No, no, my dear. I'm snug at home by my fire. Today was indescribable. I even got a brief spot on the telly."

"You deserve a toast as well." Higginbotham had turned out to be a first-rate colleague, and I wished him well.

"One small item I neglected to mention."

"Oh?" I had actually already spoken with him twice today.

"Yes. When I came home from the castle yesterday, I put the envelope on my desk."

"Which envelope?" I smiled to myself picturing Timothy Higginbotham's private celebration.

"The one I found on McCullough's body. I only rediscovered it a moment ago when I was looking for my pipe."

"Your pipe? I didn't know you smoked."

"I don't. I just like the smell of burning pipe tobacco. But I knew you'd want to know what was in the envelope." Higginbotham paused, and I heard him breathing with slow and measured breaths.

"Hello? Timothy? Are you there?"

"Yes, yes. The envelope. John McCullough had in his possession a piece of vellum or something dating back to Henry VIII's time. It was his family history."

"Obviously it was important to him if that's the only thing he carried out of the flames."

"This piece of paper makes the royal family look like a pack of mongrels and bastards."

I waited. What was John McCullough's ancestry?

"He is a direct descendant from twins. A long, long, really long time ago. Before there was a Britain. His great-great-great something or other, an earl, recorded the family history when Henry VIII was on the throne causing so much chaos in the church. It's all there. McCullough descended from one of the early Sethian brothers in England. Probably the monk who translated the Gospel that was stolen."

"A Sethian monk. That's no surprise. But you said, before there was a Britain—"

"I did." Higginbotham paused, no doubt for a sip of his wine. "Let me read to you where the lineage begins." He paused, and this time I heard him swallow a large gulp. "Judas Iscariot."

I sat stunned while Higginbotham continued. "Judas Iscariot had two sons, twins. David barJudas wrote down everything his father told him, preserving the material that later became the *Gospel of Judas*. He hid the manuscript in a dry cave until the knights came and found it. He was the first founder of the Sethian Brotherhood."

Paul had been right, that first night when he told her the same thing.

"The other son, Jesse, became a Christian believer and followed Joseph of Arimathaea when he came to bring the faith to England. Right before the time of King Henry VIII, the Earl of Standby recorded the lineage in a single hand. Since the date of 1567, the handwriting changed as generations had added names to the list."

"So McCullough was a direct descendent of Judas?"

"Yes, and isn't the irony exquisite?"

I paused. "What do you mean?"

"My dear, McCullough wasn't a descendant of the Sethian twin. He was a descendant of the Christian one."

I sat at my desk speechless as the last piece of the case fell into place. After McCullough's heart attack, he must have known he was living on borrowed time. He had to act quickly to get the manuscript back to the Brotherhood and fulfill his legacy. That's what had jolted the group into action.

"Well? What do you think of that?" asked Higginbotham.

"Frankly," I said, "it makes me glad I'm an American Heinz 57."

As I stepped outside into the night, I looked at the stars, sparkling in the clear, cold night sky. John McCullough's was not among them.

Epilogue

Five weeks later, I found myself seated by the hearth near the window at the Olde Branford Inn, drinking a glass of Perrier. The sun was setting over the ocean, cirrus clouds refracting the rays into a red glow tinged with purple.

The Guildford family had cremated Andrew and buried him in a private ceremony, but Yale had had a huge and star-studded memorial service. Accolade after accolade followed Andrew to the grave.

Malcolm's service was also private, held at Trinity on the Green Episcopal Church. The priest had obviously spent a sleepless night wrestling with what to say. His eyes were bloodshot, with bruised-looking bags underneath. The sermon, terse, held a message on forgiveness.

At least the church had allowed Malcolm a funeral. The family and close friends sang, "There's a wideness in God's mercy like the wideness of the sea." Paul held my hand through the service, looking straight ahead at the stained glass window showing scenes from the life of Christ.

After the funeral, Paul had left to go back to Dallas to finish the semester at SMU. He had accepted Yale Divinity School's offer to fly back and forth to teach his uncle's class in the spring—but he refused to serve as Interim Dean.

I had asked my boss Crenshaw for some time off. The Campus Killer's trial wouldn't get underway until January, and I wanted time to consider Crenshaw's offer as Chief of Detectives. Crenshaw had said, "The world's your oyster, Isabella. You just tell me what you want."

Last week, Paul and his parents had flown into New Haven Regional Airport. I picked them up and took them to the empty house on St.

Ronan. I cooked a big casserole of lasagna, a salad, homemade rolls, and chocolate pie. "It isn't Victoria's Secrets, but my mother said food always makes things better." I paused. "I didn't know what else to do."

Lindsey had cried. Paul said it was the first time Lindsey had ever cried in front of someone who wasn't a family member. Then she dried her eyes, sat up straight, and announced, "We can't spend Christmas in this house. Noe's taking the children to her sister's in Paris, and I think we should go with her."

Tomorrow night, Paul and I would join them for the midnight Christmas Eve service at the Episcopal Cathedral in Paris. The day after Christmas, he had booked a suite at Le Palais de la Mediterranee in Nice.

I looked out at the sunset, an especially striking one as the red glow intensified, and purple and yellow streaks grew tinged with blue in the sun's dying light. After living for eight years in the agony of rage and self-absorption, I was beginning to understand the cost of redemption, seen through the faith of a man who had suffered at least as much as I had.

I finished the Perrier, paid, and went home to pack. I had an early plane to catch.

Acknowledgements

First of all, I'd like to thank my publishers Larry and Audrey Ketchersid, who were willing to take on this book in their new company; I'd also like to thank my former professor, Robert Flynn, who introduced us. It has been very exciting working with enthusiastic and talented people and being on the ground floor of something new. I'd also like to thank Mary Reed, my publicist, for her expertise, enthusiasm, and great sense of humor.

Mimi McNamara, Graphic Artist at the National Cathedral, has done a splendid job designing the cover of this book, and I'm very grateful she agreed to work with us on it.

The Yale Divinity School has been a "home away from home" for two appointments as a Research Affiliate. I cannot thank the people there enough for their support and encouragement, especially Paul Stuehrenberg for running such a wonderful program for visiting scholars and Dale Peterson for taking an active interest in every person who walks through the door. It is a friendly, stimulating, and spiritual place.

I'd also like to thank the community across the street where I stay in New Haven, the Overseas Ministry Study Center, which feeds and sustains all who live among them. The people there create an environment of genuine Christian caring and fellowship, where God's love, inspiration, and refreshment reaches, literally, to the corners of the earth.

My home college in Texas, Midland College, has been like a family to me for the last sixteen years. Many thanks for their support and continued friendship and collegiality.

Thanks goes to Tony Walker, our tour guide through Scotland, who endured my many questions and gave me an in-depth background of the history of what is actually the country of my heritage. Thanks also goes to Jamie Arnold, a guard at Scotland Yard in London, who filled me in on what goes on in the famous and legendary British institution. Officer Joseph Avery at the New Haven Police Department allowed me to see the detectives' room and gave me valuable information about the way things work in the NHPD.

The Sethian ceremony was adapted from The Acts of John in "The Apocryphal New Testament" translated by M. R. James, Oxford, Clarendon Press, 1924.

Several people read this book and gave me good advice. My husband, Stockton Williams, and my mother, MaryAllen Meriwether, always go through and help me get manuscripts presentable. They make me look smarter than I am. Lisa Powell and Elaine Keating offered several helpful suggestions, and Peggy Nash has been a loyal writing friend through thick and thin. My friends Molly Sharpe and Janet Morris gave me excellent advice about different aspects of the book. My friend Sarah Ruden not only read the manuscript, but also kept me going with her buoyancy and gift of friendship.

My prayer group and my tennis group in Kerrville helped me hold on to my sanity during the process of getting this book written, edited, and published, and I am most grateful.

A thank you to Diane Higgins who edited the book, and going back many years, I'd like to thank two people who sat me down and taught me to write, Dr. James Yoch of the University of Oklahoma and Andrew Baird.

Again, my family and my in-laws are my greatest treasures, and I couldn't do anything without them.

304 Leslie Winfield Williams

Washington National Cathedral

Washington National Cathedral is a church for national purposes called to embody God's love and to welcome people of all faiths and perspectives. A unique blend of the spiritual and the civic, this Episcopal cathedral is a voice for generous-spirited Christianity and a catalyst for reconciliation and interfaith dialogue to promote respect and understanding. We invite all people to share in our commitment to create a more hopeful and just world.

Learn more at www.nationalcathedral.org or by calling (202) 537-6200.

About the Author

Leslie Williams is an English Professor who has taught at Midland College, University of Houston, Incarnate Word University, Northwest Vista, and has received two appointments as Visiting Scholar at the Yale Divinity School. She currently commutes between New Haven and Kerrville, Texas. She is married to Stockton Williams, an Episcopal priest in Kerrville, where their two children and five grandchildren live.

Breinigsville, PA USA
25 January 2011
254058BV00001B/38/P

9 780984 304981